*RT* BOOK *REVIEWS* RAVES ABOUT AMANDA ASHLEY

*EMBRACE THE NIGHT*

"Sensuous! Mesmerizing! Electrifying! A must read for all vampire romance fans!"

*SUNLIGHT, MOONLIGHT*

"Two highly entertaining fantasy tales for the price of one!"

*A DARKER DREAM*

"Rich in sensuality and imagery! Readers will be entranced by this haunting tale. Amanda Ashley is a masterful storyteller."

*DEEPER THAN THE NIGHT*

"The very versatile Amanda Ashley does a wonderful job . . . a fast-paced and fun-filled read!"

# TIMELESS LOVE

"Don't ask questions, *cara.* Please just hold me, touch me."

She gazed down at him, into the fathomless depths of his dark gray eyes, and the loneliness she saw there pierced her heart. Tears stung her eyes as she reached for him.

"Why are you so alone, my angel?" she asked quietly.

"I have always been alone," he replied, and even now, when he was nearer to peace of spirit than he had been for centuries, he was aware of the vast gulf that separated him, not only from Sara, but from all of humanity, as well.

Gently, she cupped his cheek with her hand. "Is there no one to love you, then?"

"No one."

"I would love you, Gabriel."

Other books by Amanda Ashley:

*Deeper Than the Night*
*Sunlight, Moonlight*
*A Darker Dream*
*Shades of Gray*
*Midnight Embrace*
*After Twilight* (Anthology)
*The Captive*

# AMANDA ASHLEY

# EMBRACE THE NIGHT

Dorchester
Publishing

DORCHESTER PUBLISHING

January 2011

Published by

Dorchester Publishing Co., Inc.
200 Madison Avenue
New York, NY 10016



ISBN 13: 978-1-4285-1084-5
E-ISBN: 978-1-4285-1229-0

The "DP" logo is the property of Dorchester Publishing Co., Inc.

Printed in the United States of America.

# Embrace the Night

# PART ONE

## ONE LOVE, ONE LIFETIME

# *Prologue*

*Salamanca, 1995*

The single headstone stood on a small rise, the luminous white marble glowing like a beacon in the gathering darkness. A thick gray mist rose up from the ground to meet the lowering clouds, but he needed no light to find his way to the grave site, or to read the inscription on the stone.

SARA JAYNE DUNCAN OGNIBENE
1865 to 1940
Beloved Wife
Gone From This Earth
Yet She Abides Forever
In My Heart

Sara. They had shared more than fifty years together. Had there been fifty more, a hundred more, it would not have been enough. She had filled the emptiness in his life, brightened the darkness that dwelled in the abyss of his accursed soul.

He groaned softly, experiencing the pain of her death anew.

"Why, Sara?"

The question, torn from the depths of his heart, echoed in the stillness.

*Why, why, why . . .*

He cursed himself for letting her go, and yet, loving her as he did, he'd had no other choice.

"Sara, beloved, come back to me."

The pain of their separation pierced him anew, as sharp as it had been the night she died in his arms.

His hand caressed the cold marble headstone, then came to rest on the earth that covered her remains. But the woman he had loved more than his own life was gone. Her soul, her essence, had departed the earth, bound for that heaven that was forever denied him.

Sara.

The other half of his heart.

His solace in a dark and lonely world.

*Sara, Sara, why did you leave me? Was my existence so repugnant you could not share it?*

He groaned, deep in his soul, knowing he was being unfair. From the beginning, she had accepted him for what he was. Loved him with every fiber of her being, with every beat of her heart. Whatever anguish he was suffering now was not because of Sara's decision, but because of who, and what, he was.

Pressing his cheek to the damp grass, he closed his eyes, remembering how it all began . . .

# *Chapter One*

*England, 1881*

He had been observing her for the last thirteen years, watching, from the shadows, as the cumbersome braces on her slender legs were changed again and again. A weakness in the lower limbs, the doctors said. That was what kept her from walking.

He had seen the hope fade from her wide blue eyes as she accepted the fact that she would never run and play like the other girls who lived in the orphanage. Later, as she grew older, he had felt her despair as she realized that she would probably never marry or have children, that she would likely live out her days alone, with no one to love her, no family to mourn her, or remember her when she was gone.

He was the only one who sensed the true depths of her despair, her heartache, the only one who knew how she yearned to run in the golden light of the sun, to walk in the silver shadow of the moon.

He was the one who heard the sound of her muffled tears in the dark of the night. For others, she put on a brave face, but alone in her room, she wept bitter tears—tears that ate at his soul like acid.

He had never intended for her to know of his existence. Never. He had wanted only to watch over her, an unseen phantom who shared her loneliness and, in so doing, eased his own.

So it was that he was lingering in the shadows outside her room late one summer night.

He knew she had spent the afternoon sitting in the park across from the orphanage, watching the younger children at play, watching the couples old and young stroll hand in hand along the tree-lined path.

Watching life pass her by.

She had skipped dinner and gone to bed early that evening, only to lie awake long after everyone else in the house was asleep. A single candle burned at her bedside, its flickering light casting pale shadows over her face.

Now, hovering in the shadows on the veranda, he felt his heart ache. She was talking to herself, her voice low and soft, but not so low he could not hear it.

"You can do it, Sara Jayne," she said, her voice tinged with determination. "I know you can. The doctors could be wrong!"

For the next five minutes, he watched her struggle to inch her way to the edge of the bed, watched as she pulled herself to a sitting position, scooting over to the edge of the bed until her legs dangled over the side, her feet touching the floor.

"You can do it." Taking a deep breath, she clutched the newel post at the head of the bed and pulled herself to her feet.

For a brief moment, she stood there, her brow sheened with perspiration, and then, bravely, she let go of the post.

He bit off a curse as her legs gave way and she dropped to the floor.

"It's hopeless," she murmured, her voice thick with despair. "No one's ever going to adopt me." She dashed the tears from her eyes. "Or love me. I'll spend the rest of my life in this place and never do any of the things other girls do. I'll never marry. Or have children . . ."

She sat there for several minutes, staring at the floor, her shoulders slumped in resignation.

It grieved him to see her steeped in such anguish. She had always tried so hard to be cheerful, to be brave. She was a beautiful young girl, on the verge of womanhood. Who could blame her for feeling that life was passing her by?

He longed to go to her, to take her in his arms and give her the comfort, the reassurance, she so desperately needed, but he dared not reveal himself.

He was about to turn away when she reached under her pillow and withdrew a small brown bottle. She stared at the bottle for a long moment, a pensive expression on her face.

And he knew, in that moment, that she intended to end her life.

Without thinking of the consequences, he barged into the room.

Sara Jayne glanced up, startled, as a tall man swept into her bedchamber. He was dressed all in black, from his soft leather boots to the heavy woolen cloak that swirled around him like a dark cloud.

"Sara, don't!"

His voice was like ebony satin, soft, mesmerizing.

Sara clutched the bottle to her breast. "Don't what?"

"Don't take your life, Sara."

She blinked up at him, too surprised by his unexpected intrusion in her room, and by his knowledge of what she intended to do, to be alarmed. "Who are you?"

"No one of importance."

"What were you doing out on the veranda?"

"Watching you."

*That* frightened her. He saw it in the way she shrank back against the pillows, in the sudden widening of her eyes as she realized that she was alone, and helpless.

"Watching me? Why?"

"I have watched over you since you were a child."

She smiled then, a faint expression of amusement and disbelief. "Are you my guardian angel?"

"Exactly."

"And is your name Gabriel?"

He ignored the sarcasm in her voice. "If you wish."

She glanced at the bottle in her hand. "And have you come to take me to heaven?"

"No," he said sadly. "That I could never do."

"To hell then?"

He shook his head. His sweet Sara would never see hell, he mused, unless she looked into the depths of his eyes.

On silent feet, he closed the distance between

them, and took the bottle from her hand.

Too late, she tried to snatch it back.

"No, Sara," he said, shoving the bottle into the pocket of his trousers. "I'll not let you take your own life. Not now. Not ever."

"I have no life," she retorted bitterly. "I've never been anything but a burden, first to my family, and now to the sisters who must take care of me."

"That's not true."

"It is! Don't you think I know it is? Why else would my mother have abandoned me?"

"Sara." He whispered her name, stricken by the depths of the pain in her eyes.

"I'm nothing but a burden," she said again. "The sisters say they love me, but I know they'd be relieved if I was gone."

"Ah, my poor sweet Sara," he murmured, and before he quite realized what he was doing, he was sitting on the edge of the bed, drawing her into his arms.

How lovely she was, with her silky blond hair and eyes as blue as a robin's egg. Sweet Sara Jayne. So lovely. So fragile.

He held her close, surprised that she didn't pull away. Instead, she burrowed into his arms, her face pressed to his chest. He felt her shoulders shake, felt her tears soaking through his shirt, the moisture warm and damp upon the coolness of his skin.

He held her, rocking her gently, until she fell asleep. And even then he was reluctant to let her go.

He cradled her to his chest until the first faint hint of dawn brightened the sky. Only then did he lower her to the bed. He gazed down at her for a long moment, and then he drew the quilt over her.

Knowing he had no right, he bent down and kissed her cheek, and then he was gone, as silent as the sunrise.

# *Chapter Two*

He reached his lair in Crosswick Abbey minutes before the sun climbed above the horizon. Bolting the door behind him, he rested the back of his head against the solid wood, his skin still tingling from the promise of the sun's warmth.

Closing his eyes, he tried to remember what it had been like to walk in the light of day, to welcome the touch of the sun on his face, to bask in its warmth.

With a muttered oath, he pushed away from the door and crossed the floor. Sinking down in the huge, thronelike chair that was the room's only piece of furniture, he stared into the blackness of the hearth.

She was in pain, and she wanted to end her life. There were all kinds of pain, he thought. Sara's wasn't physical; it went much deeper than that, piercing her heart, her soul. Sweet and sensitive, she felt she was a burden to the handful of nuns who ran the Sisters of Eternal Mercy Orphanage.

His heart ached for her. She had been born to wealthy parents, but from the day of her birth, the Duncan family had been plagued by a constant stream of bad luck. Two ships belonging to the fleet owned by her father were lost at sea; a fire destroyed a part of their home. In the following year, Adalaina Duncan gave birth to a stillborn son. Shortly after Sara's third birthday, her father was killed in a carriage accident. Only then did his wife learn that he had gambled away not only their fortune, but the shipping line as well. His creditors, previously kept at bay by his good name and his fervent promises to make good on his many outstanding notes, had foreclosed on the family estate. Sara's mother, stricken by her husband's death and the loss of her home, had abandoned her daughter, never to be seen again.

It was no wonder Sara was bitter, he mused. Perhaps he should have told her that she was the single ray of sunshine in his own miserable existence, that her life had purpose, even if it was only to bring light into one man's world of darkness.

But he couldn't tell her that. Much as he longed to give her comfort, he couldn't give her hope when he had none to give.

He felt the sun rising, felt the faint lethargy that came with the dawn, a lassitude that grew ever stronger until it rendered him powerless. When he'd first been made, centuries ago, he had been unable to withstand the overpowering weakness that had come with daylight. Drained of his strength, he had been forced to seek total darkness during the daylight hours, to sleep the restorative sleep of the undead. But as he got older, and stronger, he found that he was able to take his rest later in the day, to rise earlier at night, though the touch of the sunlight still meant death. He feared the touch of the sun, the agony of a fiery death, as he feared nothing else.

Those early days had been filled with confusion and frustration. The lust for blood had filled him with self-loathing, yet he had been unable to resist the urge to drink, and drink, and drink, until he was sated with it. His hearing, sharpened to a new awareness, was bombarded with noise. The sound of thunder was deafening. Only with long practice did he learn to shut out the thoughts of others, to regain a sense of inner quiet. His eyesight was nothing short of miraculous; his strength was that of twenty men. Like a child with a new toy, he had tested the limits of his powers, his endurance. And in the testing, he had heedlessly brought pain and death to those helpless mortals who had unwittingly crossed his path.

Filled with loneliness, cut off from mankind, he had left Italy and wandered through the world, searching for a safe haven, a new place to call home. Gradually, he had learned to control the blood lust. He had learned it wasn't necessary to drain his prey, or take so much that life was lost. He had learned to hypnotize a victim to his side, take only enough to appease his need, and leave, with the victim never realizing what had been done. And still there were times when the urge to feed was overwhelming, when even his considerable willpower wasn't enough to keep him from taking a life.

It was not an easy burden to bear, knowing he must exist on the life's blood of others or perish, knowing he was hated and feared by all mankind.

Some accepted the Dark Gift and reveled in it, as he had. Others went mad.

He slumped down in the chair, shrouded in darkness and in his own bleak thoughts. For centuries he had prowled the earth, inflicting havoc on humanity, exulting in his immortality, content to wander aimlessly, caring for no one, letting no one care for him, until the loneliness became more than he could bear. He had accepted what he was by then, had learned to control the lust for blood, and so he had sought a mate, searched the world from end to end looking for that one woman who would see past the monster he had become to the man he had once been.

He'd had no trouble finding women. He needed no mirror to remind him that he was a virile male in his prime. His hair was long and straight, as black as his soul; his eyes were as gray as the morning mist that rose from the river. His face was pleasant enough, his lips full and sensuous; his nose, while slightly crooked, was not offensive.

He'd had women. Countless women. Beautiful women. Highborn or low, they had come to him gladly, showering him with their affection, until they discovered what he was. Some turned away in disgust, some in horror. One had fallen to her death . . .

He swore a vile oath at the memory. He had loved Rosalia with all the passion of youth, and she had died because of him. There had been times since then when he had grown heartily sick of the monster he'd become, times when death had beckoned sweetly.

Thirteen years ago had been such a time. He had been on the brink of destroying himself, of walking out into the sunlight to feel the sun on his face before it destroyed him. That had been the night he had seen Sara for the first time, a small, golden-haired girl huddled in the corner of an empty room.

She had been crying softly, as if she were afraid of disturbing the quiet of the night, and the sound, so filled with sorrow, had drawn him out of his own misery. The sound of her tears had led him to an elegant manor house.

She had stopped crying the instant he picked her up, staring at him through bright blue eyes filled with tears. And then she had smiled at him, a sweet, innocent smile filled with trust, and he had vowed to protect her for as long as she lived.

He had searched the rooms, looking for the child's mother, but there was no sign that anyone lived in the house. The furniture was covered; the closets were empty.

He had cursed softly, wondering who would abandon such a precious child.

He had learned later that Sara was the child of Adalaina Duncan, and that the woman had fled her home in the middle of the night. The townspeople had assumed she had taken the child with her.

Late that night, he had taken Sara to the orphanage run by the Sisters of Eternal Mercy.

When he handed her to the nuns, she had stared up at him, her little face looking sad, as if she realized she would never see him again.

He had watched over her ever since . . .

A long, slow sigh escaped his lips as he stared into the blackened hearth. Sara. What would he do if she tried to take her life while he slept? What would his life be like without her?

*Have you come to take me to heaven?* The sound of

her voice echoed in his mind, as did his own cryptic reply: *That I could never do.* Truer words had never been spoken, he thought, for he was far beyond the reach of heaven.

*And is your name Gabriel?* she had asked, to which he had replied, *If you wish.*

A faint smile curved the corner of his mouth. He had lived many lives and worn many names, but none pleased him more than the one she had given him.

For this lifetime, her lifetime, he would be Gabriel.

# Chapter Three

With a sigh, Sara closed the book she had been reading. Another happily-ever-after ending, she thought despondently. If only real life, her life, would end like that. If only there were a Prince Charming waiting in her future, eager to carry her off on his prancing white charger; a tall dark handsome man who could look past the wheelchair and see the woman.

She stared at the closed veranda doors, remembering the mysterious man who had come to her in the dark of the night. A faint smile curved her lips. All day, she had thought of him, her imagination creating one fantasy after another.

He was a prince in disguise looking for his own Cinderella.

He was an eccentric nobleman searching for the perfect mate, and she was it.

He was a depraved monster from a childhood dream, and only she could save him . . .

A small sound of disgust erupted from her throat. No man, whether prince or monster, would ever want a woman bound to a chair. What prince would want a princess who couldn't walk? What monster could be reformed by half a woman?

Tears stung her eyes and she dashed them away with the back of her hand. Lately, all she wanted to do was cry, to wallow in self-pity. She was tired of it, ashamed of it, but she couldn't seem to stop. She was almost seventeen years old. She wanted to run through a sunlit meadow, walk along tree-lined paths, swim in the pretty blue lake behind the orphanage. And more than anything, she wanted to dance.

She glanced at the beautiful little ballerina music box beside her bed. Her one dream, ever since she'd been a little girl, had been to be a dancer. It was a hope she had held close to her heart through all the years of her childhood, a hope that had grown fainter each time the doctor had changed the braces on her legs, until, in the end, they had removed the braces altogether. Any hope she had ever had for a normal future had died that day, killed by the cold, implacable realization that she would never walk. She would never be a ballerina. She would spend her whole life in a wheelchair.

She wouldn't cry! She wouldn't!

Sara choked back a sob as the door swung open and Sister Mary Josepha came in to see to her nighttime needs before tucking her into bed.

"Sleep well, child," Sister Mary Josepha said.

After making sure the bell pull was in place in case Sara Jayne needed something during the night, the nun left the room.

Sara lay in her bed, wide awake, as silence fell over the household. She was drawing the covers up to her chin when she saw a shadow move across the gauzy curtains that covered the veranda doors.

"Gabriel?" She peered into the darkness. "Gabriel?" She called his name again, the cry echoing in the lonely corridors of her heart. "If you're there, please come in."

She held her breath, waiting, hoping, and then the doors swung open, revealing a dark figure silhouetted by the moonlight.

"Gabriel."

"Sara." He inclined his head in her direction as he stepped into the room and closed the doors behind him. "You're up late."

"I'm not tired."

"You've been crying," he remarked, his voice tinged with accusation and regret.

She shook her head. "No, I haven't."

She pulled herself into a sitting position, then lit the lamp beside the bed. "Have you been watching me again?"

Gabriel nodded. He had stood in the shadows, watching her read, watching the play of emotions on her face. It had been so easy to divine her thoughts as the story unfolded, to know that she had imagined herself as the heroine, that she yearned for the perfect fairy-tale kind of love and fulfillment that existed only in books.

"I've seen you before, haven't I?" she mused. "Before last night, I mean?" She studied his face, the deep gray eyes, the sharp planes and angles, the strong square jaw. "I remember you."

Gabriel shook his head. She couldn't remember him. It was impossible.

"You're the one who brought me to the orphanage."

"How can you possibly remember that? You were only a child."

"So it was you!" She smiled triumphantly. "How could I ever forget the face of my guardian angel?"

A muscle worked in Gabriel's jaw as guilt and self-loathing rose up within him. He was an angel, all right, he thought bitterly, the angel of death.

"And you've been watching over me ever since? Why?"

Why, indeed? he thought. He couldn't tell her she represented everything he had lost, that her innocence drew him like a light in the darkness, that he had watched her grow from a beautiful child into a beautiful woman, and that his lust had grown with her. No, never that! He shoved his hands into his pockets and curled them into tight fists. She must never know that.

"Why?" He forced a smile. "Curiosity, of course."

"I see," Sara said dryly. "Since you saved my life, you wanted to see how I turned out?"

"You could put it that way."

"And how have I turned out?"

"Beautifully," he murmured.

"Beautiful but useless."

"Sara!" He was at her side in a heartbeat. "Never say that. Never feel that."

"Why not? It's true. I'm no good to anyone."

"You are. You are good for me."

"Really?" she asked skeptically. "How?"

How, he thought. How could he explain what she meant to him?

"You can't think of anything, can you?"

"I have no family," Gabriel said quietly. "No close friends. After I found you, you became my family. Sometimes I pretended that you were my daughter . . ."

"And you left me gifts, didn't you?" Sara glanced at the ballerina on her bedside table. "You brought me presents on my birthday, and at Christmas."

Gabriel nodded.

"I always wondered why there were no cards with the gifts." She smiled up at him. "I've loved all your presents, especially the music box."

"I'm glad they pleased you, *cara,*" he said, rising smoothly to his feet. "And now I must go."

"Oh." She looked away, but not before he saw the disappointment in her eyes.

"Do you wish for me to stay?"

"Yes, please."

With a sigh, he drew a chair up beside her bed and sat down. "Shall I read to you?" he asked, glancing at the book she'd been reading.

"No, I finished it. But you could tell me a story."

"I'm not much of a story teller," he remarked and then, seeing the disappointment in her eyes, he acquiesced with a slight nod. "Many years ago, in a distant country, there was a young man. He came from a very large family. A very poor family. He was sixteen when a mysterious illness spread through their village. He watched his whole family die, one by one, and when they were all gone, he laid them side by side in their cottage and then set it on fire.

"For many years, he traveled the land, and then,

when he was nine and twenty, he met a woman, and for the first time in his life, he fell in love, so much in love that he never questioned who she was, or why she would see him only at night.

"And then one day he contracted a fever, and he knew he was going to die the same horrible death that had claimed his family. Though he was loath to admit it, even to himself, he was terribly afraid to die.

"The woman he loved came to him when he was on the very brink of death. Weeping from pain and fear, he begged her to save him.

" 'I can do it,' she said. 'I can do as you wish, but the price will be dear.'

" 'Anything,' he said.

" 'And if the price is your soul, will you still pay it?'

"Foolish man that he was, he agreed. And the woman, whom he had thought was an angel, carried him away in a dance of darkness. And when he awoke again, he realized he'd struck a bargain, not with an angel, but with a devil. And though he would now live forever, he would never live at all."

"I don't understand," Sara said, frowning. "Who was the man? Who was the woman? How could he live forever, but not live at all?"

"It's only an old fairy tale, Sara," Gabriel replied. He glanced out the window, then stood up. "This time I really must go," he said. "Rest well, *cara mia*."

"Thank you for the story."

"You are most welcome," he replied softly, and bending, he pressed a quick kiss to her forehead. "Good night."

"Will you come back tomorrow night?"

"If you wish."

"I do."

"Until tomorrow, then."

"Until tomorrow," she called as he moved through the doorway. "Sweet dreams."

A muscle twitched in Gabriel's jaw as he vaulted over the railing that enclosed the veranda. Sweet dreams, indeed, he mused bitterly.

And landing lightly on the damp ground, he disappeared into the darkness, as silent as the rising sun.

# *Chapter Four*

For Sara, the hours of the day had always passed slowly. Bound to her chair, there wasn't much she could do to pass the time. There were no other girls in the orphanage her age, so she had little companionship. True, she loved to read. She had a fine hand with a needle. She enjoyed painting. But they were all leisurely occupations, and none of them made the hours hurry swiftly by.

Sometimes, Sister Mary Josepha came to sit with her, regaling Sara with stories of her childhood in Sicily. Sister Mary Josepha had been the oldest daughter in a household of ten daughters and two sons. She told of milking cows and goats, of gathering eggs, of shaving her younger brother's head because he threw her favorite doll down the well.

But on this day Sister Mary Josepha was tending the babies, and the other nuns were busily preparing for the Sabbath. And never had Sara yearned for the hours of daylight to end as much as she did now. For Gabriel would come with the darkness.

She was too excited to do more than toy with her food.

"Is something wrong, Sara Jayne?" Sister Mary Louisa asked.

Sara glanced up guiltily. "No, Sister."

"You've hardly touched your supper."

"I'm not very hungry. May I please be excused?"

Sister Mary Louisa and Sister Mary Josepha exchanged glances; then Sister Mary Louisa nodded. "I shall be in later to help you get ready for bed."

With a nod, Sara went to her room and closed the door.

She was the only girl in the orphanage who had her own room, a fact she had never appreciated more than now. They had told her it was because she was the eldest, because it was difficult to carry her chair up and down the stairs, but Sara thought it was because they knew she would most likely be in their care for the rest of her life, a fact Sara had gradually come to accept years ago as she watched one child after another leave the orphanage for a new life.

It had been painful, watching couples come to the home, watching them pass her by with hardly a glance when they realized she was crippled. She couldn't blame them for wanting younger children, children who were whole. But it had hurt just the same.

With a toss of her head, she put such thoughts aside. What did it matter now, when Gabriel was coming?

She brushed her hair until it gleamed like a newly minted gold coin, and all the while she kept glancing at the veranda doors, knowing it was too early for him to appear, yet growing more anxious with each passing minute.

Sister Mary Louisa came in to help her get ready for bed, helping her with the chamber pot, helping her into her nightgown, helping her get into bed.

"Don't forget to say your prayers, child," the nun said.

"I won't, Sister. Good night."

"Good night, Sara Jayne. God bless you."

The minutes ticked by, and still he didn't come. She heard the tower clock chime eight, heard muffled voices as the sisters herded the other children upstairs to bed.

Gradually, the house fell silent. She heard the clock chime nine, ten.

Had he forgotten? Or simply changed his mind? Perhaps he'd never meant to come at all.

She was about to extinguish the night light when she felt a breath of air whisper past her cheek. Glancing over her shoulder, she saw him outlined against the veranda door.

"Gabriel! You came!"

"I said I would, did I not?"

Sara nodded as happiness welled up inside her.

"Have I come too late?"

"No."

She held out her hand, and after a moment's hesitation, he crossed the room. And then, to her utter astonishment, he dropped to one knee, took her hand in his, and kissed it.

The touch of his lips swept through her like wildfire.

Images imprinted themselves on her mind: the

black silk of his hair, the dry warmth of his lips, the width of the shoulders beneath the voluminous folds of the black cloak.

And then he lifted his head, and she gazed into his eyes.

Fathomless gray eyes that seemed to see into her and through her.

Eyes filled with an immeasurable anguish that went deeper than sorrow.

Abruptly, he rose to his feet, as if he feared she had seen more than she should. His hand disappeared inside his cloak and reappeared with a book.

"For you," he said.

It was a volume of poetry, exquisitely bound. The pages were of fine parchment edged in gold leaf.

She would not have cared if the book were old and ragged, not if it came from him. But this . . . aside from her music box, it was the most beautiful thing she had ever seen.

"Thank you." She gazed up at him, clutching the book to her breast. "Will you read it to me?"

"If you wish."

She held it out to him, felt a shiver of delight race up her spine as his hand brushed hers. After removing his cloak, he lowered himself to the floor, his back braced against her bed.

Opening the book, he began to read. The poem was a song of unrequited love, filled with dark imagery and sensual innuendo.

His voice was deep, resonant, mellifluous. It conjured up images of moonlit nights, of faraway places and forbidden desires, of fair maidens and armored knights on white chargers, of love lost and love found.

The lamplight cast deep shadows over his profile

and haloed his hair with silver.

He turned the page, and his voice filled the room, winding around her, cocooning her, until she was no longer a helpless invalid, but a fairy queen holding court on a golden cloud, a sea nymph riding the back of an enchanted porpoise, an elf dancing on the petal of a fragrant blossom.

There was magic in his voice, in the wondrous rhymes, in the very air around them.

She gazed at his profile and saw an arrogant warrior riding fearlessly into battle, a swarthy outlaw demanding justice, a proud knight in tarnished armor.

She had no idea how long she had been staring at him before she realized he had stopped reading.

She felt the color rush to her cheeks as his gaze met hers, and she felt suddenly confused, as if she had just awakened from a dream. It had all seemed so real, and as she looked deep into Gabriel's eyes, she realized that he had been the warrior, the outlaw, the knight in tarnished armor.

Gabriel stared at her as if seeing her for the first time. Her eyes, as blue as the sky he had not seen in over three hundred years, were no longer the eyes of a child, but the eyes of a girl on the brink of womanhood. In a single glance, he noticed for the first time that there was no longer any hint of girlishness in her face or form. Her lips were full and naturally pink. Her neck was slender, graceful. Her hands were soft and smooth, and he felt a sudden shaft of heat spiral through him as he imagined her arms holding him, her hands caressing him.

She took a deep breath, and he noticed that she

had taken on the full, pleasantly rounded shape of a woman.

But most startling of all was the realization that she was looking at him as if he were a man.

In a single fluid motion, he rose to his feet and dropped the book into her lap.

For a long moment, he held her in the heat of his gaze and then he reached for his cloak. The dark wool swirled around him like fog on a dark night as he settled it over his shoulders, and he was gone.

"Gabriel?" She blinked several times, wondering if she had, indeed, dreamed the whole thing. She picked up the book, still warm from his touch, and laid her cheek against the cover.

She hadn't imagined it. He *had* been there.

Closing her eyes, she prayed he would come to her again.

He melted into the rising mists of darkness, welcoming the cold of the night, embracing the chill wind that blew off the river.

He had read to her from an ancient book of poetry, and she had stolen into his heart and caught a glimpse of his soul. She must have seen the darkness there, an emptiness that was deeper and blacker than the bowels of hell.

Why hadn't she been afraid?

Others had looked into his eyes and run away in fear; those who had not run fast enough, or far enough, had died.

Why hadn't she been afraid? How could he ever face her again?

He felt the anger rise up within him, and with it the lust for blood, the urge to kill.

He tried to ignore it, but on this night the hunger would not be denied.

Like a dark wraith, he prowled the near-deserted streets until he found what he was looking for, a homeless drunkard lying in the stinking refuse of an alleyway.

Like the angel of death, he hovered over the man, his long black cloak shrouding them in darkness as silent as the grave . . .

Sated, yet filled with self-disgust, Gabriel stormed into the long-neglected monastery where he had made his home for the past thirteen years. It was dark and gloomy inside, and he was content to leave it so. He had other dwellings: an ancient castle in Salamanca, a spacious apartment on a secluded street in Marseilles, a cottage in the Highlands of Scotland. The castle was his favorite abode. It was even older than he was, but he had refurbished it inside and out, until it again stood upon the hill as proud and glorious as it had once been.

But this place . . . he found it ironic that one as cursed as he should dwell within its walls, that a place that had once been hallowed by the presence of hundreds of righteous, God-fearing men should now be inhabited by a demon most foul.

Crosswick Abbey had once been a beautiful edifice, home of the Brotherhood of the Sacred Heart, but now the whitewashed stone walls were gray and crumbling; the stained-glass windows that were still intact were dulled by years of dust and neglect; the cross that had once adorned the steepled roof had decayed long since.

Why hadn't she been afraid?

He walked past the chapel, past the long row of small, cold cells, into the high-ceilinged room that had once been used to welcome visitors to the abbey. It was the largest room in the building save for the chapel.

He dropped into the huge, high-backed chair he had taken for his own. For the first time in decades, he was filled with self-loathing for who and what he was. What right did he have to survive at the cost of another's life? What right did he have to inflict his presence on a child as pure and sweet as Sara Jayne? She would be horrified if she knew what manner of creature came to her in the dark of the night.

He stared at the blood on his hands, and knew he could not see her again.

She waited for him the next night, and the next. And when a week passed and still he did not come, she refused to leave her room, refused to eat, or to drink anything except a little water now and then.

With the covers pulled up to her chin, she stared at the veranda doors, waiting, knowing he would not come.

Sister Mary Josepha and Sister Mary Louisa hovered over her, begging her to eat something, weeping softly when she refused to answer their questions. Kneeling at her bedside, they prayed for her soul.

"What is it, Sara Jayne?" they asked time and again. "Are you ill? In pain? Please, child, tell us what's wrong."

But she couldn't tell them about Gabriel, so she only shook her head, silent tears tracking her cheeks.

The doctor came, only to go away shaking his head. She overheard him tell the good sisters there was nothing physically wrong with her; it was only that she had lost the will to live.

And so she had. With a sigh, she closed her eyes. Soon, she would no longer be a burden to anyone.

He stood on the balcony and stared at the rain, wondering why it reminded him of tears, and then, riding on the heels of the wind, he heard the sound of weeping.

Between one breath and the next, he was down the stairs and out the rusty iron gate, running with demon speed through the night, her name like the prayer of the damned on his lips.

He vaulted the wall of the orphanage with ease, crossed the grounds as silent as a shadow. Pausing at the veranda door, he peered inside. She lay beneath a heavy quilt, as still as death.

The complete absence of sound within the room echoed in his heart like thunder.

A wave of his hand opened the door and he stepped inside, then hurried to her side.

"Sara!" He threw back the quilt and lifted her into his arms. Her skin was dry and cold; her lips were blue. "Sara!"

She was dying. The knowledge struck him to the heart. She was dying, and it was his fault.

Without stopping to think of right or wrong, without pausing to consider the consequences, he opened the vein in his wrist and pressed it to her lips.

"Drink, Sara," he urged.

He waited for what seemed an eternity, but she didn't move. Frantic, he forced her lips apart, held his bleeding wrist over her mouth, and stroked her throat to make her swallow.

Not too much, he thought. He didn't want to initiate her, only bring the color back to her cheeks.

He removed his wrist from her mouth, and the wound healed almost instantly. "Sara?"

Her eyelids fluttered a moment and then she was staring up at him. "Gabriel?"

He cradled her against his chest, relief rushing through him. "I'm here."

"You didn't come. I waited and waited . . . and you didn't come."

"I won't leave you again, *cara.*"

There was a bowl of broth and a glass of water on a tray on the bedside table. The soup had gone cold, but he warmed it with the heat of his gaze.

"Sara, I want you to eat this."

"I'm not hungry."

"Please, *cara,* for me."

"All right . . ."

Obediently, she swallowed several spoonfuls of the clear broth.

"No more," she murmured.

He put the bowl on the table, then drew her into his arms again. "Sleep now."

"Will you be here when I wake?"

"No, but I will come to you tomorrow night."

"On your honor, you promise?"

"I have no honor, *cara,* but I promise I will be here tomorrow night."

She summoned a faint smile, then, with a sigh, her eyelids fluttered down once more.

He held her for as long as he dared, his fingertips drifting over her hair, sometimes caressing the gentle curve of her cheek, until he felt the distant heat of the sun making its way over the horizon.

Only then did he let her go.

Only then did he admit that he would do anything, even surrender his own life, to keep her safe.

She woke feeling better than she had in months. Inexplicably, her legs felt stronger, and even though she attributed it to her imagination, it seemed as though she could feel the blood flowing through her useless legs. Sitting up in bed, she wiggled her toes, something she'd never been able to do before.

The sisters proclaimed her recovery nothing short of a miracle.

Her appetite had returned, as well. Sitting at the breakfast table a half hour later, she ate everything Sister Mary Carmen placed before her, and then asked for more.

She didn't miss the surprised looks that passed between Sister Mary Carmen and Sister Mary Louisa.

Later, sitting outside, she watched the younger children at play, and for the first time in her life, she wasn't jealous of their ability to run and jump.

Lifting her face to the sun, she offered a silent prayer to God, thanking Him for the beauty of the day, for the gift of life, for Gabriel. . . .

Unable to help herself, she laughed softly as happiness bubbled up inside her. Gabriel had promised to come to her that night. More important, he had promised never to leave her again.

Later, she read a fairy tale to several of the children. Perhaps it wouldn't be so bad to spend the rest of her life here, Sara thought as she turned the pages. She could become a nun, if they would have her; if not, they might let her stay on and teach.

She paused in the story, looking over the top of the

book into the faces of the children sitting on the grass at her feet. Such sweet faces, innocent and trusting, so eager to love and be loved.

Six-year-old Elizabeth smiled up at her, her eyes alight with anticipation as she waited for Sara to finish the story.

She could be happy here, Sara mused. If she could never have a child of her own, at least she could have children around her, children who needed love. And who could sympathize with them more, understand them more, than she?

She read another story, and then waved good-bye as Sister Mary Josepha called the children away. It was nap time.

Left alone, Sara gazed at the flowers that bloomed in wild profusion along the walkways. Today, with the sun shining and her heart filled with the certainty of seeing Gabriel, life seemed wonderful, perfect, filled with promise.

Today, with thoughts of Gabriel crowding her mind, anything seemed possible.

"Hurry to me, beloved," she whispered. "Hurry to me."

# Chapter Five

He was on the brink of awareness when he heard her voice.

Startled, he sat up, wondering if he had dreamed it. And then he heard it again, her voice, as loud and clear as if she stood beside him.

*Hurry to me, beloved. Hurry to me.*

Beloved . . .

He closed his eyes, basking in the sound of that single word. Beloved. If only it were true.

He dressed hurriedly, anxious to see her again, to see her smile, hear her voice caress his name.

He raced through the night, his preternatural speed carrying him quickly to where she waited for him.

She was sitting up in bed, an angel in a high-necked, long-sleeved gown. Her hair fell over her slender shoulders in endless waves of honey gold.

His heart quickened when he met her gaze and

his eyes, those fathomless gray eyes that held all the sadness of the world.

She hardly realized he had stopped dancing, stopped singing, so lost was she in the depths of his gaze. He held her body to his with both arms now, and she could feel every inch of his hard masculine form pressed against hers. The sadness in his eyes was burned away by a sudden blaze of emotion that she did not recognize. She felt the heat of it spiral through her, making her aware of him in ways she had noticed only in passing before. He was tall and muscular. His shoulders and chest were broad. She could feel the heat of his body, the maleness of it, where it touched hers.

How well they fit together, she mused, and even as the thought crossed her mind, she became acutely aware of her own body, of a sudden restlessness. She wanted him to hold her closer, tighter. She wanted him to kiss her, the way the prince kissed the princess in the fairy tale.

"Gabriel . . ." She leaned toward him, until all she saw was his face, his eyes.

"No." With a choked cry, he carried her back to the bed, dropping her onto the mattress as if her skin burned his hands.

"What is it?" she asked, confused. "What's the matter?"

"What's the matter?" He laughed, a harsh sound devoid of humor. "Ah, Sara, you foolish child. If you only knew . . ."

"Knew what?"

He clenched his hands at his sides in an effort to still the monster rising within him. Not for centuries had he satisfied his unholy desire with a girl as young, as pure, as Sara. Not since he'd first been made vampire had he quenched his thirst with the blood of an innocent.

"Gabriel?"

Ah, the sweet, trusting sound of her voice as she whispered his name, the unconscious yearning, the untapped passion. He could hear every beat of her heart, hear the thrumming of her blood as it pulsed through her veins, thick with desire. It was almost more than he could bear.

He closed his eyes and drew in a deep, calming breath. This was Sara, his Sara. He could not violate her. He would not take her blood, though to do so would be ecstasy.

"Gabriel, are you ill?"

"No." The word was one of harsh denial. "But I must go."

"So soon?"

"Yes." He opened his eyes and forced a smile. "I'll see you tomorrow night."

"Tomorrow night." She repeated the words, holding them close to her heart.

"Good night, *cara,*" he said, his voice thick, and then he was gone, running as if he, himself, were being pursued by demons.

He ran for hours, unable to outrun his loneliness, his longing, and then, filled with self-loathing, he entered the monastery. He had no need of a light as he made his way down the long, winding staircase that led to the underground catacombs where the monks had buried their dead. It was a dark place, musty with age and decay.

To punish himself, he climbed into the coffin he rarely used. Grasping the lid, he brought it down with a resounding thud, burying himself in the smothering darkness he hated.

"Monster," he murmured, and the word echoed off the sides of the oak casket. "Demon. Ghoul. Fiend. You will not touch her, you misbegotten spawn of the devil," he declared, his voice growing thick as the heavy sleep of the undead dragged him down, down, into the deep abyss of oblivion.

"You . . . will . . . not . . ."

He woke the following evening, a moment of panic rising within him as he opened his eyes to eternal darkness. And then he remembered where he was.

Muttering an oath, he climbed out of the coffin. He had not used it in more years than he could remember, preferring to take his rest in the big thronelike chair upstairs.

He stared at the burnished oak for a long time, reminding himself of what he was. Not a man, but a monster, fit for nothing but death and darkness.

His steps were heavy as he climbed the stairs. Deep in thought, he changed his clothes, combed his hair, donned his cloak.

As if to further punish himself for wanting what could never be his, he went out into the shadows, a bloodthirsty beast stalking its prey.

*This is what you are.* The words echoed and reechoed in his head as he bent over his hapless victim. *Don't let her sweetness fool you into thinking you're still a man, capable of loving, of being loved. You're naught but a monster, every man's nightmare . . .*

A short time later, he was walking toward the orphanage. And all the while, he tried to convince himself to stay away from her. His Sara, his angel of light, should not be contaminated by the darkness of his soul.

He was still trying to talk himself into staying away as he vaulted the orphanage's high stone wall.

She was waiting for him. He had expected to find her tucked into bed, but she was sitting in her chair, facing the veranda doors. Her goodness, her sweetness, reached out to him, washing over him like sunlight.

"A new dress," he remarked as he crossed the threshold.

She nodded shyly. "I made it."

"It's lovely," he murmured. And, indeed, it was. The deep blue darkened her eyes, the full sleeves reminded him of angel's wings. "You are lovely."

His words brought a flush to her cheeks. "Thank you."

"So lovely." He held out his hand. "Would you go out with me, *cara*?"

"Out?" She looked puzzled. "Out where?"

"Wherever you like."

"I couldn't . . . shouldn't . . . anywhere I wish?"

"Anywhere."

"The ballet?"

"If you wish."

She smiled, radiant with happiness. For as long as she could remember, she had longed to go to the ballet, to see *Swan Lake, Giselle, The Sleeping Beauty, Don Quixote*. She had studied the lives of many of the great ballerinas, like Marie Taglioni, Fanny Elssler, Carlotta Grisi, Francesca Cerrito, and Marie Salle.

And now her dream was about to come true. Then she glanced down at her dress, and her happiness dissipated like dew beneath the sun.

"I can't go. I don't have anything suitable to wear."

"You will," he said cryptically, and before she could ask questions, he was gone.

"Gabriel!" Shoulders sagging, she stared into the darkness, wondering if he was gone for the night.

An hour later, he was back. "For you," he said, and with a flourish, he reached inside his cloak and withdrew a gown of ice-blue satin.

Sara glanced at the dress, at Gabriel, and back at the dress, unable to believe her eyes. "For me?"

"You don't like it?"

Not like it? It was the most beautiful thing she had ever seen. She looked up at him, too dazed to speak.

"Can you . . . shall I . . ." He swore softly. "Will you let me help you change?"

She felt her cheeks flame as she nodded. Deftly, he helped her out of her dress and into the gown, lacing her up with such casual nonchalance that it eased her embarrassment. The satin was smooth and cool against her skin, a sharp contrast to the heat of his touch.

There were slippers and gloves to match. He pulled them from beneath his cloak, making her wonder if he was conjuring them from thin air.

She felt like the princess in a fairy tale. "How do I look?"

"See for yourself," he said, and lifting the mirror from the wall, he held it in front of her.

She did look like a princess, she thought. The gown was a study in simple elegance, the bodice fitted, the full skirt sweeping the floor. Fine white lace edged the scalloped neckline.

"It's the most exquisite thing I've ever seen," she

said, mesmerized by the miracle the gown had wrought in her appearance. Her eyes seemed bluer; her cheeks were flushed with excitement. "Where did you get it?"

"Does it matter?" he asked as he replaced the mirror, careful to keep to one side so that she wouldn't notice that his form cast no reflection in the glass.

Sara shook her head.

"Ready?"

"Ready."

Effortlessly, he lifted her into his arms and carried her out onto the veranda.

"You can't carry me all the way to the opera house," she remarked as he started across the yard.

"No need." He gestured to the surrey waiting outside the gate. "We'll ride."

It was like a dream, a wonderful dream, the ride through the streets, the feel of the breeze in her hair, the warmth of his shoulder next to her own, the brush of his thigh against hers when he shifted on the leather seat.

The ballet had already started when they arrived. As if he did it every day, he lifted her from the seat and carried her into the theater, nodding at the doorman, climbing the stairs with ease, carrying her into a private box.

Gently, he placed her in one of the red velvet chairs, then sat down in the other one.

She couldn't believe she was there. Her gaze swept the theater, from the frescoes painted on the ceiling to the heavy drapes that framed the stage. Leaning forward, she stared at the people seated below—elegant women gowned in lustrous silks and satins, handsome men attired in black evening clothes. And she was a part of them. She lifted her chin, feeling as if she belonged, as if she were, indeed, a princess.

And then, very slowly, she faced the stage.

A sigh of wonder, of awe, escaped her lips as she saw the ballerina for the first time. The dancer moved like a feather on the wind, light, airy, graceful. Each movement was perfection, perfectly timed, flawlessly executed.

Mesmerized by the sinuous blending of music and dance, Sara forgot everything but the woman who seemed to float effortlessly across the stage, her tiny feet encased in white ballet slippers.

They were doing *Giselle,* created by Carlotta Grisi in Paris in 1841. The story was one of Sara's favorites. She watched, entranced, as the peasant girl, Giselle, fell in love with the handsome Albrecht, a nobleman disguised as a peasant boy. She wept softly when Hilarion, who also loved Giselle, told her the truth about Albrecht. Upon learning that her beloved was betrothed to another, Giselle died of a broken heart.

"So sad," Sara murmured as the curtain came down on the first act. "So sad, but so beautiful."

"Yes," Gabriel said, his hooded gaze locked on Sara's face, his voice husky. "So beautiful."

More than beautiful, he thought. Her cheeks were rosy with delight, her eyes were shining, her lips slightly parted. He could hear the excited beat of her heart, hear the blood humming through her veins, feel his own heart beating in cadence with hers.

Hands curled into tight fists, he shoved them into the pockets of his trousers, trying not to stare at the pulse throbbing in the hollow of her throat, trying to forget that she carried his blood in her veins. Trying not to think of what it would be like to savor the sweetness of her lifeblood.

With a supreme effort of will, he forced such thoughts away and concentrated on the music, on the look of delight on Sara's face.

Sara leaned forward as the curtain went up on Act Two, fascinated as Giselle was transformed into a Wili, a spirit who haunted the woods at night, enticing men to dance until they expired of exhaustion. Tears stung her eyes as Hilarion was killed by the Wilis and Myrtha, Queen of the Wilis, forced Giselle to attempt to destroy Albrecht in the same way. But Albrecht was spared, first by taking shelter under the cross on Giselle's grave, and then by dancing with Giselle until dawn, when Giselle returned to her grave.

When it was over, Sara sat back in her chair, a soft sigh escaping her lips. "Thank you, Gabriel," she said, her voice tinged with awe.

"You're welcome, *cara*."

"Wasn't she wonderful? I don't think Grisi could have done it better. Do you think Albrecht was really in love with Giselle? How could a nobleman make a whole village believe he was a peasant?"

Gabriel shrugged. "People believe what they want to believe," he said, and sat back in the seat, content to listen as Sara spoke enthusiastically of the costumes, the music, and always the ballerina.

When the theater was empty, he lifted her into his arms and carried her down the stairs and out to the surrey. Removing a robe from under the seat, he placed it over her lap, picked up the reins, and clucked to the horses.

It was a clear night, cool, with a slight breeze. A

full moon hung low in the sky.

As they rode through the moon-dappled darkness, Sara was again aware of the man beside her. Inside the theater, she had been caught up in the magic of the music and the dancing, but here, in the quiet of a late summer night, alone with Gabriel, the ballet seemed far distant.

She glanced at him from the corner of her eye, studying his profile, noting the way the moonlight turned his hair to silver. He was a handsome man, dark and mysterious. And lonely.

The thought struck her with the force of a blow, and she realized that loneliness surrounded him, that it was his aloneness that called out to her above all else.

Too soon, they reached the orphanage and he was carrying her into her room.

Gently, he placed her in her chair and suddenly the magic was gone. She was Sara again.

"The dress," she said, blinking back her tears. "I can't keep it."

He nodded his understanding. There was no way for her to explain to the nuns how she came to have such an expensive gown.

Keeping his face impassive, he carried her to the bed, quickly divested her of the elegant blue dress, and helped her into her night rail. Kneeling at her feet as if he played ladies' maid every day, he removed the satin slippers, drew the gloves from her hands.

"I had a wonderful time," Sara murmured. "Thank you."

"Until tomorrow night, then," he said. Taking her hand in his, he lifted it to his lips and kissed her palm. "Sleep well, *cara*."

She blinked back a tear, and he was gone.

# *Chapter Six*

He walked the streets for hours after he left the orphanage, his thoughts filled with Sara, her fragile beauty, her sweet innocence, her unwavering trust. She had accepted him into her life without question, and the knowledge cut him to the quick. He did not like deceiving her, did not like hiding the dark secret of what he was, nor did he like to think about how badly she would be hurt when his nighttime visits ceased, as they surely must.

He had loved her from the moment he first saw her, but always from a distance, worshiping her as the moon might worship the sun, basking in her heat, her light, but wisely staying away lest he be burned.

And now, foolishly, he had strayed too close. He had soothed her tears, held her in his arms, and now he was paying the price. He was burning, like a moth drawn to a flame. Burning with need. With desire.

With an unholy lust, not for her body, but for the very essence of her life.

It sickened him that he should want her that way, that he could even consider such a despicable thing. And yet he could think of little else. Ah, to hold her in his arms, to feel his body become one with hers as he drank of her sweetness . . .

For a moment, he closed his eyes and let himself imagine it, and then he swore, a long, vile oath filled with pain and longing.

Hands clenched, he turned down a dark street, his self-anger turning to loathing, and the loathing to rage. He felt the need to kill, to strike out, to make someone else suffer as he was suffering.

Pity the poor mortal who next crossed his path, he thought, and gave himself over to the hunger pounding through him.

She woke covered with perspiration, Gabriel's name on her lips. Shivering, she drew the covers up to her chin.

It had only been a dream. Only a dream.

She spoke the words aloud, finding comfort in the sound of her own voice. A distant bell chimed the hour. Four o'clock.

Gradually, her breathing returned to normal. Only a dream, she said again, but it had been so real. She had felt the cold breath of the night, smelled the rank odor of fear rising from the body of the faceless man cowering in the shadows. She had sensed a deep anger, a wild, uncontrollable evil personified by a being in a flowing black cloak. Even now, she could feel his anguish, his loneliness, the alienation that cut him off from the rest of humanity.

It had all been so clear in the dream, but now it made no sense. No sense at all.

With a slight shake of her head, she snuggled deeper under the covers and closed her eyes.

It was just a dream, nothing more.

Sunk in the depths of despair, Gabriel prowled the deserted abbey. What had happened to his self-control? Not for centuries had he taken enough blood to kill, only enough to ease the pain of the hunger, to ease his unholy thirst.

A low groan rose in his throat. Sara had happened. He wanted her and couldn't have her. Somehow, his desire and his frustration had gotten tangled up with his lust for blood.

It couldn't happen again. It had taken him centuries to learn to control the hunger, to give himself the illusion that he was more man than monster.

Had he been able, he would have prayed for forgiveness, but he had forfeited the right to divine intervention long ago.

"Where will we go tonight?"

Gabriel stared at her. She'd been waiting for him again, clothed in her new dress, her eyes bright with anticipation. Her goodness drew him, soothed him, calmed his dark side even as her beauty, her innocence, teased his desire.

He stared at the pulse throbbing in her throat. "Go?"

Sara nodded.

With an effort, he lifted his gaze to her face. "Where would you like to go?"

"I don't suppose you have a horse?"

"A horse?"

"I've always wanted to ride."

He bowed from the waist. "Whatever you wish, milady," he said. "I'll not be gone long."

It was like having found a magic wand, Sara mused as she waited for him to return. She had only to voice her desire, and he produced it.

Twenty minutes later, she was seated before him on a prancing black stallion. It was a beautiful animal, tall and muscular, with a flowing mane and tail.

She leaned forward to stroke the stallion's neck. His coat felt like velvet beneath her hand. "What's his name?"

"Necromancer," Gabriel replied, pride and affection evident in his tone.

"Necromancer? What does it mean?"

"One who communicates with the spirits of the dead."

Sara glanced at him over her shoulder. "That seems an odd name for a horse."

"Odd, perhaps," Gabriel replied cryptically, "but fitting."

"Fitting? In what way?"

"Do you want to ride, Sara, or spend the night asking foolish questions?"

She pouted prettily for a moment, and then grinned at him. "Ride!"

A word from Gabriel, and they were cantering through the dark night, heading into the countryside.

"Faster," Sara urged.

"You're not afraid?"

"Not with you."

"You should be afraid, Sara Jayne," he muttered

under his breath, "especially with me."

He squeezed the stallion's flanks with his knees and the horse shot forward, his powerful hooves skimming across the ground.

Sara shrieked with delight as they raced through the darkness. This was power, she thought, the surging body of the horse, the man's strong arm wrapped securely around her waist. The wind whipped through her hair, stinging her cheeks and making her eyes water, but she only threw back her head and laughed.

"Faster!" she cried, reveling in the sense of freedom that surged within her.

Hedges and trees and sleeping farmhouses passed by in a blur. Once, they jumped a four-foot hedge, and she felt as if she were flying. Sounds and scents blended together: the chirping of crickets, the bark of a dog, the smell of damp earth and lathered horseflesh, and overall the touch of Gabriel's breath upon her cheek, the steadying strength of his arm around her waist.

Gabriel let the horse run until the animal's sides were heaving and covered with foamy lather, and then he drew back on the reins, gently but firmly, and the stallion slowed, then stopped.

"That was wonderful!" Sara exclaimed.

She turned to face him, and in the bright light of the moon, he saw that her cheeks were flushed, her lips parted, her eyes shining like the sun.

How beautiful she was! His Sara, so full of life. What cruel fate had decreed that she should be bound to a wheelchair? She was a vivacious girl, on the brink of womanhood. She should be clothed in silks and satins, surrounded by gallant young men.

Dismounting, he lifted her from the back of the horse. Carrying her across the damp grass, he sat down on a large boulder, settling her in his lap.

"Thank you, Gabriel," she murmured.

"It was my pleasure, milady."

"Hardly that," she replied with a saucy grin. "I'm sure ladies don't ride pell-mell through the dark astride a big black devil horse."

"No," he said, his gray eyes glinting with amusement, "they don't."

"Have you known many ladies?"

"A few." He stroked her cheek with his forefinger, his touch as light as thistledown.

"And were they accomplished and beautiful?"

Gabriel nodded. "But none so beautiful as you."

She basked in his words, in the silent affirmation she read in his eyes.

"Who are you, Gabriel?" she asked, her voice soft and dreamy. "Are you man or magician?"

"Neither."

"But still my angel?"

"Always, *cara*."

With a sigh, she rested her head against his shoulder and closed her eyes. How wonderful to sit here in the dark of night with his arms around her. Almost, she could forget that she was crippled. Almost.

She lost all track of time as she sat there, secure in his arms. She heard the chirp of crickets, the sighing of the wind through the trees, the pounding of Gabriel's heart beneath her cheek.

Her breath caught in her throat as she felt the touch of his hand in her hair, and then the brush of his lips.

Abruptly, he stood up. Before she quite knew what

was happening, she was on the horse's back and Gabriel was swinging up behind her. He moved with the lithe grace of a cat vaulting a fence.

She sensed a change in him, a tension she didn't understand. A moment later, his arm was locked around her waist and they were riding through the night.

She leaned back against him, braced against the solid wall of his chest. She felt his arm tighten around her, felt his breath on her cheek.

Pleasure surged through her at his touch, and she placed her hand over his forearm, drawing his arm more securely around her, tacitly telling him that she enjoyed his nearness.

She thought she heard a gasp, as if he were in pain, but she shook the notion aside, telling herself it was probably just the wind crying through the trees.

Too soon, they were back at the orphanage.

"You'll come tomorrow?" she asked as he settled her in her bed, covering her as if she were a child.

"Tomorrow," he promised. "Sleep well, *cara*."

"Dream of me," she murmured.

With a nod, he turned away. Dream of her, he thought. If only he could!

"Where would you like to go tonight?" Gabriel asked the following evening.

"I don't care, so long as it's with you."

Moments later, he was carrying her along a pathway in the park across from the orphanage.

Sara marveled that he held her so effortlessly, that it felt so right to be carried in his arms. She rested her head on his shoulder, content. A faint breeze played hide-and-seek with the leaves of the trees. A lovers' moon hung low in the sky. The air was fragrant with night-blooming flowers, but it was Gabriel's scent that rose all around her—warm and musky, reminiscent of aged wine and expensive cologne.

He moved lightly along the pathway, his footsteps making hardly a sound. When they came to a stone bench near a quiet pool, he sat down, placing her on the bench beside him.

It was a lovely place, a fairy place. Elegant ferns, tall and lacy, grew in wild profusion near the pool. In the distance, she heard the questioning hoot of an owl.

"What did you do all day?" she asked, turning to look at him.

Gabriel shrugged. "Nothing to speak of. And you?"

"I read to the children. Sister Mary Josepha has been giving me more and more responsibility."

"And does that make you happy?"

"Yes. I've grown very fond of my little charges. They so need to be loved. To be touched. I had never realized how important it was, to be held, until . . ." A faint flush stained her cheeks. "Until you held me. There's such comfort in the touch of a human hand."

Gabriel grunted softly. Human, indeed, he thought bleakly.

Sara smiled. "They seem to like me, the children. I don't know why."

But he knew why. She had so much love to give, and no outlet for it.

"I hate to think of all the time I wasted wallowing in self-pity," Sara remarked. "I spent so much time sitting in my room, sulking because I couldn't walk, when I could have been helping the children, loving them." She glanced up at Gabriel. "They're so easy to love."

"So are you." He had not meant to speak the words aloud, but they slipped out. "I mean, it must be easy for the children to love you. You have so much to give."

She smiled, but it was a sad kind of smile. "Perhaps that's because no one else wants it."

"Sara . . ."

"It's all right. Maybe that's why I was put here, to comfort the little lost lambs that no one else wants."

*I want you*. The words thundered in his mind, in his heart, in his soul.

Abruptly, he stood up and moved away from the bench. He couldn't sit beside her, feel her warmth, hear the blood humming in her veins, sense the sadness dragging at her heart, and not touch her, take her.

He stared into the depths of the dark pool, the reflection of the water as black as the emptiness of his soul. He'd been alone for so long, yearning for someone who would share his life, needing someone to see him for what he was and love him anyway.

A low groan rose in his throat as the centuries of loneliness wrapped around him.

"Gabriel?"

Her voice called out to him, soft, warm, caring.

With a cry, he whirled around and knelt at her feet. Hesitantly, he took her hands in his.

"Sara, can you pretend I'm one of the children? Can you hold me, and comfort me, just for tonight?"

"I don't understand."

"Don't ask questions, *cara*. Please, just hold me, touch me."

She gazed down at him, into the fathomless depths of his dark gray eyes, and the loneliness she saw there pierced her heart. Tears stung her eyes as she reached for him.

He buried his face in her lap, ashamed of the need that he could no longer deny. And then he felt her hand stroke his hair, light as a summer breeze. Ah, the touch of a human hand, warm, fragile, pulsing with life.

Time ceased to have meaning as he knelt there, his head cradled in her lap, her hand moving in his hair, caressing his nape, feathering across his cheek. No wonder the children loved her. There was tranquility in her touch, serenity in her hand. A sense of peace settled over him, stilling his hunger. He felt the tension drain out of him, to be replaced with a near-forgotten sense of calm. It was a feeling as close to forgiveness as he would ever know.

After a time, he lifted his head. Slightly embarrassed, he gazed up at her, but there was no censure in her eyes, no disdain, only a wealth of understanding.

"Why are you so alone, my angel?" she asked quietly.

"I have always been alone," he replied, and even now, when he was nearer to peace of spirit than he had been for centuries, he was aware of the vast gulf that separated him, not only from Sara, but from all of humanity, as well.

Gently, she cupped his cheek with her hand. "Is there no one to love you, then?"

"No one."

"I would love you, Gabriel."

"No!"

Stricken by the force of his denial, she let her hand fall into her lap. "Is the thought of my love so revolting?"

"No, don't ever think that." He sat back on his heels, wishing he could sit at her feet forever, that he could spend the rest of his existence worshiping her beauty, the generosity of her spirit. "I'm not worthy of you, *cara*. I would not have you waste your love on me."

"Why, Gabriel? What have you done that you feel unworthy of love?"

Filled with the guilt of a thousand lifetimes, he closed his eyes, and his mind filled with an image of blood. Rivers of blood. Oceans of death. Centuries of killing, of bloodletting. Damned. The Dark Gift had given him eternal life. And eternal damnation.

Thinking to frighten her away, he let her look deep into his eyes, knowing that what she saw within his soul would speak more eloquently than words.

He clenched his hands, waiting for the compassion in her eyes to turn to revulsion. But it didn't happen.

She gazed down at his upturned face for an endless moment, and then he felt the touch of her hand in his hair.

"My poor angel," she whispered. "Can't you tell me what it is that haunts you so?"

He shook his head, unable to speak past the lump in his throat.

"Gabriel." His name, nothing more, and then she leaned forward and kissed him.

It was no more than a feathering of her lips across his, but it exploded through him like concentrated sunlight. Hotter than a midsummer day, brighter than lightning, it burned through him, and for a moment he felt whole again. Clean again.

Humbled to the core of his being, he bowed his head so she couldn't see his tears.

"I will love you, Gabriel," she said, still stroking his hair. "I can't help myself."

"Sara . . ."

"You don't have to love me back," she said quickly. "I just wanted you to know that you're not alone anymore."

A long, shuddering sigh coursed through him, and then he took her hands in his, holding them tightly, feeling the heat of her blood, the pulse of her heart. Gently, he kissed her fingertips, and then, gaining his feet, he swung her into his arms.

"It's late," he said, his voice thick with the tide of emotions roiling within him. "We should go before you catch a chill."

"You're not angry?"

"No, *cara*."

How could he be angry with her? She was light and life, hope and innocence, long walks on bright summer days. He was tempted to fall to his knees and beg her forgiveness for his whole miserable existence.

But he couldn't do that, couldn't burden her with the knowledge of what he was. Couldn't tarnish her love with the truth.

It was near dawn when they reached the orphanage. Once he had her settled in bed, he knelt beside her. "Thank you, Sara."

She turned on her side, a slight smile lifting the corners of her mouth as she took his hand in hers. "For what?"

"For your sweetness. For your words of love. I'll treasure them always."

"Gabriel." The smile faded from her lips. "You're not trying to tell me good-bye, are you?"

He stared down at their joined hands; hers small and pale and fragile, pulsing with the energy of life, his large and cold, indelibly stained with blood and death.

If he had a shred of honor left, he would tell her good-bye and never see her again.

But then, even when he had been a mortal man, he'd always had trouble doing the honorable thing when it conflicted with something he wanted. And he wanted—no, needed—Sara. Needed her as he'd never needed anything else in his accursed life. And perhaps, in a way, she needed him. And even if it wasn't so, it eased his conscience to think it true.

"Gabriel?"

"No, *cara*, I'm not planning to tell you good-bye. Not now. Not ever."

The sweet relief in her eyes stabbed him to the heart. And he, cold, selfish monster that he was, was glad of it. Right or wrong, he couldn't let her go.

"Till tomorrow, then?" she said, smiling once more.

"Till tomorrow, *cara mia,*" he murmured. And for all the tomorrows of your life.

# *Chapter Seven*

Images flashed through his mind—scattered images of writhing flames, of frightened children crying, of women weeping hysterically.

Pain seared through him. Excruciating, nauseating pain.

He fought through the layers of oblivion, his gaze opening on darkness. He knew immediately that it was still daylight and for a moment he lay there, confused. Never before had anything save the threat of imminent danger disturbed the heavy lethargy that weighed him down during the light of day.

Sara!

He knew in that moment that her life was in danger, that the pain that had seared through him had been her pain. His hands clenched at his sides as he tried to rise. It was like trying to fight his way out of quicksand, and he fell back, breathing heavily, fear making his heart beat fast.

Sara!

His mind screamed her name, echoing and reechoing like rolling thunder.

Sara!

She was hurt, perhaps dying, and until sundown there was nothing he could do.

Never before had he felt so helpless, so cursed. From the depths of his heart, he cried out, beseeching a kindly heaven to help her, to spare her life.

"Please. Please. Please."

Just that single word, repeated over and over again, as he was dragged down into the darkness.

When he woke, he could still feel her pain, her anguish, and he knew she was still clinging to life.

*I'm coming, Sara.* He sent his thoughts across the miles, from his heart to hers. *Hang on,* cara. *I'm coming.*

"He's coming . . ." Struggling through a morass of pain, Sara repeated the words again and again.

"Lie still, child," Sister Mary Josepha said. "You must lie still."

"But he's . . . coming. I've . . . I've got to . . . be ready."

Sister Mary Josepha glanced up at Sister Mary Ynez. "Who's coming? Who can she talking about?"

Sister Mary Ynez shook her head. "Maybe she's thinking of her father. Will you stay with her while I look in on the others? I fear Elizabeth will not survive the night."

Sister Mary Josepha nodded. "Poor child," she murmured. And bowing her head, she began to pray.

* * *

Gabriel walked down the narrow hallway, his nostrils filling with the odor of alcohol and antiseptic, of strong carbolic and ether. Of blood. So much blood.

The hunger rose within him, stabbing at him, wrapping around him. Blood. Warm and sweet.

He turned down another hallway, and the lust for blood was overshadowed by pain. Sara's pain. She was unconscious, but her silent screams of agony reached out to him, tearing at his heart, his soul.

On silent feet, he approached the doorway. She was lying on a narrow bed, covered by a thin white sheet. An elderly nun sat in a straight-backed wooden chair beside the bed, a well-worn rosary clutched in her gnarled hands.

The nun glanced up as he stepped into the room, her rheumy blue eyes widening in horror. "What are you doing here?"

Gabriel said nothing, his guilt over what he was rising up to choke him in the face of the old nun's purity of heart and soul.

"Spawn of the devil," she whispered, "why are you here?"

Her words cut him to the quick. "I mean her no harm, Sister, I assure you."

Sister Mary Josepha clutched her rosary to her breast, her thumb caressing the ivory crucifix. "Be gone!"

Gabriel shook his head. "I must see her, if only for a moment."

Though she was aged and small of stature, the nun bravely put herself between Gabriel and Sara.

"You will not have her." Sister Mary Josepha lifted the crucifix, thrusting it toward him. "Be gone, I say!"

Gabriel took a step backward and then, drawing on his revenant power, he gazed deep into the nun's eyes, delving into her mind.

"Sit down, Sister," he said quietly.

Slowly, her movements stiff and unnatural, the nun moved to the chair and sat down.

Gabriel passed his hand in front of her face. "Sleep now," he said, his voice quiet, soothing.

He felt a moment of resistance, but the old nun was powerless against the dark power of three hundred and fifty years. Her eyelids closed, her head lolled forward, and she was asleep.

On silent feet, Gabriel moved to the bed and gazed down at Sara. Revulsion and a wave of pity rose within him as he stared at her, at the blistered skin on her arms, her hands. He drew back the sheet, tears welling in his eyes as he saw the ugly burns on her chest, her legs. Miraculously, her face had been spared.

She moaned then, a soft cry of agony that tore at the very edges of his soul. He placed his fingertip against the pulse in her throat. Her heartbeat was slow, her life force weak. She was dying.

"No!" The word was ripped from his throat.

And then he was lifting her in his arms, carrying her swiftly from the room, from the hospital, the power of his mind blinding those he passed to their presence.

With preternatural speed, he raced toward the abbey. Sara lay limp in his arms, hardly breathing. She seemed to weigh nothing at all and he carried her effortlessly.

"Please don't let her die. Please don't let her die."

The words were a prayer in his heart, even though

he didn't believe that God would hear him.

When he reached the abbey, he carried her into his room and laid her on the floor. A blink of his eye started a fire in the hearth. Removing his cloak, he spread it before the fireplace, then placed her on it, his heart pounding with fear. She looked so still; her skin, what little hadn't been burned, was as pale as death.

With a sob, he slit the vein in his wrist, parted her lips, and let his blood drip into her mouth. One drop, two. A dozen. How much would it take?

When he judged she'd had enough, he drew the fur-lined cloak around her, then gathered her into his arms. Rising, he sat down in his chair and gazed into the flames.

He held her throughout the night, wondering how the fire had started, listening to her soft moans of pain, her erratic breathing. She sobbed for her mother, her father. Once, she cried his name, begging him to come to her, to help her.

"I'm trying, *cara*," he murmured. "I'm trying."

He felt dawn approaching and knew the time had come to leave her. He held her as long as he could, held her until his body felt drugged, heavy. Reluctantly, he laid her on the floor in front of the hearth, wishing he had a bed for her, blankets. Clothes. And hard on the heels of that thought came the hope that she would have need of those things, that he had given her his accursed blood in time. That he had given her enough. He had no food to give her, only a bottle of aged red wine. He left it on the hearth where she would be sure to see it if she woke, and then, having done all he could, he left her.

On feet that felt as heavy as lead, he made his way

down to the catacombs and secured the door. With Sara in the house, he would have to take his sleep with the rest of the dead.

He rose as the sun was going down, the smell of rain heavy in the air. He took the stairs two at a time, ran down the narrow hallway to his room.

Sara lay as he had left her, her blond hair spread like a golden halo around her head.

Murmuring her name, he knelt beside her. Drawing back his cloak, his gaze swept over her from head to foot, and then he let out a long sigh of relief. She was healing. Not as swiftly as he would have, but she was healing. Her skin still looked raw in places, but the blisters were shrinking, drying.

Gently, he covered her once more, and then he closed his eyes as relief washed through him. She would be all right.

"Gabriel?"

He opened his eyes to find her staring up at him, her brow furrowed in bewilderment.

"How do you feel?" he asked.

"Terrible. What happened?"

"There was a fire at the orphanage."

"A fire! How did it start?"

"I don't know."

"Do you know if Sister Mary Josepha and the other nuns survived the fire? And the children . . . ?" She blinked back a tear as she thought of all the sweet dear children she had grown to care for. Had they been burned, as well?

"I don't know, Sara, but I'll find out."

"Thank you."

She glanced over his shoulder. "Where are we?"

"This is where I . . . live."

"Here?" She stared at the room, empty save for a large, thronelike chair. There was a faded space on one wall where a large crucifix had once been. She thought it odd that the room's only window was covered by a thick black cloth. "What is this place?"

"It used to be a monastery."

"And you live here?" She frowned as vague memories of the night of the fire began to surface. "I seem to remember being taken to the hospital. How did I get here?" She stared at him, waiting for an explanation.

"Are you hungry?" he asked, abruptly changing the subject.

"No. I want to know why I'm here."

"Thirsty?"

It was obvious he wasn't going to answer her, and she was too muddled by all that had happened to pursue the matter.

"I am thirsty," she said, her throat feeling suddenly dry.

With a nod, Gabriel poured her a glass of wine, and she reached for it, her hand halting halfway to the glass.

He saw the horror in her eyes as she gazed at her hand, at the reddened skin, the ugly yellow scabs left by the blisters.

"Sara . . ."

"My hand. What happened to my hand? My arm?" She threw the cloak aside, the fact that she was naked not registering as she looked at the raw red patches that covered her arms and legs and chest.

He saw the scream rising in her throat, the panic

in her eyes, and cursed himself for not thinking to prepare her.

"Sara, listen to me, you're all right."

"All right? How can I be all right?" She stared at him, then slowly shook her head. "I don't understand. Why doesn't it hurt?"

"I . . ." He took a deep breath. "I gave you something to aid in the healing."

"Something?"

"A new medicine. Sometimes it works miracles." He drew the cloak around her. "Rest now, *cara*. Sleep is the best healer of all." He stroked her hair. "Don't be alarmed if I'm not here in the morning," he said. "I may have to go out, but I'll be back by nightfall."

She nodded, and then she closed her eyes and curled into his arms, as trusting as a babe.

He held her until he was certain she was asleep, and then he went out. She would need something to wear when she woke. Clothes. Shoes. Undergarments. A comb and brush and pins for her hair. A bed to sleep in.

Unmindful of the rain, he went into the city. The shopkeepers all knew him. His material wants were few, but he always bought the best, the most expensive, and the tradespeople were eager to serve him. The shops that had closed for the night eagerly opened their doors, anxious to do his bidding.

He bought bread and cheese, a variety of fruits and vegetables, a bottle of vintage wine. He bought a small curved settee covered in blue and green striped damask, a matching footstool, a small table inlaid with ivory, a box of scented candles, a Persian rug, a narrow bed with an elaborately carved headboard, sheets and linens, a pillow stuffed with feathers.

Entering one of the ladies' shops, he picked out several colorful frocks, undergarments, silk stockings, a pair of shoes with silver buckles. Ribbons in rainbow colors for her hair. A bonnet trimmed with feathers and lace. Perfumed soap for her bath. A dark blue cloak trimmed in ermine to keep her warm. A sleeping gown. A dressing gown of rose-colored velvet. He bought her a box of chocolates, a feather fan, a pair of gloves, another book of poetry, a bouquet of spring flowers, an elegant crystal vase to put them in.

He was on his way home when he passed a toy shop. The doll in the window immediately caught his eye, and he bought that, too.

Loading all his goods into a rented wagon, he drove back to the abbey.

Sara was still asleep in front of the fire. Moving quietly, he carried the furniture into the room, placing the bed against the wall where the crucifix had hung. He made the bed as best he could, smoothing the linens over the plump mattress.

Sara stirred but didn't wake up when he carried her to the bed. Removing his cloak, he drew the sleeping gown over her head, trying not to stare at her softly rounded curves. He tucked her in, pressed a kiss to her cheek, and then carried in the rest of the furniture. He spread the rug on the floor, placed the settee and the footstool in front of the hearth.

He put the table by the bed, then placed the chocolates and the book of poetry on top, within easy reach, along with a glass of water. The flowers added a touch of color to the drab room.

He filled a small basket with bread and cheese and

fruit, covered it with a napkin, and placed it upon the table, as well.

He left the clothing in the boxes, anticipating her excitement when she saw her new finery. He put the doll within reach of her hand where she would be sure to see it upon waking.

For a moment, he stood in the center of the room, pleased with the changes he'd wrought. Amazing, what a rug and a few pieces of furniture could do, he mused. But it was the woman who gave the room life, the woman who drew him, her life force beckoning the revenant within him while her goodness, her innocence, enticed what little was left of the man he had once been.

Helpless to resist her, he knelt beside the bed and took her hand in his, wanting to be near her for as long as he could.

The fire burned brightly, but it was Sara's presence in the room that warmed him.

She woke slowly, still caught in the web of her nightmare, and then, as if someone had doused her with cold water, she remembered that it hadn't been a nightmare at all. There had been a fire at the orphanage.

All too vividly, she remembered waking up, her throat burning, her eyes stinging, as tongues of fire licked the edge of her bed. Unable to escape the flames, she had screamed until she was hoarse, sobbing for Gabriel, her angel, to come and save her. She remembered the awful horror that had coiled within her, the terrible certainty that she was going to die. And then the flames had touched her, licking at her skin . . .

She held up her arm and stared, disbelieving what she saw. The skin, which last night had been raw and red, was almost healed.

Throwing back the covers, she examined her chest, her legs, but saw only the glow of pink healthy skin.

It was impossible. A miracle. She lifted her hand, turning it this way and that, unable to believe the proof of her own eyes.

She frowned a moment, bemused to find herself clad in a modest white sleeping gown. A faint blush heated her cheeks as she realized that Gabriel had dressed her for bed, that he had seen her unclothed while she slept.

And then she saw the doll and she forgot everything else.

The ballerina was made of fine china, her face beautifully painted. Her eyes were big and blue, her lips a delicate rose. She wore a tutu of pale pink tulle; dainty pink ballet slippers covered her feet.

"Oh . . ." Reverently, Sara reached for the doll. It was the loveliest thing she had ever seen. "Carlotta," she whispered. "I shall name you Carlotta."

Sara glanced around the room, hoping to see Gabriel. It was then she noticed the pretty little table beside the bed. Wide-eyed, she stared at the flowers, the book, the heart-shaped box of chocolates, the wicker basket covered with a linen cloth.

Pulling herself into a sitting position, she reached for the book, carefully turning the pages, and then she reached for the chocolates, her mouth watering.

Candy of any kind had been a rare treat in the orphanage. She quickly gobbled down two pieces, and then laughed. The whole box was for her, to eat at her leisure. She touched the flowers, her fingertips caressing the velvety petals. Flowers. No one had ever given her flowers before.

Feeling like a queen, she nibbled a third chocolate, then took a drink of water, wondering all the while where Gabriel was.

After a time, she drew the basket onto her lap and peeked inside to find a small loaf of honey bread, a wedge of cheese, grapes and apples.

Such luxury, she thought, to sit in bed and indulge. She spent the rest of the morning reading. When noontime came, she finished the food in the basket, then took a nap.

When she woke, it was almost dark. Sitting up, she glanced around the dusky room, the need to relieve herself uppermost in her mind.

She was on the verge of tears, afraid she would disgrace herself, when Gabriel entered the room.

"You're looking well, *cara,*" he remarked, and then frowned at the expression of distress on her face. "What is it? What's wrong?"

"I need . . . I need to . . ." Her cheeks burned with embarrassment. How did a lady tell a man that she needed a bedpan?

But there was no need. Understanding dawned in the depths of Gabriel's eyes. Wordlessly, he swept her into his arms and carried her down a long hall lined with narrow cells.

He stepped into the first cell, uncovered the chamber pot in the corner, raised her gown, and placed her on it.

Avoiding her gaze, he left the room.

She couldn't face him when he returned.

"Sara? Sara, listen to me. You needn't be embarrassed. I'm only sorry I didn't anticipate your needs sooner. Forgive me."

She mumbled something completely inane under her breath, wishing he would just go away and leave her alone. It had been bad enough when the nuns tended her, but this was beyond enduring. She wanted him to think of her as a woman, not a helpless child.

"Sara . . ."

She heard the sound of his footsteps as he crossed the floor, and then he was kneeling in front of her, taking her hands in his.

"Sara, look at me."

"I can't."

"It's a perfectly normal function of the body."

She felt her cheeks grow hotter.

"If you're going to stay here with me, you had best get used to my helping you."

"Stay here?" She looked up then. "Do you mean it?"

"If you wish it."

"Oh, I do."

"Good, then let's have no more foolishness." He swung her into his arms and carried her back to her bed. "Did you enjoy the poetry?"

"Yes, thank you. Thank you for everything. Especially for Carlotta." She caressed the doll's hair. Perhaps she *was* just a child, Sara thought, to be so overjoyed with such a gift.

"I've brought you something to eat," he said, and reaching into a box, he withdrew a steaming platter, placed it on a tray, and set it in her lap. "I hope you like it."

"It smells wonderful," Sara replied. "But aren't you going to eat?"

His gaze slid away from hers. "I've eaten."

"Oh." She didn't know where to begin. The plate was piled high with chicken in a creamy sauce, vegetables dripping with butter. There was a chunk of warm bread dripping honey.

He placed a glass of wine on the table, then inclined his head. "Enjoy your meal, *cara*."

Gabriel stood beside the fireplace, gazing at the flames, while she ate. The smell of the chicken sickened him, and yet he yearned to be able to sit beside Sara, to share the meal with her, as a normal man might have done.

He had not eaten solid food in centuries; indeed, the very thought made him physically ill. Fresh blood was his diet now, that and an occasional glass of red wine.

He glanced at her over his shoulder. She looked vibrant and alive. Cursed though he might be, his blood had saved her. The hideous burns and blisters had all but disappeared. In another day or two, they would be completely gone.

He stared into the flames again. Tomorrow . . . how long could he keep her here? How could he bear to let her go?

She'd been here but a day, and already his life was made richer. Caught in the web of sleep in his lair, he had felt her presence in the room above. For the first time in over three centuries, he had slept without feeling alone.

And yet, he couldn't condemn her to a life with him, a life that was no life at all. He couldn't let her spend her days in this dreary place, cut off from the rest of humanity, just so he could have the pleasure of her company at night, feel her nearness while he slept.

"Gabriel?"

He turned to face her, realizing she had been speaking to him for several moments. "I'm sorry, *cara*, did you say something?"

"I asked if you would share a glass of wine with me."

"Of course."

She watched him cross the room, his steps fluid, his cloak swirling out behind him. He moved like moonlight on water, she thought. It was as if his feet never touched the floor.

He refilled her glass and handed it to her. Smiling her thanks, she took a sip, then offered him the glass.

His dark gray eyes met hers as he turned the goblet in his hand, drinking from the place where her lips had been.

A quick heat uncurled within her as their eyes met. There was something sensual, erotic, in watching him, in knowing that his mouth was where hers had been only moments before.

She licked lips gone suddenly dry as his presence seemed to fill the entire room. The light of the fire danced in his hair, limning the ebony-colored strands with gold. The expression in his eyes grew intense, as if the heat of the flames burned within their depths. She studied the breadth of his shoulders, familiar with the latent strength that resided within him. He was dressed all in black, always in black.

He hadn't moved, and yet he seemed to be all around her, filling her senses, until all she could see or hear was Gabriel. All she could taste or touch or smell was Gabriel.

Her heart pounded within her breast, a low steady beat, like that of a distant drum.

She opened her mouth to speak his name, but no sound emerged save that of a sigh.

*"Cara . . ."* He took a step toward her, one hand stretched in entreaty. Clad in her long white gown, with the wealth of her golden hair falling over her shoulders, and the light of the flames reflected in the depths of her blue eyes, she looked like a madonna, an angel.

He folded his hand into a fist and clenched it at his side. She was an angel, he thought, and he was a monster who had no right to touch her, to want her.

He took a step backward, and she had the feeling that he was withdrawing from her, that there was more than distance separating them. The thought frightened her.

"Gabriel?"

"You should rest, Sara."

"I rested all day. Can't we go out?"

"Perhaps tomorrow night."

"Have I done something to displease you?"

"No!"

"Then what's wrong?"

"Nothing. You've been through quite an ordeal. You need to conserve your strength."

"But I feel fine." She looked up at him, a slight frown creasing her brow. "Why do I feel fine?" She stared down at her hands as if she'd never seen them before. "Why am I healing so fast? Gabriel, I'm frightened."

"Don't be." He took a step toward her, wanting,

needing, to hold her, yet afraid to get too close, afraid he wouldn't be able to control the hunger her nearness aroused. "There's nothing to be afraid of."

"But the fire . . . Gabriel, it burned me. I . . ." She took a deep breath. "I should have died. I was dying. I remember hearing Sister Mary Josepha tell Sister Mary Louisa that my death would be a blessing. I remember Father Dominic standing over me, giving me last rites."

She gazed up at him, her eyes filled with confusion. "What happened to me, Gabriel? Why didn't I die?"

"I can't explain it, *cara*. Only trust me. Believe me when I tell you that there's nothing to fear."

But she couldn't help being frightened. All day, she had avoided asking herself these questions. In the light of day, she could pretend everything was all right, that nothing out of the ordinary had happened to her. But she couldn't pretend anymore. She'd been badly burned, but it didn't hurt. Already, the signs of injury were disappearing; in a few days they'd probably be gone.

A soft oath escaped Gabriel's lips as he saw the anguish, the confusion, in Sara's eyes. Two long strides carried him to her bedside. Sweeping her into his arms, he carried her to his chair and sat down, cradling her in his arms as if she were a child.

He gazed deep into her eyes, bending her will to his. "Go to sleep, *cara*. There is nothing to fear. Sleep, *cara mia*. Sleep . . ."

He felt the tension drain out of her as her eyelids grew heavy. Moments later, she was asleep.

# *Chapter Eight*

With the power of his mind, Gabriel willed Sara to sleep throughout the next day.

He rose with the onset of dusk. Changed his clothes. Left the catacombs, bound for the orphanage.

Dissolving into mist, he entered the building that had been Sara's home for the past thirteen years. In all that time, he had never ventured into any room but hers. The acrid smell of smoke hung over the house.

He moved down the hallway, peering into the kitchen, the parlor. A large room filled with books and toys, easels and paints, was located at the end of the hallway. Inside, two nuns watched over a dozen children engaged in a variety of activities.

Instinctively, he passed by the chapel, and the small rooms where the nuns slept.

The upstairs was mostly bedrooms. The room

above Sara's was only a blackened shell. Part of the floor had burned away; he could see where the flames had burned their way down the wall behind Sara's bed. It was a miracle she had survived, that she hadn't been burned even worse than she was.

He found several of the nuns gathered together in a small upstairs room, quietly discussing the fire, and the condition of one of the children who had been badly burned. He heard Sara's name mentioned several times.

And then Sister Mary Josepha entered the room.

"I spoke to Father André," she said. "He thinks I imagined the whole thing. But I didn't! I know what I saw." Tears welled in the old nun's eyes. "He took Sara Jayne," she said, her voice filled with despair. "That monster took her."

"Perhaps we should notify the police," one of the nuns suggested.

"What could they do against such evil?" Sister Mary Josepha shook her head. "They probably wouldn't believe me any more than the good father did."

"We must do something," another nun said.

"But what?" Sister Mary Josepha shook her head again. "I was powerless against him." She clutched the cross that dangled from a braided rope around her waist. "I've never felt such evil. Oh, my poor Sara, to be at that fiend's mercy."

An hour later, he entered the monastery. He freed Sara's mind from sleep as he locked the door behind him.

She was yawning when he entered the room.

Sara smiled at him uncertainly. "Where have you

been?" she asked as he removed his cloak.

"I went to the orphanage," Gabriel replied, dropping his cloak on the foot of the bed. "How do you feel?"

"All right." She glanced away, afraid to ask questions, afraid of the answers.

"None of the sisters was badly hurt," Gabriel said, answering the unspoken question in Sara's eyes. "One child was badly burned. One died."

"Who?"

"I didn't ask her name."

Sara closed her eyes, murmuring a silent prayer for the child's soul, giving thanks that no other lives had been lost.

"Sara?"

She looked up at him through eyes shiny with unshed tears, grateful that the nuns who had cared for her had been spared.

"Are you all right?"

She nodded, blinking back her tears. "Does Sister Mary Josepha know where I am?"

Gabriel shook his head. "No, I didn't have a chance to speak to her. I learned of the fire from someone else. No one seems to know how it started."

"Do you think I could send her a message and let her know I'm all right?"

"If you wish."

"You never told me why you brought me here."

"Does it matter?"

She blinked up at him, confused by the peculiar light in his eyes, by the sudden warmth that suffused her. Of course it didn't matter, she thought; she'd rather be here, with him, than anywhere else.

"No, but . . ." She plucked nervously at the bedclothes. "I can't believe I slept the whole day."

"You needed the rest."

She made a soft sound of assent. "And now I need to . . . you know."

With a nod, he carried her into the monk's cell, waiting in the corridor while she relieved herself. It would be so easy, he thought, so easy to mold her mind to his way of thinking, to make her long to stay with him always. He could arrange it so she would be content to sleep days so that she might spend her nights with him. What bliss, to keep her by his side, to watch her blossom into womanhood, to be the one to teach her of the ways between a man and a woman. It would all be so easy, but so wicked, because he wasn't a man at all . . .

A startled cry drew him quickly to her side.

"What is it?" he asked, glancing around.

"My legs, they feel so strange."

Gabriel frowned. "Strange?"

"They tingle, like someone is poking me with pins and feathers."

Dropping to his knees, he lifted her gown and ran a hand along her right calf.

"That tickles! Gabriel, I've never had any feeling in my legs before. What's happening?"

He rocked back on his heels, then shook his head. "I'm not sure."

Frowning, he carried her back to his chamber. Was it possible that the power of his blood had healed her infirmity? There was, he thought, but one way to tell.

Gently, he stood her before him, her feet touching the ground. "I'm going to let you go, Sara."

"No!" she clasped his shoulders.

"Only for a moment. Trust me." He relented a little when he saw the fear in her eyes. "Here, hold my hand."

She stared at him, her eyes wide with apprehension, as he took her hand in his, and then let his other hand fall away from her waist. She swayed unsteadily, but didn't fall.

"Gabriel," she breathed. "I'm standing."

He took a step back, his hand still holding hers. "Come to me, Sara."

She shook her head, afraid to move for fear of falling.

His gaze held hers, dark and mesmerizing. "Come to me, Sara. Don't be afraid. I won't let you fall."

"I can't." But even as she spoke the words, she was moving, sliding her left foot forward, shifting her weight, sliding her right foot up. One step. Two, and then she stumbled and fell into his arms.

He lifted her easily, holding her close to his chest.

"I walked!" she exclaimed, her voice filled with wonder. "Gabriel, I walked."

He smiled down at her, his heart pounding with joy. His blood, his demon blood, had saved Sara's life, and now it seemed it had returned the strength to her legs. Even if his soul spent eternity in hell, he would ever be grateful for the Dark Gift that had brought such happiness to Sara's eyes.

"Put me down," she said, wriggling in his arms. "Put me down. I want to walk!"

And she did walk. With his help at first, and then, slowly, haltingly, she walked from one end of the room to the other on her own.

"Perhaps you should rest now," Gabriel suggested.

Sara shook her head. She could feel strength flowing through her, feel her legs growing stronger with each passing moment. "It's a miracle!" she said fervently. "Nothing less than a miracle."

A miracle, indeed, Gabriel mused. A little of his accursed blood had the power to restore her strength, but even as he watched her, he couldn't help but wonder if she would think the miracle worth the price if she knew how it had been wrought.

Holding her arms away from her sides, she twirled around, her gown billowing around her ankles.

"A miracle! Gabriel, I can walk. Do you know what that means? I can walk." She threw her arms around his neck and hugged him tight. "If I can walk, I can run! If I can run, I can dance!"

With boundless energy, she twirled around the room, her eyes shining, her hair floating around her shoulders like a golden nimbus.

"I'm going to dance!" she shouted, her voice echoing off the stone walls. "I'm going to dance and dance and dance!"

She grabbed his hands and twirled him around, laughter bubbling in her throat. "Isn't it wonderful?"

"Aye, *cara,*" he agreed, her happiness flooding his damned soul like sunshine. "It's wonderful."

Abruptly, she stopped twirling. "Dance with me, Gabriel."

With a slight nod, he took her in his arms and began to waltz her around the room.

Sara tilted her head back. "We need music. Won't you give us some?"

"If you wish," he murmured, and he began to sing a slow song from his youth, of love lost, of love found.

He had an incredible voice, deep and rich, filled

with such passion and longing it brought tears to her eyes.

They danced together as if they had done so a thousand times before. The sound of his voice wrapped around her, adding to the magic of the night. She looked into his eyes and saw a tiny flame that grew and grew until she felt the heat of it envelop her.

And then he was kissing her, his lips warm, gentle, hungry. The heat of his hands seared her skin. The beat of his heart thundered in her ears. And she was drowning in sensation, smothering in a blanket of desire.

She kissed him back, shivering with delight, with fear. His tongue stroked her lower lip, and fingers of flame exploded within her. She pressed against him, yearning to be closer. His chest was hard and solid. She felt his arms tighten around her waist. His breath was warm against her face, labored, rasping.

"Gabriel . . ." Her voice sounded heavy, drugged.

*"Cara . . ."*

It took every ounce of willpower he possessed to put her away from him. The scent of her, the softness of her, stirred his desire, not only for her sweet body, but for the vital essence of her life. The hunger raged through him, urging him to take her, here, now, to satisfy the awful thirst only her blood could quench.

He heard her gasp and knew that the blood hunger was visible in his eyes.

With an oath, he turned away. He stared into the fire, and the flames exploded upward with a mighty roar.

"Gabriel!"

"Go to bed, Sara Jayne."

"But . . ."

"Go to bed, Sara!"

She didn't argue this time. Jumping into the bed, she pulled the covers up to her chin, her gaze focused on Gabriel's back. He was breathing heavily, his hands clenched at his sides.

"Good night, Sara," he said, his voice gruff.

"Good night."

He took a deep breath, and then, without looking back, he left the room.

She stared after him, confused by what had happened, by the unholy light that had burned in the depths of his eyes. But surely she had imagined that. A trick of the flames, perhaps. Yes, that was it.

With a sigh, she snuggled deeper into the covers, then wiggled her toes.

She could walk! Tomorrow she would explore the abbey. She would go outside and run barefoot through the grass. She would write the good sisters and tell them she was well, that she was more than well!

And tomorrow night, she would dance in the light of the moon. With Gabriel.

Murmuring a heartfelt prayer of gratitude for the miracle that had been bestowed upon her, she gazed at the thick black cloth that covered the window, wondering absently why Gabriel had put it there. Perhaps she would ask him tomorrow . . .

She dreamed of blood and death, of the darkness of eternal damnation, of the loneliness of hell.

She dreamed of demons with blood-red eyes and teeth as sharp as daggers.

And woven into the tapestry of her dreams, like a

fine gold thread, she saw Gabriel, heard him singing to her, his eyes sad, filled with a haunting loneliness she couldn't comprehend.

Gabriel . . . she saw him lying in a dark place, surrounded by death . . .

With a cry, she sat up, the covers clutched to her breast. For a moment, she was tempted to get out of bed and search for Gabriel, but the thought of wandering through the dark abbey, alone, in the dead of night, was more frightening than the nightmare that had awakened her.

Murmuring a fervent prayer, she slid under the covers and closed her eyes.

There were no more bad dreams.

Cloaked in the shadows of a quiet street far from the abbey, Gabriel felt Sara's restlessness. Though he had not taken her blood, there was a bond between them, an unbreakable link that had been forged when the first drop of his blood had passed her lips.

There were some who believed that to taste the blood of a vampire was to condemn oneself to the same life of darkness, but he knew it was not true. In ancient times, people had believed there were other ways to become a vampire—dying in a state of sin, dying after being cursed by one's parents. Some thought death by drowning, or committing suicide, might turn a person into a creature of the night. Being the seventh born was said to be another way to receive the curse. Midwives said that children born between Christmas and Epiphany, or children born with teeth, or with a caul, were destined to become vampires. Children whose mothers failed to eat enough salt during pregnancy were also believed to be cursed.

Fables, he thought. Foolish fables told to frighten children. Had they been true, the world would have been overrun with vampires long ago.

There was only one way to become a vampire, and that was an exchange of blood. The victim must be drained of his lifeblood to the point of death, and then drink the blood of the vampire.

In all the years since he'd been made, he had never bequeathed the Dark Gift to another. He had offered it only once, to Rosalia, begging her to ease his loneliness, to share eternity with him, but the mere idea had filled her with revulsion. In her haste to get away from him, she had fallen to her death.

Since then, he had kept his secret to himself, mingling with mortals only when his own company was no longer enough, when he needed to hear the sound of laughter, to be in the midst of those who were vital and alive.

After centuries of reveling in being a vampire, he had come to curse the loneliness of his existence, the selfish need for blood, the smell of death that was ever present in his life, but now he felt only joy.

Sometimes he felt as though he were being ripped apart. He yearned for a normal life, yearned for the sunlight, for the chance to marry and have children, to love and be loved. And yet, he enjoyed the powers that came with being a vampire. He had seen centuries come and go. He could change his form. Most people believed bats were the vampire's animal of choice, but he found it most unpleasant to squeeze his essence into such a small shape, and much preferred to turn into a wolf, though these days he did it rarely.

He possessed the strength of twenty mortal men; he had the power to hypnotize others, to bend them to his will. He had control over animals, over the wind and the rain. He could climb walls with the agility of a spider. In the blink of an eye, he could change shape, or dissolve into a swirling gray mist. But the novelty of such tricks, amazing as they might be, had dimmed long ago, and now, for the first time in years, he yearned to be mortal again so that he might love Sara.

Sara . . . she was asleep again, protected from him by her youth, her innocence.

Fiend though he might be, he would not defile her.

# *Chapter Nine*

Sara woke feeling wonderful. Jumping out of bed, she twirled round and round. It hadn't been a dream. She could walk!

She smiled when she saw an old wooden bathing tub in one corner of the room. A huge kettle filled with water hung from a tripod over a low fire. Bless Gabriel, he thought of everything.

She took a leisurely bath, her heart bubbling with joy as she propped her legs on the lip of the tub and wriggled her toes. She could walk!

Hunger drove her from the tub. She found some bread and cheese and a small bottle of wine in a basket. Wrapped in a blanket, she ate standing up, marveling that such a thing was possible. She could stand. She could walk, and suddenly a whole new world had opened before her eyes.

Sara glanced at the box of chocolates on the bedside table, at the room, though there was little to see—the bed she had slept in, the table, Gabriel's chair.

Several large boxes at the foot of the bed drew her eye, and she wondered why she hadn't noticed them before. She hesitated for a moment, not wanting to poke into them if they belonged to Gabriel, but her curiosity got the best of her.

A riot of color met her eyes as, one by one, she opened the boxes. She found delicate convent-made underwear: pantalets edged with lace, a camisole bedecked with a pale blue ribbon, a corset, a petticoat made of organdy, a pair of kidskin gloves, shoes with silver buckles, silk stockings.

Another box held a straw bonnet trimmed with a white feather and pink ribbons.

And dresses! Beautiful dresses fit for a queen. She draped them over the bed, her hands lingering over each one. The rose-pink silk was a study in simplicity with its scalloped neckline and long fitted sleeves. The blue challis was trimmed in yards and yards of delicate lace. There was a muted rose, green, and blue plaid taffeta, a floor-length gown of burgundy velvet.

In other boxes, she found a dressing gown of rose-colored velvet, a dark blue cloak trimmed in ermine. She'd never owned such costly clothing in her life. One box held dozens of ribbons in all the colors of the rainbow; another held a white feather fan. She opened the fan carefully; then, pretending she was a highborn lady bored with life, she fanned herself.

A highborn lady, indeed, Sara thought with a laugh, and closing the fan with a flourish, she stared at the bounty spread on the bed.

She stroked the ermine trim on the cloak as if it

were still a living thing. The cost of the cloak alone would have put food on the table at the orphanage for a month. Why had Gabriel bought her such elegant things? Where would she ever wear them?

Where? Here and now, she thought, and hastily pulled on the undergarments, then reached for the dress of rose-pink silk. It felt like heaven and fit as if it had been made for her. She glanced around the room, hoping to find a looking glass, but there was none in evidence. She tried each dress on, fretting over the lack of a mirror.

Perhaps she'd find a looking glass in one of the other rooms, she thought, and made her way down the hall, peeking into the tiny cells where the monks had once lived as she passed by.

Barefoot, she padded silently from room to room, all thought of a looking glass forgotten as she explored the old abbey.

The chapel, long neglected, still retained a hint of its former beauty. Some of the stained-glass windows had been broken, but others were still intact. A shaft of sunlight streamed through the window over the altar, the colored glass tinting the sunbeams.

Sara knelt at the altar, her gaze fixed on the window. It depicted a small blue pool in the midst of a green meadow. The Christ figure stood beside the pool holding a tiny lamb in the crook of one arm. Other lambs and sheep were gathered at his feet.

Sara glanced to the left where another window depicted Christ's agony on the cross. It was so beautiful, so lifelike, that tears stung her eyes. She stared at the nails in His hands and feet, unable to imagine the pain He had suffered, or His willingness to shoulder the sins of the world, to suffer, bleed, and die as an atoning sacrifice for all mankind. She had never doubted His love for her. And now He had blessed her with a miracle.

She knelt there for a long time, enveloped in a sense of peace and love as she offered a quiet, heartfelt prayer of gratitude for the ability to walk.

Leaving the chapel, Sara peered into what looked like the infirmary. Four iron bedsteads lined one wall. The mattresses, made of straw, had long since disintegrated. A huge lacy spider web dangled from one corner.

She paused at the refectory door. Several long plank tables, covered with years of dust, were situated in neat rows, and she imagined the monks sitting there in the high-backed wooden chairs, eating in silence while one of the brothers read to them from the scriptures. She saw another spider web, and there was a nest of some kind in the massive stone fireplace.

She went from room to room, expecting to find Gabriel, or at least some sign of him, but there was nothing anywhere to indicate that he lived in the abbey. No food in the kitchens, no clothing in any of the rooms, nothing.

Toward the back of the monastery, she found a narrow door. Thinking it led outside, she opened it to find a long stone stairway. Darkness rose up to meet her; darkness and a dank, musty smell.

Curious, she placed one hand on the wall and took a step down. Her breathing seemed suddenly loud as she took another step, and then another, until she came to a second door.

She tried the latch, but it was locked.

She stood there for a long moment, her senses reeling. Gabriel's image rose in her mind, and with it a vision of darkness, a foreboding coupled with a strong feeling of pain and anguish.

"Gabriel?"

Was he in there? Hurt, maybe?

She tried the latch again, turning it this way and that.

*Go back.*

She whirled around, her hand pressed over her heart. She fully expected to find someone standing behind her, but there was no one there. Had the words come from her own mind then, a warning from some sixth sense, or had they been spoken by some unseen entity?

She glanced at the door again, felt the hair rise along her arms. She took a step backward and then, overcome by a sudden overwhelming sense of evil, she bolted up the stairs and ran for the sanctuary of her room.

Inside, she slammed the door, then stood there, breathing heavily.

Gradually, her heartbeat returned to normal, and she told herself she had imagined the whole thing, that she was just letting her imagination get the best of her. But she didn't believe it. Not for a moment. She had sensed evil, something so sinister, so dark, that it had touched her most primal fear and sent her running for the safety of her room as though her very soul were in danger.

She wished that Gabriel was there to soothe her fears, to assure her that all was well. She wondered again why there was no food in the kitchens, why she had found nothing to indicate his presence.

Surely if he lived here, she would have found clothing, a razor, a hairbrush, something.

Curling up in his chair with the book of poetry, she determined to ask him where he spent his days. She wanted to know how he earned his living, and why he lived here, in this cold place. And maybe, if she could summon the nerve, she would ask him what evil lurked at the bottom of the stairs.

It was just at dusk that Gabriel entered the room. Sara glanced up from her book, her spirits lifting at the mere sight of him. Clad in a full-sleeved white shirt, tight black breeches, and soft leather boots, he took her breath away.

Rising, she ran across the floor and threw herself into his arms.

Gabriel closed his eyes as his arms closed around Sara. She fit into his embrace as though her form had been sculpted to complement his. Her scent rose all around him, warm and feminine. And alive.

For endless moments, they clung to each other.

For Sara, it was like coming home after a long absence.

For Gabriel, it was like walking in the sunshine.

After a time, Gabriel drew back so he could see her face. "Is anything wrong?"

"Not anymore."

"I don't understand."

"I missed you," Sara explained shyly. "All day, I wondered where you were, what you were doing." She placed her hand on his chest, her fingertips making random circles over his heart. "It's lonely here without you."

"I'm sorry. You must be hungry. Would you care

to go out?" His gaze moved over her. "You look lovely."

Sara lowered her gaze. "Thank you."

Releasing her, he draped the cloak about her shoulders, then offered her his arm. "Shall we go?"

He took her to a small but elegant restaurant, sipped a glass of red wine while she ate an enormous meal.

"Why aren't you eating?" Sara asked.

He hesitated a moment before he said, "I dined earlier."

"Oh."

"Finish your meal, *cara*, and then, if you'd like, we'll take a stroll in the gardens."

She ate quickly, conscious of his gaze, aware of his every movement. She loved to watch his hands. They were strong hands, expressive hands. Gentle hands. She felt a blush heat her cheeks as she recalled the kiss they had shared, the way his hands had skimmed over her body, light as the wings of a butterfly.

"Are you ready?"

She looked up with a start, the blush in her cheeks deepening as her eyes met his. "Yes."

He paid the bill, helped her with her cloak, took her hand. The night wrapped around them, dark and intimate, as they walked along a narrow, tree-lined path through the gardens. The fragrance of a hundred flowers rose up all around them, perfuming the air, but it was Sara's scent that filled Gabriel's senses, her nearness that made his heart pound in his chest. She looked like an angel in the light of the moon. A wealth of golden hair framed her delicate face, her skin glowed, her eyes were like shadowed blue pools.

The twin talons of need and hunger rose up within him, their claws piercing the darkness of his heart, his empty soul. It would be so easy to take her, to enfold her in his arms and feast upon her sweetness.

So easy.

He paused before a low stone bench. "Shall we sit awhile?"

"All right." She sat down, the folds of her pink gown spreading around her like the petals of a rose. "Where were you today?"

"I'm afraid I must ask you not to pry into my personal life."

"I didn't mean to pry," Sara said quickly, hoping to conceal the hurt caused by his censure, "I just wondered . . . never mind."

"Wondered what?"

"Where you spend your days. What kind of work you do."

"I don't work."

"You don't?"

"No. Not only am I a very private person, but a very wealthy one, as well."

"Oh."

"So," he said, forcing a smile, "how did you spend your day?"

"Trying on clothes." She placed her hand over his and gave it a squeeze. "Thank you, Gabriel. The dresses are lovely. I adore the book, and the candy, and everything else. You've been so generous."

"My pleasure."

"I went exploring today."

She felt his hand stiffen beneath hers. "Did you?"

Sara nodded. "I was looking for a mirror," she confessed, wondering if he would think her vain. "The dresses are so pretty. I wanted to see how I looked . . ."

Gabriel nodded. He should have known she'd want to primp before a looking glass, but it was the one thing he could not provide for her.

"I didn't find one, though." She stared at her hand, so small compared to his. "I . . . do you . . . ?"

"Go on."

"Do you really live in the abbey? I mean, there doesn't seem to be anything of you in any of the rooms." She shrugged. "I mean, for a wealthy man, you don't seem to own very much."

"I have a castle in Spain," he remarked. "If you're looking for wealth, I'll take you there one day."

"No, I didn't mean that!"

"I know."

"Where do those stairs go? The ones in the rear of the monastery?"

"To the catacombs. Don't go down there again, *cara*. There's nothing in those dark vaults but those who sleep the endless sleep of death."

A shiver ran down Sara's spine. "I know. I could feel it. Oh, Gabriel, it was awful."

Wordlessly, he gazed into her eyes. Never had the abyss between them seemed wider or deeper or more impossible to cross. It was a chasm with no bridge save death. Her death.

She watched him rise to his feet in a single fluid movement. "Is something wrong?"

"It grows late. We should be getting back."

She offered him her hand, felt the strength of his fingers close over hers as he helped her to her feet.

"I had a lovely time, Gabriel. Thank you."

He inclined his head in acknowledgment, then pressed his lips to her hand. "My pleasure, *cara*."

Unexpectedly, she wound her arms around his neck and pressed her lips to his. He gasped at her touch, at the warmth of her body against his own. She was like a shadow in his arms, fragile, elusive, yet loving and warm. So warm. So full of the energy of life. His heart thudded in time to the pulse fluttering in her throat, exciting his hunger, tormenting, tantalizing.

His body hardened at her nearness, and he wrapped his arms around her, drawing her closer, basking in her nearness, her youth, her innocence. Ah, but she felt good in his arms.

She moaned softly, grinding her hips against his as his tongue scorched her mouth. Her scent rose all around him, female, musky, desirable.

With a low groan, he lifted her arms from his neck and took a step backward. "We'd better go," he said hoarsely.

Tucking her hand in his, they walked back to the restaurant. He lifted her into the carriage, his hands lingering at her waist, before he vaulted up beside her. Taking up the reins, he clucked to the horse.

Later, he stood at the foot of her bed, watching her sleep, his lust for her flesh, and her blood, burning through him like a dark flame. He touched his tongue to his teeth, felt his fangs lengthen as he imagined the ecstasy that would be his, and hers, if he allowed himself to succumb to the hunger. Just one small taste, he thought. What harm could it do?

The power of his presence called to Sara's subconscious. Sleepily, she opened her eyes. She blinked once, twice, but the creature at the foot of her bed didn't disappear. Only stood there, staring down at her through eyes that glowed with an unearthly incandescence. Even in the darkness, she could see its fangs—long and white and deadly.

It was the monster who haunted her dreams.

"I'm dreaming," she murmured shakily. "I've got to be dreaming."

She stared at the creature for what seemed an eternity, and then, like an image in water, the figure began to blur until it faded to a dark mist and disappeared.

Deep in the catacombs, Gabriel took on his own shape. The time had come, he mused with regret. He was going to have to let her go, now, while he still could.

Sara stared up at him. "Go? Go where?"

"I've made arrangements for you to attend the School of Ballet in France."

"France!" Sara exclaimed.

She looked up at him, her eyes shining. "Oh, Gabriel, do you mean it? The School of Ballet!"

"You're pleased, then?"

"Oh, yes, but I'm too old to begin."

"They are willing to make an exception in your case."

"Really? Why?"

A wry smile hovered over Gabriel's lips. "With enough money, anything is possible."

"Oh, Gabriel, you're so good to me!"

"You leave tomorrow. I've opened an account for you at my bank in Paris. All your expenses will be paid. In addition, I want you to buy yourself a new wardrobe."

"Aren't you coming with me?"

"No."

"Have I done something to displease you?"

"No! Of Course not."

"Then why are you sending me away?"

Her words brought a wistful smile to his lips. "You're a young woman, Sara Jayne. It's time you associated with other young women. And young men . . ."

"But . . ." *I don't want to leave you,* she thought, frightened at the prospect of being parted from him. He was the only constant left in her life, the only security she had.

"You must trust me in this, Sara," he said. "It's for your own good. All the arrangements have been made."

"It's like a dream come true," she said, and wondered why she wasn't happier. Only moments ago, she had been ecstatic at the thought of going to Paris, but that was before she realized it meant being parted from Gabriel.

"You're too generous, Gabriel. I don't know what to say."

"Thank you will suffice."

"It hardly seems enough."

"The look in your eyes is thanks enough," Gabriel replied quietly. "A coach will pick you up in the morning, so I will bid you good night, and good-bye."

"Won't I see you in the morning? Aren't you going with me?"

"I'm afraid not. Business calls me away."

"So this is good-bye, then?"

"For now."

She realized abruptly that she might never see him

again. The thought smothered her excitement as effectively as pouring water over a fire. "Will you come to visit me?"

He hesitated a moment before answering, "If I can."

"You seem anxious to be rid of me," she remarked, not meeting his gaze. "I thought . . ."

Gabriel took a deep breath and let it out in a long, slow sigh. "Thought what?"

"That you cared for me."

"Of course I care, Sara."

"No, I mean . . ." She felt a crimson tide wash up her neck and into her cheeks. "I thought you were starting to care for me the way a man cares for a woman." She risked a glance at his face. "Last night, when I kissed you . . . Did I displease you? Is that why you want to send me away?"

"No, Sara." He reached for her hand, then thought better of it and shoved his hands into his trouser pockets. "It's just that you're so young, *cara* . . ."

"And you're so old?"

"Older than you can imagine," he answered with a trace of bitterness. "I want you to see the world you've been missing. I want you to have a chance to spread your wings."

"But . . . I'll miss you."

Pain lanced Gabriel's heart. She might miss him for a week, perhaps a month, but he would miss her through all the endless days and nights of eternity.

# *Chapter Ten*

Gabriel sat in his favorite chair, staring blankly into the darkness. Five years had passed since he'd sent Sara to France. Five years was but a moment in the life of a vampire, he thought ruefully, yet each day of those years had seemed an eternity.

He had found no joy in his existence with Sara gone from him. Reading held no pleasure; there was no solace in music. He haunted the ballet, torturing himself as he gazed at the ballerina and imagined Sara in her place.

He fed in spurts. He had no appetite and fed only when the hunger grew excruciating, clawing at his insides like a wild beast until he thought he would go mad. Only when the hunger grew unbearable did he leave the abbey, prowling through the back streets for nourishment.

Even then, he took little, only enough to sustain

his existence, hating what he was because it kept him from what he wanted.

Five years . . . She would be almost twenty-two now, a woman grown. And suddenly he knew he had to see her again, just once, and then he'd go to ground and sleep until her life was over and she was eternally safe from his hunger.

She was starring in *Giselle* at the Paris Opéra. The theater was an amazing piece of architecture, Gabriel mused as he made his way to his box. He knew the history of the opera house well. He had been living in Paris when Charles Garnier designed the building. Work had begun in the summer of 1861; the facade was unveiled in 1867. Work on the building had come to a halt during the Franco-Prussian War of 1870, and the unfinished opera house had been used as an arsenal and a warehouse for storing food and wine.

Gabriel had left Paris during the siege. Not for him the ugliness and cruelty of war. Food had been scarce. Zoo animals had been killed and the carcasses sold to restaurants. The rich ate elephant meat; the poor had dined on dogs and cats and rats. Paris had been on fire, people starving; the streets had been red with blood.

It wasn't until January of 1875 that the grand staircase was thronged with the first of many distinguished guests.

Gabriel sat forward in his seat, his gaze riveted on Sara's face as she took the stage. It was amazing, what she had accomplished in five short years. The audiences wondered how she had come so far so fast. It was nothing short of a miracle, they said, mystified by her phenomenal rise to fame. But for Gabriel there was no mystery involved. It was the blood, *his* blood, that had wrought the miracle, enabling her to accomplish in a few years what it usually took decades to achieve.

While waiting for the curtain to go up, he had listened to the conversations around him, an easy task for a vampire. Everyone had been talking about Sara, marveling at how effortlessly she danced. Her performances were impeccable, they all agreed, her interpretations inspired.

And now, as he watched, he could only concur. Her feet hardly seemed to touch the floor, so that she seemed to float across the stage, as fluid as water, lighter than air. Her face was radiant, her eyes glowing, as she danced, and he knew that for this short space of time, she was Giselle. She had perfectly captured every nuance, every emotion.

When the final curtain came down, he sat back in his seat and closed his eyes. Her performance had been flawless. He knew then that she had been born to dance. What he had just seen could not be taught; it had come from within her heart, her soul.

*You wanted only to see her,* he reminded himself. *Now you must go.*

But his feet refused to obey the promptings of his mind, and he found himself standing in the shadows outside the stage door, waiting for one more glimpse of her face.

He sensed her nearness even before she emerged from the theater. At first, he saw only Sara, her vivid blue eyes sparkling, her long blond hair falling like a heavenly cloud about her slim shoulders.

And then he noticed the man at her side, the proprietary grip of his hand upon her arm.

A low growl rose in Gabriel's throat. His first instinct was to attack, to rip out the man's throat with his bare hands. And then he saw the way Sara smiled at the young man, the happiness in her eyes, and he felt as if someone had driven a stake through his heart.

Dissolving into mist, Gabriel followed them as they walked down the street to a small cafe. Inside, they sat at a back table, talking about the evening's performance. The man, whose name, Gabriel learned, was Maurice Delacroix, praised Sara's dancing.

"I was good, wasn't I?" she said, but there was no boasting in her tone, or in her expression. "It was odd, but I felt as if . . ."

"As if?"

"I don't know. I can't explain it, Maurice. I wish . . ."

Maurice leaned closer, his hand enfolding hers. "What do you wish, Sara?"

"I wish Gabriel could have seen me dance tonight. I think he would have been pleased."

Maurice withdrew his hand from hers as if he'd been stung. "Gabriel again! When are you going to get over your infatuation with your benefactor?"

"I'm not infatuated. I just miss him, that's all." Sara stared at the candle sputtering in the middle of the table. The short time she had spent with Gabriel seemed so long ago, yet she had never forgotten him.

At first, she had written to him, but she had no last name for him, no address save Crosswick Abbey, and her letters had come back with the notation that they were undeliverable. Yet her bank account was always full. She had felt guilty spending his money when she couldn't even acknowledge his generosity with a note of thanks.

For a time, she had refused to spend his funds, and when two months passed with no withdrawal, she had received a short letter from Gabriel urging, almost demanding, that she indulge herself at his expense. It was the only letter she had received from him, and she had carried it with her until it grew dog-eared around the edges. Fearing its destruction, she had placed it between the pages of the first Paris Opéra playbill that listed her name as *prima ballerina*.

Five years. She still couldn't believe how much she had learned, how far she'd come. She was the leading ballerina. It was a miracle. Most dancers started at a very young age and studied for years, yet the most intricate steps had come to her easily.

She was recognized on the street. Men sent her flowers and trinkets. She had received numerous proposals of marriage. She had danced before royalty. She had done all the things she had ever dreamed of, and still her life was lacking. She wanted to dance for Gabriel. She wanted to dance *with* Gabriel, to feel his arms around her once more, to gaze into the depths of his haunted gray eyes, to hear him sing his sad songs. More than anything, she yearned to wipe the sorrow from his eyes, to make him smile, to hear him laugh.

"Sara?"

Startled, she looked up.

"I asked if you're ready to go?"

"Yes." She smiled at Maurice. He was a handsome young man, tall and lean, with the inborn grace of a dancer. His hair and eyes were chocolate brown; his lips were full and sensual.

"I'm sorry," she said contritely. "I haven't been very good company tonight, have I?"

As always, he forgave her instantly. "Not very. Come, I'll walk you home."

He lingered at the door until she rewarded him with a kiss, and then, whistling softly, he went down the stairs, turning to wave before he disappeared around the corner.

In the quiet of her room, Sara turned on the lamp and got ready for bed. Sitting at her dressing table to brush her hair, she thought again of how lucky she was. She had everything she had ever wanted. Her apartment was large and airy. The parlor was painted white; the furniture was dark mahogany, the sofa and chairs covered in varying shades of blue. Her bedroom was spacious and airy even though it had only one window. The walls were pale blue; the quilt on her bed was in shades of blue and rose, as was the carpet on the floor.

She had enough clothes to outfit three women, money to spend as she wished. For the first time in her life, she had friends her own age, friends who shared her passion for the ballet. Despite the fame and popularity that set her apart from the other dancers, she was well liked by those she worked with.

She had danced in London, in Rome and Venice, in Madrid. She had performed for kings and queens, for orphans and others who could not afford the price of a ticket to the ballet.

She should have been happy. She *was* happy, most of the time. But tonight . . . for some reason she couldn't stop thinking of Gabriel, wondering where he was, if he was well, if he ever thought of her at all.

With a sigh, she extinguished the light and slid under the covers, and after saying her nightly prayers, she bid a silent good night to Gabriel, hoping that somehow he would know she hadn't forgotten him.

He stood at her window as he had so often stood on the veranda at the orphanage, watching her sleep. She had been beautiful as a young girl, but now, in the bloom of womanhood, she was exquisite. Her skin was translucent ivory, her hair spread across the pillow like a golden flame. Her lashes made dark crescents on her smooth cheeks. Her lips were ripe and pink, like the petals of a wild rose. Beneath the covers, he could see the outline of her body, young and supple and amply endowed. Her legs were long and straight; strong from years of dancing on point.

He looked at her, and he ached deep inside, ached with the loneliness of 350 years, with the memory of her laughter, her smile, the chaste kisses they had shared.

A low groan rose in his throat. Three hundred and fifty years of solitude, of existing on the fringe of life, sustaining himself with the blood of others. He had studied with the most brilliant minds of the ages, traveled the world over, seen the rise and fall of countless civilizations, and yet he hadn't been a part of the world of men for over three centuries. Times had changed. Places had changed, yet he remained the same. Always the same. Always alone. Afraid to trust. Afraid to love . . .

Unable to help himself, he melded his mind with

hers, and there, in the safe netherworld of sleep, he made love to her, seducing her with his thoughts, molding her body to his with the magic of his revenant power . . .

She woke with his name on her lips, her skin damp, her breathing labored, her whole being filled with a languorous sense of warmth and fulfillment.

A blush burned her cheeks as the memory of her dream surfaced in her mind. She had been dreaming of Gabriel, dreaming that he was making love to her. His hands had been hot and impatient as they caressed her, his voice raw with desire. His lips had scorched her breasts, her throat. She remembered the feel of his teeth at her neck, the heat of his tongue as he laved the pulse at her throat. And his eyes . . . they had burned with an all-consuming fire, searing away every thought but the desire to please him.

It had been the most real, most provocative dream she had ever had.

She took a deep, steadying breath, and her nostrils filled with his scent.

Startled, she sat up, clutching the sheet to her breasts.

"A dream," she murmured, her gaze peering into the dark corners of her room. "That's all it was. A dream."

Yet she could not shake the feeling that he had been there.

He went to the theater every night for the next ten days, seeing the joy on her face as she danced. He followed her when she left the opera house, despising himself for spying on her, unable to stay away.

She seemed to be ever in the company of the young man he had seen her with that first night, and the thought that she cared for that weakling mortal filled him with a monstrous rage.

They held hands, and he wanted to rip the boy's arms from his body.

They kissed good night at her door, and he was sorely tempted to tear the boy to shreds, to claw the flesh from his handsome young face until nothing remained.

He hovered near her window, watching as she brushed her lustrous hair, and he burned for her, burned as though the sun had found him in the darkness.

He could force her to love him. The knowledge was ever there, tempting, beckoning. He could hypnotize her with his revenant power so that she would do anything he asked, or he could take her blood and bind her to him for as long as she lived. She would be his slave then, mindlessly adoring, obediently doing whatever he asked. She would live for him, beg him to take her blood, willingly die for him, if he but said the word.

But he didn't want a slave. He wanted her devotion, freely given.

Filled with self-disgust, ashamed of the cowardice that kept him from confronting her openly, he dissolved into mist and returned to his lair, an abandoned cottage on the outskirts of Paris. It was an ideal place, located in a small clearing off the side of a badly rutted road, hidden from casual view by a grove of trees and shrubs gone wild.

Assuming his own form, he prowled the empty

rooms. He had sent Sara away to make a life for herself, and that was what she had done. She had dreamed of being a dancer, and now she was a *prima ballerina*, the toast of the Paris Opéra. She had an apartment of her own, friends, a young man who obviously adored her. What need did she have for an ancient vampire?

He paused before the darkened window and stared at the glass. Had he been mortal, his reflection would have stared back at him, but he cast no shadow, no reflection, because he was not alive, not in any sense of the word.

He should have died long ago. What was the point of his existence? He contributed nothing, gave nothing. He was naught but a parasite feeding off the fear of mankind, existing on the lifeblood of others, never giving, always taking . . . but no, that wasn't entirely true. He had given Sara a few drops of his blood, and given the world a ballerina without equal.

Sara . . . He had loved her for almost twenty years. It was a pitifully short time compared to the span of his life, yet they had been the most rewarding years of his entire unearthly existence. He had thought, when he lost Rosalia, that he had lost all reason for continuing, but he knew now that what he had felt for Rosalia was as nothing compared to the love he felt for Sara. But Sara, too, was lost to him now, and he had only himself to blame.

For once in his life, he had tried to be noble, to do the right thing, and it had cost him the one thing he held dear above all others.

He sensed the coming of dawn, felt his skin begin to tingle with the rising of the sun. He stared at the brightening sky. He had lost Sara, and he had nothing left to live for. He had only to stay where he was, to let the golden rays of the sun find him, and his existence would soon be over. A few moments of excruciating pain as his body burst into flame, and the hollow shell that had once housed his immortal soul would be destroyed.

He felt a sudden yearning to see the dawn, to watch the sun rise above the horizon. Hands clenched at his sides, he stepped out into the yard and stared at the heavens, and waited.

For the sunrise. For the fiery death it would bring.

Slowly, the sun climbed over the horizon, its brightness blinding to a man who had not seen it in over three hundred years. Like a master painter, the sun splashed her light across the sky, streaking the dark canvas with colors—fiery crimsons and brilliant golds.

Mesmerized by the wonder of it, he stood there, feeling a heat he had not felt for over three hundred years, seeing the clear golden light of the sun, inhaling the scent of dew-kissed grass and damp earth.

He ignored the pain for as long as he could, and then a shriek rose in his throat as a molten shaft of sunlight found him, burning the skin on his face and hands, penetrating his clothing like the fires of hell. The smell of charred flesh stung his nostrils as his skin began to smolder.

With a harsh cry of agony, he bolted through the doorway and ran down the cellar stairs. Crawling into the long wooden box that served as his resting place, he closed his eyes, cursing the cowardice that had overcome his determination to put an end to his existence.

Writhing with pain, he willingly gave himself over to the sleep of the undead, embracing the darkness that enveloped his soul, surrendering to the blessed oblivion that blocked all thoughts of Sara from his mind, and blotted out all his useless dreams of a mortal life even as it swallowed the agony that enflamed him.

Sara woke with a cry on her lips, shaking with pain and fear as flames engulfed her.

Sitting up, she stared wildly around the room. Dawn was lighting the sky, and she took a deep, steadying breath. It had only been a dream, after all.

She fell back against the pillows and closed her eyes. Only a dream, but it had been so real. Her first thought upon waking was that she had been reliving the fire at the orphanage, but now she realized it hadn't been the orphanage at all, nor had the pain she felt been her own.

Gabriel . . . His name rose up in her mind, and with it came an image of scorched flesh.

Gabriel. He had been much on her mind these past ten days. On her mind, and in her dreams. Once, sitting in the cafe near the opera house, she had imagined she'd seen him standing in the shadows.

"Gabriel." His name whispered past her lips, soft as a sigh, fervent as a prayer, as she drifted back to sleep.

And deep in the cellar of a distant cottage, a creature of the damned heard her voice, and wept blood-red tears.

# Chapter Eleven

He woke with the coming of darkness. Woke to pain and a ravenous hunger that would not be denied. The touch of the sun had left him weak, and he knew he had to feed, and soon. It was the only way to ease the pain burning through him, the only way to rejuvenate his seared flesh.

He climbed carefully out of the box. Each movement brought torment; colorful curses hissed in six languages filled the air as he removed his singed clothing and changed into a pair of loose-fitting breeches and a shirt made of fine lawn.

Feeling every one of his 379 years, he climbed slowly, painfully, up the cellar stairs to stand in the doorway, his head hanging.

The hunger burned inside him, a relentless flame that would not be quenched.

He donned a greatcoat, turned up the thick fur collar, and left the cottage. In his weakened state, it took him more than an hour to reach the city. And all the while the ravenous wolf of his hunger clawed his insides until he was nearly mad with it, and with the throbbing pain of his seared flesh.

He turned down an alley reeking with filth, and waited. . . .

The production was *Sleeping Beauty*, and Sara was dancing the role of Aurora.

He sank back in his chair, his gaze fixed on Sara as she danced with the four princes, holding an exciting and delicate balance on one foot as she was passed from one suitor to the next.

He watched with rapt attention during her solo, awed by her steps, which were light and quick, expressing her youth and joy, her hopes for the future. His throat convulsed as she pricked her finger on the spindle. It was only make-believe, but the thought of her blood, red and vital, made his mouth water as she collapsed into enchanted sleep.

He sat back, lost in his own thoughts, as the prince saw a vision of Aurora, but his full attention was aroused once more when the prince awakened Aurora with love's first kiss . . .

If only real life ended as happily as fairy tales, he mused ruefully. If only love's first kiss would restore him to the life he had lost . . .

Hardly aware of what he was doing, he left the theater, his thoughts turned back 379 years. He had been born in a small village outside Vallelunga, Italy. His mother, who had given birth to ten children, had been old before her time. His father, too, had been worn out with the burden of providing for such a large family.

Gabriel, who had been Giovanni Ognibene back then, had been the eldest son. He had hated the poverty in which they lived, hated the crowded house, the long hours in the fields, the constant struggle for survival. He had yearned for a different life, a better life, and the opportunity had come on a cool spring morning.

He had agreed to gentle a headstrong young stallion for one of their neighbors and he had been hard at work when a portly, gray-haired man stopped to watch him. The man had been impressed with the way Gabriel handled the horse, so impressed he had offered Gabriel a job working in his stables. For Gabriel, it was the opportunity of a lifetime. Salvatore Musso was a wealthy man who owned a large villa in Vallelunga.

Gabriel had readily accepted the position. He had bade his parents a cheerful good-bye, promising to send money home and to visit often.

He had worked hard during the next six months, earning Musso's respect, making friends with the man's son, Giuseppe.

He had been sixteen when he received word that his parents were ill. He had left for home immediately, but it had been too late. A mysterious fever had swept through the village, and he had watched his family die, one by one. First his mother, then his sisters, his brothers, and finally his father.

Only then, when all those he loved were dead, had he realized how much he had loved them. Deep inside, he had felt as if their deaths had been his fault.

At the urging of the village priest, Giuseppe's parents had taken Gabriel into their home. At first, mourning the loss of his family, he had kept to himself, but as time passed, he discovered a whole new world, a world of wealth and aristocracy, a world where people never went to bed hungry, where servants did the work, where everyone dressed in fine clothes.

It was a world he had never seen before, a world he wanted for his own.

Giuseppe's parents had been most generous. They had fed him and clothed him, but fine clothes could not disguise Giovanni's lack of social grace. Still, he had tried hard and learned quickly, and he'd had one thing in his favor: he was young and handsome and the women adored him. They were willing to make allowances for his cloddish manners, willing to teach him the dances of the day, to instruct him in etiquette and proper decorum. He had quickly learned the polite phrases, the art of dancing and fencing, the proper way to sit a horse, to greet royalty. But always, in the back of his mind, had been the knowledge that he was only pretending.

He had been nine and twenty when he accompanied Giuseppe to Venice. It had been a time of laughter, of parties that seemed never-ending. It was there he had met Antonina Insenna. She had beguiled him from the start, and he had quickly fallen prey to her dark beauty. She had been a woman of untold wealth and power. To others she had appeared coolly self-assured, aloof, but for Giovanni she had smiled, and when she smiled, he was lost.

Nina had been everything he had thought he wanted in a woman: beautiful, desirable, mysterious. The fact that she was older than he only added to her mystique, as did her refusal to see him during the day, and though they had spent every evening together, she had refused to let him stay the night. And because he had thought himself in love, because she had been a woman of the world, full of fire and mystery, he had seen only what he wanted to see.

And then, on an afternoon in later summer, he had met Rosalia Baglio, a young woman of quiet, incomparable beauty. He had been smitten with her from the first, and she with him. He knew then that what he had felt for Antonina was not love, but lust.

He began to avoid Nina's company, preferring to spend all his time with Rosalia. They had met openly and in secret, pledging their love and devotion, even though he had feared she could never be his. Rosalia came from a wealthy family, while he had no money of his own, no lands, no title.

It had been inevitable that Antonina should discover that he had left her for another woman. Her wrath had been terrible to see. She had threatened to tell Rosalia of their affair, threatened to kill him, to kill Rosalia in front of his very eyes, but in the end she had done none of those things.

"You will regret this, Gianni," she had told him on what he had thought would be their last night together. "The time will come when you will beg me for that which only I can give, and the price will be dear."

He had not believed her. And then, after a wild night of carousing and drinking with Giuseppe and a few friends, he had taken sick with a fever. Giuseppe's parents had summoned the physicians. They had bled him to exorcise the bad humors from his body. They had forced vile concoctions down his throat, but to no avail. Two days later, the doctors went away, shaking their heads, and he had known he was going to die.

He had been trying to accept the fact that his life was over before it had begun when Antonina appeared in his room as if by magic.

"I can help you, Giovanni," she had promised in her soft, silky voice. "Only say you will be mine for one night, and all will be well. I will restore your health, Gianni, and give you riches beyond your wildest dreams."

"Too late," he had moaned, the fear of dying rising up within him. "Too late."

"Not too late, *cara mia,*" she had said. "Only give me your promise."

And because he had been in excruciating pain, because he had been terrified of dying, because he had wanted so very badly to marry Rosalia, he had agreed to do whatever Antonina wished.

As soon as he had given Antonina his vow, a change had come over her. All softness seemed to vanish from her face, and her eyes had glowed with a fierce and terrible light.

She had sat down beside him on the bed and drawn him into her embrace and kissed him. Her lips had been as cold as the grave, and when he tried to pull away, her arms had tightened around him and she had laughed softly, a dry sound, like old bones rattling.

Fear had shot through him and he had struggled harder to escape her, but in vain. His strength was as nothing compared to hers.

With ease, she had held him down, her body covering his as she kissed his eyelids, his cheek, his mouth, her lips gradually burning a path to the side of his neck.

He had gasped when he felt her teeth prick the skin, the sensation one of mingled pain and sensual pleasure. And then he had felt himself drowning, suffocating in darkness and fear. Her skin had grown warmer as his own grew cold, and he had known he was on the brink of death. His heartbeat had slowed, his breathing had grown shallow and labored, and he had been swallowed up in darkness, smothered in terror unlike anything he had ever known or imagined.

He had looked at her blankly, not comprehending, as she bit her own wrist and pressed it to his mouth.

As if from far away, he had heard her voice. "Drink, Giovanni."

He had been too weak to resist when she pressed her bleeding wrist to his mouth. "Drink, Giovanni," she had urged. Again.

He had obeyed because he lacked the will to do otherwise. And like a river at flood tide, life had flowed back into him, filling him. He had closed his eyes, moaning with pleasure as he drank and drank and drank.

When she took her wrist from his mouth, he had opened his eyes, intending to ask for more. But then he had seen Antonina hovering over him, her lips stained with blood, and he had known it was his blood.

He had stared at her in horror. "What have you done?"

She had smiled at him, and he had seen her teeth, the canines long and sharp.

"I have fulfilled my promise," she said. "I have restored your health, and given you wealth and power. You are now immortal, Giovanni Ognibene, and with immortality comes power, and the ability to gather the wealth of the world."

Rising, she had pulled a white silk handkerchief from her pocket and delicately wiped the blood, his blood, from her lips. He had shuddered with revulsion when she used that same handkerchief to wipe her blood from his mouth.

She had remained at his side while his body sloughed off the last of his humanity. His senses, now sharper than before, were bewildering, frightening. Colors had been brighter, the candlelight had hurt his eyes, the slightest sound had bruised his ears.

She had told him, in a voice devoid of emotion, that he must have blood to live, that food would sicken him, but he had refused to believe her.

With amusement, she had left the room, returning a short time later with a handful of succulent grapes. To prove her wrong, he had eaten them all. A moment later, pain had knifed through him and he had dropped to his knees, his stomach retching violently.

"It's almost dawn," she had said, her gaze darting to the window and back. "You can sleep with me today. Tomorrow night, you will fulfill your promise, and then you must find a place to rest. You must line your bed with the earth of your homeland, should you ever decide to leave Italy."

He had stared at her, uncomprehending.

"You are a creature of the night now," Antonina had explained. "You cannot die. Exposure to the sun will kill you. Holy water will burn your flesh. You cannot procreate, but you will live forever." She paused, her hand on a small wooden chest. "I promised you wealth, Giovanni, and here it is. Use it wisely."

Two nights later, frightened and confused, he had gone to Rosalia and told her everything. Looking back, he wondered why he had been so thoroughly unprepared for the stark expression of revulsion that rose in her eyes, for the terror that had sent her stumbling away from him. He could still hear her screams as she fell down the winding staircase to land with a sickening thud on the floor below. He had known even before he reached her side that she was dead. He had left Italy the next night.

He had thought it would be an easy thing, living by night and sleeping by day. He had assumed he would be able to walk among mortals, to dance and laugh and make love as before, but it was not to be. The hunger, new and untamed, roared to life whenever he allowed himself to mingle with humanity. In the beginning, unable to help himself, he had satisfied his thirst nightly, often at the expense of some poor mortal's life. Only after many decades had he learned to control his beastly appetite, to take a few drops instead of a life.

He had learned, to his dismay, that while he looked human, he was an outcast, a creature who would never again belong to the family of mankind.

He had learned, over the centuries, what true loneliness was . . .

And now he stood in the shadows of the cafe, watching Sara. Dressed in a gown of palest pink, she looked as fresh and natural as a wild rose. Her young man sat beside her, his hand holding hers, his gaze rapt upon her face, and who could blame him? She was a vision, an angel, fair of face and form, with a laugh as soft as a sigh, and a smile more radiant than the sun.

Envy rose within Gabriel, and his hands clenched into fists. It took every ounce of his self-control to keep from crossing the room and breaking the young man's neck. One quick twist would do it. Just one.

*Sara, my sweet Sara, why did I ever let you go?*

She looked up then, her head turning in his direction, her gaze probing the shadows.

Had she heard his thoughts? Did she know he was there? But that was impossible.

And yet she was rising, walking away from the table. He stood in the shadowed corner, his body trembling as she drew near. He could feel her gaze searching the darkness. But for the terrible weakness that plagued him, he would have dissolved into mist and disappeared.

"Gabriel?"

"Go away."

"Gabriel! Is it you?"

"Don't come any closer, Sara."

She stopped, confused. "What's wrong?"

"Go away."

She licked her lips nervously, wishing she could see him more clearly, but he seemed one with the shadows. "I'll go," she said, "but only if you promise to come to me later."

"I cannot."

"I've missed you, Gabriel."

"Have you?"

"Yes." She took a step forward. "You're in pain, aren't you?"

"How do you know that?" he asked sharply.

"I felt it when it happened. I feel it now."

"Go, Sara, please go."

"You'll come to me later tonight?"

"Yes." The word was torn from his lips.

* * *

Two hours later, he knocked at the door of her apartment. Like a callow youth courting his first girl, he stood in the shadows, uncertain and a little afraid.

He heard Sara's voice telling someone named Babette she was dismissed for the night. A moment later, Sara opened the door, and he was overcome with a rush of wild emotion.

"Gabriel! I'm so glad to see you. Come in, come in."

"The lights," he said, hugging the shadows. "Put out the lights."

She frowned at him a moment, then went to do as bidden. Only then did he enter the room, quietly closing the door behind him.

For a moment, he stood there, guilt rising up to meet him. She had no idea what she had invited into her home.

"Gabriel?"

"How are you, Sara?"

"Fine. And you?" He heard the underlying note of concern in her voice. "Won't you sit down?"

With a nod, he sat down on the damask-covered settee.

"Can I take your cloak?" she asked.

He shook his head, retreating into the concealing folds of the hooded garment.

She stood in front of the sofa, her hands toying with the wide blue sash of her dress. "I'm glad you're here. I've missed you."

"You were wonderful tonight," he said.

She flushed with pleasure. "You were there, at the opera house?"

"Indeed. I've never seen anything more beautiful, *cara.* Truly, you were born to dance."

"I do love it so."

He took a deep breath, his hands clenching beneath the voluminous folds of his cloak.

"And the young man who was with you at the cafe? Do you also love him?"

"Maurice?" She laughed softly. "He is just a friend."

"But he would like to be more?"

"Yes."

"Do you love him?" The words were harsher this time, demanding an answer.

"Perhaps, a little."

"Has he asked you to marry him?"

She didn't answer immediately. He could hear the sudden, nervous hammering of her heart, hear the blood rushing through her veins, heating her cheeks.

"Has he?" Gabriel prompted.

"Yes. He said we should marry and start our own ballet company." The thought made her smile. "He said we would tour the world."

He felt the rage building within him as he imagined her married to her young man, walking with him in the sunlight, giving him children . . .

Summoning centuries of self-control, he fought down the urge to strike out. He had no right to intrude in her life, no right at all. Maurice was the kind of man she deserved. Young, handsome, ambitious. Someone who shared her love of the dance, someone who could share the days and nights of her life.

Someone mortal.

He wanted to kill him.

"If you wish to marry him, I shall see that you're well taken care of. I have a rather large apartment in Marseilles. It shall be yours on the day you wed, as well as a generous monthly allowance."

"I couldn't—"

He held up a hand, silencing her arguments. "You have no parents to provide for you, and I would not see you totally dependent on whoever you decide to wed."

Hurt and confused because he seemed anxious to see her wed to another, Sara took a step forward, then sat down on the opposite end of the settee.

"Is that why you came here, to marry me off to someone else?"

"What do you mean?"

She lowered her gaze. "I've never stopped thinking of you, Gabriel. Every night, I hoped you would come to see me, that you were missing me, longing for me, as I have been longing for you."

She looked up at him, her gaze quietly pleading. "I know you thought I was just a child, that I was too young to know my own mind, my own heart, but I love you, Gabriel. I loved you then, and I love you now."

"Don't!"

"Why? Why can't I love you?"

She reached out to him, and he jerked away. The movement dislodged the hood, allowing her to see his face for the first time.

"Gabriel! What has happened?"

"Nothing," he said, replacing the hood. "An accident."

Before he could stop her, she sprang to her feet and lit the lamp.

"No!" He covered his face with his hands, only then realizing what a mistake it had been to come here.

He cowered before her as she lowered the hood, then pulled his hands away so she could see his face.

"Oh, Gabriel," she murmured, her throat constricting with horror. "My poor angel."

He turned away, not wanting her to see the ruin of his face, not wanting to see the pity he knew would be reflected in her eyes.

A low groan, half pleasure, half pain, rumbled in his throat as Sara drew him into her arms, rocking him gently, as a mother would comfort a wounded child.

"Tell me what happened," she urged.

"I was burned . . ." His voice was low, muffled against her breasts.

"Burned!" A vivid image of the fire at the orphanage flashed through her mind, and with it, the memory of pain, horrible, excruciating pain. "Oh, Gabriel," she murmured, "I thought it was only a dream."

"A dream? What are you saying?"

"I dreamed of you, dreamed that you had been badly hurt. It was so real. I felt the heat burn my skin . . ."

She was examining his hands and arms as she spoke, her eyes filling with tears as she saw his burned flesh. "How did it happen?"

He closed his eyes for a moment, her touch soothing him as nothing else could. "It doesn't matter. I was careless. It's not as bad as it looks."

"Does it hurt dreadfully?"

"Not now."

Sara drew him into her arms again as if she knew that her touch brought him solace. "How long will you be here?"

"I . . . I don't know." He had planned to see her dance, to assure himself that she was well and happy, and then leave. But now . . . how could he leave her now? Her very nearness was like a soothing balm to his troubled soul; her touch brought surcease from the pain of his wounds.

"Stay," she entreated. "Please stay."

"I don't want to complicate your life."

"How could you do that? You're my guardian angel, remember?"

"I remember, *cara*." With an effort, he withdrew from her arms. "I must go now."

"You'll come tomorrow night?"

"If you wish."

"I do, very much. Will you meet me outside the opera house? We could go to dinner."

"No. I shall come to you here. At midnight."

She rose with him, her eyes shining with happiness because she would see him again. "You won't change your mind?"

"No, but your maid, Babette, must not be here."

Sara nodded. She supposed it was natural that he wouldn't want anyone else to see him. "Won't you . . . will you . . . ?"

Gabriel frowned at her. "What is it you wish, *cara?* You have only to name it, and it's yours."

"Won't you kiss me good night?"

He nodded slightly, intending to do no more than brush his lips across hers. As if suspecting as much, she stood on her tiptoes, her hands gently cupping his ravaged face as she pressed her mouth to his.

Light exploded through him, brighter than the glow of a thousand candles. It flowed through him, clean and pure, filling his mind with images of warm summer days and sun-kissed mornings bright with dew.

Stunned, he stumbled backward, and after murmuring a hasty farewell, he took his leave before she could see the blood-stained tears that dampened his cheeks, before he fell to his knees at her feet and begged her to see past the monster he had become and love the man who no longer existed.

# Chapter Twelve

"What do you mean, you can't see me after the show?"

Maurice stared at her, his brow furrowed, his eyes mirroring his confusion.

"I have an appointment," Sara replied.

"An appointment? With whom?"

"An old friend." An exasperated sigh escaped Sara's lips. "If you must know, I'm meeting Gabriel."

Understanding replaced confusion in Maurice's eyes, but only for a moment as jealousy quickly took its place. "So, he's finally come to see you after all these years."

"Yes."

"Do you think it's wise for you to meet with him alone?"

"What do you mean?"

"How will it look, the two of you being alone together in your room?"

Sara felt a blush stain her cheeks. It wasn't proper to entertain a man alone in her apartment. But Gabriel wasn't just any man. He was her benefactor; but, more than that, he was her friend, the closest thing to a family that she had. But it wasn't that thought that brought the flush to her cheeks. It was the knowledge that she wanted to be more to him than a protégée. Much more.

"It will be all right," Sara said, keeping her voice carefully cool and calm. "After all, he's been supporting me for the past five years. I can hardly refuse to see him." She hated lying to Maurice. It wasn't Gabriel who had insisted on seeing her. Quite the opposite, in fact.

"Someone should be there with you," Maurice insisted. "A chaperon, if you will."

"Babette will be there," Sara lied.

Maurice laid his hand on her arm. "I love you, Sara. I only want what's best for you."

"I know." She gazed into his eyes, wishing she could return his affection, but she belonged to Gabriel heart and soul, had been his since the first time she saw him on her veranda.

"Marry me, Sara," Maurice implored. He dropped to one knee and took her hand in his. "I know I'm not nearly good enough for you, but you'll be rich in love if nothing else, I promise you that. Only say yes."

"Maurice . . ."

"It's him, isn't it?" Maurice rose to his feet, his eyes blazing with anger and jealousy. "You're infatuated with that old man."

"What makes you think he's old?"

"Isn't he?"

Sara frowned. She'd never given any serious

thought to Gabriel's age. Thinking of it now, she realized she truly had no idea how old he was. To look at him, one would guess him to be in his late twenties, and yet he seemed much older, much wiser.

"Sara?"

"I don't know how old he is, and I don't care. I'm not running off with him, Maurice. He's only coming by to see how I'm doing."

"Then it won't matter if I'm there."

"I'm afraid it will matter very much."

"Sara . . ."

"I don't wish to discuss it any further, Maurice. Quick, give me a kiss for luck. There's my music."

She danced that night as never before, certain that Gabriel was somewhere in the audience. Her solo was for him and him alone. When she looked at the prince, it was Gabriel's face that loomed in her mind; it was Gabriel's kiss that awakened her from her enchanted sleep.

She had hoped he would be waiting for her outside the theater, but he was nowhere to be seen. Maurice insisted on walking her home.

She bade him good night at the door, assuring him she would be fine.

She dismissed Babette for the night, bathed quickly, slipped into a modest dark blue velvet dressing gown with a froth of lace at the throat. She lit several candles, filled a bowl with apples and cheese, placed a bottle of wine and two glasses on the table.

She was all aquiver by the time she heard his knock at the door.

Taking a deep breath, she crossed the room and opened the door.

He stood in the shadows as before, his face hidden in a hooded cloak as dark as the night.

"Gabriel," she exclaimed, her voice filled with joy. "Come in." She closed the door behind him, wishing she could keep him there forever. "Let me take your cloak."

"No."

"You needn't hide your face from me."

"Sara . . ."

She walked toward him, her hand out. "Let me take your cloak, Gabriel. It's warm in here, and you'll be more comfortable without it."

"I was thinking of your comfort."

"Your face doesn't distress me."

With a sigh of resignation, he removed his cloak and handed it to her. He knew how hideous he must look, the skin on his face and arms discolored and puckered by the heat of the sun, yet her smile faltered hardly at all as she looked at him.

Sara carried his cloak into her bedroom. For a moment, she pressed her face to the finely woven wool, breathing in his scent, and then she placed it carefully on the bed, her hands running over the material, pretending it was Gabriel her hand caressed and not his cloak.

When she returned to the parlor, he was sitting on the far end of the sofa, away from the candles that flickered on the table.

"Would you like something to eat?" Sara asked, gesturing toward the bowl of fruit and cheese. "Some wine?"

"A glass of wine," he said.

She filled two glasses, then sat down beside him.

"You were wonderful tonight," Gabriel remarked.

"I have never seen anyone dance with such intensity, such joy."

"It was for you," Sara confessed quietly. "I knew you were out there, watching me, and I wanted to make you proud."

"You've done well, Sara Jayne. You are a ballerina without equal, just as you always dreamed."

"I owe it all to you, and I thank you for it with all my heart."

"No, *cara*. It was always there, within you. So, tell me, where do you go from here?"

"There's talk that the company will go on tour in the fall."

Gabriel nodded. "All the world should see you dance, *cara*," he said, and then frowned. "What's wrong?"

"I love dancing," Sara said, "but it isn't enough."

"You have the world at your feet. What more do you want?"

"I want you at my side."

As always, he retreated from her at the mention of anything personal between them.

Drawing on her courage, she put her goblet aside and then, taking his untouched glass from his hand and placing it on the table, she slid across the sofa and placed her hand on his shoulder.

"Tell me you don't care," she said, her gaze intent upon his face. "Tell me you don't want me, and I'll never speak of it again."

"You know better than that," Gabriel replied, his voice rough. "I've wanted you, hungered for you, for years."

"Then why are we apart?"

"Because it is for the best."

"For whom?"

"For you, *cara*. You must trust me in this."

"No! You must trust *me* in this. It makes no sense for us to be apart."

"It makes more sense than you will ever know. You would do well to forget you ever knew me. Marry your young man. Dance for the world. Have children, and teach them to dance. It's what you were born for."

Sara shook her head. "No, Gabriel," she said fervently. "I was born for you."

With slow deliberation, she moved closer, until only a breath of air separated them.

And then she said the words he could not resist, and he knew he was lost. "Let me hold you."

His resolve melted like warm wax as she drew him into her arms. If he had any weakness besides his need to avoid the sun, it was his need to be held by this woman. She was sunlight to his darkness, eternal life to his infinite damnation.

For a long while, she held him close, and then she kissed him. She didn't close her eyes, nor did he. She saw the flame, bright as molten gold, that leaped into his eyes, felt the raw animal power, the naked hunger, the overwhelming need that engulfed him as her mouth closed on his. He wanted her. Oh, yes, he definitely wanted her.

And she wanted him. She wanted to feel his strength, wanted him to possess her, fully, completely, masterfully. Wanted him to take her with all the power at his command, to show her what it meant to be loved.

She looked into his eyes and she felt herself

drowning, sinking down, down, into darkness, into light.

Gabriel moaned her name as he drew her closer, his arms wrapping around her, strong and sure. Her breasts were crushed against his chest, his hands stroked her back, slipped under her gown to caress the curve of her calf.

She gasped, startled by the intimacy of his touch, by the pleasure that shot clear through her.

She was drowning in sensation, helpless to resist the power of his touch, the hunger in his eyes. Eyes that burned fever bright, igniting tiny flames within her heart, her soul, filling her with a warmth that flowed through her veins, making her restless for something she didn't understand.

With a sigh of surrender, she closed her eyes and gave herself up to the magic of his touch.

It was her total lack of fear, her complete trust in him, that was his undoing.

An animal-like growl of pain rose in his throat as he devoured her mouth with his. She was sunshine and light, goodness and hope, the innocence of youth, everything that was forever lost to him. He kissed her deeply, searching for salvation, wishing for humanity. She was soft and supple in his arms, willing, eager, a foolish moth racing toward the flames of destruction, and he didn't have the strength to protect her.

His hands delved beneath her gown to find living flesh and skin softer than velvet, smoother than satin. In moments, her gown was on the floor. In another moment, his clothes joined hers. And then she was in his arms, a study in perfection from the crown of her head to the soles of her feet. And she was his. His for the taking.

He loved her gently, his hands trembling, his voice ragged with the effort to hold back, until his body was on fire for her. He was on the verge of making her his when he heard her soft cry of pain.

Horrified, he froze, his body poised over hers. Only then did he realize that the hunger was also burning through him, that his kisses were no longer gentle, that his fangs had almost pierced the fragile skin at her throat.

Not knowing how close she was to danger, she arched beneath him, seeking fulfillment for the restless wanting of her body.

With a growl, he drew away and turned his back to her.

"Gabriel?"

Her voice was low and uneven, filled with confusion.

"Forgive me," he said gruffly. "I didn't mean . . ."

"Gabriel." She placed a tentative hand on his back, felt his whole body shudder at her touch. "I want you."

"No, Sara," he replied, his voice ragged. "Don't ask me."

"I don't understand."

"Please let me go." It was a cry of anguish, a plea for her to be strong because his need for her made him weak and vulnerable.

"No!"

"It's for the best."

"It's not!" Embarrassed and hurt by his rejection, she sat up, her arms crossed over her breasts. "I wish I'd never left England," she said, fighting back her tears. "I wish I was still in that awful chair. You loved me then. I know you did."

He closed his eyes, his hands balling into fists, as her unhappiness washed over him. He never should have come here, he thought. Never should have seen her again. He hadn't meant to cause her pain, only to ease his own.

He could wipe it all from her mind. He had only to look into her eyes, to bend her will to his. He could make her forget that he existed . . . but to do so would be like ending his existence, he thought bleakly, because if he didn't exist for Sara, there was no point in going on.

And because he was basically a selfish man, because he'd been alone for too long, he turned around and took her hand in his.

"Sara?"

She looked up at him, and he cringed before the misery in her eyes.

"Please, Gabriel," she murmured. "Please don't leave me. I need you so."

"And I need you. Tell me, *cara*, if I stay, will you do as I ask without question?"

"Yes."

"Anything I say? Even if it makes no sense to you?"

A slight frown lined her brow. "I don't understand."

"It's quite simple. I'll stay, but only if you promise to do whatever I ask, without question, no matter how odd it might seem at the time."

"I promise."

"Then you must dismiss your maid from your employ."

"Babette?"

Gabriel nodded.

"Very well, but why?"

"Without question, *cara*, remember? Now," he said quietly, "put on your gown. It's late, and you need your rest."

"But . . ." Sara bit off the word. She would do whatever he asked, without question, just as she had promised. But not asking questions was far harder than she had anticipated.

"It's not too late to change your mind," Gabriel remarked.

Sara shook her head, and he turned away to don his own clothing. He heard the soft rustling of her gown as she slipped it on.

Only then did he turn to face her. "You're so young, Sara. I don't want to hurt you."

"You won't . . ."

He held up his hand, silencing her. "It's late. I want you to go to bed. I'll see you tomorrow night, at the theater."

"All right."

"Good night, *cara*. Sleep well."

"Good night, my angel. Will you dream of me?"

"As always," he replied, bending to kiss her cheek. "As always."

# Chapter Thirteen

He was waiting for her outside the theater the following night. Clad in evening clothes and a black cloak, he was quite the handsomest man she had ever seen, Sara thought. And he was waiting for her.

Cheeks flushed with anticipation, she ran to him, not caring who saw, or what anyone thought.

Gabriel crushed her close, as if he had been waiting his whole life for this moment, and then he placed her hand on his arm and led her away from the opera house.

"Your face looks ever so much better," Sara remarked, astonished at the miraculous improvement in his appearance. His skin, which had been badly discolored and puckered only the night before, showed little trace of the earlier damage.

"The burns were mostly superficial," Gabriel explained with a shrug.

"But . . ."

"We're here," he said, and guided her into a small restaurant that was dark and cozy. He asked for a table in the rear, away from the crowd, and smoothly steered their conversation to the night's performance.

Sara ordered something to eat, but Gabriel only asked for a glass of dry red wine.

"Don't you ever eat?" Sara asked.

"I dined earlier."

Sara studied him thoughtfully, then shrugged, too excited by his presence to fret over such a small thing.

Sara had finished eating, and they were discussing the company's upcoming production of *Swan Lake* when Maurice appeared at the table.

Sara looked up, startled. "Maurice, what are you doing here?"

"I wanted to meet your mysterious benefactor."

"Oh." She glanced at Gabriel. "Maurice, this is Gabriel . . ." She hesitated, realizing she didn't know Gabriel's last name. "Gabriel, this is Maurice Delacroix, a member of the company."

"Will you join us?" Gabriel asked.

"I'm sure Maurice has other plans," Sara said, pinning Maurice with a look that clearly said "go away."

"Not at all," Maurice replied. He slid into the booth beside Sara.

Gabriel ordered a glass of wine for Maurice and another for himself.

There was a moment of awkward silence as Gabriel stared at the younger man. Uncomfortable under Gabriel's probing gaze, Maurice quickly drained his glass.

"Sara tells me you've been most generous in your

support," Maurice remarked. "Do you sponsor many dancers?"

"Just one."

"I see. Sara has told me very little about you. Have you always had a fondness for the ballet?"

"Yes," Gabriel replied, a small smile hovering at the corners of his mouth. "Always."

"How long will you be in Paris?"

"I'm not sure." Gabriel let his gaze move over Sara in a long, slow glance that could only be interpreted as possessive. "I've not been to Paris for many years. It's a beautiful city, don't you agree?"

Maurice glared at Gabriel, all too aware that the man wasn't talking about the city at all. "You seem a man of the world," he said, his voice harsh. "No doubt even a city as lovely as Paris will soon lose its appeal."

"Perhaps."

"I've asked Sara to marry me."

"It was my understanding she had refused your suit."

"For the moment, but I hope to change her mind. Perhaps she would be more willing to say yes if she knew she had your blessing."

Gabriel laughed softly. His blessing, indeed. "Sara doesn't need my permission to wed. I've already told her I will support whatever decision she makes."

Abruptly, Sara rose to her feet. "I'm tired of being discussed as if I weren't here," she declared. "I'm going home."

Maurice sprang to his feet. "I'll see you home."

"I brought Sara here," Gabriel said, rising, "and I will see her safely to her door."

He held out his hand and Sara took it without hesitation. "Good night, Maurice," she said softly.

"Sara . . ."

Gabriel fixed Maurice with a hard stare. "The lady said good night."

Maurice took a step backward, repelled by the coldness in the other man's eyes, by the sudden, unexpected sense of evil. With a last glance at Sara, he left the restaurant.

Sara smiled apologetically at Gabriel as they walked home a short time later. "I'm sorry he made a scene."

"He's smitten with you," Gabriel replied. "Anyone can see that."

Sara tilted her head back so she could see Gabriel's face. "And I'm smitten with you."

"Are you, *cara*?"

"I've told you so often enough. Don't you believe me?"

"I believe you."

They reached her apartment a short time later. Inside, he helped her off with her cloak, then shed his own as she lit the lamp, then turned to face him.

"Will you stay the night?" she asked.

"A bold question for a maiden," Gabriel mused with a wry grin. "Are you asking me to spend the night, or to make love to you?"

"Both," she answered, and knew she was blushing furiously.

"And if I refuse?"

The light went out of her eyes. Her shoulders sagged dispiritedly. "Are you going to refuse me again?"

"Sara . . ."

"Is it me?"

"No!"

"Then, is there something wrong with you? Some reason that you can't, or won't . . ." Her voice trailed off. She had no idea how to phrase her question delicately, and lacked the courage to ask it outright.

"There is noting wrong with me in the way you mean. It's only that you're so young."

"Are you going to bring that up again? Would you like me better if I were old and wrinkled? Shall I lock myself in a tower somewhere until you think I'm of the proper age?"

He laughed then, a deep masculine laugh filled with humor. She had never heard him laugh like that before, had rarely seen him smile. It transformed him, making him seem younger, more approachable.

Gabriel held out his arms. "Come to me, Sara."

She went to him without hesitation, burrowing into his embrace, her face pressed to his chest. She closed her eyes and drew in a deep breath, surrounding herself with his scent, his touch. His lips moved in her hair as his hands gently stroked her back, her shoulders. And then, muttering an oath, he swung her into his arms and carried her into the bedroom.

His hands, those large hands which could have easily torn her in two, trembled as he placed her on the bed and undressed her, but Sara hardly noticed, for she was trembling too, with trepidation, with anticipation. His eyes blazed with desire as he quickly shed his own clothing, then stretched out on the bed beside her and drew her into his arms.

"You must tell me if you want me to stop," he said, his voice husky. You must tell me if I hurt you, or frighten you."

"Frighten me?"

"I've wanted you since the day I watched you change from a wide-eyed little girl into a beautiful young woman," he confessed. "Wanted and waited. If my passion frightens you, you must tell me."

Sara nodded, though she didn't fully comprehend his meaning. She knew little of what went on between a man and a woman, only what she had read in books. Hardly an education, she thought, for the books always ended with a chaste kiss and happily ever after.

But there was nothing chaste about Gabriel's kisses. They roared through her like wildfire, burning out of control, igniting tiny flames wherever his mouth touched her flesh.

She clutched him to her, her nails raking his back and shoulders, fearful of the turbulent emotions that smoldered inside her, yearning for something that seemed just out of reach.

He whispered to her in French, in Italian, speaking words of love and quiet assurance as his hands added fuel to the fire.

Emboldened by his caresses, she let her hands wander over him, her fingertips restless, inquisitive, as they learned the texture of his skin, felt the powerful muscles that bunched and relaxed beneath her questing hands.

She felt him shudder at her touch, heard him gasp. With pleasure, she wondered, or pain? But she couldn't stop touching him. His skin was hot beneath her palms, his breathing erratic. And she was smothering in his heat, gasping for air.

She knew a moment of fear as he grabbed both her hands in one of his, imprisoning them above her head as he rose over her. She stared up at him, her heart pounding furiously.

In the dim light of the room, he seemed larger than life. His hair fell over his shoulders like a dark cloud; his eyes were turbulent, like the sky before a storm.

His eyes . . . surely it was a trick of the candlelight that caused his eyes to glow with that blood-red flame.

Gabriel saw the terror rise in her eyes, and knew that his own must be glowing with the hunger for blood. It took every ounce of his considerable self-control to keep from burying his fangs in her neck as he merged his flesh with hers.

Sara cried out, a low cry of pain, of fear, as their bodies came together. With a groan, he claimed her lips in a brutal kiss, and all thought fled her mind, swallowed up in the ecstasy that exploded deep within her, sending frissons of delight coursing through every inch of her body.

She was his now, she thought exultantly. Only his. He would never leave her, never send her away again.

"Sara, are you all right?" he asked, his voice muffled against her shoulder.

She uttered a languid moan of assent, a soft feminine sound that indicated she had been thoroughly pleasured.

Elation bubbled up inside Gabriel. He had claimed her body without damning her soul. For the first time in centuries, he felt like a man instead of a monster. It was a glorious feeling, but all too brief, for hard on the heels of exhilaration came a deep sense of regret, an aching sense of remorse because he knew deep in the empty recess of what had once been his heart that he had defiled something pure and clean.

She felt the change in him, the sudden sense of withdrawal. With a low cry, she wrapped her arms around him and held him close.

"Sara," he groaned, "what have I done?"

"I love you, Gabriel," she whispered fervently. "Please don't spoil this moment for me. Please don't say you're sorry for what happened."

A violent tremor racked his body. "Sara . . . hold me."

She heard the anguish in his voice, the threat of tears, and she clutched him to her. Holding him as tightly as she could, she wondered what darkness lurked in his past that could cause him such anguish. Sometimes it seemed he feared her touch as much as he craved it.

"Go to sleep, Gabriel," she murmured. "I'll keep your demons at bay."

"Ah, *cara*," he replied, his voice raw and edged with pain. "If only you could."

"Sleep, my angel," she crooned, and in moments she felt his body relax, heard the slow, even tenor of his breathing that told her he was, indeed, asleep.

He woke with a start, his flesh tingling with the awareness of dawn. Sara was lying beside him, her head pillowed on his shoulder.

She stirred as he slid out of bed and began to pull on his clothes.

"What are you doing?" she asked sleepily.

"I must go."

"Why?"

"No questions, *cara,* remember?"

He dropped a quick kiss on her brow and ran from the room, bolting down the stairs and out into the street. The sky was still gray, but even as he ran down the street, he could feel the promise of a new day, the faint heat of the sun.

The memory of the burns he had received the last time he faced the sun spurred him on. With preternatural speed, he traveled through the narrow streets until he reached the abandoned cottage.

He released a long sigh when he was safe inside. Panting heavily, he made his way to the basement, thoughts of Sara uppermost in his mind as he climbed into the narrow box where he slept away the daylight hours.

Sara thought about Gabriel as she rehearsed later that day, wondering why he had left so abruptly. Every time someone entered the room, she glanced up, hoping it would be Gabriel.

Later, back in her apartment, she kept expecting him to appear, but late afternoon faded to early evening, and he still didn't arrive.

Had she done something wrong?

She was a bundle of nerves when she arrived at the theater. Twice, during her warm-up, she forgot the steps, and for the first time ever, she didn't feel like dancing.

She took the stage reluctantly, knowing her performance would be less than perfect. And then she saw him, sitting in the front row, and it was as if she had suddenly grown wings.

As she had once before, she danced only for Gabriel, and when the performance was over, the audience gave her a standing ovation. But she heard only Gabriel's applause, and it was the sweetest sound she'd ever known.

Hurrying to her dressing room, she quickly changed into her street clothes. She was on her way out of the building when Maurice caught up with her.

"You were sensational tonight," Maurice said. "Where are you going in such a hurry?"

"Gabriel's waiting for me."

Maurice swore under his breath as he caught hold of her arm and dragged her to a halt. "I don't want you seeing that man anymore."

Carefully and deliberately, she pried his fingers from her arm. "Excuse me?"

"You heard me."

"I will see who I want, when I want. And right now, I want to see Gabriel."

"There's something not right with that man," Maurice exclaimed.

"What do you mean?"

"I'm not sure, but last night, when I looked into his eyes, I . . . I can't explain it except to say he's evil, Sara Jayne. Stay away from him."

"Evil! What are you talking about?" Sara demanded, yet even as she waited for his answer, an image appeared in her mind, an image of Gabriel's eyes glowing blood-red as he rose over her.

"Sara, listen to me . . ."

"No! I love Gabriel, and he loves me. Now leave me alone."

Maurice stared after Sara as she ran down the corridor toward the exit. Somehow, he had to save her from making the worst mistake of her life.

# *Chapter Fourteen*

She was too excited to sit in a cafe, too happy to eat, so they went for a long walk in the moonlight, her arm tucked possessively through his.

Once, he paused in the shadows to kiss her brow and she wound her arms around his neck, hugging him close, shamelessly pressing her body against him.

"Gabriel, I . . ." Sara bit down on her lower lip, wishing she had the nerve to ask him to make love to her again. She was eager for his touch, but, knowing little of men, she wasn't sure if he was plagued by the same restless yearnings that kept her tossing and turning far into the night.

"What is it, *cara?*"

"I . . . nothing."

Gabriel gazed deep into her eyes and knew, in that instant, what she wanted. Wordlessly, he pivoted on his heel and headed for her apartment.

Inside, he closed the door, then held out his arms. With a small cry of relief, she stepped into his embrace, sighing as his arms wrapped around her.

"Is it terribly wicked of me to want you so?" she asked, refusing to meet his gaze.

"No, *cara mia*."

"I couldn't think of anything but you all day," she confessed shyly. "When you left so abruptly this morning, I was afraid I'd done something to displease you."

He shook his head, the anguish in her voice stabbing him to the heart.

"Will you have breakfast with me tomorrow?" she asked tremulously.

"I cannot."

"Why?"

"No questions, Sara."

"But . . ."

"I mean what I say."

"Will you dine with me tomorrow night then?"

He hesitated a moment, his eyes shadowed with doubt.

"I'm quite a good cook," she said, hoping to reassure him.

"I'm sure you are."

"You'll come to dinner then?"

"If you wish."

She gazed up at him, her blue eyes shining with happiness and love. "Won't you kiss me now?"

Slowly, gently, he lowered his head and claimed her mouth with his own. As always, holding her, touching her, filled him with light, driving away the darkness in which he had lived for so long.

Carrying her into the bedroom, he made love to

her with exquisite tenderness, telling her with each heartfelt kiss, each stroke of his hands, each word that whispered past his lips, how much he adored her.

Her love enveloped him, surrounding him with the purity of her heart, the generosity of her spirit. She offered him her love, nothing held back, and he grabbed it with both hands, clinging to her goodness, telling himself that he couldn't be a monster, not when Sara could love him so completely.

He held her in his arms while she slept, his gaze never leaving her face. Her lashes lay like dark fans upon her cheeks. Her lips were full and pink, faintly swollen from his kisses. Her hair fell over the pillow and across his chest like streaks of sunlight. He lifted a lock of her hair and brushed it across his face, inhaling the scent, delighting in the touch of each silken strand.

"So beautiful, so innocent," he murmured, his voice thick with anguish. "Will you ever forgive me for what I've done?"

Her eyelids fluttered open and she gazed up at him, a soft smile curving her lips, her eyes aglow with the love in her heart.

"What have you done, Gabriel, that I should forgive you?"

"I've stolen your innocence," he whispered. "Taken that which I had no right to take."

Her hand reached up to caress the unyielding curve of his jaw. "You didn't steal it. I gave it to you."

"Ah, *cara*, you have no idea what you've done."

"I've made you happy," she said confidently. "Can you deny it?"

"No."

"I have no regrets," she said, her eyelids fluttering down. "None at all . . ."

And for that one brief moment, neither did he.

He sat at the table, amazed at the abundance of food she had prepared—roast beef, potatoes smothered in a thick gravy, carrots swimming in butter, Yorkshire pudding. Surely she didn't expect the two of them to consume it all!

The very thought of swallowing even a forkful of cooked meat made him physically ill, but he kept his face impassive as she sat down across from him and lifted her glass.

"To us," she said.

"To us," he repeated, and touched his glass to hers.

To spare her feelings, he sampled everything she had prepared and lavishly praised her culinary efforts, and then, as soon as he could, he made an excuse to go outside, where he retched violently.

Breathing heavily, he drew in deep gulps of air, willing his tortured stomach to relax. For one doomed to subsist on a warm liquid diet, a meal of meat and vegetables was impossible to digest.

When he was again in control, he returned to the parlor. Sara was waiting for him, a curious look in her eyes, but for once she asked no questions.

They spoke of the theater, of the weather, which had been unusually clear, of her new understudy, and then, hesitantly, Sara blurted the question that had been troubling her.

"What if I become . . . with child?"

"You needn't worry, *cara*. I am unable to have children."

He watched the play of emotions flit across her

face: relief at first, then sympathy, then regret.

"Do you wish to have a child?" he asked.

"Yes, of course. Someday . . ."

"And you shall."

"But how . . . I mean . . . I don't want anyone but you."

"I'm afraid you will soon tire of me, *cara*."

"I won't!"

"I think you will. In time, my way of life will begin to feel like a prison, and when that time comes, I shall let you go."

She frowned at him, not understanding. "What do you mean?"

"I like to keep to myself. I don't care for large groups of people, for parties. I like to dine alone." He covered her hand with his. "Forgive me, Sara, I didn't mean to hurt you. I enjoyed this meal with you very much, but the truth remains that I prefer to dine alone. My life is set a certain way, and I find it difficult to change, even for you."

"I'm not asking you to change anything," she said petulantly.

"But you are. Don't you see?"

"No." She stood up and turned her back to him. "I think you're tired of me already, that you're just trying to find a polite way to tell me good-bye without hurting my feelings."

She whirled around to face him, and she looked so young, so vulnerable, he ached inside. Tears shimmered in the depths of her eyes and sparkled on her lashes.

"Is that it? Are you tired of me so soon?"

Rising, he closed the distance between them and took her hands in his. "No, *cara*, I'm not tired of you.

Should we spend a thousand years together, I would never tire of you. Believe that." He lifted her hands to his lips and kissed first one and then the other. "Perhaps I should go."

"No!" She bit down on her lip, and he could see she was trying to gather her composure, her dignity. "I mean, I'd like for you to stay."

"If you wish."

"I don't mean to be a burden to you."

"That you could never be. Come now, dry your eyes."

Obediently, she wiped away her tears.

"What can I do to make you smile again?" he asked indulgently. "Shall I buy you a pretty new frock? A bauble of some kind? Your own opera house? Tell me, *cara,* what would you like?"

"For you to love me."

"I do love you, Sara," he replied fervently. "I love everything about you."

"Show me?"

With a wordless cry, he swept her into his arms and lowered her to the floor. And there, on the colorful Persian rug in front of the hearth, he made love to her in such a way that she would never doubt his feelings for her again.

Maurice stood in the shadows across the street from Sara's apartment, waiting.

His hands clenched and unclenched as he imagined Sara in her benefactor's arms, willingly surrendering to Gabriel what she so adamantly refused to give to him.

He swore softly. What was there about that man that attracted Sara? Admittedly, Gabriel was handsome in a dark, brooding sort of way. Admittedly, he was rich. He was also suave, arrogant, and sinister.

Maurice shook his head. It was inconceivable to him that Sara was unaware of the latent evil that lurked in Gabriel's hooded gray eyes. She was an innocent, pure of heart and soul. Surely she could sense the danger that radiated from the man.

But days had passed, and he realized that she was so smitten with Gabriel that he might have been one of Satan's minions and she wouldn't have cared. It was the fact that she might be in mortal danger that had finally convinced Maurice he had to do something, that he had to prove to Sara that Gabriel was not the man she thought he was.

But then, Maurice wasn't sure just what kind of man Gabriel really was, or what harm he intended for Sara Jayne. He only knew that there was something not right about Sara's benefactor, and that was why he was standing here in the shadows, waiting.

He straightened, a warning chill slithering down his spine when he saw the door to Sara's apartment house open. A moment later, a tall figure swathed in a hooded black cloak descended the stairs.

Gabriel.

Maurice waited until the man was well ahead of him, and then began to follow him.

It was like trying to follow a shadow. The night seemed to embrace Gabriel like a long-lost lover. It surrounded him, enveloped him, became one with him.

Maurice was running now, his footsteps muffled by the damp grass alongside the road.

And then, as if swallowed up by the night, the man disappeared.

Maurice blinked, and blinked again, unable to believe his eyes. One minute Gabriel had been there, a dark silhouette against the night, and the next he was gone.

A coldness, like that of the grave, swept over Maurice as he turned back toward the city.

"Slow down, Maurice, you're not making any sense."

"I'm telling you, Sara, the man disappeared right before my eyes. One minute he was there, and the next he was gone." Maurice shivered as he followed Sara Jayne into her apartment, carefully locking the door behind him.

Sara made a low sound of exasperation. "Are you trying to tell me you think Gabriel is a ghost or something?"

"I don't know what he is, but he isn't human."

"You're letting your imagination run away with you," Sara chided. "It was cold and foggy last night, that's all. He probably turned a corner and you lost sight of him."

"No!" Maurice grabbed her by the shoulders and shook her. "Listen to me, Sara Jayne, you've got to stay away from that man. He's evil."

"Maurice, you're hurting me!" She twisted away from his grasp, then stood rubbing her shoulders. "This isn't funny."

"Damn right it isn't!" He took a step toward her, then stopped when he saw the warning in her eyes. "Has he . . . have you . . . ?"

Sara glared at him, her eyes narrowed. "Have I what?"

"Never mind, I can see that you have. Why, Sara Jayne? What is there about this man that attracts you? Can't you sense the evil that surrounds him?"

Sara sat down on the sofa and smoothed her skirts. "I think you should go now," she said, her voice coolly polite.

Maurice took a deep breath. "Sara Jayne, please listen to me." He began to pace the floor, too agitated to stand still. "I know you think I'm overreacting, that I'm just jealous because you've been spending so much time with him, but that's not it, I swear! You're in danger. Promise me you'll be careful. Next time he comes here, forget your infatuation with him and . . ."

Maurice's voice trailed off and he stared at her. She didn't believe a word he was saying.

"I'll see you later, at the theater," he said, thoroughly disheartened. "Please be careful."

She saw Maurice to the door, then stood there for a long moment, watching him walk away. He'd always seemed like such a level-headed young man, his feet solidly planted on the ground. This babbling about Gabriel disappearing in the mist was ludicrous. Evil, indeed! Gabriel had never shown her anything but kindness . . .

Evil . . . unbidden came the memory of the peculiar red glow she had seen in his eyes when they made love. But that had been nothing more than a trick of the light . . .

She had never seen him during the day . . . But surely a man of Gabriel's wealth was extremely busy. Even on the Sabbath? taunted a small voice of doubt.

With a shake of her head, Sara thrust her troubling thoughts aside, refusing to give heed to Maurice's foolish accusations. Gabriel was no more evil than she was!

He was waiting for her outside the opera house that night. She studied him carefully as they walked the short distance from the theater to her apartment. Elegant was the first word that came to her mind. As usual, he was dressed in black evening clothes. His linen was snowy white; his cravat impeccable. His cloak was as black as the night, and she had the sudden fanciful notion that Gabriel was a part of the night, dark and mysterious. He moved with an unusual gracefulness for such a big man; his steps were incredibly light, as if his feet hardly touched the ground. She would have given anything to be able to move like that.

Her gaze moved to his face. Just looking at him made her smile. He was so handsome. The burns that had once marred his smooth flesh were gone as if they had never existed. There was a ruddy glow to his cheeks. His hair was the color of midnight, his eyes as gray as the storm clouds swirling overhead. And his lips . . . ah, those lips that kissed her with such mastery, such passion.

She felt an odd little quiver in her stomach as his hand tightened on her arm. Soon, she thought, soon he would kiss her again.

"You're very quiet this evening," Gabriel remarked as they reached her door. "Is something wrong?"

"No. I was just wondering . . ."

He lifted one thick black brow in question as they entered the parlor. "Wondering?"

She crossed the room and lit one of the lamps. "If we were going to make love tonight."

She turned to face him, and he thought he had never seen anything as lovely as Sara Jayne Duncan, with her guileless sky-blue eyes and her cheeks burning with embarrassment.

He lifted a lock of her hair and let it fall through his fingers. "You've not grown tired of me then?"

"Oh, no."

"Ah, Sara," he murmured, "your innocence humbles me."

"Hardly innocent anymore," she replied with a saucy grin.

"Indeed." His voice was quiet, filled with self-reproach.

"Gabriel! You're regretting what we've done again, aren't you?"

"No."

She lifted her chin so she could see him better, her hands fisted on her hips. "You're lying. If I don't regret it, I don't know why you should."

"You're too—"

She stamped her foot angrily. "Don't you dare tell me I'm too young!"

"I won't." He cocked his head to one side, his eyes alight with amusement. "Is your temper tantrum over?"

"I'm not having a temper tantrum. I'm simply tired of being treated as if I were a child. Look at me, Gabriel. I'm a woman, with a woman's needs, a woman's desires."

"You are indeed," he murmured. "Sometimes it's hard for me to remember that you're all grown up."

"Maybe this will help you remember," she suggested, and throwing her arms around his neck, she kissed him.

There was nothing childish about her kiss, he admitted. Nothing at all. He felt the taste of her spread to all his senses as desire flared between them, more potent than brandy, hotter than a thousand suns.

She moaned softly, pressing herself against him, and he had no thought to deny her.

He removed his cloak and her pelisse and dropped both over a chair; then, taking her by the hand, he led her into the bedroom. With exquisite tenderness, he undressed her, the heat in his eyes chasing away the chill of the room. She was vaguely aware that it was raining. Lightning flashed across the sky; there was a dull rumble of thunder.

Gabriel's gaze held hers as he undressed, and then he lifted her in his arms and carried her to the bed, stretching out beside her.

She looked like a porcelain angel, he thought, a seraph newly fallen to earth, her eyes the color of the daylight sky he had not seen in more than three hundred years, her hair the color of the sun at midday.

He pressed a finger to her lips when she started to speak. And then, as if she were made of delicate crystal that might shatter at any moment, he made love to her. His hands moved over her, barely touching her skin, yet her whole body sprang to life, quivering, reaching, yearning toward him. He kissed her, his lips skimming her eyelids, the curve of her cheek, the smoothness of her brow. She felt his teeth graze her throat, his breath like the desert wind, heard a groan rumble deep in his throat.

She arched beneath him in silent invitation, her hands reaching for him, wanting to touch the hard wall of his chest, to span the width of his shoulders, to draw him to her, inside her, forever.

"Forever," he whispered, and she wondered if he had read her mind.

And then he was a part of her, his breath mingling with hers, his heart beating with hers, and she knew that if he loved her forever, it would not be long enough.

# *Chapter Fifteen*

Sara was filled with disappointment and a keen sense of loss when she woke to find him gone.

She pressed her face into the pillow and drew in a deep breath, inhaling his scent, wondering why he had refused to stay the night. It would be so wonderful to awaken in Gabriel's arms, to make love to him first thing in the morning, when the world was new.

Maybe tonight she would ask him to stay. Maybe this time he would agree.

Smiling, she slid out of bed. Tonight, she thought. She would see him again tonight.

"Aren't you tired of the ballet?" she asked later.

They were sitting in their favorite cafe, at the table Sara had come to think of as theirs. As usual, she ordered a light meal; as usual, he had only a glass of dry red wine.

Gabriel lifted one black brow. "Are you tired of dancing?"

"Of course not!"

Gabriel smiled at her then. "And I never tire of watching you dance. You have such passion, such life."

His words brought a flush of pleasure to her cheeks. Her dancing *did* have more passion, she mused, and she owed it all to Gabriel. He had transformed her from a girl into a woman, and it had changed the world. Now, when she danced, the music seemed to have more meaning, more depth; her body seemed better able to express deep emotion, whether it was Aurora's love for the prince in *Sleeping Beauty*, or sorrow for lost love in *Giselle*.

A last bite, and she pushed her plate away. She wiped her mouth with her napkin, hiding behind the cloth while she summoned her nerve.

"Gabriel?"

"Yes, *cara?*"

"Why don't you move in with me?"

"No."

"Why not? We spend every night together anyway. It would be ever so much easier if you lived with me."

"I told you before, *cara,* I have my own way of life. I don't wish to change it."

"But . . ."

"No, Sara, either we go on as before, or we end it now."

"That's not fair!" She stared at him for a moment, and then frowned as a horrible thought occurred to her. "You're not married, are you?"

"No."

"Then why? Please, Gabriel, it would be so wonderful to wake up in your arms."

"No questions, Sara Jayne, remember?"

"No questions, no questions!" She threw her napkin down on the table. "I'm sick of those two words."

Gabriel sighed heavily, knowing he was being unfair. But he could not explain his reasons to her. To do so would be to lose her forever, and he wasn't ready to let her go, not yet.

He lifted his glass, drained the last few drops of wine, and rose to his feet. "Shall we go?"

With a curt nod, she stood up and walked swiftly toward the door, acutely aware that he was close behind her even though his footsteps made hardly a sound. Sometimes she had the feeling that he walked on air.

Outside, Gabriel took her arm, but instead of turning south, toward her apartment, he turned north, toward a small park. He could feel Sara's anger in her rigid posture, in the tension of her arm beneath his grasp. In all honesty, he couldn't blame her for being angry, and yet, even if he wanted to explain why they couldn't live together, what could he say?

*Sorry,* cara, *I'm a vampire. In the three hundred and fifty years of my dark existence, I've trusted no one to know where I take my rest during the day. And you would not want to see me then, my body hard and unmoving, with the stillness of a sleep that is like death. You don't want to see me when I rise, when the hunger is upon me, when my eyes look like death and no mortal is safe in my presence . . .*

They turned down a narrow path. Few people frequented this place after the sun went down, but Gabriel had no fear of the dark, or of mortal man.

The park was beautiful in the moonlight. A faint

breeze whispered through the leaves, singing songs to the night. Drifting shadows played hide-and-seek with the light of the moon.

He sensed the man's presence as they drew near the small pond located at the far reaches of the park.

"Your purse, *monsieur,*" the man said. Moonlight glinted off the blade of the knife in his hand.

"I'm afraid my purse is empty," Gabriel said coolly.

The man's gaze moved over Gabriel in a long, assessing glance, noting the high quality of his clothing, his expensive leather boots, the fine wool of his cloak.

"I think not," the brigand said with a sneer. He made a threatening gesture with his knife. "Give it over, now."

"No."

The thief lunged forward, but before he could strike, Gabriel's hand closed over the man's forearm in a viselike grip.

Sara gasped at the look of horror that flickered in the man's eyes as Gabriel's hand inexorably tightened around his wrist and the knife fell from nerveless fingers.

She felt a rush of nausea at the sound of the bones being slowly, deliberately crushed. The blood drained from the man's face; a shrill scream of agony bubbled in his throat as tears welled in his eyes.

"Mercy, my lord," the man begged. "Please . . ."

"Gabriel, let him go!"

Gabriel's back was toward her, and she saw him stiffen at the sound of her voice, as if he had suddenly remembered she was there, watching.

Taking a step forward, Sara placed her hand on his shoulder. "Please, Gabriel, please let him go."

Abruptly, Gabriel released his hold on the brigand's arm and the man fell to his knees, his ruined arm cradled against his chest.

"Don't come here again," Gabriel said, and taking Sara by the hand, he led her back toward the street.

"I've got to stop," she said weakly, "Please, I'm . . ."

"Sara, what is it?"

"I'm going to be sick."

Gabriel wrapped his arm around her waist, supporting her as she retched.

When the spasm passed, he wiped her mouth with his handkerchief, then swept her into his arms and carried her home. And all the while he was berating himself for behaving so savagely in her presence. Why hadn't he simply given the man his purse? Certainly he could afford the loss of a few francs.

When they reached Sara's apartment, Gabriel put her to bed, fetched a glass of water to rinse her mouth, and then fixed her a cup of hot tea heavily laced with brandy.

"Better?" he asked when she set the empty cup aside a few moments later.

Sara nodded, then glanced away. She could still hear the awful sound of the man's bones breaking as Gabriel crushed his wrist. The memory of it sickened her even as she marveled at Gabriel's superhuman strength.

Superhuman. She remembered Maurice's words: *There's something not right with that man,* he had said. *Can't you sense the evil that surrounds him?*

Sara looked up into Gabriel's face, gazing deep into his eyes, but it wasn't evil she saw reflected in the smoky gray depths, only love and concern.

"What is it, *cara?*" he asked. "What troubles you?"

"That man . . . you broke his wrist as if it were made of kindling."

"I was angry."

Sara shook his head. "It was more than that."

"What are you trying to say?"

"I don't know. I . . . it was awful."

"I'm sorry you had to see it." Bending, he brushed her cheek with his knuckles. "Go to sleep, Sara."

"Gabriel . . ."

"No questions, tonight, *cara.* You need to rest."

"But . . ."

His gaze caught and held hers. "You're tired, Sara Jayne," he said, his voice low and hypnotic. "Go to sleep. We'll talk tomorrow."

"Tomorrow," she repeated drowsily, and then her eyelids fluttered down and she was asleep.

He sat beside her as long as he dared, and then he left the house.

Maurice waited in the shadows across from Sara's house, listening as a distant clock chimed the hour. Five A.M.

Shivering in the chill air, he shifted his weight in the saddle, wishing he had thought to wear gloves.

He had just decided to call off his vigil when the door to Sara's apartment opened and a dark shape descended the stairs and blended into the night.

"You won't get away from me this time," Maurice vowed.

And filled with a sense of purpose and determination, he touched his heels to the horse's flanks.

Lost in thought, his steps uncharacteristically slow and heavy, Gabriel made his way toward the abandoned cottage. Sara wanted him to move in with her, and she wouldn't accept his excuses forever. For the first time, he considered telling her the truth. Perhaps, if she loved him enough, she would be able to accept him for who and what he was. Perhaps she'd keep his secret, be content to share her life with a man who was not a man at all.

He made a low sound of disgust deep in his throat. And perhaps she'd offer to ease his thirst, as well, or even join him in his hellish existence.

And perhaps dogs would sing and pigs would fly.

Revulsion for what he was rose up within him, as hot and bitter as bile. Even if she wished it, he would never condemn her to the kind of existence he led. She was a creature of light and beauty. To condemn her to a world of endless darkness would be cruelty of the worst kind.

He should leave her, he thought bleakly. Walk out of her life and never return. But, selfish bastard that he was, he knew that was something he could not do. He had lived in solitude for most of the last two hundred years, rarely mingling with humanity, but with Sara he had dared to take a small step into the mortal world. He had sat beside her while she dined in her favorite cafe. He had ventured into the Paris Opera and watched her dance.

He had dared to make love to her—and for those brief moments, the darkness that enveloped him had been swallowed up in her light. Miraculously, his desire for her flesh had tempered his lust for blood. Holding her in his arms, loving her, had given him a reprieve from the ugliness of his existence. For that alone, she had earned his love and his everlasting gratitude.

Sara . . .

Her goodness permeated him. He had the oddest feeling that if he could find the courage to tell her what he was, to confess his innumerable sins against humanity, her love would shrive the guilt from his soul.

He could not leave her, he thought as he entered the cottage and closed and locked the door. If it meant his life, he could not leave her. Not so long as she would have him.

His feet made no sound as he descended the narrow stone stairway that led down to the cellar. There were stout locks on both sides of the thick oak door. By night, the lock on the outside of the cellar door kept his resting place secure; by day, the lock on the inside ensured that no one would come upon him while he slept.

Entering the cellar, he closed the door behind him and turned the key in the lock.

Silently, he crossed the dirt-packed floor, removed his cloak, and climbed into the long, sturdy pine box that served as his resting place.

Closing his eyes, he let his imagination take flight. Sara, clothed as the Princess Aurora, pirouetted within the corridors of his mind, and he was the prince. But in his ballet, it wasn't the prince who awakened the princess from sleep with a kiss, but the princess who willingly gave the prince a single drop of her precious blood and saved him from a life of eternal darkness . . .

Leaving the horse tethered out of sight in a copse of trees, Maurice moved stealthily toward the cottage, his footsteps muffled by the damp earth.

So, he thought with satisfaction, this was where the devil lived.

His heart was pounding like a wild thing when he reached the south side of the cottage. Hardly daring to breathe, he peered into the window. The room was empty. Frowning, he made his way around the cottage, pausing to peer into each window.

As near as he could tell in the darkness, all the rooms were empty.

Puzzled, he made his way toward a clump of brush and hunkered down on his heels. A short time later, dawn brightened the sky and he crept toward the cottage again. The faint light afforded by the rising sun confirmed his earlier suspicions: the rooms were all empty. So, where was Gabriel? Had he gone back to town? Or was there perhaps a room below?

He tried the windows and door. All were securely locked. Strange, he thought, that a house long abandoned would be locked from the inside. Stranger still that Gabriel, who possessed a great deal of wealth, chose to live in an abandoned cottage on the outskirts of town.

Feeling his courage expand with the dawn, Maurice found a good-sized rock and then, taking a deep breath, he broke one of the windows with it. He listened for a long moment, waiting to see if the noise had been overheard, and when nothing happened, he climbed over the low sill.

He paused inside the room, his heart pounding so loudly it would have been impossible to hear anything else, and then, summoning his nerve, he walked from room to room. A heavy layer of dust covered the floor; lacy cobwebs adorned the corners of the ceilings. A rat had made a nest in the kitchen hearth.

A wave of unease overtook him as he came to a flight of steps that led down, to the wine cellar, he supposed.

A fine sheen of perspiration coated his brow and dampened his hands as he took the steps one by one until he reached the door at the foot of the stairs.

He wiped his palm on his trouser leg, placed his hand on the latch. Instantly, he was overcome with a deep, primeval fear that went beyond terror as an image of blood-red eyes shining within a cavernous skull rose within his mind. And with that death's-head image came an overwhelming sense of doom.

It was more than he could endure. With a hoarse cry, he bolted up the steps. The cold sweat of fear momentarily blinded him, and then he was running through the small cottage, diving through the broken window, impervious to the blood that oozed from his hand when he gashed it on a shard of broken glass.

As if pursued by all the hounds of hell, he vaulted into the saddle and raced away from the cottage and the terrifying evil that dwelled within.

The scent of blood, hot and fresh and rank with fear, drifted down the stairs that led to the cellar, rousing Gabriel from the lethargy that imprisoned him.

He sat up, his senses suddenly alert. Lifting his head, he sniffed the air, much as a wolf might sniff the wind, and he caught it again, the tantalizing odor of freshly spilled blood.

Someone had been inside the cottage.

Head cocked to one side, he closed his eyes and listened. And waited.

But the danger was past. Whoever had invaded his sanctuary had fled, leaving nothing behind but a few drops of blood and the lingering smell of fear.

He would have to find a new resting place, he mused as he slowly surrendered once more to the darkness of his deathlike sleep. Either that, or destroy the mortal who had dared violate his lair.

A faint smile twisted his lips. For Sara's sake, he would spare Maurice's life. For now.

# *Chapter Sixteen*

"What is it, Maurice?" Sara asked. "You look as if you've seen a ghost."

"Sara Jayne . . ." He stumbled into her apartment, the fear that had choked him at the cottage still strong.

"What have you done to your hand?" she asked.

Maurice glanced at his hand. The neckerchief he had wrapped around the cut was soaked with blood.

"It's nothing," he muttered, too agitated by what had happened in the cottage to be concerned about his injury. "Saints above, Sara Jayne, he's a monster!"

Exasperated, she closed the door, then drew her dressing gown more tightly around her. "Haven't you given up that absurd notion yet? Is that why you got me out of bed at this hour of the morning? To tell me that Gabriel is a monster?"

"It's true. Come with me and see for yourself."

"And just what did you see?"

"Nothing."

"Maurice, you're not making sense."

"I didn't *see* anything except a locked door. It's what I felt, Sara Jayne. Never in all my life have I felt such evil. You've got to believe me. He's unholy."

"Sit down," Sara said. "I'll get you a glass of brandy. And then I'll bandage your hand."

With a weary nod, Maurice sank down on the sofa and closed his eyes. He couldn't forget the horror that had surrounded him in the cottage, the terrible sense of evil, of danger. Of death.

"Here," Sara said, handing him a glass of brandy. "Drink this. It will help ease the pain."

While he sipped the brandy, she washed the blood from his hand, covered the shallow cut with salve, and bandaged it with a strip of clean cloth.

"I'm going to get dressed now," she said, "and then we'll go have a look at that cottage."

"Maybe that's not such a good idea."

"I want to see it for myself."

They reached the cottage an hour later. In the brilliant light of early morning, the dwelling looked peaceful enough. It was obviously deserted, Sara thought, and had been for a long while by the look of it. The vines had gone wild, climbing over the trellis and spreading around the house. The windows were dirty; the chimney was in disrepair.

"Maybe we shouldn't go any closer," Maurice said.

"Don't be silly. We've come this far. I'm going inside."

Resolutely, she approached the cottage, then walked around to the back until she came to the window Maurice had broken. She could see several dark brown stains on the sill, and she shuddered, knowing it was from the cut on Maurice's hand.

Picking up a rock, she broke away the last shards of glass from the frame. Then, lifting her skirts, she started to climb over the sill.

"Wait." Maurice laid a restraining hand on her shoulder. "You'll ruin your skirts. I'll go through the window and open the front door."

"Very well," Sara agreed.

Moments later, the front door opened with a loud creak and Sara stepped into the cottage. The room she found herself in was empty, but she thought it might have once been rather nice.

Holding her skirts away from the floor to keep them clean, she walked toward the next room. She could hear Maurice following her, his footsteps hesitant.

She walked through each room, and then turned to confront Maurice. "There's nothing here. I don't think anyone's lived here for years."

"Don't you feel it?"

"Feel what?"

With a shake of his head, Maurice grabbed Sara's hand and led her down the cellar stairs. As soon as they reached the door, he felt the short hairs rise along the back of his neck.

"Don't tell me you can't feel *that?*" he exclaimed.

"I'll tell you what I feel," Sara retorted. "I feel silly for listening to you."

"He's behind that door," Maurice said. "I know it."

"That's ridiculous. Gabriel's a wealthy man. What would he be doing here, in this old place?"

Yet even as she spoke the words, she remembered the deserted abbey in London.

"Put your hand on the door and tell me what you feel."

Filled with a sudden sense of unease, Sara placed her hand on the door. And in that instant, she knew Maurice was right. Gabriel was behind that portal. She could feel his presence as strongly as she felt Maurice's hand on her shoulder.

But it wasn't a sense of evil that assailed her, but rather a sense of confusion and doubt. Why was he here?

"Gabriel?"

*Be gone!*

It was his voice, loud and clear in her mind. And in that moment, she didn't want to know why he was there, didn't want to know what secrets he was hiding.

"Do you feel it?" Maurice asked.

"No. Let's go."

"What's wrong?" Maurice asked. His fingers closed around the crucifix in his jacket pocket. It was large and costly, made of solid silver. "Why are you in such a hurry to leave?"

"We have a rehearsal this afternoon. I want to have time to eat lunch first. Come along, Maurice, there's nothing scary here."

He followed her because he was eager to be away from the place, but he didn't believe her words for a minute. She had felt something, and whatever it was had drained the color from her face.

He rose as soon as the sun had set. After drawing water from the well behind the cottage, he bathed, then changed his clothes and packed a few of his belongings.

With preternatural speed, he made his way into town and secured lodgings at the best hotel Paris had to offer. After unpacking his clothing, he ordered a bouquet of flowers and a midnight supper for two, and then he left the hotel.

For an hour, he walked the streets. For Sara, he would reenter the mainstream of humanity. He would take her to parties; he would take her dining and dancing, though he would have to be careful to avoid mirrors and other reflective surfaces. If she wished, he would accompany her to London when the company left Paris.

He sat in his usual box during her performance, mesmerized, as always, by her beauty. She moved with an inherent grace that was enchanting. Each step, each movement of her hand, each facial expression, was perfection.

And Maurice . . . Gabriel let his gaze rest upon the young man. What was he going to do about Maurice? The man didn't know anything, and yet he suspected far too much. Gabriel's first instinct was to kill Delacroix, but that he could not do. Sara liked the young man. But for her affection, Maurice would be dead even now.

Muttering an oath, Gabriel dismissed Maurice from his mind and lost himself once again in the magic that was Sara Jayne.

As always, she flew into his arms when the show was over, her eyes shining with happiness and the knowledge that she had danced beautifully.

"Where shall we go tonight?" she asked, slipping her arm through his.

"My hotel?" he answered casually.

"Your hotel?" She hesitated only a moment. "Yes, I'd like that."

She was surprised when he summoned a carriage, and even more surprised when they arrived at the Hotel de Paris.

"Is this where you stay?" she asked, her eyes growing wide as they stepped into the lobby of the hotel.

Never in all her life had she seen anything so grand. The carpets, the tapestries, the long, winding staircase. A chandelier to rival the one at the Opéra hung from the intricately carved and painted ceiling.

His room was equally grand. Heavy velvet draperies covered the windows. A matching spread covered the enormous brass bed. The furniture was rich red mahogany, the settee of fine damask.

She made a slow circle, taking everything in, frowning when she noticed there was no looking glass.

Before she could comment on the lack, there was a knock at the door and a young man entered the room pushing a tea cart with one hand and carrying a huge bouquet of flowers in the other.

Gabriel took the flowers. Bowing low, he handed them to Sara. "For you, *cara*."

"They're beautiful, Gabriel," she murmured, touched by his thoughtfulness. "Thank you."

"Shall I serve you, *monsieur*?" the young man asked.

"That won't be necessary."

The young man's eyes widened as Gabriel pressed several coins into his hand. "Thank you, *monsieur*. And if you have need of anything else, please let me know." With a bow, he left the room.

"Enjoy your meal, *cara*," Gabriel said. He placed

the tray on the small table near the window and lifted the cover. "I hope the pheasant is to your liking." He held her chair for her, then took the opposite seat.

"It looks delicious," Sara said. She cocked her head to one side and smiled. "I suppose you've already eaten?"

Gabriel nodded. "But don't let that spoil your dinner."

"I'm used to it," she said with a sigh. "Are you sure you won't share it with me?"

He glanced at her plate briefly, his stomach churning at the mere idea of digesting such a conglomeration of meat and vegetables. "I'm sure."

He filled their glasses with wine, then handed one to her. "To you, my sweet Sara," he said, touching his glass to hers. "May life bring you all the happiness you deserve."

She looked at him over the rim of her glass as she took a drink, felt the heat that arced between them as their gazes met.

"To us, my angel," she said, lifting her glass to his. "May we share all our tomorrows."

"It is my fondest wish," Gabriel replied ardently.

The fervor of his words and the refulgent look in his eyes enveloped her in a warm haze. Lost in the promise of his hooded gray eyes, she began to eat, though she hardly tasted a thing.

She couldn't stop watching him. He sipped his wine while she ate, and she yearned to lick the drops from his lips. He placed his empty glass on the table, his fingers making lazy patterns on the stem, and she yearned to feel his hand caress her skin.

He smiled, as if he knew her thoughts, and she felt

the blood rush to her cheeks, but she couldn't stop staring at him, couldn't keep from admiring the width of his shoulders, the sheer masculine beauty of his face.

He wore a loose-fitting white shirt, dark brown trousers, and brown leather boots, and she thought how perfect he would be to play the part of the prince in *Sleeping Beauty*, for his kiss had surely awakened her, to life, to love. To passion.

"What did you do today?" Gabriel asked as she pushed her plate away.

"Do?" She was filled with a sudden sense of unease as she recalled going to the cottage with Maurice. In the excitement of performing and then coming to Gabriel's hotel, she had all but forgotten Maurice's ramblings.

A slight frown drew Gabriel's brows together. "Is something wrong, *cara*?"

"Wrong? No, nothing's wrong. Why do you ask?"

"You're a poor liar, Sara."

"What do you mean?"

"Something is troubling you. What is it?"

"Nothing!"

He didn't believe her. She felt her mouth go dry as his gaze pierced hers. She could almost feel those deep gray eyes probing her heart, her soul. Her mind.

"Nothing's wrong," she said again. "Maurice and I went for a drive this morning."

"Indeed?" Gabriel said, his voice silky smooth. "Tell me, how is your young man?"

"He's not *my* young man," Sara retorted, glad for the apparent change of subject. "We're just friends."

"He seems to have injured his hand."

Sara bit down on her lip. "Yes, he . . . he cut it on a piece of glass."

"How unfortunate."

"Yes. We stopped at a small cottage. That's where Maurice cut his hand."

"I hope you looked after it for him. Cuts can be nasty things. Deadly, should infection occur."

Sara nodded. They weren't talking about anything as mundane as a minor cut, she thought, her mind racing. Gabriel was warning her to be careful. But to be careful of what?

"It was a quaint little cottage just outside of town. No one was living there. We climbed in through a broken window in the back."

Why was she telling him this? She had the oddest feeling that he already knew, that he was somehow drawing the words from her mind.

"And what did you see there, *cara?*"

"Nothing . . ." She tried to draw her gaze from his and failed. She hadn't *seen* anything, but she *had* heard his voice. All day, she had tried to tell herself it had only been her imagination, but she knew now that it had indeed been Gabriel's voice. "You were there, weren't you?"

"No questions, *cara.*"

"You were there," she said again, with more conviction this time. "Why? Are you engaged in something illegal?"

"No questions!" His fist came down on the table with such force her silverware skittered across the surface, knocking over her empty wine glass.

"Maurice said . . ." Abruptly, she pressed her lips together, fear for Maurice's life making her suddenly cautious. For the first time since she had known Gabriel, she was truly afraid of him.

"I should like to go home now." She clasped her hands in her lap to still their shaking, but she could not stay the tremor in her voice. "Please."

Gabriel rose stiffly to his feet and pulled out her chair. "As you wish, *cara*," he said quietly.

She watched him out of the corner of her eye while she drew on her evening cape and gloves, fearing he would try to detain her, but he remained by the table, his hands clenched at his sides, his deep gray eyes filled with pain and self-reproach.

"Good night." She was trembling so badly she could scarcely speak the words.

A sad smile lifted the corners of his mouth. "Good-bye, Sara Jayne."

# *Chapter Seventeen*

The next two weeks were the most miserable of Sara's life. She filled her mornings with long rehearsals, and her afternoons with Maurice. He took her shopping, to lunch, on long walks, on a picnic. She refused to discuss Gabriel or the cottage, refused to relate what had happened between herself and Gabriel at the hotel.

She took a nap late each afternoon, then went to the theater. She tried to lose herself in her dancing, but she found no joy in it. Her feet felt like lead; her heart seemed to be made of wood. The ballet mistress scolded her nightly, admonishing her to pay attention, to listen to the music, but to no avail. There was no joy in her heart, no music in her head, nothing but the sound of Gabriel's voice bidding her good-bye.

If her days were long, and her dancing less than perfect, her nights could only be described as hellish.

She was tormented by nightmares—dark dreams filled with phantoms and fiends, ghouls with eyes that glowed, demons with fangs dripping with blood. Her blood.

Night after night, she woke in a cold sweat. On several occasions, she slipped out of bed and lit the lamp, checking in the mirror to make certain there were no bites on her neck.

As bad as those dreams were, there were others that were worse—horrible nightmares in which the fiends that chased her had Gabriel's voice, Gabriel's eyes.

These dreams started innocently enough. They would be walking in the park, or they would be dancing while he sang to her, and then, gradually, she would be overcome with a sense of dread. A shroud of darkness would overcome her, stealing the strength from her legs so that she couldn't run, and then he would be there, bending over her, enveloping her in the folds of his cloak until she was aware of nothing but the blood-red glow in his eyes and the smell of her own fear. And then he would smile, exposing his teeth, the canines long and sharp.

And then the true terror began, flooding through her with each wild beat of her heart as he bent over her. Horror would clog her throat, trapping her scream inside, so that she could only stare up at him, as helpless as a kitten caught in the jaws of a wolf. She would feel his lips on hers, his hands caressing her back. And then, just as she had convinced herself there was nothing to be afraid of, she would feel the sharp sting of his teeth at her neck.

Taut with fear, she would close her eyes, waiting for the pain, but there was no pain, only a gradual awareness of sensual pleasure that started deep within her and vibrated outward. To her horror, she would tilt her head to the side, exposing more of her neck to the ravages of his teeth. Heat would pulse through her, its warmth hypnotic, so that, when he finally drew away, she cried out in protest, begging him to take more, to take it all. At her words, he would laugh softly and then plunge his fangs into her neck again, a low growl of demonic ecstasy rumbling in his throat as he drained the blood from her body.

She would wake up screaming then, her body trembling violently, the bedclothes soaked with perspiration.

After the first few nights, she tried to stay awake, but after a strenuous day of rehearsing and dancing, her body demanded rest.

She had tried sleeping with the light on, but even that failed to banish the demons that haunted her, and when that didn't help, she asked one of the other dancers to stay with her for a couple of days, thinking Jean Marie's presence might keep her nightmares at bay, but her screams frightened Jean Marie so badly that the girl packed up her things and left while it was still dark outside.

As a last resort, she asked Maurice to come and spend the nights on the sofa. It didn't stop the dreams, but it was good to have him there when she awoke in tears, good to feel the solid strength of his arms around her, to hear his voice telling her that everything would be all right.

Another week passed, and then another. Maurice proposed to her again, and when she refused him, he asked candidly if she would consider letting him move in with her.

"I'm here most nights anyway," he said with irrefutable logic. "And it would be so much more convenient if my belongings were here, as well."

"I don't know . . ." Sara shook her head. "I don't think that's a good idea."

"You're not thinking of a reconciliation with him, are you?"

"No. Whatever we had is over. It's just that . . ." She shrugged, and then smiled at him. "I just can't. What would people say?"

"All right, Sara Jayne," he said good-naturedly. "We'll let it go for now. But I promise you, we'll talk about it again. Soon." He winked at her. "I'll be by to pick you up later."

She kissed him good-bye, then went to sit by the window. Why was she so reluctant to share her life with Maurice? He loved her. He was kind, thoughtful, fun to be with, intelligent, generous. He would make a fine husband, yet she made excuses for not wanting to share her apartment with him, excuses that had never occurred to her when Gabriel had taken her in his arms.

Gabriel. She missed him, missed him more than she wanted to admit. She relived every moment she had spent with him, from the first time she had seen him on her balcony at the orphanage to the last night in his hotel room. She remembered being held in his arms while he danced her around the room, remembered the joy they had shared when she discovered she could walk.

She glanced at the ballerina doll Gabriel had given her. He had been kindness itself in those days at the abbey, buying her gifts, singing to her, caring for her. He had taken her to her first ballet, letting her see for herself that it was as beautiful, as wonderful, as she had imagined. He had taken her riding on his horse, letting her experience the stallion's marvelous speed and power. He had fulfilled her every wish, her every dream. The clothes in her closet, the food on her table, the very apartment in which she lived, were all possible because of Gabriel's generosity.

But, more importantly, he had made her feel loved, cherished. Even when she had been trapped in her wheelchair, he had made her feel beautiful, desired. It was a rare gift, the ability to make another feel important. Until she had met Gabriel, she had always felt as if she had been a burden, first to her family, and then to the nuns. But Gabriel had given her a sense of self-worth, and she knew that, even if she were still bound to her chair, he would still find her desirable.

He had given her something else, as well. He had allowed her to comfort him. Clearly she recalled the night in the park, when he had knelt at her feet and begged her to hold him, to comfort him. A single tear slipped down her cheek as she recalled the abject loneliness she had read in the depths of his eyes, his hunger for the gentle touch of her hand.

She loved him. Loved him with her whole heart, and nothing that had passed between them could change that simple fact. She loved him. And he loved her.

They'd been apart almost three weeks when Sara gathered her courage and went to his hotel. She had dressed with care in a long-sleeved white silk blouse and a pink skirt. She wore a wide-brimmed white hat trimmed with feathers and flowers, and a pair of white gloves.

Taking a last glance in the mirror, she left her apartment, her heart beating double-time at the thought of seeing Gabriel again.

She lifted her chin defiantly as she walked up the stairs to Gabriel's room, ignoring the disapproving glance she received from the hotel clerk. She knew he was probably thinking she was a harlot, since no lady deserving of the name would call on a man who was not a relative unless she was adequately chaperoned. But what she had to say to Gabriel was best said in private.

She knocked on his door twice, then stamped her foot. She should have known he wouldn't be here. He was never about during the day; in fact, she couldn't ever remember having seen him before dusk.

What *did* he do all day that he was never available?

Frowning, she went outside and summoned a carriage to take her back to her apartment, and then, before she could change her mind, or question her reasoning too closely, she instructed the driver to take her to the cottage on the outskirts of town.

"Shall I wait, *mademoiselle*?" the driver asked.

"Yes, please. I shan't be long."

"Very well, *mademoiselle*." Touching his finger to his hat brim, he parked the carriage in the shade afforded by a tree a short distance away.

Lifting her skirts, Sara made her way to the front door, only to find that it was locked. Making her way to the back of the house, she peered through the broken window.

"Gabriel," she called softly. "Are you here?"

She listened a moment, and then repeated her

question, a little louder. Again, no answer, only a strong impression that he was inside.

With a grimace, she gathered her skirts and climbed over the low sill, letting out a sigh of exasperation as she snagged her petticoat on a piece of glass.

And then she was inside the cottage. The absolute quiet of the place was overwhelming. Was it her imagination, or could she hear the house breathing? She was certain she could hear the hammering of her heart.

"Gabriel?"

Hardly daring to breathe, she tiptoed through the house, her apprehension growing with each step.

And then, as if drawn by a magnet, she found herself at the cellar door.

She lifted a trembling hand, intending to knock on the door, when her courage deserted her. Whatever lay behind that door, she didn't want to know.

She was about to leave when the door swung open and she found herself face to face with Gabriel.

He was not happy to see her.

"*Cara,* what are you doing here?"

"That's what I was going to ask you."

Gabriel crossed the threshold and closed the door behind him.

Sara met his gaze and frowned. "Are you all right?"

"Fine," he replied tersely. In truth, it took a great deal of effort for him to stand there. He judged it to be mid day, when his strength was at its lowest ebb. It was possible for him to stand there now only because there was almost no light at the bottom of the stairs, and because he'd needed so badly to see her face one more time.

"Are you sure?" Sara asked doubtfully. "You look a trifle pale . . ."

"I'm fine." He leaned his shoulder against the door jamb in what he hoped was a casual pose. "What do you want, Sara?"

"Couldn't we go upstairs and talk?"

"I'm rather busy at the moment."

"Busy?"

"No questions, *cara*."

She bit down on her lip, resisting the urge to scream at him, to insist that she would no longer be bound by that ridiculous promise, but something in the depths of his eyes warned her to keep silent.

Gabriel clenched his hands in an effort to keep the overpowering lethargy at bay. His gaze was drawn to her throat, to the pulse throbbing there. He hadn't fed in several days, and her nearness, coupled with the knowledge that she could appease his demon thirst, was a temptation he feared he could not long resist. Even now, he could smell the blood flowing in her veins, hear the rapid beating of her heart.

"Sara, you must go. I'll come to you tonight if you wish. We can talk then."

She nodded, bewildered by his apparent weakness, by the strange pallor of his skin, the sudden harsh rasp of his breathing. Was he ill? She glanced at the door behind him, wondering what secrets he was hiding there.

"Sara . . . please . . . go."

"I'll see you tonight?"

"Yes," he rasped. "Tonight."

He watched her climb the stairs, and then he fell

back against the door, his strength nearly gone.

He released a deep sigh when he heard the front door close. Then, and only then, did he return to his retreat.

The image of Sara's face, lined with concern, followed him into oblivion.

She knew Gabriel was in the audience even before she set foot onstage. The knowledge that he was there, that he would be watching, set her pulse to racing. For the first time in almost three weeks, she felt like dancing.

Maurice slanted her a quick, questioning look during the *pas de deux*, and she knew he was aware of the change in her. How could he help it, when her feet suddenly felt lighter than air, when her leaps were effortless, joyful, when her solo was once again filled with passion and *joie de vivre*?

He was at her side the minute the final curtain came down. "He's here, isn't he?"

"Who?"

"Don't be coy, Sara Jayne. You know very well who. Gabriel. He's out there, isn't he?"

"I don't . . ." She nodded her head, knowing it was useless to lie. "Yes."

"You can't mean to meet him!"

"I do."

"I won't permit it."

"I think you forget yourself, Maurice."

"I forget nothing! I remember how frightened you were when you left his hotel the last time. I remember the nightmares that haunted your sleep, that made you afraid to be alone. He was the cause of that fear, those nightmares. And now you mean to start it all again!"

"I'm sorry. I have to see him, at least one more time."

"Why?" Maurice's voice and expression were filled with anguish, with a deep-seated need to understand. "Why, Sara Jayne? What hold does he have over you?"

"None, it's just that I owe him so much—"

"You owe him nothing!"

"But I do. Don't you understand? He's given me everything I have. Everything! My apartment, my clothes, my dancing, I owe it all to him."

"And what does he expect in return?"

"He's never asked me for anything."

Maurice made a low sound of disbelief.

"It's true! He's the nearest thing to family that I have, Maurice. I can't hurt him."

With a sigh of resignation, Maurice turned away, his steps heavy as he left the stage. He had never thought of himself as a brave man, or a foolish one, but surely what he was contemplating proved that he was the most courageous of men or a complete and utter fool.

Sara studied Gabriel carefully as they sat in their favorite cafe later that night. Earlier, she would have sworn he had been ill. His skin had been stretched taut over his skin, his eyes had burned as with a fever, his voice had been harsh and edged with pain. But now he looked strong and fit. He was clad in black, as usual. There was a ruddy glow to his cheeks, a gleam in his eye. Sara shook her head. Had she imagined it all?

"Something troubles you, *cara?*" he asked, and his voice was as deep and resonant as always.

"No, nothing."

"What did you want to see me about?"

"I wanted to apologize for my actions the other night. I had no right to question you. I ask you to forgive me."

As always, her honesty humbled him. "You have every right to your questions, *cara,*" he replied quietly. "I am only sorry I cannot give you the answers you desire."

"Are you in some kind of trouble? Is that why you're hiding out in that cottage?"

How like her, he thought, to be worried about him. "No, Sara, I'm not in trouble. Not the kind you mean, at any rate. I told you before, I lead a very secluded life, one that must seem strange to a woman such as yourself."

"I . . . had you been ill since I saw you last?"

A muscle worked in Gabriel's jaw. He must have looked like death itself when she saw him at the cottage that morning, and now she was wondering at his apparently miraculous improvement.

"No, *cara,* I have not been ill, not the way you mean." He had been soul sick, though, he thought bleakly. He had missed seeing her each evening, missed the joy of her laughter, the warmth of her caring. He had missed watching her dance. It had only been his overwhelming desire to see her again that had given him the strength to rise while the sun still commanded the sky.

"This afternoon . . ." She caught her lower lip between her teeth, afraid to pry further for fear of making him angry.

He met her confused gaze. It would be so easy to clear her mind of her questions and doubts, so easy to mesmerize her with his revenant power, to wrap her in the illusion that all was well. But he could not do that, not to Sara. The very thought of invading her mind was repulsive. And yet, she deserved an explanation of some kind. Unfortunately, he had none to give but the truth, and that was trapped in his throat.

"More wine?" he asked instead.

Sara nodded. "Please."

"So, *cara,* what is it you wish to do now?"

"What do you mean?" She sipped her wine, her gaze fixed on Gabriel's face.

"Do you wish me to be gone from your life?"

"No!"

Her quick denial, the fervor in her tone, pleased him beyond words, and saddened him beyond pain.

"We cannot go on as before, Sara. You have too many questions that I cannot answer." He looked deep into her eyes, his own filled with sadness. "And you're afraid of me now, I think."

"I'm not," she said quickly, but she was lying, and they both knew it.

"You have nothing to fear from me, *cara.* I would never hurt you."

"And Maurice?"

"No harm will come to the boy, but he is delving into things which do not concern him. If he persists, he will live to regret it."

Sara nodded, her mouth suddenly dry.

He felt her confusion, her fear, and it sickened him to know he was the cause. Now he truly hated what he was, hated it because it was keeping him from the one thing he wanted more than his next breath.

"Sara . . ." Whispering her name, he leaned across the table and reached for her hand. "I wish there was no need for secrets between us. I wish, with all my heart, that we could go on as before, but I fear that is impossible now."

"What are you saying?"

"I'm leaving Paris tomorrow."

"Leaving? Why? Where are you going?"

"It's for the best. I've kept you at my side long enough. I want you to live your own life. Marry. Have children."

"No . . ."

"You have so much ahead of you, *cara*. I want you to live your life to the fullest, to experience all that life has to offer."

"Why are you doing this?" She was weeping now. "I said I was sorry."

Gabriel glanced around the cafe, aware of the curious looks coming their way. He tossed a few coins on the table to pay for Sara's meal and the wine, draped her cape over her shoulders, and led her from the cafe.

She sobbed quietly on the short walk to her apartment.

"Gabriel . . ."

He silenced her words with a kiss, then drew her into his arms and held her close until her tears subsided. He removed her cape and gloves, and then, with a gentleness that bordered on awe, he undressed her and carried her to bed. He quickly shed his own garments, then slid in beside her and gathered her into his arms.

"Please don't leave," she murmured.

"Don't think of it now," he chided softly, and claimed her lips in a kiss that was filled with a bittersweet passion.

He made love to her all the night long, his hands memorizing the incredible smoothness of her skin, the silky texture of her hair, the tantalizing taste of her lips. He buried his face in her neck and drew in a deep breath, drowning in the sweet scent of her warm, supple flesh.

His hands adored her, his voice caressed her, surrounded her, until she could think of nothing but Gabriel—the wonder of his body, the magic in his hands, the sweet caring in his voice as he whispered her name.

And then his flesh merged with hers and they were one being. Two hearts beating as one, two souls joined together. He buried himself deep within her, sheathing himself in her warmth, burying his darkness in the light of her touch. Enveloped in her warmth and humanity, he let himself forget, for the moment, that he was in reality a demon disguised as a man.

He made love to her thoroughly and completely, until she fell asleep, sated and exhausted, in his arms.

He held her until he felt the stealthy approach of the dawn, and then he kissed her one last time.

Rising, he dressed quickly, then wrote her a short note, telling her that he had left the city while she slept, begging her to go on with her life.

He left the note where she would be sure to find it, and then he pressed a gentle kiss to her brow.

"Farewell, *cara,*" he murmured.

And knew at that moment that if he still had a heart, it would be breaking.

# Chapter Eighteen

Shrouded in the shadows, Maurice watched Gabriel leave Sara Jayne's apartment and then, as he had before, he followed the man to the deserted cottage.

At last, the time had come. He had spent most of the night preparing for what he intended to see accomplished before the sun set on the morrow.

He prayed that he had the courage to see it through.

He hoped that Sara Jayne would forgive him.

Hidden in the darkness, he watched Gabriel unlock the door to the house and step inside.

And then he waited.

Not until the sun was well above the horizon did he approach the dwelling, pulling the small wagon he had hidden in the trees the day before.

He walked around the house, peering in each window, assuring himself that Gabriel was nowhere to be seen. And then he lifted the first cross from the back of the wagon.

Two hours later, the cottage was surrounded by wooden crosses. They were placed against the walls of the house, in front of the windows, on the roof, over the chimney. Holy water, stolen from several church fonts, had been brushed around the door frame and each window, and then he had poured a narrow stream of holy water around the cottage itself. As an extra measure, he had strewn garlic around the foundation. He only hoped he had correctly interpreted the signs, and that Gabriel was indeed a vampire, and not some other form of night creature.

Maurice shuddered. As a young man, he had enjoyed reading novels about vampires: *Wake Not the Dead* by Tieck, *The Pale Faced Lady* by Alexandre Dumas, *La Morte Amoureuse* by Gautier.

In literature, the preferred method of destroying a vampire was a wooden stake through the heart, but, at least for the moment, Maurice lacked the courage to face Gabriel in his lair. According to legend, a vampire could not cross an unbroken circle made of holy water. If he could not leave the house, he could not feed. If he could not feed, he would weaken. And then Maurice would break down the cellar door and do what had to be done.

He walked around the house three times, studying his handiwork, wondering how long it would take for Gabriel to weaken to the point that he would no longer be a threat.

She read the note four times. Her cheeks were wet with tears, the paper stained with her sorrow, when she finally put the note aside.

He was gone.

". . . for your own good," the note said, "I want you to get on with your life. Marry Maurice. Have children . . ."

But she didn't want to marry Maurice, didn't want to have his children. She wanted Gabriel. She had wanted him ever since the first night he had come to her in the orphanage. He had been her solace, her hope, her joy. He had made her feel beautiful.

And now he was gone.

She was tempted to go to the cottage, to see for herself, but she couldn't face the pain that would bring.

Maurice came to call on her later that afternoon, his brown eyes warm with caring as he invited her to lunch.

"Not today, Maurice," she said. "I want to take a nap before I go to rehearsal."

"All right. Shall I come by for you later?"

Sara shrugged. "If you wish."

"Till later, then," he said. He gave her hand a squeeze, planted a kiss on her cheek, and took his leave.

Sara stared at the closed door, overwhelmed by a sense of emptiness, of loss.

She was going to leave Paris. There were too many memories here. Perhaps she'd go to Italy . . . but no, Gabriel had a villa there. Spain, then? She shook her head. Gabriel owned a castle in Salamanca. Back home, to England? But, no, there were too many memories there, as well.

She sighed in exasperation. She might just as well stay where she was, she thought bitterly. She'd take his memory with her wherever she went.

Maybe she *would* marry Maurice. He loved her, adored her, would never leave her. But she would never love him as he deserved.

Her steps were like lead as she went into her bedroom and crawled into bed. Sleep was the answer, she mused as she crawled under the covers. Sleep was forgetfulness.

He woke with the setting sun, his decision to leave Paris weighing heavily upon him. This morning, before sleep enveloped him, he had decided to go home to Italy, to go to ground and sleep for a hundred years. Perhaps, after such a long rest, he would be able to forget her.

With a low oath, he acknowledged it for the lie it was. He would never forget her. Not if he survived another 350 years.

Rising, he changed his clothes, his mind and his heart warring within him. Go. Stay.

Crossing the room, he unlocked the door, his nose wrinkling against the overpowering smell of . . . garlic?

He took the stairs two at a time, then came to an abrupt halt as his gaze settled on the large wooden cross visible through the kitchen window.

He walked from room to room, his anger growing with each step. In the bedroom, he placed his hand on the sill where Maurice had broken the window. And quickly jerked it away. Muttering an oath, he glanced at his hand. The skin was burned as though he'd touched a living flame.

Holy water! Crosses. Garlic.

Maurice.

Like a lion in a cage, he prowled from room to

room. He was trapped within this place, caught like a fish in a net by that pretty-faced boy.

He loosed his rage in a long, anguished cry. And then, refusing to believe what he knew to be true, he put his hand on the door latch and wrenched it open. But in spite of his determination, he could not step through the door, nor bear to face the heavy wooden cross which burned his eyes with a greater intensity than the sun at noon-day.

With a cry of frustration, he slammed the door, his anger rising with his hunger.

Muttering curses in a dozen languages, he paced the floor until the rising sun drove him below.

Three weeks passed, and he was in agony. Hunger clawed at him, relentless, merciless in its intensity. And as the hunger grew, so did his weakness, until he could barely climb out of the shallow wooden box where he took his rest. Rest! He had not truly rested in the last seven days. His skin was shrinking, stretched taut over his frame. His eyes burned. And always, the hunger screamed through him, clawing at his vitals until he thought he would go mad with the pain.

Three weeks without nourishment, save for the blood of one small rat that had foolishly crossed his path. The thought filled him with revulsion, yet he would gladly have drained the blood from a dozen rodents if he but had the chance . . .

A low moan rose in his parched throat. Had he truly sunk so low? He stared at his hands. With their shrunken flesh, the fingers looked almost skeletal.

He cursed himself for being foolish enough to stay in the cottage after Maurice had learned the location of his lair. He cursed himself for not disposing of the troublesome young man when he had the chance, for not summoning Delacroix to his side when he still had the power to do so.

*Sara . . .*

On legs that would barely support him, he walked slowly from one end of the cellar to the other.

*Sara, Sara.*

If he could only see her one last time . . .

*Sara . . .*

She woke with a start, the sound of Gabriel's voice ringing in her ears. He was in pain, crying her name.

Had it been a dream? She sat up, her gaze sweeping the room. Was he here? But that was impossible. He'd left town weeks ago.

"Gabriel?"

*Sara . . . Sara . . .*

He needed her. In minutes, she was dressed and out the door. She fretted as she waited for a hack, tapped her foot impatiently as the carriage made its way toward the cottage. He was there. She knew it, just as she knew that he needed her.

She told the driver to stop the carriage before the cottage came in sight. She thrust the fare into his hand and began to run, her feet flying over the ground.

She was light-headed and out of breath by the time she reached her destination. Eyes wide, she stared at the cottage. There were wooden crosses everywhere, even on the roof. The heavy odor of garlic assailed her nostrils.

She tried the door, but it was locked. Lifting her skirts, she went around to the back of the house and climbed through the broken window.

"Gabriel?"

*Go away!*

"Gabriel, where are you?"

*Go away!*

Taking a deep, calming breath, she went into the kitchen and down the stairs that led to the cellar door. She was surprised to find the door unlocked, and more surprised by the sudden and total terror that engulfed her as she lifted the latch and crossed the threshold into darkness so thick it was almost palpable.

"Gabriel?" Her voice was soft and low and shaky.

"Go away!"

She peered into the darkness, trying to see him. "Gabriel, where are you?"

"Sara, for the love of heaven, get out of here while you can!"

"I'm not leaving. You called me, and I'm here."

Tears stung his eyes. She had heard his anguished cries, and she had come to him.

He pressed his forehead against the cold stone wall and closed his eyes, striving for control.

"Please, Sara, go away."

"What's wrong, Gabriel? Won't you tell me?"

"I'm . . . not well."

"I'll help you. Only tell me what to do."

"No." He placed his hands on the wall on either side of his head, his fingernails raking the cold stones. "Please . . . go. Please . . . I don't want to hurt you."

"Tell me what you need, and I'll get it for you."

"What I need?" His voice was shrill, edged with pain and despair. "What I need! Ah, Sara," he murmured brokenly. "If you only knew."

"I'll get it, Gabriel, I promise, whatever it is. Only tell me."

She took another step into the room. Her eyes had become accustomed to the darkness and she could see him now, a black shape huddled against the opposite wall.

She took another step, and he whirled away, his cloak swirling around him as he stumbled toward the far corner.

"Gabriel, my angel, please let me help you."

"Angel . . . angel . . ." He laughed then, a horrible sound that bordered on hysteria. "Devil, you mean. Go away from me, my sweet Sara. Go away before I destroy you as I destroyed Rosalia."

"I'm not leaving," Sara said firmly. And before she could change her mind, before her imagination could frighten her away, she crossed the room and gathered him into her arms.

She felt his whole body tense at her touch.

"Gabriel . . ."

For a moment, he closed his eyes, absorbing her nearness, her warmth. Ah, how he had craved her touch, yearned to hold her, to be held by her. He shuddered as the hunger rose up within him, hot and swift, the need, the pain, more than he could bear.

The heat of her hands penetrated his clothing. He could hear the soft whisper of blood stirring through her veins, smell it, taste it. . . .

"Gabriel, please tell me what to do."

With an inhuman growl of despair, he whirled around to face her. "Go away!"

Sara stared up at him, at eyes that blazed in the

darkness like hell's own fires, and knew she was looking into the face of death.

"What has happened to you?" she asked, her voice quivering with barely suppressed terror.

"Nothing has happened to me. This is what I am."

He bared his teeth, and Sara took a step backward. Even in the darkness, she could see his fangs, sharp and white and deadly. And the unearthly red glow in his eyes.

"Now will you go?"

His voice was ragged, his hands clenched at his sides as he struggled to control the hunger that burned through him.

Sara took a deep breath, fighting down the urge to run away as fast and as far as she could.

"No, Gabriel," she said with quiet determination. "I'll not leave you again."

The room was growing lighter, and she realized the sun had come up, that its light was slowly creeping down the stairs.

With a low cry, Gabriel spun away, his cloak swirling around his ankles like black smoke. Taking refuge in a corner untouched by the sun's searing brightness, he dropped into a crouch, his head lowered, his arms shielding his face.

*Vampire.*

The word echoed in her mind.

"Yes, Sara." Gabriel's voice, taut with pain, spoke to her from the shadows. "Vampire. That is what I am."

She shook her head. Vampires were creatures of fantasy and illusion, like Santa Claus. "I don't believe it."

"It's true nonetheless. Go now."

"You need blood."

He made a harsh sound that hovered somewhere between laughter and despair. "I thought you didn't believe."

"If you need blood, take mine." Were those her words? Sara wondered, unable to draw her gaze from his bowed head. Was that her voice, calmly urging him to take her blood?

"No!"

"Will it help you?"

She took his silence for assent. "Then take it, my angel. Take as much as you need."

"No!" He screamed the word, but, ah, the mere thought of it, to taste the very essence of her life . . . "No, I won't. I can't. Please, go away."

Relief washed through him as he heard her footsteps cross the floor and climb the stairs. She was leaving. Had he the right, he would have given thanks to the Almighty.

A moment later, his head jerked up and a feral growl rumbled in his throat as the scent of blood, tantalizing and sweetly fresh, reached his nostrils.

He whirled around to find Sara standing before him, her left arm extended. His gaze was instantly drawn to the small pool of blood welling from the shallow cut she had inflicted in her wrist.

Blood. Warm. Fresh. The essence of life. An end to the horrible agony knifing through him, a pain that grew ever worse now that the promise of relief was near.

Sara's blood.

Hands clenched at his sides, he shook his head. "No," he gasped. "Sara . . . no."

He shook his head as she walked toward him, helpless to resist when she pressed her bleeding flesh to his lips.

With a low cry of despair, his mouth locked on her arm, tasting her sweetness, feeling the life-giving fluid flow through him, easing the awful hunger that plagued him like the fires of hell.

Time lost all meaning as he gave himself over to the pleasure of satisfying a craving over which he no longer had control.

Sara . . . the essence of life, of light . . .

Sara!

He released her immediately, his heart pounding with fear as he gazed into her eyes. Had he taken too much?

"*Cara mia,* how do you feel?"

She blinked up at him. "I don't know. A little faint." Her gaze moved over his face, amazed to see that he already looked better. The deadly pallor was fading. "Do you need more? Is it enough?"

Was that her voice, sounding so calm as she asked him if he had taken enough of her blood? Had she finally gone mad? She should have been repulsed by what had just happened, sickened to think that he needed blood to survive, horrified that she had given him hers. But she wasn't repulsed or sickened or horrified. She was, in fact, sorry he hadn't taken more.

Had she imagined it, or had she actually felt a sense of pleasure that bordered on ecstasy when his mouth closed over her wrist? It was very strange, she thought. Very strange indeed.

"Sara." There was a wealth of misery in his voice as he ripped a strip of cloth from his shirt tail and wrapped it around the gash in her wrist, then turned away.

He could not face her. He felt naked and ashamed. She had seen him at his worst. Stripped of his dignity, of the thin mask of humanity, she had seen him for the monster he truly was, something no other mortal had ever witnessed and survived.

"Gabriel?"

"I'll be all right."

"You're sure? Perhaps you should . . ."

"I'm sure! Sara, please go now."

"No, I don't want to leave you."

He didn't think he'd taken enough blood to initiate her, but what if he had indeed taken too much? He didn't want to enslave her in that way, didn't want to strip her of her free will so that she would be forever bound to him, afraid to be without him. He didn't want to own her body and soul; he wanted her love, freely given.

Hands balled into tight fists, he turned to face her. "Please go," he said gently. "I need to be alone."

She didn't want to leave him. Didn't want to ever be away from him again, but the quiet pleading in his voice convinced her to go. "Very well. If that's what you want."

He felt a momentary surge of relief. If she was willing to leave him, even for a short time, all would be well.

She placed her hand on his arm, felt him tremble at her touch. "I'll be back later."

"No."

"I'll be back," she repeated in a voice that brooked no argument.

"Sara?"

"Yes?"

"The cross in front of the house. Remove it."

"All right."

"You must also wash the door frame."

"Anything else?"

"A circle made of holy water and garlic surrounds the house. Break it."

"I will."

He nodded, resenting the fact that he'd had to ask her for anything else when he'd already taken so much. "You know I can't stay here any longer."

Of course he couldn't stay here. It was no longer safe. Why hadn't she realized that before?"

"We've got to get you out of here," she said. "I'll be back in a little while. You rest until then."

"It's morning. I can't go out."

"I'll think of something," she said, and hurried away before he could argue further.

Outside, she took a deep breath, wishing she had thought to ask the carriage to wait. But perhaps a good long walk was just what she needed. Ordinarily, she would have been afraid to be out walking on a lonely road at dawn, but not now. She concentrated on putting one foot in front of the other, refusing to think of what he was as she made her way back to town.

When she reached the city, she hired a closed carriage, dismissed the driver, and drove to her apartment.

Inside, she walked through the house, closing all the drapes. In her bedroom, she covered the curtains with a heavy quilt, so that no light at all filtered into the room. Then, laden with every blanket she could find, she drove back to the cottage.

Not wanting Sara to see him in his deathlike sleep, Gabriel roused himself when he sensed her approaching. Moving sluggishly, he reached for his cloak. Sewn into the lining was a fine layer of earth from Vallelunga. His native soil, necessary to his survival when he was away from his homeland.

It took all his strength, all his willpower, to meet her at the door. Had the sun been any higher in the sky, it would have been impossible.

"Come," she said, and covering him with three layers of blankets, she led him out of the cottage and into the carriage.

He huddled on the floor of the conveyance, the blankets spread over him, while she drove back to the city. He could feel the sun searching for him, feel its insufferable heat, knew that he would die in unspeakable agony if Sara betrayed him now.

It was still too early for there to be many people about. When they reached her apartment, she quickly unlocked the door, then ran down the steps to help Gabriel inside, guiding him into the bedroom.

He shook off the blankets, then sighed as the darkness closed around him.

"Do you need anything?" she asked.

"I need to be left alone," he said, and his voice was low and heavy, as if he had been drugged.

"All right."

"Promise me you won't come in here until after dark."

"Why?" she asked, and then, before he could reply, she made an impatient gesture with her hand. "I know. No questions."

"I would think you had all the answers you needed by now."

"Go to sleep, Gabriel. I promise not to disturb your rest."

He waited until she left the room, and then, after spreading his cloak on top of the counterpane, he stretched out on her bed and closed his eyes, the taste of her blood still hot on his tongue, her scent surrounding him, as he fell into darkness.

# *Chapter Nineteen*

He woke at dusk. For a long while, he stayed where he was, recalling what had happened earlier in the day. Filled with rage, his body racked with pain, the hunger slicing through him like hot knives, he had been on the very brink of madness. And then Sara had come to him, offering him the surcease he needed. And he, cursed wretch that he was, had taken it.

Even now the thought of what he had done filled him with self-loathing.

Why had she helped him? Once she knew what kind of monster he was, why had she brought him here?

"Because I love you."

He sat up at the sound of her voice. "Don't."

"You said that before, remember?" Sara remarked as she entered the room. "I said I loved you and you told me not to."

"You should have listened."

"That story you told me, about the young man who traded his soul for another chance at life, that was you, wasn't it?"

He nodded, too ashamed to speak.

She sat down on the foot of the bed and studied him through wide, guileless eyes.

"How old are you, Gabriel? You would never tell me before."

"I was born in the winter of 1502."

She frowned a moment. "But that would make you . . ."

He nodded. "Three hundred and eighty-four years old."

It was impossible, inconceivable. And yet she knew it was true.

"You always said you were too old for me," she mused, and then she began to laugh uncontrollably.

Gabriel watched her from beneath hooded lids, his emotions in turmoil. He had made love to her, had given her his blood and taken hers. Though he had not taken enough of her blood to initiate her, they now shared a bond that could never be broken.

Sara looked at him, helpless, as her hysterical laughter dissolved into tears. And then he was holding her, his face buried in her hair. She felt his shoulders shake and she knew he was crying, too.

"Gabriel?" She drew away, her own tears forgotten in her need to comfort him.

A single tear hovered in the corner of his eye. A tear tinged with blood. Very carefully, she wiped it away with a corner of the bed sheet.

She stared at the bright red stain on the white linen and realized, for the first time, the full horror of who and what he was.

Vampire.

The undead.

Creatures who slept in coffins by day and prowled the darkness at night, preying on the weakness, and the blood, of others.

Gabriel was a vampire.

He saw the knowledge in her eyes, saw the realization that came as she recalled incidents from the past.

"That's why I never saw you eat," she said tonelessly. "Why I never saw you during the day. Why the burns on your face healed so quickly . . ."

She gasped as another startling realization came to the fore. He was the monster who had plagued her nightmares not so long ago.

"It's true," he said flatly. "All of it. Look at me, Sara. What do you see?"

"I see the man I love." She spoke the words confidently, but he saw the doubt shadowing her eyes.

Gabriel shook his head. "No, Sara, I'm not a man. I exist, but I don't live. I grow old, but I don't age. Face it. Accept it."

She looked at him warily, wondering why she wasn't more afraid. Sadness dragged at his features; his eyes were haunted, filled with more pain than a mere mortal could ever endure.

"Do you despise me now?" he asked.

"No."

"But you're afraid of me."

"A little."

"I won't hurt you, *cara*. Believe that. And if you can't believe my words, then look inside my mind and see the truth for yourself."

"Look inside your mind? What do you mean?"

"We share a bond, Sara. A blood bond. If you but try, you can read my thoughts."

"Is that why I heard you calling to me?"

Gabriel nodded, waiting for her to take the next logical step.

"But I heard you before you took my blood."

He nodded again, his hands clenching as he watched her try to fit the pieces together.

"Have you taken my blood before?"

"No."

"You gave me yours." It wasn't a question, but a statement of fact.

Time hung suspended while she waited for his answer.

"Yes."

"When I was burned," Sara said. "That's why I got better so fast. You gave me your blood, and it made me strong. It made me walk . . ."

"Yes."

"But that wasn't the first time, was it? You gave me your blood when I wanted to die because I thought I was never going to see you again. I remember now. You came to me in the night. I thought it was another dream, but it was real, wasn't it?"

"Yes."

"You saved my life. Twice."

"And you have saved mine, miserable though it might be."

He yearned to hold her, to bury himself in her sweetness, but he could not. In spite of the blood bond between them, he felt as if a chasm as wide and deep as hell separated them.

She licked her lips, needing, dreading, to ask the

question that had been gnawing at the corner of her mind.

"Am I a vampire now?"

"No!" The word was torn from his throat. "I would never bring you over, Sara. You must believe that if you believe nothing else."

The relief in her eyes was like a dagger in his heart.

"Sara . . ." He glanced at the open door, then slid out of bed. "Someone's here."

"Maurice," Sara said, rising. "I forgot he was coming by."

"Go then."

"Will you be here when I get back?"

"No. I'm going to Spain."

She stared at him, wanting him to stay, yet afraid of what it would mean if he did. Vampire. The mere idea was vile, repugnant. Unbelievable.

Before she could speak, she heard Maurice's knock at the door again.

"You'd best go let him in before he breaks down the door," Gabriel said dryly.

"Don't go," she said, and left the room, closing the bedroom door behind her before he could reply.

She ran to the front door and opened it, forcing a smile. "Good evening, Maurice."

"Sara." He frowned. "You're not dressed," he said, taking in her disheveled appearance. "Am I early?"

"No, I'm late. Sit down. Have some wine. I won't be but a moment."

"Hurry, *cheri*. We dine at seven."

"I will."

She paused outside her bedroom door, took a deep breath, and stepped inside.

Gabriel was standing at the window. He glanced

at her over his shoulder as she closed the door behind her.

He didn't look like a demon now, she thought. That horrible red glow was gone from his eyes; his skin no longer looked like old parchment. He looked like Gabriel again, human, masculine, and devastatingly attractive. Suddenly she yearned to be in his arms once more, to hear his voice whispering her name, to taste his kisses. Man or monster, she loved him, would always love him.

Gabriel met her gaze, though it was difficult for him to look at her now. Only a short time ago, she had seen him at his worst, seen him as he really was. Few people had ever seen him when the hunger was fast upon him and lived to tell the tale.

He wished he could hold her.

He wished she would go away.

"Was there something you wanted, Sara?"

"I . . . Maurice is here. We're going out to dinner."

The faintest glimmer of amusement flickered in Gabriel's dark eyes.

"Yes," he murmured dryly, "I was thinking of going out for . . . dinner . . . myself."

He watched the color drain from her face as she absorbed his meaning.

"How can you make jokes about . . . about what you do?"

"Believe me, Sara, there's nothing funny about it."

"Have you . . . ?"

"Have I what?"

"Have you killed a great many people?"

He shrugged, trying not to be offended by the revulsion in her voice, by the morbid curiosity in her eyes.

"Not many," he replied coldly. "Are you in fear for your life now?"

"No! I just thought . . . I mean . . ."

"It isn't necessary for me to kill to survive. I no longer require a great deal of blood, nor do I need it each day."

His gaze held hers. He wanted suddenly to hurt her, to shock her, or perhaps he merely needed to remind himself of the vast gulf between them.

"If I'm desperate, the blood of animals will suffice. In extreme cases, I've been known to dine on the blood of rats."

"Why are you telling me this? Do you think it will make me love you less? Are you still trying to drive me away?"

He couldn't look at her any longer, couldn't abide the overwhelming pity, the faint glimmer of revulsion, that lingered in her eyes.

Cursing softly, he turned to stare out the window again. "You'd better go," he said tersely. "Your young man is waiting for you."

She wasn't much company at dinner that night. She picked at her food, remembering what Gabriel had said. *If I'm desperate, the blood of animals will suffice. In extreme cases, I've been known to dine on the blood of rats . . .* Had he been serious, or was he merely trying to drive her away? And yet, deep down, she knew that everything he had said was true. He lived only by night. He fed off the blood of other living creatures. How could he exist like that?

She stared at the dark red wine in her glass. Gabriel drank wine. It was the only nourishment she had ever seen him take. How could he drink blood?

"Sara Jayne?"

She glanced up, aware that Maurice had asked her a question. "What?"

"You seem distracted."

"I'm sorry."

"Is anything wrong?"

"No."

"Have you by chance been out to the cottage?"

"Why do you ask?"

"Have you?"

"Yes. I assume that's your handiwork, all those crosses, and the garlic?"

Maurice nodded.

"What did you hope to prove?"

"He's a vampire, Sara Jayne. I'm sure of it."

"Don't be ridiculous," she scoffed. "There's no such thing."

Maurice shrugged. "Maybe, maybe not. But if he isn't a vampire, then all I've done is waste my time. And if he is . . ."

"If he is?"

"Then he won't be able to leave the cottage." Maurice sat back in his chair, his expression suddenly suspicious. "You didn't touch anything, did you?"

"No," she said quickly. Too quickly.

"You're a terrible liar, Sara Jayne."

"That's what Gabriel says."

"Where is he?"

"I don't know. When I saw him last, he said he was leaving Paris."

"Are you sorry he's going?"

"I don't know." She looked at Maurice, her gaze unwavering. "But I know I shall miss him every day for the rest of my life."

* * *

Gabriel walked slowly through the castle. It was an amazing piece of work. Built over four hundred years ago of stone and wood, it was a sight to behold, from its turrets and towers to the moat and drawbridge. At one time, it had housed a hundred knights. Now its high stone walls sheltered a monster.

He moved through the Great Hall with its tapestries and long trestle tables, through the kitchens that hadn't been used in over three hundred years. Climbing the winding stone staircase, he wandered from chamber to chamber, pausing now and then to stare out one of the windows into the darkness.

Removing a key from his inside coat pocket, he unlocked the door to the dungeons and walked down the damp stone steps. Ancient instruments of torture lined one wall; a score of iron-barred cells bore mute evidence to a less civilized time. The walls were damp; the air was musty.

Returning to the Great Hall, he sank down in the thronelike chair that had belonged to the lord of the castle and stared into the enormous fireplace at the far end of the room.

The silence of the castle was absolute. The Hall was in utter darkness, as black as his soul.

He closed his eyes, and Sara's image came quickly to mind, her beautiful face framed by a wealth of honey gold hair, her eyes now filled with laughter, now shining with love, now cloudy with desire. Sara . . .

He saw her dancing the part of Aurora in *Sleeping Beauty*, an ethereal creature of beauty and light as she pirouetted across the stage during the Rose

Adagio; he saw her as Giselle, lamenting her lost love . . .

With a mighty curse, he forced her image from his mind.

Determined to pretend for a while that he was a mortal man, he decided to hire some men to come out and replace the rotting wood he had noticed on the drawbridge; he would hire a couple of women to sweep and clean.

In a week or so, Necromancer would arrive, along with the young man he had hired to act as stableboy.

Gabriel grunted softly. Perhaps he'd buy a couple of mares and raise horses. It would give him something to do to pass the time, something to think about besides Sara . . .

He glanced around the Hall, filled with a sudden yearning to see it filled with people, to hear the laughter of children, the gossip of women, to imagine, for a little while, that he was like any other man. For a moment, he closed his eyes and pretended that Sara was his wife, that she had come to him without fear or doubt, that she had agreed to be his for as long as she lived . . . for a moment, it was a dream sweeter than life itself. But the thought of watching her age and die was more than he could bear, and he put the image from his mind.

He was a creature of the night, destined to spend his existence alone. A bitter smile twisted his lips. After 355 years, he should have learned to accept it.

A fortnight later, the castle was humming with activity. He had hired two men to come during the day to keep the castle in good repair, and a woman to look after the house. He purchased three blooded mares to breed with his stallion, which had arrived the week before.

If the hired help found it odd that the master of the castle never appeared during the day, they did not mention it, at least not in his hearing. If the stableboy thought it most peculiar that the horses were bred at night, and that the master took the stallion out only after dark, he kept it to himself.

In a short time, the castle seemed to have roused from a deep sleep. The moat was cleared of debris, the windows were washed clean, the floors were swept daily, the tapestries had been aired. One of the maids planted a flower garden, weeds and briars were removed, trees were pruned.

Determined not to sit in his castle and brood over what could never be, Gabriel paid several visits to the local tavern, where he sat alone in the back of the room, his only companion a bottle of red wine. He knew the villagers were curious about his identity. Rumors and gossip abounded, implying that he was everything from a defrocked priest to an eccentric nobleman.

Well, he thought, let them speculate.

Several times, he heard Sara's voice in his mind, calling to him, begging him to come back. He felt her pain, her loneliness, her confusion, but he never answered her, and finally he closed his mind against her, refusing to torture himself by listening to her cries.

His only joy was in riding his big black stallion. Each night, he raced across the dark land, reveling in the horse's speed and power, remembering how Sara had shrieked with delight the night he had taken her riding. She had urged him to go faster,

faster. Cheeks flushed, her lips parted, she had turned to face him. His Sara, so full of life . . .

He reined the stallion to a halt and sat staring into the distance. Sara. What was she doing now? Had she decided to marry Maurice? Gabriel's hands curled into tight fists as he thought of the young man's treachery. Were it not for Sara, he might still be imprisoned in that cottage, writhing in pain as a relentless thirst drove him slowly mad. Maurice and Sara . . .

Sensing his agitation, the stallion shifted uneasily beneath him. Gabriel spoke to the horse and the animal quieted immediately.

And still Gabriel sat there, staring sightlessly into the distance, his mind filling with images of Sara in Maurice's arms, in Maurice's bed.

Gabriel threw back his head as a long, anguished cry rose in his throat, and then he urged the stallion into a run, flying like the wind across the darkened land.

But he could not outrun his misery, or the image of Sara with another man.

A mortal man who could walk with her in daylight.

A man who could give her sons.

She had finally put him from her mind. She stopped trying to read his thoughts, stopped trying to send her thoughts to him. She spent her every waking hour with Maurice, mentally extolling his virtues, telling herself that she loved him. They danced onstage together. He was the prince to her Aurora, the Albrecht to her Giselle. They shared candlelit dinners after the theater. They went walking together in the early afternoon. They spoke of marriage. She let him kiss her, and occasionally she endured his caresses, but she refused to let him move in with her.

She went on a shopping spree and bought herself a new wardrobe: hats, shoes, petticoats, gowns and day dresses, feather fans, lacy parasols, a sleeping gown of gossamer silk.

She redecorated her apartment in shades of mauve and white.

She indulged her every whim. She danced as she had never danced before.

And at night, alone in her bed, she cried herself to sleep.

He felt a presence when he stepped into the Hall—a presence he recognized. And loathed.

She was wearing a dress the color of fresh blood. Her hair, black and glossy, fell over her shoulders in loose waves. Her complexion was glowing, and he knew she had fed recently.

"What are you doing here?"

"Giovanni, *mon amour,* is that any way to greet an old friend?"

"We are not friends," Gabriel retorted sharply.

"Lovers, then," Antonina purred. "Even better."

Crossing the room, she ran her hands across his shoulders and down his arms, appreciating the solid feel of him, the latent strength that rippled beneath her fingertips.

She felt her blood stir as she gazed up into his eyes. "Ah, Giovanni, I have missed you."

Gabriel took hold of her hands and pushed her away. "What do you want, Nina?"

She pouted prettily. "Do I have to want something?

It's been decades since we last met, *cara mia*. I just wanted to see how you are."

"I'm fine. Go away."

"Don't be rude, Gianni." She walked around the Hall, running her fingertips over the ancient tapestries, pausing at a narrow window to gaze into the courtyard below.

"Why are you here?" she asked without turning around. "Who are you hiding from?"

"I'm not hiding from anyone," Gabriel replied. *Except Sara. Except myself.*

Antonina glanced at him over her shoulder. "You cannot lie to me, Gianni."

She stared deep into his eyes, and even from across the room, he felt the heat, the power, of her gaze. A thousand years she had walked the earth. He knew of no vampire older, or more powerful, than Antonina Insenna.

"Have you fallen in love again, Giovanni? Is that why you have buried yourself in this dreary castle?"

She had always been the most perceptive of women, Gabriel thought bleakly. There was no point in lying to her, yet he could not bring himself to admit the truth.

"When I buried Rosalia, I vowed never to love again," he replied curtly.

"You once loved me," Antonina said. "Remember? Ah, those long summer nights we spent together, *cara*—"

"Don't call me that!"

Antonina lifted a delicate black brow. "Did she hurt you, Gianni? Is that why you've come here, to lick your wounds?" She moved toward him, her footsteps so light she seemed to float across the floor.

"Come out with me, Gianni," she crooned, her dark eyes shining with the lust for blood. "Let us hunt together."

Slowly, Gabriel shook his head. "Go away, Nina," he said wearily. "I don't want you."

She drew herself up to her full height, her expression regal, haughty.

"You wanted me once, Giovanni Ognibene. Can you deny that it was good between us?" A knowing smile teased her lips. "I see that you remember the nights we spent together. In all these years, *mon amour,* I have not found another lover to compare with you."

He stared at her, hating her because what she said was true. They had been good together. She had loved him with the passion and strength and endurance that only a vampire could possess. She had been insatiable, hungry for his touch, and he had delighted in it. At the time, he had thought it was because he was a superb lover. He knew now that, even as a mortal, she would have been insatiable, forever lusting for more.

Eager to put some distance between them, he walked to the fireplace and rested his hand on the mantel. "You haven't told me why you're here."

"I'm lonely," she said petulantly. "Lonely and bored. Won't you amuse me for a little while, Gianni, for old times' sake?"

"No."

"Once you wanted what only I could give you," she said, her voice brittle. "Now I want what only you can give me."

Gabriel shook his head. "There are other vampires

in the world, Nina. Seek your pleasure from one of them."

"But none of them are you, Gianni. You owe me a debt. Were it not for me, your body would have been food for the worms these last three hundred and fifty years."

"I can't give you what you want."

"I'm not asking for your love, Giovanni, only a moment of your time."

"No. You have nothing to tempt me with this time, Nina. You can't offer me life. I have no need of gold." He breathed a weary sigh. "Go away."

Her eyes narrowed ominously, her lips thinned, and he wondered how he had ever thought her beautiful.

"So," she hissed, "you would deny me a single night in your bed?"

"I would deny you a single minute."

"Think carefully, Giovanni," she warned. "Think about your little ballerina."

In an instant, he was across the room, his hand locked around her throat. "You will not touch a hair on her head! Do you hear me? Not a hair!"

She laughed in his face. "Do you think to threaten me, Giovanni?"

"It is no threat, Antonina. If you dare to lay a hand on Sara, I will drag you out into the sunlight and watch you burn."

She made a low sound of disbelief. "You would die for this mortal woman?"

"If need be. Look at me, Nina. Never doubt that I mean what I say. I will burn beside you rather than let you harm Sara."

"You fool! Do you think I have survived for a thousand years by being intimidated by the likes of you? Be careful where you rest, *cara.* I have those who will do my bidding by day. They will not hesitate to drive a stake through your ungrateful heart, and then bring me your head." She glared at him defiantly. "And what do you think will become of your little ballerina then?" She laughed softly, wickedly. "I should hate to destroy a creature as handsome as you, *mon amour.* Perhaps I shall bring her over instead. Would you like that?"

Gabriel's hands wrapped around her throat, choking off her breath. He wished fervently that he could squeeze the life from her body, but such a thing was impossible.

With a cry of frustration, he let her go, then wiped his hands on the sides of his trousers, as if touching her had somehow defiled him.

Rage flickered in the depths of her hell-black eyes. "You will regret this night, Giovanni. I promise you, you will regret this night!"

"Nina!" Fear for Sara's life rose up within him. "Damn you, Nina, come back here!"

But it was too late. She was gone in a swirling gray mist, her voice trailing behind her like smoke. *You will regret this night . . .*

Gabriel ran a hand through his hair. Damn! What had he done? Why hadn't he given Nina what she wanted? A night of his time. What difference would one night have made?

He glanced out the window. The sky was growing light, changing from black to indigo. Antonina would have to go to ground soon, as would he.

Muttering an oath, he found a scrap of parchment and quickly wrote a list of directions, advising his servants that he had been called away in the middle of the night, leaving instructions that the crate in the basement was to be shipped to Paris immediately, along with his horse. He left enough money to pay for his passage, as well as a generous gratuity. As an afterthought, he invited his servants to take up residence in the castle until he returned, if they so desired.

With the last detail taken care of, he went below to seek his rest, confident that his instructions would be obeyed without question.

His last thought, as the darkness carried him away, was of Sara.

# *Chapter Twenty*

She was never going to see him again. Finally, after three long months, she had resigned herself to that fact. She had stopped looking for him in the audience while she danced, she had stopped searching for his face in the crowds that lingered outside the theater, she had stopped waiting for his knock at the door.

And she had told Maurice that she would marry him in the spring.

She glanced at him now as he donned his hat and coat. He was indeed a handsome young man, lean and fit from hours of dancing and exercise. The ballerinas in the corps de ballet eyed her with envy because she had everything. She was the *prima ballerina*. Her name was well known in Venice and London and Paris. And she was going to marry Maurice, the *premier danseur* of the company. Perhaps, one day, they would even form their own ballet company.

She walked him to the door of her apartment, accepted his kiss, bade him good-bye.

Closing the door, she leaned back against it and closed her eyes. She had everything she had ever wanted, so why was she so unhappy? Why did she have to force herself to smile when she was with Maurice? Why did his kisses leave her cold and unmoved?

Because of Gabriel. Always Gabriel. Forever Gabriel. He was out of her life, but he would never be out of her heart, and try as she might, she would never make it so.

"Gabriel." His name was a sob on her lips.

*"Cara."*

She whirled around, her heart climbing into her throat at the sound of his voice, at the world of tenderness in his endearment for her.

"Gabriel!" She stared at him, unable to believe he was there, that she hadn't conjured his image from the depths of her aching heart.

He wore black breeches, black boots, and a dark green shirt. His cloak fell from shoulders even broader than she remembered. His hair was the color of ebony, his eyes the dark gray of storm-tossed clouds.

The silence stretched between them.

She longed to run into his arms, to lay her head on his chest and cry out all the unhappiness of the past three months.

He yearned to hold her close, to assure himself that she was well.

But she was afraid of being rejected.

And he was afraid that if he touched her again, he would never, ever let her go.

And then she saw the aching loneliness in the depths of his eyes and knew she would risk anything, even the pain of rejection, to comfort him, if only for a moment.

And he knew that he had been fighting a losing battle since the moment he first held her.

*"Cara."*

Just that one word. That was all he said. But it broke the barrier between them. In less than a heart-beat, she was enfolded in his arms, tears of joy flowing down her cheeks. And he was murmuring her name over and over again, his loneliness banished forever by the sight of her tears—tears of love, of happiness, of acceptance.

He held her close for a long moment, feeling as though he had come home at last, and then he bent his head and brushed his lips across hers. And she melted into him, her arms stealing around his waist, holding him as if she would never let him go.

He kissed her again, more deeply this time, letting himself absorb her warmth, her sweetness.

"Ah, *cara,*" he murmured, "if you only knew how much I've missed you."

"No more than I missed you." She gazed into his eyes. "I tried to call you with my mind."

Gabriel nodded. "I heard you."

"Why didn't you answer?"

"You must know why."

"Because you're a . . ."

"Vampire."

She nodded, wondering why the word was so hard to say. In her heart, she knew it was true, but deep inside she believed that if she never said the word, the truth would go away.

"Sara." He rested his chin on the top of her head.

"Why have you come back?" she asked tremulously.

"Do you want me to go?" He had told himself that if she no longer held any affection for him, he would find Nina and do whatever she asked in exchange for her promise to spare Sara's life.

"No! Oh, Gabriel, nothing's the same without you. Please don't leave me again."

"I won't," he promised. "If you're sure you want me to stay, I'll stay."

"I'm sure."

"And what of Maurice Delacroix?"

Maurice! Guilt washed through her. She had promised to marry Maurice in the spring.

At her silence, Gabriel drew back so he could see her face. "What is it, *cara?*"

"I . . ."

A sudden heaviness settled over Gabriel. Had she fallen in love with the other man in his absence? "Sara?"

"I . . . I didn't think I would ever see you again," she stammered, "so . . . so I . . ." She swallowed hard. "I told Maurice I'd marry him."

"I see."

"But I don't want Maurice! I want you."

"Do you?"

"Yes! You've got to believe me. I only said I'd marry him because it didn't matter. If I couldn't have you, it didn't matter. Don't you see?"

"Has he made love to you?" He spoke the words calmly, as if her reply was of no real import, knowing all the while that he would kill Delacroix with his bare hands if he'd dared do more than kiss Sara good night.

"Of course not," Sara replied indignantly. She studied Gabriel's face anxiously. "You believe me, don't you?"

He nodded, a soft smile curving his lips. "I would know if you were lying, *cara*."

Gently, he enfolded her in his embrace once again, conscious of the warmth of her skin, the life that flowed through her, the steady beat of her heart. She was so young, so alive.

"Gabriel? You didn't tell me what made you decide to come back after all this time."

He let out a long sigh, knowing she deserved the truth. "I'm afraid I've put you in danger, Sara."

"Me? How?"

"It's a long story. Come, let us sit down and be comfortable."

Taking her hand, he led her to the sofa and sat down, drawing her down beside him. He glanced around the room while he gathered his thoughts, absently noting that the furnishings were new.

"You remember the story I told you about how I came to be a vampire?"

Sara nodded.

"The woman who brought me over came to see me in Spain. She wanted me to be her lover again."

Sara stared up at him, her eyes filled with jealousy at the thought of Gabriel caressing another woman. "You never told me she'd been your lover."

"It was a long time ago. I thought she was the most beautiful woman I'd ever seen."

"Oh. And did you . . . did she . . . ?"

"No, *cara*," Gabriel replied quietly, "we didn't. But when I refused, she became angry and threatened my life." He paused a moment. "And yours."

"Mine? But why?"

"She is also jealous, *cara*."

Sara frowned. "How does she know about me?"

Gabriel shrugged. "I don't know. Perhaps she's been following me."

"And she threatened to kill me?"

"Not exactly."

Sara sat very still, her whole body suddenly cold. "What, exactly?"

"She threatened to make you one of us."

"No!" There was a wealth of horror, of revulsion, in that single word of denial.

"That's why I came back, Sara. To protect you, if I can."

"*If* you can?"

Gabriel nodded. "She's a very old and very powerful vampire. I'm not sure I have the ability to thwart her."

Sara stared at him, more afraid than she had ever been in her life. If Gabriel, who was possessed of supernatural strength and power, wasn't sure he could protect her, what chance did she have?

Vampire. She loved Gabriel with her whole heart and soul, yet she knew she would rather be dead than become what Gabriel was, a man cut off from humanity, from God. She didn't want to live off the blood of others, to spend endless days in darkness. She wanted a home, a husband, children . . .

She began to shiver convulsively, and Gabriel drew her into his arms and held her tight. Though he made no conscious effort, he could read Sara's thoughts, and he quietly damned himself for not acquiescing to Nina's demands. He should have remembered how spiteful she could be. He should have done anything, promised anything, to temper her anger. Perhaps it wasn't too late . . .

"No!"

Startled, he glanced down at Sara to find her staring up at him, her wide blue eyes filled with jealousy.

"Don't even think of going to that . . . that woman."

"It might be for the best, *cara*."

"No."

"Sara, she has the power to hypnotize others to do her will. If she manages to destroy me, you'll be at her mercy."

"I don't care. I won't let you go to her."

Gabriel raised one black brow. "*You* won't let me?"

Sara shook her head. "You're mine now. I won't share you with her or any other woman."

"Ah, my sweet Sara, what a tiger you are."

"I love you, Gabriel."

"Sara . . ."

"I know," she replied. "I know." And taking him by the hand, she led him into her bedroom and closed the door.

"Are you sure, *cara?*"

She looked deep into his eyes, remembering the nights he had come to her in the orphanage, the nights he had taken her to the ballet, to the opera. He had saved her life, turned her dream of being a ballerina into reality. She had once thought him an angel; now she knew that he was not an angel at all, but a man who was cursed to spend his life in darkness, a creature of the night.

The man she loved.

"I'm sure, Gabriel," she whispered.

"Are you?"

He turned her so that she was facing the looking glass in the corner, and then he stood beside her, his arm wrapped around her waist.

They stood side by side, but only her reflection stared back at them.

"I'm a vampire, Sara Jayne. I can only share half of your life. I can't give you children. I'll never grow old. Can you live with that?"

She glanced at Gabriel, standing beside her, and then stared at the mirror again. She could hear him. She could touch him, yet he cast no reflection at all.

"Sara?"

"Are you still trying to get rid of me, Gabriel?" She reached up to caress his cheek, but in the glass she was touching only empty air. "Don't you know that's impossible?"

"I just want you to be sure."

With a sigh, she took him in her arms and kissed him, her tongue seeking his as she rubbed her breasts against his chest. "I'm sure, my angel," she whispered. She ran her hands over his shoulders, down his arms. "Very sure."

With a low growl, he swung her into his arms and carried her to the bed. Eager now, he removed her clothing, his body trembling with yearning as her soft curves were revealed to his gaze. How beautiful she was! And she wanted him. It was incredible.

When he started to undress, she stayed his hand, then bent to the task herself, letting her hands glide over his chest as she removed his shirt, reacquainting herself with the hard planes of his body.

He groaned low in his throat as her hands aroused

him. And then he couldn't wait any longer. Pressing her down to the mattress, he covered her body with his, her name a sigh on his lips as their bodies merged and became one.

She held him close, murmuring his name over and over again as the passion between them burned hotter, brighter, rivaling the energy and the heat of the sun.

She was all the light he would ever need, soft and warm, her touch filling the emptiness of eternity, driving the loneliness from his heart.

He felt her shudder beneath him, heard her gasp his name. A moment later, he threw back his head, his body convulsing one last time.

For a long moment, he held her close, his face buried in the curve of her neck. Knowing he must be crushing her, he rolled onto his side, his body folding around hers, holding her close. Too soon, the dawn would be upon them. But for now, for this brief span of time, she was his to hold, and to love.

He stirred with the coming of dawn, and his movements awakened Sara. Propping herself up on one arm, she watched him dress.

"Where are you going?"

He made a vague gesture with his hand. "I need to find a new lair."

"Stay."

"No."

"Why not?"

Why, indeed? She knew what he was; he had no need to hide himself from her.

"You can rest in here, as you did before."

"I would have your promise that you won't enter the room until nightfall."

She sat up, the covers tucked under her arms, and he thought how beautiful she looked, with her hair falling over her shoulders in glorious disarray, her lips slightly swollen from his kisses.

"Why?" Sara asked candidly. "Don't you trust me?"

His unflinching gaze met hers. "With my life, *cara*, but I would rather you didn't see me while I sleep."

Head cocked to one side, she regarded him curiously, wondering what he didn't want her to see.

"Please, *cara*."

"Very well." She swung her legs over the edge of the bed and stood up, quickly gathering the clothing she would need for the day.

"Sara, be careful today. Nina could be in Paris. She might have summoned help. Keep the doors and windows locked. Don't open the door for anyone you don't know."

"I have a rehearsal this afternoon."

"Is Maurice picking you up?"

A flush rose to her cheeks. "Yes."

"Good. Stay close to him. Be sure he brings you home."

"A most unusual request," she teased, "coming from you."

"I don't want you to be alone."

"What about you? What if she sends someone after you?"

"I'm not totally helpless during the day, Sara," he said, hoping to ease her mind. And it was true, up to a point.

She worried her lower lip with her teeth for a moment, then sighed. "Maybe I should stay home."

Gabriel clenched his fists at his sides, wishing again that he had agreed to spend the night with Nina, to pleasure her as she desired. But for his stupid pride, his revulsion at the idea of being Nina's plaything, even for one night, Sara would not now be in danger.

"Gabriel?"

"I think you'll be all right, *cara*. After rehearsal, I want you to buy some garlic and hang it over your doors and windows. Have you a cross? Good, wear it when you go out."

"You're frightening me."

"I know, but you need to be prepared."

He gathered her into his arms, wishing he could spend the day at her side. He thought briefly of taking her away from Paris, but wherever they went, Nina would find them. She would sense his presence, as surely as he could sense hers.

"I love you, Sara Jayne. Be careful."

The sun was up. He could feel the strength draining from his body, and he sat down on the edge of the bed as the lethargy slowly began to steal over him.

"Sara, cover the window."

"What? Oh!" She flew out of his arms and quickly hung a heavy quilt over the window, effectively blocking out the small amount of light that had penetrated the curtains. "Is that better?"

"Fine. Come, sit beside me."

She did as he asked, her arm sliding around his waist. "What's it like when you sleep during the day?"

"It's like death, *cara*. When I was first made, it frightened me more than anything else. I learned to accept the darkness, the blood, but every time the sun came up was like dying all over again."

She tightened her arm around him, not knowing what to say.

"Gradually, as I grew stronger, I discovered I could stay awake for a short while after the sun came up, and rise before the sun set, so long as I stayed out of the light."

"Do you dream while you sleep?"

"No. And yet, there have been times when I was aware of you, of what you were doing. When the orphanage caught fire, I knew you were in pain, but there was nothing I could do." He gazed into her eyes, remembering how helpless he had been. "It was a terrible feeling, knowing you needed me and there was nothing I could do."

"But you did help me," she reminded him. "If not for you, I'd still be confined to that chair."

"And now, because of me, your life is in danger."

"I don't care! I wouldn't trade a minute of the time we've had together. Not a minute. And maybe she won't come looking for us. Maybe she was only bluffing."

"Maybe," Gabriel said. And maybe the sun wouldn't shine and the rain wouldn't fall.

He held her a moment longer, and then sent her away. "Your promise, *cara,*" he said, not wanting her to see him when the deathlike sleep was upon him. "Remember your promise."

"I remember." She kissed him one more time, then left the room, quietly closing the door behind her.

# Chapter Twenty-one

She was too nervous to sit still, consumed by curiosity about why Gabriel had so adamantly insisted that she not enter the room while he slept.

She wandered through the apartment, straightening this and that, while she waited for Maurice, her thoughts as unstable as a kaleidoscope. Gabriel was a vampire. Maurice wanted to marry her. The company was going to London in the spring. Nina wanted her dead . . .

Sara shuddered at the thought. How did one fight against a vampire?

She fingered the small silver cross at her throat. It was hard to imagine that anything so small as a crucifix, or so common as garlic, had the power to repel a vampire, yet she remembered that Gabriel had been unable to leave the cottage until she had broken the circle of garlic and holy water.

Vampire . . . She had seen him when the hunger

was on him, seen the unholy light that had glowed in his eyes, seen his fangs, and yet it was still inconceivable that such things existed.

Yet her blood had revived him.

His blood had made her whole.

He had said he would never turn her into what he was, and she believed him, and yet, far in the back of her mind, in a corner where she didn't look too closely, lingered a niggling doubt. What if the lust for blood overcame him? What if he changed his mind and decided he'd like to have a vampire companion to keep him company through the ages?

She tried to imagine drinking the blood of others to survive, and felt her stomach recoil in horror. She tried to imagine what it would be like to live always in darkness, never to see the sunlight again, never to walk in the morning rain, or lie on the grass and watch the clouds drift across a lazy summer sky. Never to bear a child.

To live forever and never grow old . . . she had to admit that had a certain appeal.

With a shake of her head, she went to stand by the bedroom door. Leaning close, she listened, but heard nothing. A sleep like death, he had said, a sleep with no dreams.

Only her promise to stay away kept her from peeking inside.

She jumped, startled, when she heard a knock at the front door.

It was Maurice. "Ready?" he asked.

"Yes, just let me get my wrap."

They were rehearsing *Swan Lake,* but Sara couldn't concentrate on the steps or the music. Her mind kept visualizing Gabriel sleeping the sleep of the undead in her apartment. In her bed. And when she wasn't thinking of Gabriel, she was worrying about being stalked by Nina or one of her minions.

They were in the middle of the second act when the ballet mistress called a halt with a sharp tap of her baton.

"Sara Jayne, are you dancing with us today or not?"

"I'm sorry, Madame Evonne," Sara stammered, her cheeks flushing with embarrassment. "I'm . . . I'm afraid I'm not feeling well."

Madame Evonne drew herself up to her full five feet, two inches. "Do you wish to be excused?"

"Yes, please."

"Very well. Ginette, you may take Sara Jayne's place." Madame Evonne fixed Sara with a cool glance. "Shall we expect you tonight?"

Sara lifted her chin, refusing to be intimated by the dour-faced ballet mistress. "Yes."

"Very well." Madame tapped her baton on the floor and the music began again.

Sara felt Maurice's gaze on her back as she left the floor. Backstage, she settled her hat on her head, put on her cape, drew on her gloves, and left the theater, only then remembering Gabriel's admonition to have Maurice see her home.

Sara glanced up and down the street; then, with a sigh, she hailed a hack to take her to the market.

The clerk looked at her oddly as she filled a basket with strings of garlic.

She stopped at a small church on the way home and filled a bottle with holy water, praying that she would be forgiven for her theft, but at the moment, she felt she had more need of the precious fluid than did the priest.

She breathed a sigh of relief when she reached home. Inside, she pulled off her cape and gloves and removed her hat. For a moment, she paused outside her bedroom door, her curiosity again tempting her to peek inside. Only her promise to Gabriel to let him rest undisturbed kept her hand from the latch.

With a shake of her head, she turned away from the bedroom and began affixing garlic around all the windows and the front door. When that was done, she took the bottle of holy water and sparingly dribbled the liquid across the floor in front of the door and along the windowsills.

As she sprinkled holy water over and around the windows, it occurred to her that such precautions would not only keep Nina out, they would also serve to keep Gabriel in.

She'd treated every room but the bedroom where Gabriel slept when there was a knock at the door.

"Who's there?" she called, images of a female vampire with bloody fangs jumping to the forefront of her mind even though it was still daylight.

"It's Maurice. Sara Jayne, are you all right?"

"I'm fine. I'll see you at the theater tonight."

"Are you sure you're all right?" Maurice asked. "Can I get you anything?"

"I'm fine, really."

"Sara Jayne, please let me come in."

"Not now, Maurice. I'm taking a nap. I'll see you tonight."

"Very well, *cheri*," he agreed with obvious reluctance. "*Au revoir.*"

Sara pressed her forehead against the door. She

wouldn't be able to keep Maurice at bay for long. They were supposed to be engaged, after all. He wouldn't be pleased to learn that Gabriel had come back into her life. Somehow, she'd have to find the words to tell him that she was breaking their engagement. He wouldn't like that, either, but she knew now that she could never marry Maurice, or any other man. Her heart and soul belonged to Gabriel, now and always.

Gabriel.

A vampire.

It was still hard to believe, to accept. In spite of all she had seen, all he had said, it still seemed like a nightmare, too hideous to be true . . .

She felt suddenly cold all over as she recalled the nightmares that had plagued her here in Paris not so long ago.

They hadn't been nightmares at all, she thought, recalling the horrible images that had invaded her sleep, the visions of a fiend with hideous fangs and blood-red eyes. They'd been a premonition of things to come. She knew that now, because Gabriel was the demon in her dreams.

Heavy-hearted, she went into the parlor and sank down on the sofa. What was she going to do about Gabriel? About Maurice? About Nina?

She stared at the strings of garlic around the windows, praying they would keep Nina's evil at bay.

And what about Gabriel? If Nina was evil, what did that make Gabriel?

He survived by feeding on the life's blood of others. She could visualize him lurking in the shadows of the night, waiting to prey on the unwary, his fangs penetrating living flesh.

It was too horrible to contemplate, too awful to envision, and yet it was true.

Feeling suddenly chilled to the depths of her soul, she huddled in a corner of the sofa, shivering uncontrollably.

"Oh, Gabriel," she murmured, "what are we going to do?"

*Come to me.*

His voice, deep, resonant, was calling her.

Like a sleepwalker, she rose to do his bidding.

Her hand trembled as she reached for the latch, and then she was inside the room.

Gabriel's cloak lay like a splash of black paint against the snowy counterpane.

"Sara . . ."

He held out his hand, and she went to him, her heart beating wildly as she placed her hand in his. Images of fangs and blood-red eyes flitted down the corridor of her mind.

Gabriel dropped her hand and looked away. "The cross," he said, his voice harsh. "Take it off."

She slipped the delicate silver chain over her head, her mind whirling with images of Gabriel as he had looked that day in the cellar of the cottage, his eyes burning, his flesh taut, pale.

With an effort, she shook the ghastly images away. Turning away from the bed, she dropped the crucifix into her jewelry box and closed the lid.

He met her gaze then and she saw the hurt lurking in the depths of his eyes. Such changeable eyes, she thought, sometimes dark with passion, sometimes filled with an eternity of loneliness, sometimes blazing with an unholy light . . .

"You're afraid of me." It was a bold statement of fact, not a question.

"Yes." She looked at him curiously. "Why aren't you . . . how can you . . ."

"Be awake?"

Sara nodded. "I thought you slept during the day."

"It's nearly dusk," he explained. In another hour or so, his full strength would return.

"I didn't mean to disturb you."

"It's all right, Sara. I could feel your distress, your confusion. I had hoped to put your mind at ease, but it seems I've only frightened you more."

She didn't deny it, and the knowledge that she was truly afraid of him sliced through him like a knife.

"I'm sorry, Sara Jayne," he said gruffly. "I never meant to draw you into my life."

She stared at him, mute, unable to find the words to express what she was feeling and thinking. He had given her so much. For her dancing alone, she owed him a debt she could never repay, but now . . . willing or not, she had been drawn into a world she would never understand, a world she had never dreamed existed except in nightmares. And as much as she loved Gabriel, she wasn't sure she had the courage to face what he was.

From his place on the bed, Gabriel watched Sara's face. Even if he hadn't been able to read her mind, her every thought, her every emotion, was clearly etched on her face, in the clear depths of her eyes.

She had been so certain she loved him, so confident of her ability to accept him for who and what he was, and now she had come face-to-face with the ugly reality of his existence, and she couldn't accept it.

Feeling sluggish, he sat up and ran a hand through his hair. He could not blame her for her fears, could not fault her for being afraid.

He watched her leave the room, returning moments later to hang garlic around the bedroom's single window. The pungent smell sickened him, but he would have to endure it for Sara's sake.

Their gazes met when she turned away from the window.

"Did Maurice bring you home this afternoon?"

"No, I left early."

"I told you to stay with Maurice."

Sara shrugged. "I couldn't concentrate, so I came home."

"Dammit, Sara Jayne, I don't want you going out alone."

His obvious concern brought quick tears to her eyes.

"Sara . . ."

She went to him then, and he wrapped his arms around her, tucking her close to his side.

Sara relaxed against him, her earlier fear seeming foolish now. This was Gabriel. He would never harm her. With a sigh, she snuggled against him.

Moments later, she was asleep.

Gabriel held her close, his nostrils filled with a multitude of odors—the fragrance of Sara's hair, the scent of her skin, the tantalizing aroma of the blood flowing through her veins. And over all the smell of the garlic that clung to her hands, yet he knew he would have walked though a field of the vile stuff to hold her close.

His internal clock told him night was fast approaching. Soon it would be time for Sara to go to the theater.

Soon Nina would be on the prowl. Was she here, in Paris, even now? How could he thwart her if she truly intended to do Sara harm? If he agreed to do as she asked, would she agree to leave Sara alone, or would her pride demand that she carry out her threat? If he could find her lair, he might be able to lie in wait and destroy her when she was at rest. The question was, would he be able to do what had to be done before she discovered his presence, before the daylight destroyed him, as well?

He held Sara as the shadows grew long, felt his strength slowly increase as the sun went down. And still he held her close, listening to the steady sound of her breathing.

"Are you coming to the theater tonight?" Sara asked.

"I'll be there." He grinned at her. "But only if you clear the door."

Laughing softly, she removed the garlic from the lintel and washed the holy water from the floor.

"Is Maurice coming to pick you up?" Gabriel asked, helping her with her wrap.

"Yes, but I'd rather go with you."

Gabriel shook his head. "No, go with Maurice. I'll follow along behind."

"Why?" She drew a deep breath. "You don't think Nina is here, do you?"

"I don't know, but if she is, I'd like to take her by surprise if I can." Gabriel cocked his head to one side, then grunted softly. "Maurice is here."

A moment later, there was a knock at the door.

"Be right there," Sara called.

"Let Maurice bring you home."

"All right." She rose on tiptoe, brushing her lips across his, and then she opened the door and stepped outside.

Maurice stared at her, his brow furrowed. "What's that smell?" he asked. "Garlic?"

"Yes," Sara said quickly. "Shall we go?"

She took Maurice's arm and urged him down the steps. It was full dark now and her heart began to pound as he helped her into the carriage. Was Nina out there somewhere, waiting?

Maurice settled onto the seat beside her and took her hand in his. "How are you feeling?"

"I feel fine," Sara replied. "Why do you ask?"

Maurice frowned at her. "You left rehearsal today because you weren't feeling well. I just wondered . . . what's wrong, Sara?"

"Nothing."

"Don't lie to me, Sara Jayne. You've never missed a rehearsal before, not even that time you sprained your wrist. What's going on?"

"Nothing. I was just tired. Can't I be tired once in a while? I work hard every day."

"Sara Jayne, I know something is bothering you." He gave her hand a slight squeeze. "We're engaged to be married," he remarked quietly. "I had hoped you would share your troubles with me."

Sara glanced down at their joined hands. She should tell him now, she thought, tell him their engagement was off now that Gabriel had returned.

"Sara Jayne?"

"There's nothing wrong."

With a sigh, Maurice released her hand and sat

back against the seat. "Whatever you say."

Sara was relieved when they reached the theater a few minutes later.

The opera house was filled to capacity that night. Even so, she had no trouble locating Gabriel. Her gaze was drawn to him, and even amid a sea of faces, his stood out. She felt his pride in her, his desire for her, and as she moved across the stage, she forgot everyone and everything else and danced for him, only for him.

Maurice watched Sara's face as she danced. Her skin seemed to glow; her eyes were radiant. And her dancing . . . never had she moved like that, her slender body swaying, turning, leaping gracefully across the stage, every nuance sensual, inviting.

From his seat in the balcony, Gabriel, too, watched Sara dance. She was dancing for him, tempting him. He saw the fire in her eyes when she glanced his way, recognized the hunger there, the promise of the night to come.

During the intermission, he left the theater, walking its perimeter, but he detected no sign of Nina, sensed no other immortal nearby.

With that in mind, he went to the stable where he had left Necromancer, speaking softly to the stallion, making sure the horse was being well cared for in his absence.

Leaving the livery barn, he went to a nearby clothing store and purchased several changes of clothing, which he dropped off at Sara's apartment before returning to the theater.

When the performance was over, he applauded as loudly as everyone else, and then made his way out of the theater, lingering in the shadows, his revenant senses testing the air for any sign of Nina, but he perceived no threat.

Blending into the shadows, he waited to make sure that Maurice saw Sara safely home.

The drive home was uncomfortably silent. Inside the carriage, Maurice sat across from Sara, his arms crossed over his chest, his expression impassive.

Sara kept her gaze lowered, but she could feel Maurice's steady regard, feel the tension that hummed between them. Several times, she started to speak, to tell him their engagement was a mistake, that it was over, but she couldn't summon the nerve, couldn't find the words to say what was in her heart.

When they reached her door, Maurice bid her a curt good night.

She watched him climb into the carriage, and then, with a sigh, she closed the door.

She knew Gabriel was waiting for her before she turned around. In a heartbeat, she reached for him, her mouth searching hungrily for his.

She felt him hesitate, and then his arms were locked around her waist and he was holding her close, letting her feel the need pulsing through him. He kissed her deeply, his tongue teasing hers. His hands slid up her back, unfastening her gown, delving through layers of cloth to find the warm satin of her skin.

Sara moaned softly as Gabriel's hands skimmed her flesh, bringing all her senses to life. She pressed herself against him, her fingers playing over his arms and shoulders. She drew off his cloak, his shirt, wanting to see him, to touch him. His skin was cool to her touch, his body like something sculpted from marble, hard and beautifully formed.

Excitement bubbled up inside her as he carried her to bed. Lowering her gently to the mattress, he began to undress her, his mouth gliding over her lips, the curve of her neck, the hollow of her shoulder, until she was writhing beneath him, wanting more, wanting it all.

She moaned softly as he drew away to remove his boots, his trousers. For a moment, he stood beside the bed, a dark silhouette against the blackness of the room. She could feel the tightly leashed power that emanated from him. The fact that he was no ordinary man was both frightening and seductive.

And then he was on the bed beside her, enfolding her in arms like steel, pressing her down into the mattress, his voice murmuring her name, and she forgot everything but the wonder of his touch, the magic of his voice, the need that shimmered in the depth of his eyes.

"I love you, *cara mia*," he whispered, his voice low and husky. "Now and for always."

"Yes," she gasped. "Oh, yes."

With a cry, he buried himself within her warmth, and there was no more loneliness, no more darkness.

And as his body merged with hers, she felt herself become a part of him. For a few brief moments, her mind linked to his and she felt the terrible loneliness that had plagued him for three long centuries. For the first time, she understood the vast gulf that stretched between Gabriel and humanity. She understood his loneliness, his emptiness, his overwhelming need for the touch of a human hand.

Her touch. Her hand.

Whispering his name, her eyes filled with tears, she offered him all that she had, her heart, her soul, her love, and prayed that it would be enough.

# *Chapter Twenty-two*

He held Sara in his arms while she slept, one hand lightly stroking her hair. Time and again, he had tried to warn her away, but no more. From this night forward, she would be his. He would watch over her, protect her. He would destroy her enemies, destroy himself rather than allow anyone to harm her.

In the hour before dawn, he made love to her again, and then, too soon, the sun was climbing over the horizon. He gazed at her for a few more minutes, reluctant to leave her, knowing he must.

"Have you a basement?" he asked.

Sara frowned at his odd question. "No."

"An attic, perhaps?"

"There's a small crawl space in the ceiling above my closet. Why?"

"I can't expect you to abandon your bed every day at dawn."

"I could stay here, with you."

"No."

"Please, Gabriel. I hate having to leave you after we've made love. It makes me feel like a . . . a . . ."

His eyes darkened. "Like what, Sara? A *puttana?*"

"Yes, if you must know! I want to go to sleep in your arms."

"You won't like waking up next to a corpse."

"You're not a corpse!"

"That's exactly what I am," he said with a weary shake of his head. "You still don't understand, do you? I'm not alive. I haven't been alive for over three hundred years."

"Stop it!" She pressed her hands over her ears, refusing to listen. She knew what he was. How could she not? But why did he have to dwell on it? Why wouldn't he let her forget?

Gabriel took a deep breath, his hands clenched at his sides as he fought down his anger, his frustration.

"I'm sorry, Sara," he said quietly. "Forgive me."

She nodded, her eyes brimming with tears. "I only want to be with you."

"I know. Don't you think I want it, too?" His gaze met hers and she saw the anguish in his eyes. "Don't you think I'd love to fall asleep beside you, to have your face be the first thing I see when I awake?"

"We could go away," she said. "I could sleep during the day and spend my nights with you."

"Is that what you want, to give up dancing, to give up all you've worked for, to be with me?"

"Yes."

It was tempting. For a moment, he let himself imagine what it would be like to have Sara there beside him, to fall asleep in her arms, to reach for her when he awoke.

But he had to give her a chance to think it through, to fully understand what kind of life she would have if she chose to stay with him.

"You're a young woman, Sara. You have your whole life ahead of you. Think of what you'd be giving up. You'll never have a normal life if you decide to stay with me."

He ran his fingertips over her cheek, loving the warmth of her skin, wishing, as he had wished so many times before, that he was a mortal man again, that he could live with her and love her as he yearned to do.

He looked deep into her eyes. "Once you are truly mine, I will never let you go."

The possessiveness in his gaze, the intensity in voice, gave her a moment's pause. He was telling her, warning her, that if she decided to stay with him, her decision, once made, would be irrevocable.

He saw the sudden apprehension rise in her eyes, knew the very moment when she remembered that he was no ordinary man, that she wouldn't be able to decide she'd made a mistake and walk away.

"We'll talk more about it later," he said.

Sara nodded. Reaching for her robe, she slid out of bed and began gathering the clothes she'd need for the day. As an afterthought, she took the little silver cross from her jewelry box.

"Till tonight," she said, kissing his cheek.

"Tonight."

For Sara, the daylight hours passed slowly. She had little to occupy her time since she dared not go outside alone. After eating breakfast and washing her few dishes, she wandered through the apartment, finally settling down on the sofa with a book. But she couldn't concentrate. She kept hearing Gabriel's words in her mind: *Once you are truly mine, I'll never let you go.*

Wasn't that what she wanted, to be his forever?

She sat there for hours, her mind replaying every moment they had spent together, weighing her love for him, her need to be with him, against her desire to continue dancing, to have a home and a family.

*You'll never have a normal life if you stay with me,* he'd said. But did she want a normal life if she couldn't share it with Gabriel?

How could she live with him, knowing what he did to survive? How could she live without him?

How would she feel as the years passed by and she grew old, older, while he stayed forever young? Would she hate him then? Would he turn away from her when she was no longer young and pretty?

She could become what he was . . .

She glanced at the bedroom door, and after a long moment of indecision, she did what she had been longing to do, what she had promised not to do.

One hand clasping the cross she had slipped over her head when she left the room earlier, she opened the bedroom door a crack and peered inside.

Gabriel had dressed and now lay upon his cloak, his arms folded over his chest, his eyes closed. His skin looked more pale than usual. She stared at him for a long moment, but he didn't appear to be breathing. He looked, she thought morbidly, like a corpse laid out for burial.

*I'm not alive,* he'd said, and for the first time she believed him.

A sound behind her made her start, and she

whirled around to find Maurice standing in the doorway.

"What are you doing here?" she whispered.

Maurice glanced at Gabriel, then shook his head. "I knew it," he murmured. "I knew he had come back. There was no other explanation for the way you've been acting these past few days."

Sara crossed the floor toward the door, but Maurice held his ground.

"Now do you believe me?" he said, nodding in Gabriel's direction. "The man's a vampire, Sara Jayne. He must be destroyed."

"No!"

She tried to close the door, but Maurice grabbed her by the arm and half dragged, half carried her into the room Babette had used. Taking the key from the lock, he shoved Sara inside and locked the door.

"Maurice!" Sara pounded on the door with her fists. "Maurice, let me out!"

"No, Sara Jayne. He must be destroyed, now, while he's helpless."

"Maurice!" She screamed his name. "Don't!"

Ignoring her cries, Maurice went outside and retrieved the sack he'd left on the steps.

Reentering the house, he opened the sack, his hand clutching the cross he wore while he gazed at the contents, quietly praying for the courage to do what had to be done. And then, heaving a determined sigh, he withdrew a sharp wooden stake and a hammer from the sack and went into Sara's bedroom.

Gabriel lay as before.

Unmoving.

Undead.

Fear rose up in Maurice as he gazed at the man on the bed. Not a man, he reminded himself, a monster, a fiend who lived off the blood of others, a demon who must be destroyed before he turned Sara Jayne into what he was.

It was the thought of Sara that gave Maurice the courage to lift the stake. He could hear Sara Jayne pounding on the door, screaming for him to stop, as he positioned the sharpened end of the hawthorn stake over Gabriel's heart.

Holding his breath, he raised the hammer, his gorge rising at the mere idea of what he was about to do.

He was bringing the hammer down when Gabriel's hand closed around his forearm.

The hammer fell from a hand gone suddenly numb as Maurice stared down into the face of death. Gabriel's eyes blazed with an unholy fire; his lips were drawn back in a feral snarl, revealing sharp white fangs.

With his free hand, Gabriel tore the cross from the chain dangling down Maurice's chest. The silver burned his palm as he threw the crucifix across the room.

"Did you think to kill me so easily?" Gabriel asked as he tossed the stake after the crucifix.

Maurice couldn't speak. Cold sweat beaded his brow and trickled down his back as he stared at the monster lying on the bed.

Sara's voice, crying, pleading, filled the silence.

"What have you done to her?" Gabriel asked, his voice low and silky and dangerous.

Maurice opened his mouth, but no words came out, and he shook his head vigorously, his whole body trembling. He winced as Gabriel tightened his hold on his arm.

"Fool," Gabriel said. "Did you truly think a puny mortal like yourself could destroy me? I've survived for over three hundred and fifty years, little man."

"But . . ." The word squeaked past Maurice's lips.

"You thought to find me helpless," Gabriel mused. "You should not have put your faith in those silly stories about vampires. Only the very young ones are totally helpless during the hours of daylight." A wry grin twisted Gabriel's lips. "As you are helpless."

"Please . . ."

Gabriel arched one brow. "You don't wish to die?"

"No."

"Neither do I."

Maurice licked lips gone dry. Gabriel was toying with him as a cat might play with a mouse before the kill. He tried to look away from those horrible blood-red eyes, but he couldn't move.

Drawing Maurice closer, Gabriel reached up with his free hand and wrapped his fingers around Maurice's throat. He could feel the blood rushing through the man's veins, smell the overpowering scent of fear that rose from every pore. He had not fed in several days . . .

"Have you ever thought of being dinner?" he asked mildly.

Maurice shook his head, his stomach churning at the thought of Gabriel feeding on his blood.

Gabriel grunted softly. "Have you ever thought of being a vampire? I could arrange it, you know."

"No!"

"Careful, little man," Gabriel warned. "You're in no position to offend me."

Maurice glared at him, his eyes filled with fear and defiance. "Go ahead, kill me, you bastard, but do it and get it over with."

Gabriel regarded Delacroix for a long while, faintly amused by the man's unexpected show of courage.

"I'm not going to kill you," he said, loosening his hold on Maurice's throat.

Horror darkened Maurice's eyes. "You don't mean to turn me into what you are?" He shook his head. "I would rather be dead."

"Listen to me, Delacroix, listen very carefully. Sara's life is in danger." He saw the accusation in Maurice's eyes. "Not from me, but from another vampire. A very old, very vindictive vampire."

"I don't understand."

"There's no reason you should. Suffice it to say that I'm afraid of her. . . ."

"Her?"

Gabriel nodded.

"And you're afraid of her?" Maurice asked incredulously, unable to believe that Gabriel was afraid of anything, living or dead.

"The female of the species is always more dangerous, more deadly. Nina is vexed with me, and she intends to get even with me by hurting Sara. I can't protect Sara from Nina during the day."

"What can I do against a vampire?"

"Nina is no threat during the day. But she's been known to hypnotize others to do her bidding. And that, my friend, is where you come in. I'm letting you live so you can protect Sara while I rest."

"I understand." Maurice swallowed hard. "And when the threat to Sara is past, what then? Will you kill me for what I tried to do today?"

"Only if you try it again."

"And what of Sara?"

"What about her?"

"You aren't . . . you wouldn't . . ."

"Make her what I am? No, I would never do that." With a sigh, Gabriel released his hold on Maurice's arm. "Get out. And take your cross with you. You might have need of it."

With a nod, Maurice scooped up the crucifix and fled the room. Closing the door behind him, he slid to the ground, the heavy silver cross clutched tightly in his hands. Never, he thought, never had he been so afraid. So close to death. Or worse.

Gradually, he became aware of Sara's cries. Pushing himself to his feet, he walked on unsteady legs to the bedroom and unlocked the door.

Sara studied Maurice's face, her heart heavy in her breast. "Did you?"

"No."

"Oh, thank God," Sara murmured.

She started to step past Maurice when he caught her arm. "I thought he was going to kill me."

Sara's eyes widened. "What happened?"

"He woke up when I put the stake to his heart." Maurice shivered with the memory. "I've never seen anything so awful as the look in his eyes."

Sara nodded. She, too, had seen that look. It had chilled her to the depths of her soul.

"He could have killed me," Maurice said, "but he let me live because of you."

Taking her hand, Maurice led her into the parlor and sank down on the sofa. "He told me about Nina, said I was to protect you during the day." Maurice paused, willing his hands to stop trembling, but he couldn't shake off the fear that had gripped him. "What are we going to do, Sara Jayne?"

"I don't know."

Maurice glanced around the room, at the garlic hanging from the windows and over the door. "Do you really think that will keep her out?"

"It kept Gabriel inside the cottage."

"Yes, but from what he says, Nina is stronger than he is. What if she's immune to something as mundane as garlic?"

"I sprinkled the windowsills with holy water, too. I don't care how strong she is, I don't think she can cross that."

"And if she can?"

"I don't know!" Sara jumped to her feet and began to pace the floor. "I'm just as frightened as you are."

Her words were like a slap in the face. Squaring his shoulders, Maurice stood up and gathered Sara into his arms.

"I'll protect you with my life, Sara Jayne," he said quietly. "I swear it on the life of my mother."

# Chapter Twenty-three

Nina stood in the darkness across from the opera house. Dressed all in black, she blended into the shadows, watching Giovanni.

He was waiting, she thought, waiting for his little ballerina to emerge from the theater.

She could sense his mind probing the night, searching, Nina knew, for her.

Nina smiled. Did he honestly think he could keep her from exacting revenge, that he could protect that silly little mortal woman?

The smile died on her lips as she recalled how he had refused to share a single night with her. In a thousand years, no man had ever refused her and lived to tell it.

But she would not kill Gianni—it would be so much more satisfying to destroy his woman.

Or so she told herself. It was a lie, and she knew it, but she refused to acknowledge that she simply could not bring herself to destroy him, that even now, after all these years, after the way he had coldly dismissed her, he was the only man she had ever truly cared for, and he had refused her because of another woman.

Jealousy rose up within her, as bitter as gall. It was unthinkable that a man who had once adored her had spurned her in favor of that doe-eyed creature with her innocent blue eyes and pale blond hair.

Eyes narrowed, she stared at Giovanni, and at that moment she hated him, hated him as fervently as she loved him.

In a thousand years, she had desired many men, made love to many men, but she had loved none of them. She was too selfish to give anyone a part of herself. It seemed ironic, somehow, that the only man with whom she wanted to share a part of her existence did not want her.

And for that, the woman would pay.

And through the woman, Giovanni would pay.

But not too soon, she thought, shielding her presence from Gianni.

Not too soon . . .

# *Chapter Twenty-four*

Gabriel walked behind Sara and Maurice, his eyes and ears attuned to every drifting shadow, every sound. His senses told him that no one was following them. He detected no trace of a supernatural being, and yet he knew, somehow he knew, that Nina was nearby.

His gaze narrowed as he stared at Maurice's back, wondering if he would have to destroy the man once the danger to Sara was past. Or if, by some slim chance, Maurice would destroy him.

He could feel Maurice's hatred, his distrust and revulsion, but stronger than those emotions was the man's jealousy.

But it wasn't Maurice who held his attention. It was Sara. She moved with innate grace, her gown flowing around her ankles, the moonlight shimmering in her hair. He had tried not to love her, had tried to stay away from her, but to no avail, and now he knew he would not let her go. He had told her she must decide whether she would stay with him or not, but should she decide to leave him, he had no intention of letting her go. Right or wrong, willing or not, she would be his for as long as she lived.

Sara unlocked the door to her apartment, then stood on the top step with Maurice while Gabriel went inside to make sure the house was empty.

A moment later, he motioned them inside.

Sara went from room to room, turning on lights. When she returned to the parlor, Maurice was sitting on the sofa. Gabriel was standing before the hearth, one arm braced against the mantel. She could feel the tension vibrating between them.

"Would either of you care for a cup of . . ." She looked at Gabriel and smiled sheepishly. "Tea?"

"I'd like a cup," Maurice said.

"Gabriel, would you like a glass of wine?"

"No."

She glanced from one man to the other, wondering if it was safe to leave them in the room together and then, with a shrug, she went into the kitchen and filled the teapot with water.

Maurice slipped his hand into his coat pocket, feeling a sense of relief as his fingers closed over the crucifix. "She's going to marry me," he said.

"Is she?"

"Yes."

"I don't think so."

"You can't keep her with you. It isn't natural. What kind of life can she have with a . . ."

"Monster?" Gabriel supplied softly, his eyes narrowing ominously.

"Exactly! She's a young woman. She deserves

more out of life than you can give her."

"Perhaps."

Maurice's hand tightened around the cross. "Leave her alone."

"You're a fool, Delacroix. She's mine. She's always been mine."

"You won't have her!" Maurice stood up. "Do you hear me, vampire? You will not have her!"

"Who's going to stop me? You?"

"Gabriel! Maurice! Stop it!"

"Tell him, Sara Jayne. Tell him you're going to marry me."

"Maurice . . ."

"Tell him!"

"I . . ." She bit down on her lower lip as she glanced from one man to the other. "I haven't decided what I'm going to do."

"So that's the way it is," Maurice said heavily.

"I'm sorry, Maurice. Right now I can't think of the future. For all we know, I might not even have a future."

"Nina won't have you, *cara,*" Gabriel said quietly. He crossed the room. Taking the tea tray from her trembling hands, he thrust it at Maurice. "Go to bed, Sara."

Sleep. Suddenly all she wanted to do was sleep, to forget everything, if only for a little while. Without a word, she went into the bedroom and closed the door.

"You should get some rest, too," Gabriel told Maurice. "You'll have to keep an eye on Sara tomorrow."

Maurice placed the tray on the side table and poured himself a cup of tea. He stared at Gabriel over the rim of the cup. "Who's going to protect me from you while *I* sleep?"

"You have nothing to fear from me," Gabriel replied, "though killing you would be sweet indeed."

"That makes me feel a lot better," Maurice muttered. He set the empty cup on the tray and then, with a last glance at Gabriel, he went into the spare bedroom and shut the door.

A wry grin twisted Gabriel's lips as he heard Maurice turn the key in the lock. Foolish mortal, he mused, to think he was safe behind that flimsy wooden door.

Restless, he paced the room, the smell of garlic strong in his nostrils. He stared at his palm, noting that the burn from touching Maurice's crucifix was still raw and red.

Garlic and holy water, sunlight and silver crosses—such ordinary things, and yet they had the power to weaken him, to destroy him.

With a start, he stared toward the window. And there, deep in the shadows of the night, he sensed the presence of another immortal.

Antonina.

*Yes, Giovanni, I am here.*

*Leave her. Leave this place.*

He sensed her smile, knew she could feel his gut-wrenching fear—fear for Sara's life, for his own.

*I shall have my revenge, Gianni. She shall suffer for days, but your suffering shall last for eternity.*

*Nina!*

*Too late, Giovanni. You should not have refused me. I wanted only to give you one night of pleasure. Now she shall have many nights of pain. And you will feel what she feels, Gianni. That will be my revenge.*

*Nina, wait . . .*

But she was gone.

Cursing himself, cursing Nina, he went into Sara's bedroom, needing to see her, to ascertain that she was all right.

He stared down at her for a long while. Lying there in her high-necked white sleeping gown, with her golden hair spread across the pillow, she looked like an angel newly fallen to earth. Her goodness, her generosity of spirit, made him ache for things that were forever lost to him.

Needing desperately to hold her, to touch her, if only for a moment, he slid under the covers and drew her into his arms.

She stirred at his touch. "Gabriel?"

"Go back to sleep, *cara,*" he whispered.

"Is something wrong?"

"No, love. I just wanted to hold you."

With a sigh, she snuggled against him, her arms stealing around his waist, her legs entwining with his.

He closed his eyes, reveling in her nearness. Her scent filled his nostrils; the warmth of her touch filled the emptiness in his soul, chasing away the darkness. He needed her touch, he thought, needed it to survive as surely as he needed to quench the hunger that damned him.

But there was no thought of taking her as he held her in his arms, only a sense of peace.

Sara . . . He'd known her such a short time, less than a quarter of a century. Twenty-one years, a mere moment of his existence compared to the centuries he had walked the earth. And yet, of all the years he'd known, he treasured the ones he'd spent with Sara above all others.

He felt her gaze moving over his face, her hand delving under his shirt to explore his chest in ever-widening circles.

Opening his eyes, he saw her staring at him, her expression open and vulnerable.

"Love me," she whispered. "Please, Gabriel, I need you to hold me. I'm so afraid."

And so, he thought, was he. More afraid than he'd ever been in his life. How could he go on existing if Nina destroyed the fragile creature in his arms? How would he ever live with the guilt?

With a low groan, he buried his hands in the wealth of her hair and then, slowly and deliberately, he covered her mouth with his. Her tongue met his like a streak of living flame, spreading light and heat through every inch of his body, every fiber of his being. He clutched her to him, his need for her, his fear for her, overriding any thought of gentleness. She was his woman. Right or wrong, she was his and he would defy the heat of the sun or the fires of hell to protect her.

With a low growl that was nearly a sob, he buried himself within her, sheathing himself in satin sweetness, wanting to pleasure her as she was pleasuring him. And yet he knew she would never fully understand what her love meant to him, nor could he ever hope to give back as much as he received. She was warm and alive, vital and vibrant; her very touch made him feel alive. Her trust, her nearness, meant so much more to him than the brief joining of their flesh.

Later, as the moon faded from the sky, Giovanni Ognibene gazed at the woman in his arms, and for the first time in over three centuries, he felt that he was more man than monster.

# *Chapter Twenty-five*

Sara woke slowly, filled with a deep and abiding sense of contentment, of fulfillment. Gabriel had made love to her all the night long . . .

Gabriel! She turned her head and he was there, lying beside her, his eyes closed. She glanced quickly toward the window, relieved to see that it was still dark outside, that he had not yet succumbed to the deathlike sleep that engulfed him during the day.

Lightly, she traced his lips with her fingertip, felt a surge of heat course through her when he stroked her fingertip with his tongue.

His eyelids fluttered open and she found herself gazing into the depths of his eyes—beautiful deep gray eyes fringed with thick black lashes.

"Good morning," she murmured.

"Good morning, *cara.*" His gaze moved over her face. How beautiful she was. Her lips were still slightly swollen from his kisses, her hair fell over her shoulders in a riot of golden waves, and her eyes . . . he knew he would sacrifice the next hundred years to wake up each morning and find Sara looking at him like that, her sky-blue eyes filled with love.

He kissed her softly, gently, let his hands wander over the smooth silky flesh he had possessed only hours before. How quickly he had come to know the hills and valleys of her body, just as he had come to know that she liked to have her back rubbed, that tickling her feet would make her laugh.

He kissed her again, and the slow heat that had been building between them suddenly burst into flame. With a low groan, he tucked her beneath him and merged his flesh with hers, and she rose up to meet him, her arms wrapping around his neck as she offered him her love and took his in return.

They lay locked in each other's arms for a long while, reluctant to part.

He didn't have to glance at the window to know that the sky was growing light. Soon, too soon, he would have to send her from him. And yet he couldn't help wondering what it would be like to be enfolded in Sara's arms when the darkness claimed him. He had told her that being swallowed up in the deathlike sleep had frightened him more than anything else when first he'd been made. What he hadn't told her was that, though he had long ago learned to accept it, he had never learned to like it. It was a frightening thing, to be sucked down into blackness deeper than the bowels of hell, to be helpless, vulnerable. Would the darkness that overtook him be less fearful if he succumbed to it while in Sara's embrace?

"Sara?" He spoke hesitantly, not knowing how to

ask for what he wanted, not knowing if he should.

"What?"

"Hold me."

She frowned, puzzled by the note of apprehension in his voice. "I am holding you," she said.

"Will you stay with me . . ."

"Of course."

He swore under his breath, wondering why it was so hard to ask her to hold him while oblivion swept over him.

"What is it, Gabriel?" she asked, worried now. "What's wrong?"

"Will you hold me until . . . ?"

She knew then what he wanted. "I will," she promised, unable to believe what he was saying. For the first time, he looked vulnerable. It caused all her protective instincts to rush to the fore. "I'll hold you until you're . . . you're asleep."

She pulled him closer, her arms tightening around him as she cradled his head to her breast.

With a sigh, Gabriel closed his eyes. He could hear the steady beat of her heart beneath his ear, feel the warmth of her hand stroking his back, his shoulders.

"Be careful today," he said as he felt the blackness descend on him. "Stay in the house. Keep Maurice with you."

"Why? What's wrong?"

He fought the lethargy that was stealing over him. "Nina. She's . . . here. Don't go out. Promise . . . me."

"I promise."

"Check . . . doors . . ." His eyelids fluttered down and he felt himself sinking into blackness. "Windows . . . careful . . . be careful . . ."

"I will."

"My cloak . . . ," he said, his voice urgent, faint. "Need . . . it . . ."

"I'll get it. Gabriel?"

She fought down a rising sense of terror as he went suddenly limp in her arms. He didn't look as if he was sleeping now, she thought. His body was heavy, lifeless, cold.

Telling herself there was nothing to be afraid of, she slid out of bed. Standing there, looking down at him, she began to shiver uncontrollably.

What if he didn't wake up?

She was reaching for her robe when she saw his cloak. Lifting it from the chair, she held it in her hands for a moment, and then spread it over him. It was unnerving to see him lying there like that, and she quickly gathered up her clothes and left the room.

Maurice was already up, looking as if he hadn't slept more than a few minutes. Dark bristles shadowed his jaw; his clothes looked rumpled, as though he had tossed and turned all night.

"You slept with him." It was an accusation, not a question.

The flood of color that washed into her cheeks gave him all the answer he needed.

"I'll understand if you don't want to stay," Sara said, not meeting his eyes. "I've treated you badly, and I apologize."

"I'll stay," he replied curtly, and then he grinned, a dry, humorless expression. "I don't think I have much choice."

"What do you mean?"

Maurice jerked his thumb toward Sara's bedroom. "Him. He told me to watch you. But I'd have stayed anyway. I love you, Sara Jayne. Nothing will change that."

"Maurice, I'm sorry . . ."

He waved his hand in a gesture of dismissal. "Have you got anything to eat?"

Sara nodded, eager for an excuse to leave the room. How much easier her life would be if she could have loved Maurice. Their life together would have been ideal. They shared a love of dancing, of music, of art. They could have had a good life together, had children, a home in the country, all the things she longed for, and yet, without Gabriel, she wouldn't want to dance, or live. She didn't want to bear another man's children, or live in another man's house.

She wanted Gabriel, and she knew at that moment that she would do whatever she had to do, make any sacrifice necessary, to spend the rest of her life with him.

It was Sunday, and the day passed slowly. Usually, she went to Mass, but she had promised Gabriel she wouldn't go out.

Maurice sat in the chair beside the hearth, his nose buried in a book.

Sara busied herself in the kitchen preparing a huge midday meal, though she had no appetite. How could she even think of eating with Maurice brooding in the parlor and Gabriel sleeping the sleep of the undead in her bedroom? And always in the back of her mind was Nina's threat to destroy her.

Head throbbing from the heat in the kitchen and her troublesome thoughts, she opened the kitchen door and stepped outside. The autumn air felt blessedly cool against her face. For a moment, she stared up at the sun, a sight Gabriel had not seen in over three hundred years. Gabriel.

Taking a deep breath, she closed her eyes, anxious for nightfall, for the time when she could be in his arms again.

She gasped as she felt a hand on her arm, then chided herself for her fear. She turned around, expecting to see Maurice.

But it was not Maurice. Fear snaked through her. She opened her mouth to scream, but a huge hand fastened around her throat, choking off her cry, trapping the air in her lungs until the world went black.

The smell of something burning roused Maurice. Frowning, he jumped to his feet, the book in his lap falling to the floor unnoticed as he ran into the kitchen.

"Sara Jayne, what's the . . ."

The words died in his throat. The kitchen was filled with smoke; the back door was standing open. Grabbing a towel, he opened the oven and removed a pan that held a chunk of charred meat.

"Sara Jayne?"

He felt a growing sense of dread as he crossed the room and looked outside.

"Sara?"

He walked down the short flight of steps that led to the small garden behind her apartment, but there was no sign of her.

Returning to the house, he checked the spare bedroom, hoping to find her there asleep, but it was empty.

Hesitantly, he opened her bedroom door and

peered inside. Gabriel lay on the bed, as still as death.

Shutting the door, Maurice went to the entry hall. The front door was closed, locked from the inside.

Where was she? With a low groan of despair, he sank down on the sofa, his head cradled in his hands. Where was she?

And what would Gabriel do when he woke and discovered she was gone?

He woke in the hour before dusk. Lying there, still weak, he sent his thoughts to search for Sara, and knew, in that moment, that she was gone.

"Maurice!" The word was a cry of rage, a scream of primal fear.

It vibrated off the walls, shook the glass in the windows, and filled Maurice with a quiet sense of doom.

On legs that trembled so violently he could hardly stand, he walked to the bedroom, took a deep breath, and opened the door.

Gabriel sat up, his back propped against the headboard. "Where is she?"

Maurice shook his head. "I don't know."

"Damn you! I told you to watch her for me."

"I . . . she was in the kitchen, cooking. I . . . I fell asleep. When I woke up, she was gone."

Gabriel glared at Delacroix. It had been days since he fed; the lust for blood was strong, and growing stronger. "Come here."

Maurice took a wary step backward. "No."

"You will not like what happens if I have to ask you again."

On legs that felt like stone, Maurice approached the side of the bed. He tried not to look at Gabriel, but the vampire's gaze burned into his, hot and bright and hungry.

Slowly, Gabriel swung his legs over the edge of the mattress, his gaze fixed on Delacroix. "Sit here, beside me."

Maurice didn't want to obey, but he seemed to have no will of his own. Like a puppet whose strings had been cut, he sat down beside the vampire, his heart pounding so rapidly, so loudly, he wondered if he was going to die. And then he saw the blood lust blazing in Gabriel's eyes, and a short, hysterical laugh bubbled from his lips. Of course he was going to die.

*Have you ever thought of being dinner?*

Nausea roiled through Maurice as the memory of Gabriel's voice asking that question echoed in the back of his mind.

"You're going to kill me?" There was no fear in Maurice's voice now, only a distant feeling of calm, a sense of facing the inevitable.

"No, but I need your blood, Delacroix. I haven't fed in several days, and I don't have time to prowl the streets looking for someone else."

"Will I become . . ." Maurice swallowed hard, the thought of becoming a vampire more frightening than the specter of death.

"No."

Maurice flinched as Gabriel's hands fastened on his shoulders, anchoring him in place. The vampire's eyes seemed to burn a path to his soul. Fear unlike anything he had ever known rose up within him. And then he felt it, the sharp prick of fangs at his throat, the sensation of blood being drawn from his veins. The sound of Gabriel swallowing. Revulsion rose within him, and he knew he was going to be sick.

He slid to the floor when Gabriel released him, his body feeling curiously light, empty. He doubled over, retching violently, only vaguely aware of Gabriel moving about the room.

Wiping his mouth on his sleeve, Maurice glanced up. Gabriel stood near the door, putting on his cloak. The heavy black material swirled around him, making him seem even more sinister.

"Pray I find her before it's too late, Delacroix," Gabriel said flatly. "There will be no place for you to hide if she's dead."

Using the bed for support, Maurice gained his feet. From the corner of his eye, he caught sight of his reflection in the mirror. His skin looked gray and waxy. A cold chill slithered down his spine when he saw that Gabriel cast no image in the glass.

So, he thought inanely, the stories were true. Vampires cast no shadow, no reflection. He ran a hand through his hair, took a deep, calming breath. "I'm going with you."

Gabriel snorted disdainfully. "You can hardly stand."

"I'm going."

The man had courage, Gabriel thought with grudging admiration, and it wrung an apology from him, the first of its kind he had ever made.

"Forgive me," he said, his voice rough. "I wouldn't have taken from you if it wasn't necessary."

"We're wasting time," Maurice said.

A faint smile tugged at Gabriel's lips as he headed for the kitchen door. In another time and place, he and Maurice might have been friends.

Gabriel paused outside, his senses questing, testing the air. He caught Sara's scent, and though faint, it was as easy to follow as a lighted candle in the darkness.

Sara huddled in the corner, paralyzed with fright, while the creature who had brought her to this place paced the floor, back and forth, back and forth, like an animal in a cage.

She tried not to watch him, but she couldn't seem to draw her gaze from his hulking form, from his face. From the long, wicked-looking knife that dangled from one hairy fist. She had begged him to let her go, but he had looked at her through dead eyes, his face totally devoid of expression, as though all trace of humanity, of life itself, had been destroyed, leaving only an empty shell capable of movement.

Hours passed that seemed like days. With the coming of night, total blackness descended on the deserted building, and with it a deafening silence marred only by the creature's shuffling footsteps and an occasional scurrying sound that made Sara think of rats.

Shivering, she drew her knees to her chin, her arms wrapped around her legs. Why had that creature brought her here? Why had she ever opened the door? And yet it had never occurred to her that she would be in any real danger while the sun was up, that she wouldn't be safe on the steps of her own house.

"Gabriel." She breathed his name aloud, using it as a talisman against the dark, the fear that boiled up inside her. He would come for her. She had to believe that.

"Of course he'll come."

Sara scrambled to her feet, her eyes searching the darkness for the source of that smooth, sultry voice.

"So," the voice said, "you're the little ballerina who has captured my Giovanni's heart."

"Who . . . who's there?"

"Don't you know?" the woman asked petulantly. "Surely Giovanni mentioned my name."

Sara frowned. "Giovanni? I don't know anyone named Giovanni."

A soft laugh sounded from Sara's right and she whirled around. She had heard no footsteps, no movement.

"That naughty boy, he calls himself Gabriel now. Didn't he even tell you his true name?"

Sara recoiled as she felt a hand in her hair. "Who are you? Why are you doing this?"

"All in good time." There was a smile in that voice, a cruel, calculating smile. "He may change his name, but he cannot change what he is." Again, that sultry laugh. "But to take the name of an angel! Ah, that is most daring."

Sara gasped in pain as Nina's hand fisted in her hair, jerking her head back to expose her throat. "He was mine first, my little mortal. Mine. And he will be mine again."

Even in the blackness, Sara could see the hatred blazing in the other woman's eyes, the hideous otherworldly glow that Sara recognized as a lust for blood.

"No!" Sara forced the word from a throat gone suddenly dry.

"Just a taste," Nina said, and with the swiftness of a striking snake, she buried her fangs in Sara's neck, one hand clamped over her shoulder to hold her in place.

"No!" Sara screamed as she tried to twist out of Nina's grasp, certain she could hear the blood being drawn from her veins. The mere idea sickened her, as did the touch of the woman's fingers in her hair and on her shoulder. Cold, icy fingers that felt like death.

"No, no . . ." Sara moaned, feeling her legs grow weak. A red mist swirled before her eyes.

There was no pleasure from Nina's possession as there had been in Gabriel's, only pain and revulsion, a sense of being defiled by a creature that was the embodiment of evil.

With a soft sigh of contentment, Nina released her hold on Sara.

Left to her own, Sara fell to her knees.

"He'll be here soon," the vampire remarked, delicately wiping the blood from her mouth with a black silk handkerchief. "Tell him this is just the beginning."

There was a soft sound, like wings in the night, and Sara knew that the other woman had gone.

Weeping softly, she curled up on the floor, praying for Gabriel to come and end the nightmare.

*Sara?*

She sat up, her heart thudding with hope, as his voice pierced her mind. *I'm in here!*

*I'm coming,* cara.

*Be careful! There's some sort of . . . of creature in here with me.*

*Rest easy, Sara, you'll soon be safely home again.*

No sooner had the words of assurance sounded in her mind than there was a horrible crash as the door burst open. Sara saw Gabriel silhouetted in the faint light that streamed through the portal, and behind him, she saw Maurice.

The creature had seen them, too. With a roar that sounded more bestial than human, it hurled itself at Gabriel, its teeth bared in a feral snarl, the knife slashing through the air.

Sara screamed as the blade struck Gabriel, slicing through his shirt into the flesh beneath. There was no change in the creature's expression as he brought the knife down again, opening a jagged gash in Gabriel's left arm.

Gabriel made no effort to avoid the blade, just plowed forward until his hands locked in a death grip around the creature's neck. He gave a sharp twist and the creature went limp in his hands, its neck broken. The sound of the knife clattering to the floor echoed like thunder in the empty wooden building.

And then Gabriel was beside her, gathering her into his arms, crushing her close.

"Sara, are you all right?"

"Yes," she sobbed. "But you . . ." She stared at the bright splash of crimson spreading over his shirtfront, dripping from his arm.

"It's nothing, *cara,*" he said reassuringly. "By tomorrow the wounds will have healed."

Overcome with relief that he was there, that the danger was past, she wrapped her arms around him and buried her face in his shoulder, unmindful of the blood that stained her dress and dripped from his arm to hers.

"Did he . . . did that creature . . ." Gabriel closed his eyes, hating to ask, hating to think of his Sara at the mercy of that zombielike creature. "Did he hurt you?"

"No."

Feeling weak from the loss of blood, Gabriel sank down on the floor, cradling Sara to his chest, rocking her gently. "It's all right, now, *cara*," he crooned, his hand stroking her hair, her cheek. "It's all right."

"Nina said . . ."

"She was here?"

Sara felt his whole body tense at the mention of the vampire's name. "Yes. She . . . she . . . Oh, Gabriel, it was awful. She said this was just the beginning."

Sara raised a hand to her neck, revulsion rising up within her as she felt the two small puncture wounds. "She bit me."

For a moment, Gabriel closed his eyes. It was obvious that Nina hadn't brought her over, but had she taken enough to initiate Sara? If Nina had taken enough blood, Sara would be enslaved to her forever, bound to do her bidding. Sara could still function during the day. She shared a mind bond with Gabriel. If she desired, she would be able to find him no matter where he went, no matter where he rested during the day. Was that Nina's ultimate goal, to have Sara destroy him? It was the kind of twist that would amuse Antonina's warped sense of humor, having Gabriel's lover drive a stake into his heart.

With a low groan, he gazed into Sara's eyes. "How much blood did she take from you?"

"I don't know."

"How do you feel?"

"Sick. Take me home, please."

Rising to his feet, Gabriel carried her out of the building.

Maurice had stood in the shadows while Gabriel comforted Sara. Now he glanced briefly at the creature sprawled on the raw plank floor, and then hurried outside.

There were more frightening beings than vampires lurking in the dark, he thought, and fates worse than death.

# Chapter Twenty-six

Sara felt better by the time they reached her apartment. She made Gabriel sit down in the kitchen while she removed his cloak and shirt, then washed the blood from his wounds, shushing him when he tried to tell her she was wasting her time, that he was in no danger, but she refused to listen. He was hurt and she needed to care for him, to assure herself that he was all right.

Maurice, still silent, made sure the doors and windows were locked, that the strings of garlic were in place. He sprinkled fresh holy water across every entrance, and then, feeling that he had done all he could, he stood in the kitchen doorway, watching Sara tend Gabriel's wounds. Incredibly, the wounds looked as though they were already healing.

"You're very quiet," Gabriel remarked, glancing up at Delacroix.

Maurice shrugged. "What is there to say? Nothing

in my life has prepared me for anything like this."

"I wouldn't think so," Gabriel allowed with a faint grin.

"Do you think we can truly protect Sara from that . . . that woman?"

"I don't know, but I intend to try."

"Are there more of those creatures out there?"

"As many as she cares to make." Gabriel stood up. For a moment, he gazed at Sara, his fingers caressing her cheek. It was all so impossible, he thought, their love, the problems they faced, not only now, but in the future. Should they find a way to defeat Nina, they would have to find a way to weave their lives together.

He kissed her lightly, then turned toward Maurice. "I have to go out."

For a moment, his words, and what they meant, hung in the air. Sara and Maurice exchanged glances: hers, resigned but accepting, Maurice's filled with condemnation.

A muscle clenched in Gabriel's jaw. "I won't be gone long. Lock the door after me and don't open it for anyone." He fixed Maurice with a hard stare. "Do you understand?"

Maurice nodded.

"Gabriel, please don't go."

"I wish I could stay, *cara,*" he replied, reaching for his cloak, "but I cannot change what I am, not even for you."

Sara placed her hand on his arm. "If you're in need, then take from me, but please don't go out."

"Sara, no!" Maurice's voice was sharp.

"It's my decision, not yours," she retorted.

Maurice met Gabriel's eyes. "She's been through

enough tonight." He paused, the color draining from his face. "If you need blood, take mine."

Gabriel quirked an eyebrow at Delacroix. "I know what it cost you to make the offer," he said solemnly, "but you've both been through enough for one night."

Sara followed Gabriel into her bedroom, watched while he slipped into a black shirt, drew his cloak around his shoulders. At his nod, she wiped the holy water from the sill and opened the window.

"I won't be long," he promised, dropping a kiss on her brow, and then, like a drifting shadow in the night, he was gone.

Gabriel paused in the darkness, his nostrils testing the wind, his senses searching for any sign of Nina's presence, but the night was dark and quiet, with only the soft sigh of the wind to break the stillness.

On silent feet, he prowled the darkness, the lust for blood growing ever stronger within him, fueled by the pain of his wounds, by his rage.

He searched until he found what he was looking for, a whore with pale skin and long black hair. He called her to him with the power of his mind, pretending it was Nina who stared up at him, helpless to resist, Nina's blood he was taking.

And he wished he had the power to control Nina's mind as easily as he manipulated the mind of the whore.

He was tempted to drain the girl dry, to sink his fangs into her throat and take and take until nothing remained but a dry husk, and by so doing, find a measure of release for the rage, for the sense of helplessness, that was pounding through him. Nina had sent that monster to abduct Sara, had frightened her, and then had dared to take her blood . . .

Gabriel lifted his head. A quiet word put the girl to sleep. When she woke, she wouldn't remember him, or what had happened.

He walked slowly back to Sara's apartment, wondering if Sara was now in Nina's power. Did he dare take his rest in Sara's apartment while there was a chance that Nina had enslaved Sara's mind?

As amusing as Nina might find it to have Sara destroy him, it would be a quick death, at least for him. Somehow, he didn't think Nina would find much satisfaction in that. She'd want him to suffer more, want Sara to suffer more. What was it Nina had told Sara? *This is just the beginning . . .*

He swore under his breath. There had to be a way to defeat Nina, to catch her off guard, but how?

When he returned to Sara's apartment, he found her asleep on the sofa, her head pillowed in Delacroix's lap.

Gabriel tried not to notice how well they looked together, two mortals in the prime of life. He felt a twinge of guilt, knowing without doubt that Sara and Maurice would have been married now if he hadn't returned to Paris. She would have had a chance for a normal existence with Delacroix, he thought bitterly. And yet, stronger than his guilt for intruding on her life was the violent surge of jealousy that spread through him when he saw Delacroix drape his arm around Sara's waist, the gesture blatantly protective.

"Go to bed, Delacroix," Gabriel said. "I'll look after Sara."

"If it weren't for you, she wouldn't be in any danger."

Gabriel's eyes narrowed ominously. "Don't you think I know that? Dammit, if I could undo what's been done, I would. But it's too late for that now. Nina won't rest until she has her revenge."

"Why don't you leave Sara alone, get out of her life. If you're gone, maybe that vampire woman will leave her alone."

"Maybe, but it's not a chance I'm willing to take, not when it's Sara who'll have to suffer the consequences if you're wrong."

"You haven't done much to protect her so far," Maurice said.

"Tread softly, Delacroix," Gabriel warned, "else you find two vampires seeking your destruction."

"What if she's changed her mind? What if she decides she no longer wants to spend the rest of her life with a . . . with you? Will you kill me then?"

In a single fluid move, Gabriel stepped forward and lifted Sara into his arms.

"Go to bed, Delacroix," he said, his voice as hard as flint, as cold as ice. "Get out of my sight now, while you can."

All the color drained from Maurice's face. Body rigid with fear, he stood up and started toward the spare bedroom.

"Delacroix!"

Slowly, Maurice turned around.

"Make sure the doors and windows are secure before you retire."

With a curt nod, Maurice exited the room.

"You wouldn't really hurt Maurice, would you?"

Gabriel glanced at Sara. She was staring up at

him, a troubled expression on her face.

"Have you been awake the whole time?"

Sara nodded.

"Is there any truth to what Delacroix said? Have you changed your mind? Is it him you want?"

"Will you kill him if I say yes?" Her gaze was steady on his as she waited for an answer, wondering what had possessed her to ask such a question.

The world seemed to hang suspended in time as she waited for his answer. She was acutely aware of the strength of the arms that held her, of the dark passion that blazed in Gabriel's eyes. A muscle jerked in his cheek, and then he released a sigh that seemed to come from the very depths of his being.

"I don't know, Sara," he replied quietly. "I honestly don't know."

Suddenly ashamed of playing such a cruel, coy game, she flung her arms around his neck. "You'll never have to find out," she said, her voice equally quiet. "I love you, Gabriel. No matter what happens, that will never change."

"*Cara!*"

His arms tightened around her, making it difficult to draw a breath, but it was a discomfort she could live with. Her eyelids fluttered down as he bent his head toward hers, and then he was kissing her, hotly, deeply, his tongue plundering her mouth as he carried her into the bedroom and closed the door, shutting out the rest of the world.

Gabriel lay on his back, his arm curled around Sara's waist, listening to the even sound of her breathing. He had made love to her twice before sleep claimed her, made love to her as if she were the only thing that could save him from eternal damnation. In her arms, with her body pressed to his, her voice whispering his name, vowing that she would love him all the days of her life, he felt whole, clean.

And yet, even when he had been caught up in the passion that blazed between them, he couldn't help wondering if he dared take his rest in her room.

He stayed awake the whole night long, holding her close, his gaze drawn time and again to her face. He had never known anyone so beautiful, so serene. Her hair was like the softest silk in his hands; her skin was smooth and warm, tempting his touch so that he found himself stroking the line of her cheek, the curve of her shoulder, the shape of her breast.

He had never loved anyone the way he loved her.

"She will never be yours." Nina's voice, softly mocking and filled with certainty, drifted into the room.

Easing himself from the bed, Gabriel crossed to the window and looked out into the darkness, and there, like darkness itself, he saw Nina standing in the light of the waning moon.

"Never, Giovanni," she said, and her eyes glowed like fiery coals. "If you will not love me, then you will not love her."

A violent tide of anger washed through Gabriel as he stared down at her. His hands clenched and unclenched at his sides. Had he been able, he would have leapt from the window and endeavored to wring the breath from her body. But the same tokens against evil that kept Nina out of the apartment also served to keep him in.

The sound of her laughter, filled with knowing, burned his ears like acid.

"Soon, Gianni," she said, "soon she will be nothing but dust, and then a memory."

"Nina!"

She tilted her head to the side, a devilish smile playing about her lips. "Will you beg me again for her life, Gianni? Will you come outside and grovel at my feet?"

Rebellion mingled with a strong sense of pride rose up within him. He had begged her once before to no avail. But he would do it again, if she would only swear to leave Sara alone.

With a defiant lift of his head, he met her gaze. "I would come to you if I could, *bella,*" he said with a wry grin, "but I fear I cannot leave this house."

"But you would if you could? You would come here to me, now, and beg me for the little mortal's life?"

He swallowed the revulsion that rose in his throat. "Yes."

"And what would you say?"

"Whatever you wish to hear," Gabriel replied.

"Get down on your knees, Giovanni," she said, "and let me hear what words you would speak to me."

Swallowing his pride, Gabriel dropped to his knees in front of the window. "I would tell you how lovely you are, that your beauty outshines the sun, that your lips are sweeter than nectar . . ."

"And you would not mean a word of it," she exclaimed, her anger evident in her tone, in her expression.

"I will say whatever you wish to hear," he repeated.

"I will do whatever you ask. If you need to take a life, take mine."

"You would die for her?" Nina asked incredulously. "You would give up hundreds of years of living for that puny mortal female?"

"Yes."

"Then you will suffer even more greatly than I had imagined," she remarked thoughtfully, and amid a swirl of black skirts, she disappeared into the darkness.

Gabriel watched her disappear and then, swearing softly, he rose to his feet, quietly cursing the holy water and the invisible barrier it created that prevented him from following her.

"One of us has to go out," Sara said the next evening. "You may be able to go for days with nothing to . . . to sustain you, but Maurice and I have to have something to eat."

Gabriel nodded. What she said was true. Three days had passed since Nina's midnight visit at the window. Sara had sent word to the theater that she was ill and unable to perform; Maurice had sent word that he had been called out of town due to a family crisis.

In the three days since Nina's appearance, nerves had grown taut and tempers short.

"Make a list, Sara, and I'll go," Maurice offered.

"Is that wise?" she asked, looking from one man to the other.

"He can protect you from her better than I can," Maurice said.

He was right, Sara thought, but who would protect

Maurice? "We could all go out together," she suggested.

Gabriel stared out the window into the darkness, weighing the alternatives. Would it be safer if they all went out together tonight, or to wait and let Maurice go to the market in the morning? And what if one of Nina's creatures broke into the house while Maurice was gone and he was at rest? Who would protect Sara then?

"We'll go out," Gabriel decided. "And after you have eaten, we'll go to the gunsmith. I want you both to have some sort of defense against Nina's creatures."

"A pistol?" Sara shook her head. "I don't think I could shoot anyone."

"He's right," Maurice said grudgingly. "Nina has declared war on us, and we need to arm ourselves."

"Have you ever fired a gun, Delacroix?"

Delacroix glared at Gabriel defiantly. "No, but I can learn."

Gabriel nodded. More and more, he found himself admiring the young man. He might be nothing but a dancer, but there was nothing effeminate or cowardly about him.

An hour later, they went to supper at a small restaurant near Sara's apartment. Gabriel sat in the shadows away from the windows, his face turned away while Sara and Maurice dined on roast duckling with all the trimmings.

There was little conversation at the table.

As soon as the meal was over, they left the restaurant and went to visit the gunsmith. At first, he refused to open his shop, declaring he was closed for the night, but Gabriel flashed a gold coin, and he obligingly showed them his wares. He was whistling happily when they left, having sold three pistols in the space of ten minutes.

From the gunsmith, they went to the market where Sara bought enough food to last for several days.

It was nearing nine o'clock when they returned to Sara's apartment.

Gabriel had just removed his cloak when he sensed the intruders. He managed to fire a single shot before six hulking brutes overpowered him, dragging him inside the parlor. They drenched him from head to foot with holy water, then bound his hands and feet with thick chains. When that was done, one of the creatures placed a heavy silver cross on his chest.

Maurice, who had been rendered unconscious by a blow to the back of the head when he threw himself between one of the brutes and Sara, lay face down on the floor. The strong scent of blood rose in the air.

Sara screamed, and then fell silent as another of the brutes tied a gag over her mouth, then dropped a sack over her head. Slinging her over his shoulder, he disappeared into the darkness. The last creature lumbered across the floor and opened the drapes wide before he followed the others outside.

Gabriel writhed on the floor, helpless, while the holy water penetrated his clothing and burned through his skin. The crucifix, though no bigger than his hand, lay like a tombstone on his chest, making it hard to breathe. And all the while his skin sizzled and burned.

Wild with rage and pain, he cursed himself and Nina.

But the worst was yet to come, because all too soon he felt Sara's panic. As clearly as if he were there beside her, he saw the dark hole into which two of the beasts lowered her; heard Sara's muffled screams as they covered the deep, narrow hole in the ground with a thick layer of sod so that she was literally buried alive. He saw her struggle against the ropes that bound her hands and feet. A dirty strip of cotton cloth covered her mouth, muffling her terrified cries. The thick smell of damp earth, of fear, clogged his nostrils.

*Gabriel! Gabriel, help me! Oh, please, help me.*

Her cries tore at his heart, his soul.

Ignoring the agony burning through him, he tried to move, but the cross held him immobile.

Unable to free himself, he could only lie there, listening to her cries, her prayers, her silent screams. As the hours passed, hysteria threatened to engulf her, her voice grew hoarse, faint. He felt her panic when a worm crawled over her arm. And over and over again he heard her call his name, begging him to come to her, to help her.

He tried to speak to her mind, but his powers were weak, and growing weaker, and her terror shut out every other thought.

He glanced at the window. Only a few hours till dawn, he thought bleakly. And then the early morning sunlight would pour through the window, its golden rays scalding his skin, its heat incinerating his flesh.

The horror of it, the imagined agony, made him shudder.

He closed his eyes against the excruciating pain that racked him, and then, so softly that he thought he had imagined it, he heard a groan.

"Delacroix?"

A wordless grunt was his only reply.

"Maurice! Can you hear me?"

"Y . . . yes."

A thin thread of hope spiraled through Gabriel. "I need your help."

Another groan rose up out of the darkness.

"They've taken Sara."

"What . . . can I . . . do . . . ?"

"Can you reach me?"

"I'll . . . try."

Minutes passed. Long, agonizing minutes while Maurice slowly inched toward Gabriel.

"The cross," Gabriel said, his voice a harsh rasp of pain. "Get rid of it."

It seemed as though hours went by while Gabriel waited for Maurice to summon the strength to lift his arm, to remove the heavy silver cross from his chest.

Gabriel closed his eyes in relief, felt a small measure of his strength return. Lying there, he put everything from his mind but his hatred, his rage. He let it build within him, filling him until it consumed him, and then, with a mighty flexing of his muscles, he broke the chains that bound him.

Staggering into the kitchen, he stripped off his clothes and boots and scrubbed away all trace of the holy water. His skin was badly burned; in places, it hung from him in shreds of charred flesh.

He needed blood.

Slowly, he made his way into Sara's bedroom. For a moment, he closed his eyes and inhaled, letting her scent wash over him. Moving carefully, he slipped on a loose-fitting black shirt and breeches. Returning to the kitchen, he pulled on his boots, then went into the parlor. He put on his cloak, then knelt beside Maurice. The man was barely breathing; the back of his skull had been crushed, his hair was soaked with blood.

"Delacroix?"

Maurice's eyelids fluttered open. "Sara?"

"I'll find her."

"You . . . look . . . half-dead . . ."

"I am dead," Gabriel said flatly.

A wry grin pulled at Maurice's lips. "Me . . . too . . ."

There was no point in lying to him, Gabriel thought. At best, Delacroix had only a few minutes to live.

"My blood . . ." Maurice whispered hoarsely. "Take it . . . find . . . Sara."

Gabriel shook his head. For all the hunger burning through him, as badly as he needed nourishment to heal his wounds and restore his strength, he could not take this man's blood. Not now.

"Do it," Maurice urged.

"Are you ready to die?"

Maurice stared up at Gabriel, knowing without words what Gabriel was asking him. "You can . . . save me?"

Gabriel hesitated. Under other circumstances, a little of his vampire blood would have revived Delacroix, but he was too near death now for that to be effective. "If you wish."

"Would you . . . make the choice . . . to be what you are . . . again?"

Gabriel stared out the window, his heart and mind searching for an answer. Would he make the same choice again? He thought of all he had seen and done in three and a half centuries, and then he thought of the endless darkness, the years of loneliness, the awful, unbridgeable gulf that stretched between himself and all of humanity. Between himself and the woman he loved.

Slowly, he shook his head. In 350 years, he had never bequeathed the Dark Gift to another soul.

"I don't know," he replied honestly, "but you must decide now, before it is too late."

"Will saving me . . . weaken you?"

"Yes."

In that moment, Maurice made his decision. Gabriel was Sara's only chance, and the vampire was right. There was no time to waste.

"Take . . . my blood . . ." Maurice's voice grew faint. "Save . . . Sara . . ."

"As you wish," Gabriel murmured. And then, because Sara's life depended on it, on him, Gabriel bent his head to Delacroix's neck, determined to fulfil Maurice's last request.

Gabriel spoke to Maurice's mind, soothing the young man's fear as his fangs pierced his flesh. Delacroix went limp in Gabriel's arms; moments later, Gabriel felt Maurice's heartbeat slow and grow labored as he quickly drained the life's blood from the younger man's body.

Before Delacroix's heart beat its last, Gabriel drew away. Sitting back on his heels, he watched the light fade from the young man's eyes, heard the last breath of life whisper past Maurice's lips, and with it, his very soul.

Rising, Gabriel wiped the blood from his mouth. "Forgive me," he murmured fervently. "I only pray I am not too late to save her."

# *Chapter Twenty-seven*

In the last half-hour before dawn, Gabriel carried Maurice's body into a run-down part of town and left it there, lying in an alley. The police would find him in the morning. His death would be blamed on one of the many robbers who frequented this side of town.

Returning to Sara's apartment, he cleaned up the blood, locked the door. And then, wrapped in his cloak, he crawled under her bed to wait for nightfall.

In those last moments before the deathlike sleep claimed him, he sought her thoughts, hoping to reassure her, but he found nothing. Either Nina had killed her or she was unconscious.

"Hang on, Sara," he whispered. "I'm coming."

She opened her eyes to darkness. The filthy cloth that covered her mouth tasted vile; it was hard to breathe, hard to swallow.

The endless darkness, the silence, filled her with unspeakable horror. Was this what it was like for Gabriel? But no, he had said it was like death—no thoughts, no dreams.

The earth beneath her was cold and damp. She flinched as something tiny and hairy crawled across her arm. Hours ago, she would have screamed, but her throat was raw and she had no voice left.

How long had she been in this hole? Was she going to die here?

She shuddered convulsively as she imagined herself trapped in this grave without food or water, quietly starving to death, her body growing weak, emaciated, while she went quietly mad, until the worms came to devour her flesh . . .

She shook the morbid thought aside, focusing all her thoughts on Gabriel. Surely he would come for her. If he could.

She remembered the creatures who had attacked them, and for the first time she wondered if Maurice was alive.

Had she caused his death, and Gabriel's, too? Would she die here, in this place?

Was it still night? She strained her ears, hoping to hear some sound that would tell her she wasn't alone. Even the company of those awful brutes who had abducted her would be welcome.

She tried to scream, to call for help, but no sound emerged from her throat.

*Gabriel, please help me. Gabriel, anybody, please, please, help me.*

Tears streaming down her cheeks, she closed her eyes and prayed for someone to find her before it was too late.

* * *

He moved through the night like the shadow of death, his face impassive, his eyes burning with the need for vengeance. He had drained Maurice of blood and it flowed through him, warm and vibrant with the memory of life.

He drew a deep breath, sifting the thousands of scents that assailed his nostrils, homing in on the one fragrance that was hers, and hers alone.

He felt his rage stir anew as he caught a whiff of Nina's heavy perfume, and mingled with it the pungent odor of unwashed bodies.

It took him less than an hour to find where they had taken Sara. Trust Nina to choose a graveyard for their last confrontation, he mused ruefully.

And then there was no more time to think. Like hulking beasts rising out of the mist, the mindless brutes Nina had created advanced toward him, their sunken eyes dead, soulless. But he was ready for them this time, and in less than a minute all six of them lay dead at his feet.

And then Nina was there, regal in a flowing gown of black silk. Her hair fell over her shoulders and past her waist like a river of darkness. Her skin was pale, luminescent in the light of the full moon; her eyes glowed with power and hunger and an implacable need for revenge.

"I'm here," he said, and his voice echoed off the gravestones. *I'm here, I'm here. . . .*

He didn't take his eyes off Nina as he let his mind probe the area for Sara's presence. A muscle twitched in his jaw as he caught her scent. He could feel her terror, smell the fear that paralyzed her.

"I am almost sorry you came, Gianni," Nina remarked. "I can't help but feel regret that I must destroy you."

"Change your mind." He let his glance slide over her, his expression insolent, provocative. "Let Sara go and I'll do whatever you wish."

"I told you before, it is too late for that."

"For our kind, it is never too late."

"How long, Gianni? How long would you stay with me?"

"As long as you wish."

"A hundred years? A thousand?"

"If you wish."

"You went on your knees before. Will you do so again?"

"Yes, *bella,* if that is what you want."

"I do."

Slowly, his pride rebelling, his soul filling with bitterness, Gabriel knelt at Antonina's feet.

"Speak pretty words to me, Giovanni," Nina demanded, her voice like satin over steel.

"You are the most beautiful, most desirable woman I have ever seen. There is none other like you in all the known world. Your luster outshines the sun. Your voice is like honey; your lips are like the finest wine . . ."

"You mock me!"

"I speak the truth."

"Liar! If your words were true, you would be here, in my arms where you belong, instead of begging me for the life of that mortal woman."

"Nina, even a vampire cannot chose whom he will love. I cannot deny my feelings for Sara, but I swear to you that I will do anything and everything you ask of me if you will only let her go."

"Will you make love to me, here, now?"

"Yes, *bella,* but only after you have released Sara."

"And will you return with me to Italy and swear not to return to France as long as the little ballerina is alive?"

"Yes."

Nina's eyes glowed, red and evil, and then softened as she stared at the man kneeling before her. He had not changed since she had seen him in Italy all those centuries ago. He was as young and virile and handsome as he had been then, with his dark gray eyes and smooth olive-hued skin. In a thousand years, she had not found another who stirred her blood as he did.

"Tell me the truth, Giovanni, for I will know if you lie. Do you have any true affection in your heart for me?"

"No."

She nodded, as though he had given her the answer she had expected.

"Your punishment will be long indeed, Gianni," she remarked. "For I shall demand your attention every waking minute for as long as you survive. You will be my slave. You will serve me, and hunt my prey. You will satisfy my every desire, and should you displease me while this mortal still lives, I shall return here and finish what I started." Her gaze bored into his. "Do we understand each other?"

"Yes."

"Come then, kiss me to seal our bargain."

Gabriel rose slowly to his feet, his mind replaying the distant past. He looked into Nina's eyes and wondered how he had ever found her desirable. There was no warmth in this woman, no life, no laughter.

Making love to her would be like making love to a corpse, and yet he would do it for Sara.

With an effort, he masked his distaste, took Nina in his arms, and slanted his mouth over hers. Her lips were as cold as the grave; her tongue tasted of death. He flinched imperceptibly as her arms slid possessively around his neck. Her skin felt cool and clammy.

She drew away for a moment; then, standing on tiptoe, she ran her tongue over the side of his neck. He felt the sharp prick of her fangs at his throat, shuddered with revulsion as she drew his blood into her mouth, and all the while a small voice in the back of his mind warned him that he must learn to submit without recoiling, that he must get used to the touch of her hands on his flesh, her teeth at his throat, her mouth on his.

Nina stepped back, her gaze intense, and he wondered if she could sense the depths of his revulsion.

"So, Giovanni," she remarked quietly, "we have sealed our bargain with your blood."

"And now you will keep your promise."

"Yes, as you will keep yours. She is there," Nina said, gesturing at a patch of uneven ground.

He was there in two long strides, removing the heavy block of sod, lifting Sara from the hole.

"Gabriel . . ." Her voice was hoarse, her face pale and haggard. "I knew you would come," she whispered, and collapsed in his arms.

Cradling her against his chest, Gabriel dropped to his knees, quickly removing the ropes that bound her, massaging her hands and feet.

"Leave her," Nina said curtly. "Leave her now and come to me."

Gabriel bit back his words of protest. Sara was not badly hurt, only frightened and exhausted; she would be all right.

Rising to his feet, he went to stand before Nina, his pride already rebelling at her imperious demands. In all the centuries since this woman had transformed him, no one had dictated what he would or would not do. But all that was changed now. He had surrendered control of his life to Nina in order to keep Sara safe.

But he would have his revenge. When Sara's life was no longer in danger, when she had passed through mortality and was beyond Nina's grasp, he would have his revenge.

"You remember your promise, Giovanni?" Nina asked archly. "You will be my slave. You will do whatever I wish, whenever I wish it."

"I remember."

She smiled benignly as she held out her hand. "Let us go, then. It is hours until dawn. We will hunt together, and then you will share my resting place."

"Yes, *bella.*" He took Nina's hand in his. It was cold and hard where Sara's was warm and filled with life. Heartsick that he must leave her behind, he fell into step beside Nina.

"No!" Sara's voice cut across the stillness of the night. "You can't have him! He's mine."

Nina whirled around, her face contorted with rage. "You dare defy me?"

Sara shook her head, frightened by the rage in the vampire woman's eyes.

"Then be still, mortal, before I destroy you."

"You will not touch her," Gabriel said, his hand tightening on Nina's. "Remember *your* promise."

"Gabriel, why are you going with her?"

"He's mine now," Nina said triumphantly. "He has vowed to be my slave for as long as he survives."

"No! He loves me."

"Love has nothing to do with our bargain," Nina retorted, her voice filled with disdain. "Now be gone before I destroy you."

"Is this what you want, Gabriel?" Sara asked.

"Yes."

"You're lying! You love me, not her."

"Nina spoke the truth, *cara.* Love has nothing to do with our bargain." But that, too, was a lie. Love had everything to do with it, his love for Sara.

"Come, Giovanni," Nina said, tugging on his hand. "I grow weary of this conversation."

"Gabriel, don't leave me!"

"I'm afraid I must," he said bitterly. "My mistress calls, and I must obey."

Sara knew suddenly what he had done; he had forfeited his freedom to spare her life. Had he been a mortal man, with a normal span of years, it would have been a sacrifice of untold worth, but Gabriel was a vampire. Thousands of years stretched before him, making his sacrifice beyond comprehension. She let her mind meld with his, felt the anger surging through him because Nina had the upper hand. She felt his anguish at losing her, his revulsion at the thought of spending endless nights as Nina's slave, swallowing his pride while she bent his will to hers.

Sara watched Gabriel turn away to follow Nina, and in that instant she knew she could not let him do it. Better she should forfeit the remainder of her short span of life than allow the man she loved with all her heart and soul to spend an eternity as a slave to this heartless vampire.

"No, Gabriel," she cried, and running after him, she wrenched his hand from Nina's. "I won't let you spend the rest of your life with this horrible woman on my account."

"You cannot stop him!" Nina cried, and summoning her revenant power, she lashed out at Sara, her hand striking her across the face, hurling Sara backward so that she fell against an ancient tombstone.

"Leave her alone!" Gabriel roared.

But Nina ignored him. She stared at Sara, the hatred blazing out of her eyes, burning into Sara's like a living flame.

Sara screamed and shielded her eyes as pain lashed through her.

Gabriel stood where he was, watching Nina's fury build, until every ounce of her energy was focused on the girl writhing helplessly on the ground. And then, with Sara's cries ringing in his ears, he picked up a splintered piece of wood and walked toward Nina. The wood seared his flesh, and he realized in some dim corner of his mind that it had once been a part of a cross.

But the pain scorching his hand was insignificant. His only thought was to put an end to Sara's agony.

"Nina."

He spoke her name quietly, yet it echoed like thunder in the stillness. Face contorted with anger, she whirled around to confront him, and he drove the stake through her heart.

For a moment that seemed to stretch into eternity, Nina stared up at him, her mouth open in a soundless cry of surprise, and then a torrent of blood spewed from her lips and she slowly spiraled to the ground.

In the space of a heartbeat, Gabriel was at Sara's side, drawing her into his arms, whispering her name over and over again. She huddled against him, sobs racking her body from head to heel, while he rocked her back and forth, one hand stroking her hair.

After a long while, she lay still in his embrace, her eyes closed, her arms wrapped tightly around his waist. Only then did he glance over his shoulder. There was no sign of Nina save for a handful of ashes, and even as he watched, a gust of wind caught them up and carried them away, so that nothing at all remained.

# Chapter Twenty-eight

Gabriel checked into the first hotel he saw. Fixing the desk clerk with a hard stare that proscribed any questions, he demanded a room, warned that they were not to be disturbed for any reason, then carried Sara swiftly up the stairs.

Once inside the room, he closed and locked the door. With gentle hands he undressed Sara, inwardly lamenting the horror she had endured.

She remained quietly acquiescent as a bath was prepared. He lifted her into the tub, then carefully washed her from head to foot. When he was satisfied that every speck of dirt and debris had been scrubbed from her hair and skin, he lifted her from the tub, dried her, then wrapped her in a blanket.

And still she didn't speak, not a word since he had carried her out of the cemetery. It was as if she had retreated deep into herself. He had done this to her, he thought bitterly. If he had stayed out of her life, none of this would have happened.

She didn't speak when he put her to bed, though she refused to let go of his hand. Murmuring her name, assuring her that everything would be all right, Gabriel held her in his arms until she fell asleep.

How fragile she was, he thought as his fingers skimmed her cheek. And yet, she had defied Nina, proving she had the courage of a tigress and the heart of a warrior.

Easing out of bed, he went to the window and stared into the darkness, but it was Nina's face he saw, her eyes wide with surprise and pain as he drove the stake through her heart. What had she felt in those last few moments as she felt her strength ebb, and where was she now? Had a benevolent being taken her soul to heaven, or was she even now roasting in the flames of perdition, doing penance for all the blood she had shed, all the lives she had destroyed?

What would be his fate when death finally claimed him?

He stood at the window until he sensed dawn approaching, and then he closed the heavy drapes and slid under the covers beside Sara.

Wrapping his arms around her, he drew her close, absorbing her goodness and warmth into himself, until the sun climbed over the horizon and darkness claimed him. Yet even in his deathlike sleep, he was aware of her beside him. It seemed her heart beat in rhythm with his and he knew, without knowing how he knew, that she slept at his side throughout the day.

A little before dusk, he opened his eyes to find her head pillowed on his shoulder. A moment later, her eyelids fluttered open. And then, to his delight, she smiled at him.

And then she frowned. "Where are we?"

"A hotel room."

She glanced at the window. "What time is it?"

"A little before dusk. You slept the day away, I'm afraid."

"Where's . . . what happened to . . . to Nina?"

"She's dead."

"You killed her?"

"Yes."

She didn't know what to say to that, so she said nothing. Her stomach growled loudly in the silence.

Gabriel smiled indulgently. "I think perhaps I should feed you."

"I *am* hungry," she allowed, and yet she couldn't help feeling guilty for thinking of something as mundane as food after what they'd been through the night before.

Gabriel's gaze moved over her face, lingering on her lips. "Shall I call for room service?"

"Maybe later." She paused a moment. "Where's Maurice?"

There was no easy way to say it, Gabriel thought, no way to take the sting from the words. "He's dead."

Sara shook her head, not wanting to believe even though she could see the truth of it in Gabriel's eyes.

"I'm sorry, Sara. He was a brave man. He loved you very much, more than you'll ever know."

"It's my fault," she said, her voice ragged with regret. "My fault that he's dead."

"No, *cara,* if it's anyone's fault, it's Nina's and she's paid for it."

Quiet tears slipped down Sara's cheeks as she

mourned the death of her friend.

"It's only because of Maurice that I was able to come after you," Gabriel told her, gently wiping away her tears. "We owe him a great deal, you and I." He caught her hands in his and pressed them to his lips. "Tell me what you want, Sara."

"What do you mean?"

"The danger is past now. There's no one to hurt you, and now you must decide what it is you want to do with your life."

"Don't you know? I want to spend it with you."

"Are you sure? I warned you once before that, once you were mine, I would never let you go. Are you prepared to be mine for as long as you live, to share my dark existence? Can you be happy with only me, knowing you will never have children, that I will be the only family you will ever have?"

"Yes, Gabriel." She stroked his cheek with her fingertips, then sealed her promise with a kiss. "I'll live only for you, dance only for you. I'll be your sunshine, as you'll be mine, and all my tomorrows will be yours."

Humbled, as always, by her love and her trust, Gabriel drew Sara into his arms and held her close to his heart. He would lay the world at her feet, shower her with love, and pray that his meager offerings would be reward enough for sharing the loneliness of his existence. Gazing into her eyes, he vowed to do all in his power to make her happy so that she would never have cause to regret her decision.

And then she was lifting her face to his, pressing her lips to his, and there was no more time for thoughts of the future; there was only the here and the now, and the woman in his arms.

She had spoken truly, he thought as he covered her mouth with his. She was his sunshine, the light to his darkness, and from this night forward, all their tomorrows would be one.

# PART TWO

## NOW AND FOREVER

# *Chapter One*

*Los Angeles, 1995*

He stood on the upper balcony of a mansion located in the hills overlooking Los Angeles, staring at the lights that stretched away as far as the eye could see. So many changes in the world since he had gone to ground half a century ago, he mused. Miraculous changes in science, in people and places. So many changes, while he had remained the same.

Upon rising from his fifty-five year rest, he had spent weeks reading newspapers and magazines from the world over in an effort to bring himself up to date. Only when he felt he had learned enough to function in this new age had he left Salamanca. He could not bring himself to stay in the castle now that Sara was gone.

His first instinct had been to go home to Italy, but nothing there had seemed familiar; the village where he had grown up no longer existed, and so he had left there, as well, and come to the United States, where there would be nothing to remind him of Sara, or of the life he had left behind so many years ago.

He had been a part of this new and modern world for less than a year, and already he didn't like it. Everything seemed transient, rushed, tawdry. Twentieth-century man seemed to be in a terrible rush. Food was cooked in minutes in microwave ovens, clothes no longer needed to be ironed, airplanes carried passengers from one end of the world to the other in a matter of hours. Everyone seemed in a hurry all the time, almost as if they were afraid to slow down for fear they would realize they had sacrificed quality for quantity, serenity for chaos.

There were, however, a few things the modern age had wrought that he liked very much. Television was one of them. Sports cars were another. One of the first things he had done upon arriving in the United States was to buy an automobile. He had learned to drive as effortlessly as he learned everything. He loved the speed, the thrill of driving a sleek sports car at a hundred miles an hour down a narrow ribbon of road in the dark of night, the countryside whipping past in a blur.

And yet, as much as he loved fast cars, there was no spiritual communion between machine and man as there was between horse and rider. The dark red Jaguar didn't nuzzle his arm or whinny a soft welcome. He didn't find the same pleasure behind the wheel of the car that he found on the back of his horse, and yet he loved the soft purr of the Jag's engine, the feel of the wind in his face as he roared down the highway.

He had been shocked by the change in fashion. Women paraded around in scandalously short pants and tops that barely covered their private parts, flaunting their bodies. Even dresses revealed more than they covered. And hair styles—he had been shocked the first time he had seen a woman with her hair cut above her ears. The fact that it was dyed a bright orange had hardly registered.

It had taken less time to grow accustomed to the change in men's attire. His clothing was sadly outdated, his flowing cloak no longer in style. He glanced down at the black T-shirt and snug-fitting jeans he now wore. He had to admit there was a certain comfort to these clothes that he liked, though they seemed shoddy when compared to the fine wools and linens he had once been accustomed to.

Yes, the world had changed. At first, he had been sorely tempted to go to ground again, certain that a 493-year-old vampire would never be able to adapt to such a fast-paced life.

But then he had discovered there were hordes of homeless people living on the city streets, men and women who would never be missed. A human buffet of sorts, he mused with a wry grin. Had he been so inclined, he could have killed and feasted every night without fear of reprisal.

He turned his back on the view and stared through the sliding glass door that led into the dark house beyond. Dark, he thought, like his life.

She had been dead for more than half a century, yet he felt her loss as keenly as if she had passed away only the day before.

Sara Jayne. If she had ever regretted her decision to spend her life with him, she had never admitted it.

As the years began to take their toll, he had begged her to accept the Dark Gift, but she had steadfastly refused. He had watched her grow old, watched her hair turn gray and her eyes grow dim while he stayed forever young, and yet he had loved her till the day she died, loved her wholly and completely. Toward the end, when he knew she had only hours left, he had begged her to pray for him, to ask whatever deity she believed in to be merciful to him.

They had shared 54 years together before she died in his arms. Even then Sara's last thought had been for him. Remembering how alone he had been when he first came to her in the orphanage, she had implored him to forgive her for leaving him behind, had urged him to find someone else to love.

He had buried her in the small graveyard behind the castle, in the coffin he had never used. And because he could not bear to leave her there, alone in the darkness, because he could not bear to face the world without her, he had taken care of his financial affairs, sold all his property save the castle, and then burrowed into the ground beside the casket that held her remains. He had slept there for over fifty years, sleeping away the years in the hope that the pain of her loss would have lessened when he emerged again.

It had been a futile hope; he had risen to a changed world, but his grief remained the same.

Now, gazing up at the stars, he imagined his Sara in heaven, smiling and serene, forever young, forever beautiful.

More than once, steeped in loneliness and despair, he had considered ending his existence; had he believed he had any chance at all of being reunited with Sara, he would have walked out into the sunlight years ago.

But he knew that nothing good awaited him when his existence finally ended. The best he could hope for was eternal darkness; his worst fear was that he would meet Nina in the bowels of an endless, fiery, unforgiving hell.

Upon rising from the earth, he had spent a month in the castle, but the emptiness, the loneliness, the knowledge that she was forever gone, had weighed heavily upon him. It had been torment of the worst kind to walk through the rooms she had brightened with her laugher and know she would never return, to know that she would never again be there, smiling to greet him when he rose each evening. He had arranged with a lawyer to handle his financial affairs as needed, and closed the castle.

He had spent his last night in Salamanca kneeling at Sara's graveside, bidding her a silent farewell as he relived the precious years they had spent together, and then he had fled Salamanca.

For a time, he had wandered from country to country, marveling at the changes that had taken place in the world while he had rested in the earth. Empires had crumbled, civilizations had disappeared, countries that had once been enemies had become allies. There had been much to learn, and for a time he had managed to bury his grief in the need to know. But the emptiness remained.

With a sigh, he shook his morbid thoughts from his mind. It was getting late, and the hunger was gnawing at his insides.

That, at least, had not changed.

# *Chapter Two*

She was there again, sitting alone on the gray stone bench, with only the moon for company. He had seen her in the small neighborhood park located at the end of a quiet cul-de-sac every night for the past week, felt himself drawn to her without knowing why. Perhaps it was the golden color of her hair, or simply the knowledge that she looked as lost and alone as he felt.

Tonight, she was crying. Silent tears washed down her cheeks as she stared at the swings silhouetted in the darkness. He noticed she made no move to wipe the tears away, only sat there in the dark, looking forlorn.

Before he quite realized what he was doing, he found himself walking toward her.

She looked up, startled, as he sat down beside her. He saw the sudden panic that flared in the depths of her dark brown eyes as she started to rise.

He placed a restraining hand on her arm. "Don't go," he said quietly.

She stared at him, her heart pounding wildly.

"Please," he said.

She shivered at the sound of his voice. It was deep and sexy and inexplicably sad. "Who are you?" She stared at his hand, alarmed by the strength of his grip. "What do you want?"

"I mean you no harm."

"Then let me go."

He held her a moment longer, then released his hold on her arm. "Stay a while," he urged.

"Why?" She glanced around, reassured by the presence of other people nearby. "What do you want from me?"

He shook his head. "Nothing. I saw you crying, and . . . you reminded me of someone I knew a long time ago."

She made a soft sound of disdain. "That's the oldest line in the book."

"So it is," he agreed with a wry grin. "It was old even when I was young."

She sniffed, wiping the tears from her eyes so she could see him more clearly. "You don't look so old to me."

"I'm older than you think," he replied ruefully. "Tell me, why do you weep?"

"Weep?" She laughed softly. In all her 23 years, she'd never heard anyone use that word except in books.

"You're crying," he said persistently. "Why?"

"Why do you care? You don't even know me."

He shrugged, bewildered by his attraction to this strange woman. And yet there was something about her that drew him, some indefinable essence that reminded him of Sara Jayne.

"I've seen you sitting here every night for the past week," he said with a shrug.

"Oh?"

He nodded. "I like to walk through the park in the evening," he said, his gaze lingering on the pulse throbbing in her throat.

"Don't you know it's not safe to wander around after dark in L.A.?"

"Don't you?"

"Maybe I'm hoping some pervert will come along and do me in," she retorted.

"Do you in?" He frowned at her as he sought to comprehend her meaning. Language, too, had changed drastically in the last half-century.

"Kill me," she said bluntly.

"You're not serious?"

She shrugged. "Maybe I am. Maybe I'm tired of living."

"You're so young," he muttered. "How could you possibly be tired of living?"

"Maybe because I've got nothing to live for."

She stared at the concrete path beneath her feet, wishing she had never been born. Everyone she had ever loved was dead. Why hadn't she died, too? What was there to live for now? A rainy night, a drunk driver, and she had lost her parents, her husband, her baby daughter.

"What's your name?" he asked. But he knew, knew what it would be even before she spoke.

"Sarah. What's yours?"

He hesitated a moment. "Gabriel."

"Well, Gabriel, it was nice to meet you, but I think I'll be going now."

"Will you be here tomorrow night?"

"I don't think so."

He watched her walk away, felt the pain and the despair that engulfed her, the all-encompassing sense of loneliness.

"Sarah, wait."

With an impatient sigh, she turned around, waiting for him to catch up with her. He was a tall man, with long black hair and dark gray eyes. He had the look of a foreigner, she thought, though she had detected no accent in his voice. Spanish, or maybe Italian, she decided, but she didn't really care.

"What do you want now?" she asked.

"Let me walk you home."

"Listen, Gabriel, I guess you're trying to be nice, but I'm really not in the mood for company, so why don't you just go away and leave me alone?"

"Very well," Gabriel said. Taking her hand, he bowed over it. "I'm sorry to have troubled you."

Sarah stared after him as he walked away, bewildered by his old-world courtliness. She took a few steps, then turned back, intending to apologize for her rudeness, but it was too late. He was gone.

She glanced around, wondering how he had disappeared so quickly, and then, with a sigh, she walked home, back to the quiet four-bedroom house that had once symbolized everything she held dear; a house that was empty now, as empty as her life.

Inside, she sat in the front room, sitting in the dark as she had every night since she got home from the hospital. She couldn't make herself sleep in the king-size bed she had shared with David, couldn't make herself go into the nursery. She didn't answer the phone, didn't open the mail, didn't turn on the television. She slept during the day so she wouldn't have to remember how full her life had once been.

Before the accident, each new day had been brimming with promise. On weekday mornings, she had spent a quiet half-hour with David before he went to work, packing his lunch, eating breakfast, kissing him good-bye. Shortly thereafter, Natalie would wake up, eager to be held. She'd been such a happy, contented baby, always smiling, her chubby fingers reaching out to grasp at life, eager to explore . . .

Sarah shook her head, willing the images away, not wanting to remember, unable to forget. She closed her eyes and the memory of a tiny white coffin resting amid three larger ones rose up to haunt her.

The tears came then, and she huddled in a corner of the sofa, steeped in misery, wishing the stranger she'd met in the park had been the depraved killer she had read about in the paper a few days before the accident. The woman in the story had claimed that a monster with red eyes had attacked her in an alley and bitten her in the neck. "Just like Dracula," she had claimed.

Sarah frowned. Perhaps, subconsciously, she'd been hoping to run into the blood-sucker when she started walking in the park at night.

Just before sleep claimed her, she found herself thinking of the strange man in the park. There had been a world of sadness in the depths of his dark gray eyes, but she had been too caught up in her own misery to spare a thought for his.

Now, on the brink of sleep, she wondered if he,

too, had lost a loved one. If he, too, had been wandering in the dark, searching for oblivion.

She dreamed of him that night, odd, fragmented dreams that made no sense upon awaking, but then, dreams never made sense in the cold light of day.

For a little while, she stared up at the ceiling, trying to remember what the dreams had been about, but all she could remember was the sound of his voice, lost and alone, whispering her name, and the sadness in his eyes, a sorrow that went beyond grief, beyond pain. An endless eternity of sadness, she thought.

Sarah glanced at the window, saw that it was almost dawn, and drew the covers up over her head, shutting out the light, turning her back on the memories that crowded in on her.

She went back to the park that night. Sitting on the hard stone bench, she stared at the swings, wondering why she did this to herself. On one level, she told herself she didn't want to remember, yet she came here every night and stared at the swing, remembering the sound of Natalie's laughter as her grandmother pushed her in the swing, higher and higher . . .

She knew he was there even before he appeared beside the bench. Looking up at him, she refused to admit that she had come to the park that night hoping to see him again.

"Good evening," Gabriel said. He gestured at the bench. "May I?"

She shrugged. "It's a free country."

He was wearing black again. Black T-shirt, black

jeans, black cowboy boots. Somehow, she couldn't imagine him in any other color. He was dark and mysterious, like the night, she thought fancifully, and black suited him very well.

"How are you this evening, Sarah?" he asked, and his voice was warm and thick, like sun-baked honey.

"I'm all right."

Gabriel shook his head. "I don't think so."

"You don't know anything about me," she snapped.

"I know you're grieving."

"How do you know that?"

"I can feel your pain, Sarah, your sorrow."

"That's impossible."

"Is it? You've lost loved ones who were very dear to you. A husband, a child."

She stared at him, her dark brown eyes mirroring her confusion, her anxiety. "How can you possibly know that?"

He smiled faintly. "I have a talent for reading minds."

"I don't believe in that kind of thing."

"You lost your parents, too, and you feel guilty because they died and you didn't. You come here in the evening because your house is empty, and the nighttime hours are too long and too lonely."

He had frightened her now. He could see it in the sudden tensing of her shoulders, in the way she held herself, rigid and poised for flight.

"How can you know that?" she demanded, her anger overriding her fear.

"I told you, I have the ability to divine your thoughts."

"What am I thinking now?"

"You're wishing a policeman would come by."

Sarah laughed softly. "Not likely at this time of night. They're all at Winchell's having donuts and coffee."

He laughed with her, the first time he had laughed in years, and it felt good.

The smile transformed his face, and for the first time Sarah realized that he was quite a handsome man. Feeling as though she were being disloyal to David, she quickly put the thought from her mind.

"I'd better go," she said.

"I mean you no harm, Sarah."

"I know, but . . . I'm not . . . I can't . . ." She stood up, her arms crossed over her breasts. "Good night."

He watched her walk away, and then he dissolved into a dark mist and followed her home. He stood in the shadows outside her house until he was sure she was safely inside. Only then did he turn away, hoping desperately that he would see her again.

She went to the park the next night, and the next, and the next, not knowing what it was about this strange man that drew her back to him night after night. She only knew that he seemed familiar somehow, that his very presence soothed her in some indefinable way.

Their relationship was a strange one. They sat side by side, rarely speaking, yet each drawing comfort from the other's presence.

After two weeks, Gabriel had decided their nightly encounters were destined to go on that way indefinitely, with the two of them meeting and not speaking; more than strangers, less than friends. And yet, for him, for now, it was enough. Meeting Sarah each evening gave purpose to his life, gave him something to look forward to.

And then she showed up late one night, her face whiter than new-fallen snow, her eyes shadowed and red, her whole demeanor one of abject despair.

Gabriel rose to his feet as she walked toward him, alarmed by her appearance. "Sarah, what is it?"

She stared up at him, her arms hanging limply at her sides. "It's July first," she said, her voice ragged.

Gabriel nodded, not comprehending.

"It would have been our fourth anniversary." Tears welled in her eyes and cascaded down her cheeks. "Natalie would have been two."

"Sarah . . ."

"Why?" She screamed the word at him. "Why did it happen?" Sobs shook her body as she pummeled his chest with her fists. "Why didn't we stay home that night? Why didn't I die, too?"

She hit him again and again, needing to vent her anger, to unleash the rage she had kept carefully bottled up for the past six months. And all the while she asked the same question over and over again: Why, why, why?

He had no answer, only stood there while her tightly clenched fists pounded against his chest and tears streamed down her cheeks, until she collapsed against him, like a puppet whose strings had been cut.

Murmuring her name, he swept her into his arms and cradled her against his chest, holding her effortlessly.

And still the tears came, with no sign of letting up.

Gabriel glanced around. There weren't many people wandering through the park at this time of night—a couple of kids pawing each other in the shadows, a vagrant snoring beneath a tree—yet Gabriel felt the need to get her inside, away from prying eyes.

Settling her more firmly in his arms, he started walking.

It took several minutes for Sarah to realize they were leaving the park. "Where are you going?"

"I'm taking you home."

"No! I can't go back there." She couldn't face that dark, empty house, couldn't face the memories that were waiting to engulf her. She shuddered, as though overcome with a chill. "Not tonight."

"All right."

She went limp in his arms, trusting him without knowing why, or maybe simply too emotionally wrung out to care what happened to her.

She closed her eyes, her cheek resting against his chest. Cool air feathered over her face as he walked along, his footsteps light and even, as if he were floating instead of walking. She seemed to hear his voice inside her mind, urging her to relax, to rest, assuring her that everything would be all right. And she believed him. It felt good to have someone taking care of her again, even if that someone was a stranger.

He'd gone only a few blocks when he felt the tension drain out of her and knew she'd fallen asleep.

It was a long walk to the mansion, but he carried her easily, using the power of his mind to cloak their presence as a police car drove by.

The door of the mansion opened at his bidding, then closed behind him. He carried her up the long, winding staircase and down the hall to the bedroom at the end of the spacious corridor.

She stirred as he bent over the bed to draw back the covers, her eyelids fluttering open, her brown eyes wide and bewildered as she looked up at him.

"Where are we?"

"You didn't want to go to your house, so I brought you to mine."

She knew a moment of gut-wrenching fear. For some reason, it had been easy to trust him out in the open, but here, in this unfamiliar room, she felt trapped, defenseless.

"No," she said, her voice too high, "I can't stay here."

His dark gaze held hers. "Go to sleep, Sarah," he said quietly. "You've nothing to fear."

And once again, she believed him without knowing why. She felt suddenly weightless, limp. Her eyelids fluttered down. She sighed once, and then she was asleep.

Gabriel stood at the foot of the bed, watching her for a long while. He seemed to have a habit of picking up orphans and strays, he thought ruefully, but there was something about this girl that called to him. Perhaps it was merely that her hair was the same color as Sara Jayne's had been. Or perhaps it was because this Sarah, too, was alone in the world. Whatever the reason, he felt an irresistible urge to comfort her.

Shortly before dawn, he drove to the all-night market and bought a variety of foodstuffs—an assortment of breakfast cereal, fruit, milk, instant coffee, tea, bread, butter, jelly, eggs, cheese. A jar of bubble bath that smelled like wildflowers, a bar of scented soap. A bottle of dark red wine.

Food had changed, too, he thought as he dumped

a package of meat into the wobbly shopping cart. Bread came already sliced and neatly wrapped in plastic. Milk came in various-sized containers, though he couldn't remember seeing any cows in the vicinity. Not only that, but there were now all kinds of milk: low fat, no fat, whole, raw, homogenized. In his youth, there had been but one kind of milk, the kind that came straight out of the cow, unless one preferred the milk of goats.

He tried to remember what eating three meals a day had been like as he drove home; tried to remember the taste of bread, of butter, of eggs and cheese, as he carried the brown paper bags into the kitchen and began to put things away. But he had no recollection of tastes or textures, save for the vague memory of forcing himself to eat a meal Sara Jayne had prepared for him a century ago, and all he really remembered of that experience was going outside to vomit it back up.

He grinned wryly as he opened the refrigerator. He had lived in this place for three months and this was the first time he had used the refrigerator to hold anything other than an occasional bottle of wine.

The sun was climbing over the horizon when he made his way down the short flight of stairs that led to what had once been a wine cellar.

Opening the door, he stepped inside, then bolted the door behind him, wondering if she would still be there when he woke that evening.

# *Chapter Three*

Sarah woke with a start, the last images of her nightmare clinging like cobwebs to the corners of her mind. It had been a horrible dream, filled with blazing red eyes, fangs dripping blood, and the frantic sounds of her own screams. The kind of nightmare she would have expected to have after seeing *Interview with the Vampire*. Most shocking of all was that the dream, while frightening in its intensity and realism, had seemed vaguely familiar.

Sitting up, she glanced around at her surroundings. The bedroom was huge, bigger than her own bedroom and living room combined. The walls were papered in a pale rose print. There were heavy damask drapes at the windows. An antique mahogany armoire took up most of one wall. A matching vanity table and chair stood in a corner. She thought it odd that the mirror had been removed. A delicate crystal lamp stood on the nightstand on the left side of the bed. In another corner, two cozy chairs covered in the same rose print as the wallpaper faced each other across a small glass-topped table.

She remembered where she was now. Gabriel had brought her here late last night. Not surprising, then, that it had been his face she had seen in her dreams.

She glanced around, looking for a clock, wondering what time it was.

Swinging her legs over the side of the bed, she stood up. A thick mauve-colored carpet muffled her footsteps as she walked to the window and drew back the drapes. She stared at the crimson sunset for a moment, the flame-colored sky reminding her of blood. Impossible as it seemed, she had slept the day away.

Directly below, she could see a rose garden that had long been neglected. Tree-covered hills rose beyond the high brick walls that circled the mansion. There was an Olympic-size swimming pool to the right, a dark red barn off to the left. A big black horse stood hip-shot in the adjacent corral.

Whoever Gabriel was, he had money. Turning away from the window, she let the curtains fall back into place and came face to face with the man who had haunted her dreams not only last night, but for the past three weeks, as well.

"Good evening," he said formally.

"Hi."

He was dressed in black again, and though he looked roguishly handsome, Sarah couldn't help wondering if he owned anything besides black T-shirts and jeans. Thinking of his attire made her acutely conscious that she had slept in her clothes, that she hadn't brushed her teeth since yesterday morning, that she needed a shower.

"The bathroom's in there," Gabriel said, indicating a closed door to her left.

It was disconcerting, his being able to read her thoughts so easily. She had a childish impulse to stamp her foot and tell him to stop it.

"Enjoy your bath." He left the room on silent feet—bare feet, she noticed, with some surprise.

For a moment, she stared after him; then she went into the bathroom. It was unlike anything she had ever seen. The last rays of the setting sun filtered through the skylight. The walls were papered in the same print as the bedroom. An oversized pink bathtub, oval in shape, stretched across one wall; the fixtures were gold. There was an enclosed shower, a pale pink toilet, two sinks, also pink. She found a fluffy white towel and a washcloth folded on the marble sink top, along with a bar of scented soap, a tube of toothpaste, and a toothbrush.

After locking the door, she turned on the water, then stripped off her clothes while she waited for the tub to fill. Noticing a jar of bubble bath, she sprinkled some into the water, watching as millions of rainbow-hued bubbles rose to the surface.

Feeling like a queen, she turned off the tap and sank down into the water, sighing as the bubbles surrounded her with a light flowery fragrance.

She thought it strange that were no mirrors in the bathroom, not even on the beautiful carved medicine cabinet. She wondered if he had some kind of phobia about seeing his reflection.

Closing her eyes, she let her thoughts drift. Who was Gabriel? Why was he taking care of her? Did he live here alone? If so, what was he doing with floral bubble bath and scented soap? If not, where was his wife or girlfriend?

She soaked in the tub until the water grew cool, washed quickly, then stepped out of the tub and wrapped herself in the fluffy bath sheet, wishing she had a change of clothing and underwear.

Returning to the bedroom, she saw that her clothes were gone; in their place was a dressing gown of deep rose pink velvet.

She experienced an odd sense of déjà vu as she ran her hand over the rich material, thinking it had probably cost more than her entire wardrobe. She looked around and then, unable to resist, she put it on. It felt wonderful against her skin, light and soft. Luxurious and expensive.

She had just zipped it up when there was a knock at the door.

"Sarah?"

"Yes."

"Would you care to come downstairs and have a glass of wine?"

"Yes, thank you."

She opened the door to find him standing in the hall, dressed in the same form-fitting jeans and T-shirt as before. She glanced at his bare feet. There was something incredibly intimate about the fact that neither of them was wearing shoes. The thought brought a quick flush to her face.

An emotion she couldn't put a name to flickered in Gabriel's dark gray eyes before he turned away. Thick white carpet muffled her footsteps as she followed him down the stairs, through another hall, and into a large, high-ceilinged room.

She glanced around the room while he poured two

glasses of wine. An enormous marble fireplace took up one entire wall. Flames danced and crackled in the hearth. A huge crystal chandelier reminiscent of one she'd seen in a play hung from the ceiling. The carpet beneath her feet was the same white plush that covered the hallways. *White carpeting,* she thought, and wondered absently how he kept it clean. Dark green drapes covered the windows.

There was no furniture in the room save for an antique oak side table, one overstuffed easy chair covered in a dark green print, and a big-screen TV.

A graceful archway opened onto an entry hall inlaid with black marble.

Gabriel studied her face as he handed her a glass filled with dark red wine. He sensed her nervousness at being alone with him in the house, and wondered what he could say to put her at ease.

Sarah murmured her thanks as she accepted the wine. She glanced around the room again, wondering why there were no pictures on the walls, no mirrors, no clocks. There was, in fact, nothing of a personal nature in the room. "Have you . . . have you lived here long?"

"A few months."

"It's a lovely house."

Gabriel shrugged. He had bought the mansion shortly after his arrival in Los Angeles. He had been unimpressed when the real estate agent told him it had once belonged to a very famous but reclusive movie star. He had bought the house on a whim simply because the design and the gardens had reminded him of a villa he had once owned in Italy.

"Are you married?" Sarah asked.

"No."

She didn't miss the deep sadness, the loneliness, that clung to that single word.

"Divorced?"

"No."

"Living with someone?"

He frowned. "No, why do you ask?"

"The bedroom . . . it seems . . . I mean . . . never mind, it's none of my business."

His gaze caught and held hers. "I decorated it for you."

Sarah took a step backward, frightened by the fervor in his eyes, the intensity of his voice. "For me? How? Why?"

"I knew . . ." He paused a moment. "That is, I hoped, that you would come here one day."

"But we've only known each other a few weeks."

He shrugged. "With enough money, you can accomplish a great deal in a short time. You'll find clothes in the armoire."

Sarah took another step backward, wondering why she felt as though she had been thrust into a strange and alien world. She remembered bits and pieces of an old French movie she'd seen in which a man had sold his daughter to a beast. The girl had lived in luxury, but she had been a prisoner just the same.

She shook the fanciful notion from her mind. Gabriel didn't look like a beast, and she was free to leave whenever she wished. Wasn't she?

She glanced at the oversized door visible at the end of the entry hall. It was at least eight feet high and made of solid oak. To keep the world out, she wondered, or to keep her in? She told herself she was being foolish, that she was letting her imagination run wild, but she couldn't shake the feeling that if she didn't get away now, she never would, that she would be imprisoned, like Belle in *Beauty and the Beast* except, in this case, the beast was beautiful.

"I want to go home."

He hesitated a moment, as if he meant to argue with her, and then he nodded. "I'll take you."

"No."

"Sarah . . ."

He took a step toward her, and she whirled around, the glass in her hand forgotten as she darted toward the front door. Wine sloshed over the rim of the delicate crystal goblet, splashing over the white carpet to leave a blood-red stain.

Frantic, she ran down the long marble entryway to the front door. She grabbed the ornate brass knob, twisting it right and left, but nothing happened. Overcome with panic, she dropped the glass, heedless that it shattered into a thousand pieces. She tugged on the door knob, tears of fright and frustration blurring her vision.

And then he was behind her, his hands heavy on her shoulders.

"Sarah. Sarah!" He turned her around and pulled her up against him, his arms imprisoning her as effectively as iron bars. "Listen to me. I'm not going to hurt you, I swear."

He looked down at her, and the sheer unadulterated terror in her eyes stabbed him to the heart. Abruptly, he released her and took several steps backward.

"I'm not going to hurt you," he said again. "Please believe me. You're free to go."

"The door . . . it won't open . . . I can't get

out . . . please let me go. . . ."

Moving slowly, careful not to touch her in any way, he reached around her and unlocked the door.

"My car is in the driveway," he said.

Sarah blinked up at him. "You'd let me take your car?"

"It's dark out," he said, his voice quiet and devoid of emotion. "I don't want you walking home alone."

"What I do is none of your concern."

He inclined his head, as if agreeing with her, and then he pulled a set of car keys out of his pocket and pressed them into her hand.

He really was the most stubborn, intriguing, handsome man she had ever met, Sarah mused as she slid behind the wheel of the car. A Jaguar. A brand-new Jaguar was worth a small fortune, and he was letting her take it, no questions asked. She thought of the six-year-old station wagon parked in the garage at home. Never had she imagined herself behind the wheel of a car like this.

She turned the key in the ignition and the engine hummed to life.

She drove slowly toward home, wondering what would happen if she just kept on driving, if she left her old life behind and lit out for parts unknown. Montana, maybe, or Colorado. Or maybe Alaska . . .

For a moment, it was tempting. She could sell the Jag, change her name, start a whole new life . . . but she was only kidding herself. She couldn't run far enough, couldn't hope to find a place where she could hide from her memories.

When she reached home, she moved the station wagon to the driveway, parked the Jag in the garage, and locked the door.

She thought of Gabriel as she tossed his car keys on the coffee table. What kind of man let a complete stranger borrow a $70,000 car? He hadn't even said anything about her bringing it back.

She glanced down at the dressing gown she still wore. Whom had it belonged to? He'd said he wasn't married or divorced. Did it belong to an old girlfriend, then? She caressed the soft velvet gown.

*I decorated it for you.*

His voice, soft and sensual, echoed in her mind. He had decorated a room in his house for her. Had he bought the dressing gown with her in mind, as well? How had he known pink was her favorite color?

She sat down on the sofa and switched on the TV. She didn't want to think, not about David and Natalie, not about Gabriel.

But she couldn't concentrate on the late show. It was an amusing romantic comedy starring Gene Wilder, but she was in no mood for romance, or laughter.

Reaching for the remote, she ran through the channels until she came to the country music station. She listened for a while, wondering why country songs were all so sad. It seemed nine out of ten were about love—lost love, unrequited love, old love. Maybe the whole world was unhappy, she thought. Maybe there was no such thing as happy-ever-after, not for her, not for anyone.

She stared at the television, not seeing the picture, not hearing the music. Instead, she saw the sharp planes and angles of Gabriel's face. His countenance was dark and beautiful, reminding her of a painting she had once seen of a fallen angel. Her mind replayed the hours she had spent with him, and she recalled the faint note of sorrow in his voice, the lingering aura of grief in the depths of his eyes. Was he mourning, too? He had told her he wasn't married or divorced. She wondered now if he had been married, if his wife had died, if that was why his eyes mirrored her own misery.

"Gabriel . . ."

She murmured his name aloud as she pillowed her head on her arm, rubbing her cheek against the velvet of the gown.

"Gabriel . . ."

Her eyelids fluttered down, and for the first time in six months, she didn't cry herself to sleep.

Filled with an overpowering restlessness, he walked through the spacious rooms of the mansion, imagining Sarah sitting in front of the fireplace in the parlor, bathing in the pale pink tub, sleeping in the bed, reading a book in the library, watering the plants in the garden by the light of the moon, lying naked in his arms . . .

He pushed the thought aside, remembering the terror he had seen in her eyes the night before. If she looked at him like that now, when she hardly knew him, he could only imagine the horror he would read in her eyes if she discovered what he was. But that would never happen. Never again would he become involved with a mortal woman.

And yet, like it or not, he was already involved. He had been able to think of nothing else since the first night he had seen her sitting on the bench in the park, looking lost and forlorn, her eyes damp with tears.

Except for the color of her hair, there was little physical resemblance to Sara Jayne, and yet there was something about this Sarah that called to him, that begged his attention.

Muttering an oath, he left the house. For a moment, he stood outside, breathing in the cool night air, and then he made his way to the corral, whistling for the stallion.

The big black horse trotted up to him, blowing softly as he nuzzled Gabriel's chest.

Opening the corral gate, Gabriel swung onto the stallion's bare back. He had no need of bridle or bit to control the horse, only the sound of his voice and the pressure of his knees. He patted the horse's neck, then rode out of the yard, heading for the hills behind the mansion.

He rode for an hour, his inner turmoil soothed by the motion of the horse, the wind in his face. He refused to think of the past. He was uneasy with the present; the future was a door that even he couldn't open.

Sounds and sights and smells surrounded him and he sorted them without conscious thought: the distant screech of brakes, the growl of a dog, the soft whirring of wings as an owl hunted the night. He saw the yellow eyes of a cat watching him as he passed by; he caught the combined aroma of cigarettes and perfume and lust as he rode by a parked car. It took little imagination to guess what was going on behind the steamy windows, and he felt a sudden ache in his loins, a need to be held. Sara . . .

He remembered the night he had knelt at her feet, his head pillowed in her lap, as he begged her to hold him. How long ago that had been!

Heavy-hearted, he turned the black toward home.

He knew she was there even before he rode into the yard. And then he saw her, standing on the veranda that looked out over the gardens, her long blond hair falling over her shoulders, her skin glowing in the light of the moon. Desire flooded through him once more, sharp and painful.

He reined the stallion to a halt beside the corral, then sat there, staring up at Sarah, wondering what she wanted.

His gaze held hers for a long moment, and then she turned away from the rail and descended the stairs that led to the backyard.

He felt his heart beat with anticipation as he watched her approach.

"Pretty horse," she said, stopping well out of reach of the stallion.

Gabriel nodded.

"I've never seen anyone ride without a bridle or saddle."

"He's well trained."

"He must be. What's his name?"

"Necromancer." It had been the name of all his horses.

"Necromancer?" She lifted one finely arched brow. "Funny name for a horse. Doesn't it mean someone who talks to the spirits of the dead?"

Gabriel closed his eyes. For a moment, he was swept back in time, hearing Sara Jayne's voice asking him the same question, remarking that it was a funny name for a horse, and his own reply, *Odd, perhaps, but fitting.*

He ignored Sarah's question and asked one of his own. "What are you doing here?"

"I brought your car back."

He lifted one skeptical black brow.

Sarah fidgeted under his probing gaze. Maybe he really could read her mind, she thought. And if that was true, then he knew she was lying. He had been in her thoughts constantly since last night; and if she was going to be entirely truthful, then she would have to admit that he had been in and out of her thoughts ever since the first night they met.

Gabriel lifted his right leg over the horse's withers and slid gracefully to the ground. He gave the horse an affectionate pat on the shoulder, and the stallion trotted into the corral.

Without taking his gaze from Sarah's face, Gabriel closed the gate and slid the latch into place.

Sarah clasped her hands together. Gabriel's nearness, the heat in his unblinking stare, made her decidedly nervous. Why *had* she come here? If all she had wanted to do was return his car, she could have brought it back in the morning and left it in the driveway.

Her hands felt clammy, her mouth dry. She could feel her heart beating wildly in her breast, feel the blood pounding in her ears. She stared into his eyes, eyes as gray as a winter day, as hot as the summer sun. His gaze held hers for a long while, then moved down to her lips, to the pulse beating rapidly in her throat.

"Why are you here?" His voice was dark and smooth and soft, like rich black silk.

"I'll see that you get the robe back, too." she replied, wishing she could make herself look away from his eyes.

"Keep it."

"I couldn't. It must have cost a great deal."

"It's yours," he said, sounding angry now. "I bought it for you."

"Like you decorated that room?"

"Yes."

*Black*, she thought. He was wearing black again. Not jeans and a T-shirt this time, but a heavy black sweater that emphasized the width of his shoulders. Black sweat pants hugged his long, muscular legs. Looking at him, she had the uncomfortable feeling that his constant wearing of black was not merely a fashion statement, but the color of his soul.

He crossed his arms over his chest. "You didn't answer my question."

How could she tell Gabriel why she was here? How could she confess that she had gone to the park hoping to see him there, and when he hadn't shown up, she had come looking for him, needing to see him because he knew why she sought the darkness, because he understood her grief. Because his arms were strong and invincible and his voice was low and soft.

Sarah licked her lips nervously. "I thought you could read my mind."

"I'd rather hear it from you."

"It's like I said, I brought your car back. Thanks for letting me take it."

"Liar." His quiet tone took the sting out of the word.

She glared at him, resenting him because he knew the truth, because he made her feel alive again.

"Why, Sarah?"

"All right, I missed you!" She practically screamed the words at him. "I'm lonely, and I missed you. Is that what you wanted to hear? Does it stroke your male vanity?"

Muttering an oath, he took a step toward her, but she took a hasty step in retreat.

"Thanks for the use of the Jag," she said, and lifting her arm, she threw the car keys at him, then turned and ran for the heavy iron gate that led to the street.

"Sarah."

His voice. Just the sound of his voice speaking her name. But it brought her to an abrupt halt. She didn't turn around, didn't acknowledge that he'd spoken, just stood there, waiting, her heart beating a wild tattoo.

He made no sound, but she knew he was standing behind her, and then she felt his hands, his long fingers curling over her shoulders, sliding down her arms, sending shivers up and down her spine, and he breathed her name.

"No." She shook her head. "I can't. I don't even know you . . ." She gasped as his arms slid around her waist, drawing her close so that her back was snug against his chest. "It's too soon . . ."

He drew in a deep, shuddering breath as he rested his chin on the top of her head. His body sprang to life at her nearness; his nostrils filled with the scent of her skin, of scented soap and shampoo. He could hear the rapid beat of her heart, hear the blood thrumming through her veins, warm and sweet with the vitality of life. To his dismay, he felt the bloodlust stir within him, hotter and stronger than his burgeoning desire for her flesh.

"Please," she murmured, "please let me go. I . . . I don't even know your last name."

"Ognibene." His breath was hot against the side of her neck.

"Is that . . ." She swallowed against the dryness of her throat. His arms had settled around her waist, holding her firmly against him. She cleared her throat. "Is that Italian?"

"Yes."

"You're from Italy, then?" She was babbling, but she couldn't think clearly, not with his arms around her, not with his breath feathering against her cheek. He smelled of the wind, of musky male sweat, of the night itself.

"Near Vallelunga."

"Never heard of it."

She shifted in his grasp, as though testing the strength of his hold, and he let his arms fall to his sides, though his body was still pressed intimately against hers.

Gabriel held his breath, waiting. He could feel her indecision, knew that she was as aware of the charged atmosphere between them as he was. She wanted him. And he wanted her, wanted her with every fiber of his being.

Sarah worried her lower lip with her teeth, wishing his arms were still holding her because now she had to make the decision whether to remain with her back resting against his chest, or to move away.

Prudence urged her to break all contact with this strange man, to run out the gate and never look back, but every feminine instinct begged her to stay where she was, to rest her head against his shoulder, to let him wrap his arms around her once more and hold her tight.

And then he made the decision for her. Gently but

firmly, he gave her a little push.

"Go home, Sarah," he said, his voice harsh, taut with an emotion she did not understand. He reached into his pocket and withdrew a twenty-dollar bill, which he pressed into her hand. "Get a cab and go home while you still can."

"But . . ."

His eyes burned into hers. "Stay away from the park, Sarah," he whispered savagely. "Stay away from me!"

She stared at him for a long moment, her eyes filled with confusion, and then she turned and ran for the garden gate.

He stood in the moonlight long after she had gone. On this night, he did not worry about her getting safely home. It was not yet late, and she was in far more danger from him than from anyone else she might encounter.

Hands clenched, his body rigid, he closed his eyes while the lust for blood roared through him. He grimaced as his fangs lengthened in anticipation of the hunt.

Sarah . . .

He knew why she had come to him tonight even if she refused to admit it.

Unbidden to his mind came the memory of Sarah crushed against him, her back pressed to his chest, her buttocks cradled by his thighs. The beating of her heart had sounded like thunder in his ears. Even now, he felt his desire stir to life as he remembered the scent of her blood, the heat of her living flesh.

"Stay away from the park, Sarah," he murmured, repeating the words he'd spoken earlier. "Stay away from me."

But this time the words were a plea, not a warning.

# *Chapter Four*

She had the cab drop her off at the corner market on the way home. For the first time in months, she had an appetite, not for what her mother had called "real food," but to fill a sudden, unaccountable craving for Oreo cookies.

At home, she went into the kitchen and poured a tall glass of milk, then sat down at the table and opened the package, knowing she'd regret her lack of willpower the next time she stepped on a scale.

Relishing every bite, she polished off half the package, drained the glass, and then walked through the house, turning on the lights, the TV.

She dusted the furniture and vacuumed the rugs, cleaned out the refrigerator, wrinkling her nose in distaste as she threw away an unidentified blob of something hard and brown. She scrubbed the kitchen sink, the bathroom sink and the tub, emptied the trash.

But she didn't go into the nursery. She couldn't face that room, shied away from the knowledge that, sooner or later, she'd have to take down the crib, pack Natalie's clothes in boxes, and admit that she was never coming back.

It was near midnight when Sarah treated herself to a long hot bubble bath. She closed her eyes, and into her mind came the memory of a spacious bathroom and a pale pink tub.

She would not think of him, or the room he professed had been decorated solely for her.

Wrapped in a towel, she stared at the velvet dressing gown she had tossed over a chair, vacillating between folding it up and shoving it in a drawer, or putting it on. Finally, with a huff of disdain for her weakness, she slipped it on, her hands gliding over the rich fabric.

Swathed in luxurious velvet, she sat on the sofa and searched the channels until she found an old movie.

Moments later, she was asleep.

And sleeping, began to dream.

Of being confined to a wheelchair.

Of dancing *Swan Lake* with a handsome young man.

Of flames licking at her skin.

Of a black-haired man kneeling at her feet, his head buried in her lap. She heard his words, bleak and edged with despair, as if all the sadness in the world was carried in his soul.

*Can you hold me, and comfort me, just for tonight?*

And a young woman's reply: *I don't understand.*

And then his voice again, filled with an aching

loneliness that tore at her heart: *Don't ask questions,* cara. *Please, just hold me.*

She woke with the afternoon sun shining in her face, and tears in her eyes.

And her first thought was for Gabriel.

She supposed she shouldn't be surprised to find that he had invaded her dreams again. He had, after all, been at the center of her thoughts ever since the first night she saw him in the park. But who was the girl in her dreams, the one in the wheelchair?

Her brow furrowed in a frown, she went into the kitchen and prepared breakfast, the first one she'd fixed since the accident.

Sitting down at the table, she ate the French toast, hardly tasting it. Who *was* Gabriel? It was obvious that he was rich. Filthy rich. He was also the most outrageously handsome man she had ever seen. And the most mysterious.

Last night, his words, the anger in his voice, had frightened her. *Go home while you still can,* he had said. *Stay away from the park. Stay away from me!*

And that was just what she intended to do. She had buried herself in her grief long enough. It was time to start living again, time to find a job.

She glanced around the cheery sunlit kitchen, remembering the happy Saturday mornings she had spent here, fixing breakfast for David and Natalie. It had been in this room where she had told David she was pregnant, in this room where Natalie had taken her first steps . . .

There was no help for it, she mused, she'd have to sell the house. She'd never be able to look ahead while she lived here, surrounded by memories.

A fresh start was what she needed. A new job. A new house. A new life . . .

Some of her optimism vanished as she considered the possibilities. She hadn't worked in four years. She hated moving. She didn't want a new life; she wanted her old one back again.

She wanted to see Gabriel.

With an effort, she put him from her mind. Rising from the table, she washed her few dishes, took a quick shower, and drove to the mall, telling herself she'd feel better if she got her hair done, had a manicure, and bought something new to wear.

He prowled the silent house, restless, edgy. Hungry. For blood. For the touch of a human hand. The love of a woman.

Sarah . . .

Over and over again, he paced from room to room. All were empty of furniture, of life, save for the front parlor and the bedroom he had furnished for Sarah.

Why had he bought this place, he wondered. What need had he of a mansion with eight bedrooms when he preferred to sleep in the quiet darkness of the cellar? He had no need of a kitchen or a formal dining room, no opportunity to sit in the glass-enclosed solarium and enjoy the beauty of a summer's day.

He stared out the window at the gardens, imagining Sarah there cutting a bouquet of roses, wandering along the narrow tree-lined paths, sitting in the swing, sunning herself near the goldfish pond.

Sarah.

Swearing softly, he turned away from the window. He wanted her, wanted her as he had wanted his other Sara. But he could not endure the pain of loving again, could not endure the agony of watching another woman die in his arms, her body ravaged by age or disease while he remained forever young, a mockery of life.

With a roar of impotent rage, he dropped to his knees and smashed his fist against the hearth, again and again, welcoming the pain that splintered through his hand and up his arm. Blood spurted from his knuckles, and he cursed himself for the monster he was, cursed the hunger that fed upon his anger, and fueled his unfulfilled desire.

For Sarah . . .

With an oath, he rose to his feet, needing to get out of the house. She had spent but one night here, and yet the walls whispered her name, the air was tinged with her perfume, his very soul had been branded with her essence.

On swift and silent feet, he walked the moon-dappled streets. Pity any poor human who stumbled across his path tonight, he thought darkly. For there was no compassion within him now, no mercy for those weaker than himself, only a terrible hunger coupled with a seething rage. He wanted to hurt someone as he was hurting, to drain the life out of another as the will to live was being drained from his soul.

For centuries, he had wandered the earth alone, with no one to love, no one to love him. And then he had found Sara Jayne, and she had given meaning to his existence, but, all too soon, death had claimed her. And now he, who had thought never to love again, had found another woman who warmed his heart, who possessed the same strength of spirit as the woman he had lost.

He stalked the darkness, drawn inevitably toward the park. Hoping, all the while, that she'd had the good sense to heed his warning and stay away.

His gaze pierced the darkness as soon as he entered the park. And she was there, a bright beacon in the blackness of the night.

He would leave, he told himself. He would stay just long enough to see her face, to breathe in her scent, and then he would leave.

On silent feet, he drew ever nearer, drawn toward her as though he had no will of his own.

And then he was there beside her, his whole being vibrating with her nearness as he sat down on the bench, warming himself in the welcome of her smile.

She didn't speak, but he read everything she was thinking, feeling, in the depth of her eyes. She was afraid. She was lonely. She needed comfort, the nearness of another being. She wanted him, and that frightened her more than anything else.

"Sarah . . ."

Trapped in the web of his gaze, she slowly shook her head. "I can't. I'm afraid."

"Of me?"

"Yes."

"I won't hurt you," he promised, and hoped it was a vow he could keep.

"I don't even know you," she retorted, angry with him for making her feel alive again, angry with herself for wanting this man when David was dead.

But he knew her. He looked deep into her eyes, and he knew her. Recognition mingled with shock. The improbability, the possibilities, struck him with the force of a blow. He knew her. She was older than when they'd met before. Her eyes were brown instead of blue. She had known another man. But her heart and soul remained the same.

Sara Jayne.

The wonder of it rocked him to the core of his being.

"What's wrong?" Sarah asked, alarmed by the sudden intensity of his gaze.

Slowly, he shook his head. "Nothing."

"You're scaring me."

"Sara." Her name whispered past his lips, tinged with awe. And then he knelt at her feet, his arms wrapping around her waist as he buried his face in her lap.

"Gabriel!"

"Don't ask questions," he murmured. "Please, just hold me, touch me."

She stared at his bowed head, his words echoing in her mind as she lightly stroked his hair. She'd heard those words before, only last night, in a dream. But it had been another woman's hand stroking his hair . . .

A cold chill swept through her, and she jerked her hand away from his head. What did it mean?

His arms tightened around her waist. "Don't be afraid. I won't hurt you, I swear it. Just hold me," he pleaded. "Just let me hold you a moment more."

Contentment washed through him as he felt her hand move in his hair again. Ah, the touch of a human hand, warm with compassion, flowing with life. It was the touch of Sara's hand, so welcome, so familiar.

*Sara, Sara, can it really be you?*

Tears burned her eyes as she lightly stroked his hair, caressed his nape, brushed her fingers across his cheek. She could feel his body trembling, or was it her own?

Sometime later, he raised his head, his gaze meeting hers, and in the dark gray depths of his eyes she saw a hunger so deep, a yearning so painful, that it caused her heart to ache.

Almost without conscious thought, she bent her head to his and kissed him.

And time stood still, trapped in the depths of his eyes.

And then his eyelids fluttered down and he kissed her with all the longing in his heart, with the loneliness born of more than half a century without her. Kissed her with all the love in his heart, a love which would always be hers, only hers.

Passion, need, longing. They swept through Sarah like a forest fire, burning away every doubt. She forgot everything but the need to comfort this man, to take him into herself, to fill all the empty spaces in his heart and soul. She wanted to hold him to her breast and whisper that everything would be all right, that he would never again be alone. And in some deep corner of her mind, she had the strange, overwhelming feeling that she had done it all once before.

After an eternity, he drew back. "Forgive me."

"There's nothing to forgive," she replied quietly.

His eyes were deep, dark gray. She had seen those eyes before, she thought, felt their magnetism in childhood dreams.

"Sarah, come home with me."

She started to refuse, angry that he would think she was the kind of woman who would sleep with a man she hardly knew. For, even though he hadn't said the words, she knew that was what he was asking.

Because she wanted it, too.

He stood up, his eyes burning into hers, his stance almost arrogant, but she knew now that he was vulnerable, needy. Hurting. And in that same instant, she knew that he hadn't meant to insult her at all, that he wasn't the type of man to take a woman to bed unless he loved her . . . but that was impossible. How could he love her?

How could she love him?

And then he put out his hand in silent invitation.

And she stood up and placed her hand in his.

And he felt the darkness evaporate from his soul.

And she felt the loneliness in her heart take wing.

No words were needed now. With a muffled cry, he swept her into his arms and carried her home.

This can't be happening, Sarah thought. She'd never slept with any man except her husband. She had married David right out of high school. He was the first man she had ever known, the only man she had ever wanted. Until now.

Strangely, she didn't feel the slightest bit of guilt or doubt as Gabriel carried her up the winding staircase to the pale pink bedroom.

Very gently, he placed her on her feet, and then he kissed her. And kissed her again. She quivered with anticipation as she felt his hands feather over her shoulders, down her back. His tongue slid over her lower lip and she opened for him instantly, her tongue mating with his. He tasted of wine, and she thought how appropriate that was, for his kisses were intoxicating.

Still kissing, they undressed each other, and then he swept her into his arms and carried her to bed. She drew him down beside her, not wanting to be parted from him for even a moment. His skin was firm and cool beneath her questing fingertips; his mouth was hot as it moved over her. A low groan escaped his lips as his tongue laved her neck, lingering over the rapidly beating pulse in her throat.

"Gabriel . . . Gabriel . . ." She moaned his name as his hands caressed her, bringing her body to full, vibrant life. She needed him, wanted him, as she had never wanted anything else.

With bold abandon, her hands explored the broad expanse of his back and chest; her fingertips traced the taut muscles in his arms. She marveled at the strength that lay dormant beneath her hands, the power he held in tight control as if he were afraid of hurting her.

But she wanted all of him, and she urged him on, nipping at his ear lobe, caressing him, begging him to take her.

And he did. Like a dark angel, he rose over her, his long black hair falling over his shoulders, his whole body quivering as he possessed her.

She gasped as his flesh joined hers. David had always been a gentle lover. Never demanding, often hesitant, he had frequently let her be in control. But there was no hesitation on Gabriel's part. He took her as if she belonged to him, as if it were his right. He made love to her masterfully, skillfully, powerfully, and she gloried in it. Never had she felt more fragile, more feminine, more desired.

She closed her eyes in complete surrender, her heart and soul and mind bound to his. . . .

*She was in a blue bedroom, reclining on a blue and rose quilt. Heavy blue drapes hung at the window. Candlelight flickered on the walls. And Gabriel rose above her, whispering words of love to her in French and Italian. Only it wasn't her, she thought, confused. And yet, it* was *her. She could hear his voice, touch his skin, smell the sweat of their combined bodies. His hair was like a dark cloud, his eyes turbulent, like the sky before a storm.*

*His eyes . . . surely it was a trick of the candlelight that caused them to glow like a bloodred flame. . . .*

Sarah opened her eyes, frightened by the images playing in her mind. And Gabriel was there, his dark gray eyes blazing, glowing. Surely it was only a trick of the light, she told herself, and then there was no more time for thought. Ecstasy spiraled through her and she cried his name, her nails clawing his back and shoulders as their bodies merged in perfect unison, the one giving pleasure to the other and finding pleasure in the giving.

Gabriel turned his face away, not wanting her to see the blood-lust that was surely glowing in his eyes. It had taken every ounce of his self-control to contain the hunger that seethed within him, to keep from satisfying his lust for blood as he satisfied his lust for her flesh.

And yet it wasn't lust. He had loved this woman in another lifetime. He loved her now. And he would never let her go.

"Gabriel?"

He took a deep breath and then he turned on his side, drawing her with him, his arms wrapped around her, protectively, possessively.

*"Cara?"*

*Cara*. That was what he had called the girl in the blue bedroom. The girl whose emotions and desires Sarah had felt as though they were her own.

Gabriel gazed into Sarah's eyes. "Are you all right?"

"I don't know. I . . ."

"What is it?"

"I don't know how to explain it," she said, frowning. "But when we were making love, I had the strangest feeling that I was someone else. That *we* were somewhere else."

Gabriel swore under his breath. For a moment, his mind had gone back in time, and he had imagined it was Sara Jayne in his arms. But how had Sarah known that?

"And you . . ."

A muscle worked in Gabriel's jaw. "What about me?"

"I don't know. You were different somehow. Your eyes . . ." She raised up on one elbow and gazed at him intently, then shook her head. "Never mind."

Gently, he brushed a wisp of hair from her brow, then pulled her down beside him once again.

"Gabriel?"

"Hmmmm?"

"I think I'm falling in love with you." She bit down on her lip when he didn't say anything. "You don't mind, do you?"

"No, Sarah, I don't mind."

She waited, hoping he would tell her he loved her, too, or at least say that he cared, but he only gazed at her, his gray eyes dark with desire. But, deeper than the glow of passion, she saw another emotion blazing in his eyes, one she didn't recognize.

She tried to decipher it, but it was quickly gone, and then he was making love to her again, tenderly this time, carrying her away with him to heights she had never scaled, depths she had never plumbed, ecstasies she had never imagined.

And there, in the midst of rapture beyond anything she had ever dreamed of, she glimpsed the true depths of Gabriel's loneliness, his emptiness, his need to be held, to be loved.

Tears burned her eyes as her soul merged with his. With a sob, she wrapped her arms and legs around him, holding his body close even as she whispered that she loved him, that she would always love him, that he would never be alone again.

And then they came together, hearts and bodies blending together, their tears mingling as they found that one moment of shared perfection that carried them beyond the bounds of time and space.

And for her there was fulfillment and a sense of peace.

And for him there was light and hope and a sense of coming home after a long dark journey.

With a sigh of contentment, she fell asleep in his arms.

He held her throughout the night, his body warmed by her nearness, his fingers threading through the silky softness of her hair, caressing the curve of her shoulder, the side of her breast.

She dreamed of him, and he knew her dreams. They were Sara's dreams, parts of Sara's life. But only the good parts.

He held her until dawn crept over the horizon.

Leaving the bed, he covered her with the quilt, kissed her lips, then gathered up his clothes and left the room.

Never had the cellar seemed so cold, so empty. Never had the hours until dusk seemed so far away.

As he settled down to take his rest, his last thought was of Sarah. Her scent clung to him; the taste of her lingered on his tongue. In his mind's eye, he saw her sleeping in the bedroom above, her lips swollen from his kisses, her hair spread over the pillow like a splash of molten gold.

"Sarah." He whispered her name as the darkness closed in on him, dragging him down into oblivion.

# *Chapter Five*

It was late morning when she woke. Filled with a sense of well-being, she stretched, then sat up, wondering where Gabriel was.

Rising, she took a quick shower, and then, wrapped in a fluffy white towel, she padded downstairs.

"Gabriel?"

She frowned, her confusion growing as she went from room to room. Except for the bedroom they had shared and the front parlor, none of the rooms were furnished. There was no table in the kitchen, no chairs, though there was food in the fridge.

But her curiosity was stronger than her appetite. She retraced her steps, staring, perplexed, into each room. He'd said he'd lived here for a few months. Surely a man who drove a $70,000 sports car could afford to buy a few pieces of furniture.

She couldn't shake off the feeling that the only

room that had ever been lived in was the parlor. Nor could she shake the feeling that Gabriel was here, somewhere in the house. But if that was true, why didn't he answer her?

"Gabriel?" She stood in the hallway, her hands clutching the towel. "Gabriel! This isn't funny."

With a sigh of exasperation, she went upstairs. She was about to put on the clothes she'd worn the day before when her gaze fell on the wardrobe.

*You'll find clothes in the armoire,* he'd said.

She hesitated a moment, then opened the doors, her eyes widening with wonder. There were dresses, blouses and sweaters, jeans and slacks, pumps and sandals, all obviously selected with her likes and dislikes in mind. She shook her head in amazement. She'd never owned this many clothes in her whole life.

It took her twenty minutes to decide on a pair of black pants and a lavender sweater. Barefoot, she went back down to the kitchen and fixed herself a cup of coffee.

Where was he?

It was then she noticed the narrow door. Painted the same color as the kitchen and tucked into a corner, it was almost invisible.

Setting her coffee cup on the sink top, she crossed the room and opened the door to discover a short flight of stairs, and another door at the bottom.

"Curiouser and curiouser," she murmured. And feeling like Alice in Wonderland, she made her way down the steps, her hand reaching for the doorknob.

It was locked. She looked around for a key, ran her hand along the top of the lintel. Nothing.

Sarah exhaled softly. Did the door lead to the garage? A basement? Into the garden?

She rested her hand on the door for a moment. The wood, a dark oak, felt smooth and cool beneath her fingertips.

Images flashed through her mind, images of a small cottage, of a broken window, of narrow stone steps, of another door also made of oak. A door that led to a damp cellar.

And she heard Gabriel's voice, filled with warning. *Be gone!*

With a start, she jerked her hand from the door and took a step backward. She hadn't imagined that voice. It had been real. Gabriel's voice.

Overcome with a sudden sense of foreboding, she turned on her heel and ran up the stairs, slamming the kitchen door behind her.

She ran through the kitchen, down the hall, through the parlor, and didn't stop running until she was outside in the driveway. Only then did she remember that her car was parked in the garage at home.

Breathing heavily, she ran down the long, winding driveway to the main gate. Tears of frustration welled in her eyes when she realized it was locked, and then, as if by magic, the iron gate swung open and she ran outside. She heard the gate slam shut behind her, but she didn't turn around, just kept running, driven by sheer terror.

He rose at dusk, his steps heavy as he climbed the stairs.

She was gone, and it was just as well.

He repeated those words over and over again in the next few nights—nights spent staring into the fireplace, or riding Necromancer. Sometimes he sat in the bedroom remembering, until his need for her became too painful. At those times, he went out into the night to walk the lonely streets. No one saw him. Moving with preternatural speed, he moved from one end of the city to the other, his presence no more than a breath of cool air to those he passed by.

Anger aroused the urge to hunt, to kill, but he refused to do so. He fed only when absolutely necessary, taking only enough to sustain his existence but never enough to quench his thirst, punishing himself with the hunger because it was easier to be tormented by the lust for blood than by his constant need for Sarah.

A week passed, and his anger grew, and with it the knowledge that he could take her at any time.

He was a vampire, after all. He could hypnotize her so that he could make love to her whenever he pleased. Then he would have only to summon her with the power of his mind, and she would be compelled to come to him from wherever she might be, warm and willing, unable to resist.

He could initiate her, and in that state she would do anything he wished. Anything. She would be miserable when they were apart. She would find prey for him, kill for him, worship him if he so desired.

Or he could force the Dark Gift upon her, and keep her by his side for eternity.

But he could not make her love him.

And that knowledge filled him with rage.

And it was that rage, finally, that drove him to her door.

*     *     *

Sarah sat in a corner of the couch, comfortably wrapped in a blanket, watching an old rerun of the Dick Van Dyke show. She'd seen this particular episode at least a half-dozen times, but for some reason she never tired of it.

When it was over, she turned to the country music channel, her thoughts drifting toward Gabriel. Always Gabriel, she thought, annoyed. She hardly knew the man, yet she couldn't forget him. He was ever in her thoughts, her dreams. Her nightmares. Deep down, she had the feeling that she was going slowly insane. Surely that was the only explanation for the dreams she'd been having. Sometimes she dreamed she was in England, other times in France. She spoke French in those dreams. She danced. She made love to Gabriel. Only it wasn't really her, but another woman, one with blond hair and blue eyes.

But it was the nightmares that truly frightened her, that made her sleep with all the lights on. There was nothing pleasant about those dreams, and she often woke with a start, images of bloody fangs and inhuman eyes imprinted in her memory.

Last night she had dreamed of being buried alive.

Closing her eyes, she took a deep, calming breath. They were just dreams, after all. And dreams couldn't hurt you . . .

"Sarah."

His voice was low, resonant.

She opened her eyes and he was there, standing in the doorway across the room. He was tall and dark, like an image from one of her nightmares, and she wondered why she wasn't afraid, or at least surprised. And then she knew. She had been waiting for this moment ever since she ran out of the mansion a week ago.

"What are you doing here?"

His dark gray eyes seemed to burn into her own. "I've come for you."

"What do you mean?"

"Can't you guess?"

She clutched the blanket tighter, her eyes widening in fearful understanding. Slowly, she shook her head, refusing to believe what she saw in his eyes.

And then he was lifting her off the sofa, though she had no recollection of seeing him move.

His arms were hard and unyielding as he carried her out of the house, blanket and all. And then they were moving through the night with blinding speed. Tears stung her eyes. Stores and houses and people blurred together in a mass of color.

And suddenly they were at the mansion, in the parlor, and she was sitting in the chair in front of the fireplace with no recollection of how she'd gotten there.

She saw Gabriel glance over his shoulder; there was a soft whooshing sound, and a fire appeared in the hearth.

Magic, she thought. It was some kind of magic.

"Look at me," he said, and his voice seemed to echo off the walls of the room, of her mind, her heart.

Hands clasped to keep them from shaking, she met his gaze.

"I've thought of nothing but you this past week," he said, not sounding very happy about it. "Only you."

"I . . . I've thought of you, too."

"Have you?"

Did she detect a note of hope in his voice? "Yes."

"Do you dream, Sarah?"

"Of course. Everyone dreams."

"Not everyone," he murmured. "Tell me of your dreams."

"Is that why you brought me here?" she asked, her voice tinged with sarcasm. "To listen to my dreams?"

"Tell me."

She tried to look away, but she couldn't draw her gaze from his.

"Tell me." It was a command.

"Mostly I dream about you," she said. "About . . ." She shrugged. "About the other night."

"Is that all?"

"No. Sometimes I have nightmares, horrible nightmares."

He didn't move, but she had the feeling he was leaning toward her. "Tell me," he said again.

"They don't make any sense. The girl in the dreams is me. I see what she sees, I hear what she hears. But she's not me."

She stared up at him, hoping he could help, hoping he would assure her that she wasn't going crazy. "Sometimes I speak French." She lifted one hand and let it fall in a gesture of helplessness. "I don't know how to speak French. But in my dreams I know the words, what they mean. And there's"—she swallowed, her mouth suddenly dry—"there's blood and death and you, all mixed up together. And last night"—her fingernails dug into her palms—"last night I dreamed that I had been buried alive. And you came to save me."

"Sarah." His voice was a harsh rasp, filled with agony. And he knew, knew without doubt, that it was Sara Jayne sitting before him.

"What does it all mean?" she asked.

He turned away, not wanting her to see the yearning, the hunger, that he knew must surely be plain on his face. "Are you sure you want to know?"

"Am I going mad?" she asked anxiously. "Is that what it means?"

"No."

"Why did you bring me here? What do you want from me?"

"I was going to offer you a choice."

"What kind of choice?"

"I was going to ask if you would be mine willingly, and if you said no, I was going to offer you the choice of being my slave or my equal."

She couldn't help it—she laughed. His slave or his equal? Who did he think he was? And then she felt the power of his gaze, and the laughter died in her throat.

"You're not kidding, are you?"

"No."

"How did you start that fire?"

He lifted one black brow. "An odd question at such a moment."

"How did we travel here so fast?"

"I have many talents," he said with a shrug.

"Are you a magician of some kind?" She shrank away from the word *sorcerer*; it conjured up too many dark images.

"Do you believe in reincarnation?"

"Don't tell me you think you're Harry Houdini?"

"Answer me!"

"No, I don't believe in reincarnation. Or ghosts. Or werewolves."

He crossed the room, parted the drapes, and stared out into the night. He should end this now, he thought, one way or the other. As he had so long ago, he told himself to let her go, to exit her life and never return. But, as with his other Sara, he could not do it. He could not cut himself off from the only woman who had ever loved him. Selfish to the end, he mused, determined to have what he wanted at all costs.

He stood there for a long time, absorbing the sounds of the night. A drunk was lying in a gutter less than a mile away, snoring loudly. He heard the near-silent sweep of an owl's wings as it hunted in the night. In the distance, he could hear people talking, fighting, loving.

He drew a deep breath, and Sarah's scent filled his nostrils. Her perfume. The soap she had bathed with. The fragrance of her hair. The sharp odor of fear. The intoxicating scent of the blood flowing warm and sweet through her veins.

He clenched his hands at his sides. *Sara Jayne, remember me,* cara, *come to me.*

"Sara Jayne." A shiver went through Sarah as she repeated the name. "She's the girl in my dreams."

"I know."

"How could you?"

"Because they're her dreams you're having, her nightmares."

"You mean she really exists?"

"She did."

"Did?" A coldness seemed to fill the room as she waited for his explanation.

"She was born in England in 1865. She had hair the color of yours, but her eyes were blue, like the sky on a summer day. She grew up in an orphanage. For a time, she was a prima ballerina in the Paris Opéra. She gave up a brilliant career and all hopes of a family for the man she loved." He paused a moment. "She died in 1940."

"You sound as though you knew her."

He seemed to move in slow motion as he turned around to face her. "I did."

"That's impossible."

A tight smile played over his lips. "Is it?"

"So," Sarah said, deciding to humor him. "Was she your slave or your equal?"

"She was my wife."

Sarah frowned. "But she died more than fifty years ago."

"Yes," he said, and his eyes were bleak, as gray as a winter sky. "In Salamanca."

Sarah shook her head. Maybe *he* was the one who was crazy.

"I'm tired," she said. "I want to go home."

The coldness had penetrated her skin now, making her shiver in spite of the flames. She knew he was hiding something, something she didn't want to know.

Gabriel took a deep breath, held it, then let it out in a weary sigh. "You are home."

She was truly frightened now. She searched her mind, trying to remember how one was supposed to deal with a lunatic.

"I'm not insane, Sarah, and neither are you. Search your mind. Let yourself remember."

"Remember what?"

"Who you are."

"I know who I am. What I don't know is who you are."

"You know me, Sarah. You've always known me."

"No," she said, tears of fright stinging her eyes. "Please, just let me go home."

"I can't. I can't lose you again."

"I'm not her! My name is Sarah Lynn Johnson. My eyes are brown, not blue. And I've never been to England or France or Spain."

"You were born crippled," he said. "I came to you at the orphanage. I read to you. I held you in my arms and we danced around the room. I took you to the opera . . ."

"To see *Giselle*." She shivered as the words whispered past her lips, as though someone had walked over her grave.

Gabriel nodded.

Sarah stared up at him, her expression one of disbelief and astonishment. "You took me riding on your horse. You sent me to France to be a ballerina. You saved my life when I was burned . . ."

He nodded again, his heart pounding as her memories surfaced.

"It was me. I was the one buried alive."

He saw the horror in her eyes as she recalled that night. Thinking to comfort her, he took a step forward, his hand outstretched.

"No!" She recoiled from his touch. "You're . . . you're a . . ." She shook her head, refusing to believe. "No, no, it can't be. This is all a dream, a nightmare."

His hand fell to his side. "Sometimes I wish it were." He let out a long, shuddering sigh. "The word you can't say is *vampire*. And it's true. It's what I am."

She shook her head again. He could hear the thundering beat of her heart, smell the fear that rose from her skin.

"You weren't afraid of me before," he remarked quietly. "Once, you even gave me your blood."

All the color drained from her face as she stared down at her wrist. "I remember." She spoke the words as though they had been forced from her lips. "You were in the cellar of an abandoned cottage and couldn't get out."

She lifted her gaze to his, but he said nothing, only stood there, his face impassive. She had never seen such stillness in another human being . . . only he wasn't human.

Vampire.

The undead.

Every Dracula movie she had ever seen rushed to the forefront of her mind. *Will you be my slave or my equal?* Did she really have any choice? If there was any truth to the movies, to the books she'd read, he could hypnotize her into doing whatever he wished. And now, with her gaze caught in the web of his, she believed it.

"Sarah, I'm not going to hurt you." He turned away, his hands shoved deep into the pockets of his trousers. "I admit I brought you here tonight to bring you over . . . to take you by force if you wouldn't come willingly."

"Bring me over?"

"Make you what I am." Even though he wasn't looking at her, he could see the horror reflected in her eyes, feel the increased rhythm of her heart as fear swept through her. "You needn't worry," he said wearily. "I've changed my mind."

"You loved her very much, didn't you?"

"Yes."

"Why didn't you make her a . . . a vampire?"

"She didn't want it."

He stared at her a moment, his gaze deep and mesmerizing, until she was hopelessly lost.

When she came to herself again, she was at home, sitting on the sofa with the blanket draped across her lap.

"Good-bye, Sarah," Gabriel said quietly. "I won't bother you again."

She blinked, and he was gone as if he'd never been there.

She sat there for a long while, their conversation replaying in her mind. She had lived before, had known him before. Memories crowded her mind, memories of Maurice and Antonina, of performing onstage at the Paris Opéra, of living in the orphanage, of Sister Mary Josepha. She remembered sitting in a wheelchair, remembered the panic she'd felt as fire swept through her room. And she remembered Gabriel carrying her into the night, his dark eyes frightened. He had given her his blood, saved her life, restored strength to her legs so she could walk and dance.

He had loved her until the day she died . . .

It couldn't be true. She didn't believe in reincarnation. She didn't believe in vampires. The very thought was frightening. But fascinating.

Suddenly too agitated to sit still, she went into the kitchen and fixed herself a cup of hot chocolate, and all the while memories flooded her mind, memories of another life, and woven deep into the fabric of those memories was Gabriel: Gabriel reading to her, singing to her, holding her in his arms.

Gabriel begging her to go away that day she'd found him in the cellar . . .

*"Gabriel, my angel, please let me help you."*

*"Angel . . . angel . . ." He had laughed then, a horrible sound that bordered on hysteria. "Devil, you mean. Go away from me, Sara, my sweet Sara, before I destroy you as I destroyed Rosalia."*

*"I'm not leaving," she had said, and she had crossed the room and taken him in her arms. "Gabriel, please tell me what to do," she had pleaded.*

*With an inhuman growl of despair, he had whirled around to face her. "Go away!"*

*She had stared up at him, at eyes that blazed in the darkness like hell's own fires, and knew she was looking into the face of death.*

*"What's happened to you?" she had asked.*

*"Nothing's happened to me," he had replied. "This is what I am."*

*He had bared his teeth and she had seen his fangs, sharp and white and deadly . . . And the unearthly red glow in his eyes.*

*"Now will you go?" he had growled, and she had replied, "No, Gabriel, I'll not leave you again."*

*He had been in pain, needing nourishment, needing blood, and she had offered him hers, but he had refused, begging her to go away. And she had, but only for a moment. She had gone upstairs, found a sliver of glass, and slit her wrist. He hadn't wanted to take it; she had seen the horror struggling against the hunger, and she had pressed her bleeding flesh to his lips. With a low growl of despair, his mouth had locked on her arm . . .*

Sarah gasped as a sudden heat pooled in her right wrist, and with it, the sense of someone sucking her flesh, drinking her blood. It was a strangely sensual feeling.

"I must have loved him a great deal to do such a thing," Sarah murmured, unaware that she had said "I" instead of "she."

She sipped the chocolate, oblivious to the fact that it had grown cool.

Gabriel. He had been the loneliest man she had ever known, doomed to live in the shadows of life, to dwell on the edges of humanity, always alone, forever in darkness. And she had been his light . . .

She wandered aimlessly through the house, then went back into the parlor and sat down on the sofa again, the blanket wrapped around her, her mind in turmoil as she tried to accept the fact that she had lived before, that she had willingly given up all hope of motherhood, of a normal life, to be with a vampire.

# *Chapter Six*

He stood on the balcony, his hands braced on the wrought-iron rail, watching the dark clouds tumble across the sky. It was going to rain. He could smell the moisture in the air, hear the distant sound of thunder as the storm drew closer.

It was a night that suited his mood perfectly—dark and restless.

He had lost her and found her and lost her again.

He cursed viciously for not forcing the Dark Gift upon her. She might have despised him for it, but she would have been his. Forever his. He wouldn't have to watch her grow old and die a second time . . .

Three weeks had passed since he had gone to her house. Ten days since he had last fed. Without her, he'd lost the will to go on, but the hunger burned bright within him, sharp as a Spanish dagger, as constant as the sun. He could feel his body weakening, feel his mind growing dim. But it didn't matter. Nothing mattered. And tomorrow it would all be over.

He wondered dispassionately how long it would take for him to die, if his body would burst into flame at the first fiery touch of the midday sun, or if he would writhe in agony like a worm on a hot rock. And what of his soul, if he still had one? Would it find rest at last? Or would it burn forever in the inferno of an endless and unforgiving hell?

But even the thought of spending eternity in the bowels of perdition didn't frighten him now because he was already on fire, his insides burning as the hunger raged relentlessly through his body, tearing at his insides with talons of flame.

A last meal, he thought dully. Weren't the condemned entitled to a last meal?

"Gabriel?"

He whirled around, startled by the sound of her voice.

"I knocked," Sarah said, and then, seeing his face, she took a step backward, one hand pressed to the back of his chair to steady herself. She didn't have to ask what was wrong. She knew. She had seen him like this once before, in the cellar of an abandoned cottage.

"Go away." He spoke the words through tightly clenched teeth.

Sarah nodded, intending to do just that, but her feet refused to obey and she stood rooted to the spot, unable to tear her gaze from his face. He wore a black sweater that emphasized the pallor of his skin. His eyes burned with a familiar red glow. His nostrils flared, like those of a wolf on the scent of blood . . .

"Go . . . away . . . now."

"It seems as if you're always trying to get rid of me."

He stared at her, trying to understand what she was saying, but the scent of her blood was overpowering, making it difficult to think of anything but the hunger roaring through him, growing stronger with each passing minute.

"You were lucky the last time," he said, his voice dry and brittle. "I cannot promise you will be so lucky now." He took a deep breath, willing his hands to stop shaking. "Why did you come here?"

"We need to talk."

"Talk?" He shook his head. "About what?"

"About us, about what we're going to do."

"There is no us. Go away, Sarah."

"I can't. I've spent every minute of the last three weeks remembering another life in another time, remembering the night we made love here, in this house. I love you, Gabriel."

He closed his eyes. Her words washed over him, cleansing the bitterness from his heart. Sweet words, he mused, the most welcome words in the world.

With an effort, he turned away from her. "Sarah, please . . . go away."

"You need blood." She had a sudden sense of déjà vu as she spoke the words, the same words she'd said a hundred years ago.

He would have laughed if he hadn't been in such agony. Once before he had tried to send her away, and she had stubbornly refused to go. And now it was happening again. Was this to be the pattern of his life from now on, to find her and lose her again and again, to ease his fiendish hunger with a few drops of her precious blood, to watch her grow old and die in his arms?

A harsh cry rose in his throat. He would not do it again. Could not do it again.

"Go home, Sarah. Forget all of this."

He flinched as her arms slid around his waist. It was a sign of his weakness that he hadn't heard her come up behind him. Had she been an enemy, he would likely be dead now, a wooden stake through his heart. An hour ago, a moment ago, he would have welcomed death, but now Sarah was here, and life was again worth living.

"We've been through all this before, Gabriel," she said, pressing her cheek against his back. "Take what you need."

"And what if I can't stop this time, *cara*? What if I take too much? What if I take it all?" He took a deep breath and let it out in a long, shuddering sigh. "If you decide to stay with me now, I won't watch you die, not this time. Are you prepared to live the life of a vampire?"

"I don't know. It seems like such a horrible way to live."

"Horrible?" He stared down at her hands, locked around his waist. It hadn't been a horrible existence, but it had been lonely. He remembered how it had been when first he'd been made, watching people he knew grow old and die, watching the world change, until there was nothing left of the life he had known, the world he had known. Until there was no one alive who remembered who he had been.

But then he had met Sara Jayne, and she had made it all worthwhile.

And now she was here.

Again.

Offering to ease his hunger.

Again.

"Gabriel, maybe there's a cure for what you are. I mean, surely, in this day and age, there must be something we can do."

"A cure?" He frowned. Over the centuries, he had heard whispers of such a thing from other vampires, but he had never believed it or pursued it. There had been too much to see, to learn. In spite of the loneliness, he had enjoyed his existence, and the supernatural powers that came with it.

A cure? Perhaps, but he couldn't think of it now, couldn't think of anything but the need to get Sarah out of the house before it was too late, before the ravening hunger that lived inside him became overpowering.

"We can talk about it tomorrow," he said. "But now you must go home." A shudder racked his body. Her blood. The smell of it was driving him dangerously near the edge of resistance. He could feel his fangs lengthening in response to the smell. It would be so easy to take her, to make her his for all time. "Sarah . . . please. Go home."

Reluctantly, Sarah moved away from him. For the first time, she realized it was raining. Lightning cut through the black clouds; thunder rumbled across the darkened skies. How appropriate, she thought. In horror movies, there was always a storm when the heroine's life was in danger.

She looked at Gabriel. He was still standing with his back toward her, his hands clenched at his sides. "Will you still be here tomorrow?"

"What do you mean?"

"You aren't thinking of doing something stupid, are you?"

"Stupid? No."

"You're lying."

He turned around to face her. "Am I?"

"You want to die, don't you? That's why you haven't fed."

She was very perceptive, he thought. But then, she always had been.

"I don't want you to die, and I don't want you to suffer." Sweeping her hair away from her neck, she tilted her head to the side. "Take what you need, Gabriel."

He took a step toward her, his hands clenched at his sides. His eyes were afire with an unearthly radiance, his lips slightly parted so that she could see his fangs. They looked sharp and very white.

"Run, Sarah," he whispered hoarsely. "Run, before it's too late."

"No." She fought down her burgeoning fear. He had never hurt her before. He wouldn't hurt her now.

And then he was there, towering over her, his dark eyes aglow as he grasped her shoulders in a grip like iron and pressed his mouth to her throat.

Her heart was beating wildly, louder than the thunder that rolled across the sky. Every nerve ending, every cell, seemed alive, tingling with fear and anticipation. She felt a sharp stinging sensation, and then a curious lassitude crept over her.

He was drinking her blood. She wondered why the knowledge of what he was doing didn't sicken her, and then the ability to think seemed to slip away and she was conscious of nothing but pleasure. It pooled in the pit of her stomach, flowed through her blood like warm sweet wine. She wrapped her arms around his waist, clinging to him as the only solid thing in a world suddenly spinning out of control. She could hear her heart beating a quick tattoo in her ears.

His hair lay like black silk against her cheek. She longed to touch it, but she lacked the strength to lift her arm. Her fingers clutched his sweater, and it was as if she could feel each individual thread. Colors danced before her eyes: vivid shades of red and violet and blue.

Her head fell back, and she was drifting, floating on a crimson sea, every fiber of her being awash with sensual pleasure.

She was desolate when he took his mouth away.

"Sarah?"

She blinked up at him. His face swam before her eyes, and she blinked again, wondering why she felt so strange.

"Sarah? Sarah!"

"Hmmm?" She stared up at him, though it was an effort to keep her eyes open, to focus. His skin was no longer pale. His cheeks were flushed; the bloodlust was gone from his eyes. A distant part of her mind told her that her blood had done that for him.

Gabriel swore under his breath, cursing the insatiable hunger, the weakness, that had driven him to take that which he had no right to take. One day he would take too much and it would kill her.

He cursed under his breath as he swept her into his arms and carried her into the kitchen. Filling a glass with water, he held it to her lips, insisting she drink it all. And then he carried her up the stairs and put her to bed.

"Stay with me," she begged. "Stay until the sun comes up."

"I will."

"Am I your slave now?"

"No."

"I wouldn't mind, you know, being your slave."

"I would. Go to sleep, Sarah."

"You'll be here tomorrow night? You won't destroy yourself? Promise me."

"I promise."

"We'll find a cure," she murmured as her eyelids fluttered down. "I know we will. And if we can't . . . if we can't . . ."

He listened to the soft sound of her breathing as sleep claimed her.

"And if we can't," he said, finishing her thought in his own way, "then we'll meet death together, for I won't be parted from you in life again."

The house was deadly quiet. Alone in the pink bedroom, the covers drawn up to her chin, Sarah stared out the window at the darkness, wondering what had awakened her, wondering where Gabriel was. The last thing she remembered was Gabriel bending over her, promising that he wouldn't destroy himself.

She let out a sigh. She had spent the last three weeks remembering another life, trying to convince herself it wasn't true, that she hadn't lived before. But she'd known, in the depths of her heart and soul, that everything Gabriel had told her was true. She had lived before, loved him before. And she loved him now.

With that irrefutable thought in mind, she had rented her house, furniture and all, to a young family. Then she had packed her bags and come here. Hard to believe that had been only hours ago. It seemed as though centuries had passed since she entered this house. Since she had come home. To Gabriel. What should have seemed totally bizarre felt completely right.

She had lived before. Gabriel had been her husband, and now she was back where she belonged.

She was almost asleep again when she sensed his presence in the room, and then he was sliding under the covers, taking her in his arms.

"It will be dawn soon," he whispered. "Let me hold you until then."

"We'll be together always, won't we?"

"Always."

She made a soft sound of acquiescence as she snuggled against him. Home, she thought, home at last.

She felt his lips move in her hair, heard his voice whispering her name, speaking to her in a language she didn't comprehend, and yet she understood every word.

Warm and safe, drifting on a gentle tide of love, her last thought before sleep claimed her was that she loved him, that even if they were parted again, she would find him in another life.

When next she woke, it was morning and she was alone, but she knew that he was there, somewhere in the house. Filled with a sense of well-being, she jumped out of bed. After taking a lengthy shower and brushing her hair, she pulled on a bulky white sweater and a pair of jeans, slipped on tennis shoes, then went downstairs. She ate a quick breakfast of tea and toast, then left the house, bound for the library.

She was amazed at the number of books on vampire lore—*Vampire: The Complete Guide to the World of the Undead* by Mascetti; *The Vampire Encyclopedia* by Bunson; *The Vampire in Legend, Fact and Art* by Copper; *The Terror That Comes in the Night* by Hufford; *In Search of Dracula* by McNally—the list went on and on, with books detailing how to recognize a vampire, how to destroy a vampire, how to protect oneself from a vampire, but nowhere did she find any indication that a vampire had ever been successfully transformed back into a human.

According to one book, vampires always wore black tuxedos with long tails, and a black silk cloak, which some believed was woven by the vampire himself after his transformation.

Sarah frowned. Gabriel did, indeed, wear black, she thought, but not a tuxedo, and she'd never seen him in a cape . . . but that wasn't true, she amended. In France, he'd always worn a long black cloak, only it had been made of wool, not silk.

She studied old newspaper articles, fascinated by a 1980s headline: VAMPIRE KILLINGS SWEEP THE U.S. The article reported that experts believed vampires were responsible for as many as 6,000 deaths a year, and that police were investigating dozens of eerie murders in which the bodies of the victims had been drained of blood—a double murder in New York City where there wasn't enough blood left in the bodies for the medical examiner to take a blood sample; six people in California had been murdered by a man who later admitted to drinking their blood.

In a book, she read that, in ancient times, people had believed that a dead body could become a vampire if an animal such as a dog or a cat jumped over it. And if a bat flew over a body, there was no escape from becoming a vampire. Likewise, if one's shadow was stolen, becoming a vampire was inevitable. If the deceased couldn't be buried, either because the earth would not accept the body, as with the case of evil-doers, or because the authorities would object, then the victim would more than likely become a vampire.

Sarah shook her head. How could people ever have believed in such nonsense?

How could she believe in reincarnation, in vampires?

But she had no doubt that Gabriel was what he said he was; she'd seen the proof with her own eyes. And if one was made a vampire, then surely one could be unmade, and she would not rest until she found a cure, because there were only two alternatives: living the past over again, or becoming what Gabriel was, and she knew that was something she could never do. If she was going to live forever, then she wanted it to be in heaven or paradise, surrounded by joy and happiness and those she had loved in life; she didn't want to live forever at the expense of others, not even to be with Gabriel.

She spent most of the day at the library before returning to the house. She was aware of a keen sense of anticipation as she went into the kitchen and fixed something to eat.

She was putting the dishes in the dishwasher when she sensed Gabriel's presence, and then he was standing behind her, his arms slipping around her waist to draw her back against him.

They stood that way for a long moment, with her hand stroking his while he rained kisses along the side of her neck.

"So," he said at last, "what did you do today?"

"I did some research on vampires."

"Oh? And what did you learn?"

"Everything but how to cure one."

He turned her in his arms and brushed a kiss across her lips. "I'm sure any cure you found in a book would be a waste of time, if one exists at all."

"Well, I'm not giving up. Haven't you ever heard of any vampire who returned to his former state?"

Gabriel shrugged. "There are stories, rumors of vampires who tried to reenter mortality."

"Did it work?"

"There is a legend among vampires that one of our kind was successfully transformed back to his human state."

"That's great!"

"It's only a fable, Sarah. To my knowledge, no vampire has ever regained his humanity." He drew her up against him, holding her tight. "One must go to the very brink of death to become a vampire. Crossing the chasm from death to life is not easy. It is, in many ways, like dying again."

"I don't want you to die."

He laughed softly, his breath fanning her cheek. "I'm already dead."

His words sent a chill down her spine. "So, what are we going to do?"

"I know a very old vampire, one older even than Nina. He lives in France. If there is a cure, Quillan would know of it."

"And if there isn't?"

"I don't know, Sarah. I only know I can't watch you die again."

"I'll come back to you, Gabriel. I found you in this life, and I'll find you again."

"Perhaps."

"How soon can we leave for France?"

"I don't know if he even exists anymore."

"Can you find out?"

"I'll try. I'll write him tomorrow and then we'll just have to wait and see."

She looked up at him, snatches of what she'd read coming back to her. "Can I ask you something?"

"You can ask."

"Do you really sleep in a . . . a coffin?"

"No. I could never overcome my aversion to that aspect of being a vampire. I sleep in a large box made of pine, and though it resembles a coffin in size and shape, it's just a box."

"Where is it?"

"In the basement. Would you care to see it?"

"No, I don't think so." She toyed with a lock of her hair. They needed a diversion, she thought, something to think about other than vampires and cures. "Do you have a VCR?"

He frowned a moment. VCR? Ah, a video cassette recorder, he thought, another remarkable invention. "No, why?"

"I thought it would be fun to sit in front of the fire and watch some movies."

"Then that's what we'll do."

Two hours later, Sarah was sitting on Gabriel's lap watching *Bram Stoker's Dracula*. So much for forgetting about vampires, she mused ruefully.

Earlier, they had braved the elements and driven to Circuit City where they had bought the best VCR on the market, as well as a stereo. From there, they'd gone to the Wherehouse and picked up a half-dozen videos.

For Gabriel, who had never been inside a video store, it had been quite an experience. He had wandered up and down the aisles until he came to the Horror section, his gaze drawn to the numerous vampire videos. He had chosen three while Sarah went in search of *Dances With Wolves*, *Sleepless in Seattle*, and *The Last of the Mohicans*. Their last stop had been at the market to buy popcorn and 7-Up.

Now, Sarah snuggled against Gabriel, one hand covering her eyes, as rivers of blood filled the screen. She'd tried to watch *Bram Stoker's Dracula* once before, and while she'd been fascinated by the love story between Mina and the Count, she'd sat through a good deal of it with her eyes closed, disgusted by the blood and the violence. She had cried at the end when Mina lopped off Dracula's head.

"Amazing," Gabriel remarked when it was over. "Simply amazing."

"Can we watch something funny now?" Sarah asked, slipping off his lap to eject the cassette from the VCR.

Gabriel glanced at the other two vampire movies stacked on top of the TV, then shrugged.

"We can watch another vampire movie later if you want," Sarah said, "although I'll probably have nightmares."

"You're living with a vampire, Sarah," he reminded her, his expression bleak. "If that doesn't give you nightmares, I doubt one of these silly movies will."

She made a face at him. "Very funny. I'm going to make some popcorn . . ."

Her gaze met his, and she knew he was thinking the same thing she was, that a bowl of popcorn, mundane as it might be, somehow served to emphasize the gulf between them.

"Can I bring you a glass of wine?"

At Gabriel's nod, she fled into the kitchen. They had to find a cure, she thought as she poured kernels into the hot-air popper. They had to! He might be able to live forever, but his existence was so empty. She wanted to be able to walk with him in the park on a cold rainy day, jog along the beach with the sun overhead, go to the zoo, the museum, hike the Grand Canyon. She wanted to make love in the daylight, to fall asleep in his arms, and wake up to his kisses. She wanted to have his children, grow old at his side . . .

She dumped the popcorn into a bowl, then stared into the wine she had poured for him. Always red wine. The color of blood.

She looked out the kitchen window, remembering her past life with Gabriel. At first, it had been wonderful. She had loved the castle, loved Spain, loved Gabriel beyond words. He had shown her the world, and the fact that she had to spend her days alone had been a small price to pay for the joy she had found in his arms at night. But, as wonderful as the first half of her life had been, the last half had been a torment. It had been awful, growing old while Gabriel stayed forever the same.

When she started to look like his mother instead of his wife, they had stopped going outside of the castle together because there was no way to explain the fact that Gabriel wasn't aging while everyone around him grew older.

And yet he had loved her to the end. She had never lacked for anything; she had only to mention that she wanted something, needed something, and it was hers. During the last year of her life, when she had been old and frail, he had cared for her as tenderly as ever a man cared for a woman. He had begged her not to leave him, to accept the Dark Gift, but by then it had been too late. She had been too old, and even though she had not wanted to die, she hadn't wanted to live forever as an old woman, either, and in the end, knowing she had made the right choice, she had died peacefully in Gabriel's arms. His face, unchanged in the fifty-four years they had spent together, had been the last thing she had seen on this earth.

And now she was with him again, and if they couldn't find a way to restore him to mortality, she would have to decide whether she wanted to die a second time, or become what he was.

She was reaching for the bowl when she sensed him standing behind her. Forcing a smile, she turned around to face him.

"You don't have to decide tonight, Sarah," he said quietly. "Not tonight, or this year, or the next."

"I know, but . . . I don't know what to do."

"Come and watch your movie."

She followed him into the living room, settled herself on his lap, and tried to concentrate on Meg Ryan's efforts to meet Tom Hanks, but the words made no sense, the humor seemed flat. The popcorn tasted like ashes. She didn't want to spend the next year trying to decide what to do. She didn't want to worry about it and fret over it, didn't want it hanging over her head. She wanted the decision made now.

Putting the bowl aside, she turned off the TV and faced Gabriel. "I think, if we can't find a cure, that you should make me what you are."

"Is that what you really want?"

"I don't know. And I don't want to have to decide. I just want you to do it."

"And what if you hate me for it?"

"I don't think I could ever hate you."

"Maybe not, but what if you're wrong, Sarah? I couldn't endure your hatred for the rest of my existence, however long that might be." He cupped her face in his hands and kissed her. "I'll see if I can get in touch with Quillan. After we hear from him, we can decide about the future."

Sarah nodded. She would put it out of her mind until they heard from the vampire in France. Until then . . . She smiled at Gabriel as she took him by the hand and led him upstairs to bed. Until then, she intended to spend every minute getting reacquainted with the incredible man who had been her husband.

# *Chapter Seven*

Because she didn't like spending her days with nothing to do, Sarah decided to try to find a job. She broached the subject on a Friday night while they sat in the kitchen playing rummy.

She hadn't expected Gabriel to object, but he did. Strenuously.

"I know women in your time didn't work, but I need something to do," Sarah argued. She shook her head, needing to make him understand how she felt. "I can't just vegetate on the sofa watching soap operas all day."

"Forgive me." Gabriel tossed his cards onto the table and stood up. "I didn't realize you were unhappy here."

"I'm not unhappy," Sarah said quickly. "Just bored." She looked up at him, suddenly curious. "You've lived hundreds of years. What did you do to pass the time?"

"A variety of things, some you wouldn't believe."

"Like what?"

"For a few years, I was a spy for one of the French kings. I can't remember now which one it was. Skulking around in the shadows was the perfect occupation for a man who must live always in darkness. For a time, I was a knight, and after that, a minstrel—"

"A minstrel!"

"I've been told my voice is passable."

"Would you sing for me?" Sarah asked, intrigued.

His gaze moved over her face, his expression softening. "I sang for you once before."

"Sing for me now. Please."

Gabriel thought for a moment, and then he began to sing an old Italian ballad of unrequited love.

His voice was deep, melodic, haunting. He sang in Italian, but he sang with such emotion Sarah had no trouble understanding the message. His voice wrapped around her, soft as candlelight, as poignant as a lover's last caress.

And memories flooded her mind. Memories of Gabriel coming to her in the dark of night, singing to her as he held her in his arms and danced her around her room in the orphanage, making her feel loved. Cherished. Beautiful. Gabriel. How could she ever have forgotten the magic of his touch, the power and beauty of his voice?

He held out his hand, and she took it, letting him draw her to her feet. For a long moment, he gazed into her eyes, the richness of his voice enveloping her as he drew her into his arms and waltzed her around the room.

The years faded away, and she was a young girl

again, filled with bitterness because she couldn't walk, couldn't dance, and then Gabriel had come into her life, and her whole world had turned upside down.

"That was beautiful," she murmured when the song ended. "You must have been the most sought after minstrel of your time. No doubt women swooned at your feet."

"There were those who paid handsomely for my talent," Gabriel allowed. "Some paid in coin of the realm, and others . . ." He shrugged, but his meaning was clear.

"I'm sure you must have made a fortune," Sarah said dryly.

"I had no need to work."

Taking Sarah by the hand, he led her into the parlor. Sitting down in the room's only chair, he pulled her onto his lap, his mood turning suddenly dark as he remembered the wealth Nina had showered on him the night he had been made vampire. In the years since then, he had made a multitude of wise, long-term investments. Money was the least of his worries, he thought.

"I guess I don't *need* to work, either," Sarah said, "but I need something to do, something to occupy my mind. Can't you understand that?"

He understood, but he did not like the idea of her working, of being out in the world of mortal men. He knew that wanting her to stay home was an antiquated notion, as outdated as the horse-and-buggy and gaslights. Nevertheless, he found some of the world's modern ideas difficult to accept.

"Isn't there something you could do at home to pass the time?" he asked.

"Well, I suppose I could try decorating the house." Sarah glanced around the spartanly furnished parlor. "Most of the rooms are conspicuously empty."

"Do whatever you like," Gabriel said, relieved that she had given in so readily. "Buy whatever you wish. Spend as much as you need. All I ask is that you be here when I rise."

It was in her mind to argue. She was an independent woman, after all, accustomed to coming and going as she pleased. If she wanted to work, he couldn't stop her. Modern women were no longer considered chattel, subservient to their husbands' every command, as women had been in Gabriel's time.

And yet, what was the point in arguing? She *wanted* to be here when he woke up, to spend every possible moment with him. And, deep down, she didn't really want to go to work. She knew it was old-fashioned and decidedly unpopular with the women of the '90s, but she liked the idea of being "just a housewife." What could be more important than making a home for the man she loved?

Shopping was something Sarah did well, and she went on a mammoth shopping spree. At Gabriel's urging, she indulged her every whim, buying whatever caught her fancy.

As a child, she had spent hours playing make-believe, and now, as she turned her attention to decorating the house, she pretended that she and Gabriel were no different from any other couple.

While she shopped, she pretended Gabriel was like any other man, busy at the office instead of sleeping in the cellar. She took the Jag and went shopping at the best furniture stores in town, and when she couldn't find what she wanted there, she went browsing through the antique shops. She bought a round oak table and two chairs, a lovely four-drawer chest, a drop-leaf desk.

Life fell into a pleasant routine. A hot and humid August gave way to a hotter September. When she tired of shopping, she went swimming, or lounged beside the pool, reading or just relaxing. Sometimes she rode Necromancer around the corral, reveling in the sense of power she experienced while riding the big black stallion. He was a beautiful horse, with clean lines, a coat that gleamed like ebony satin, and a silky mane and tail.

In the evening, she ate dinner before sunset, took a quick shower, then went into the parlor to wait for Gabriel, pretending he was coming home from a hard day at the office instead of rising from a deathlike sleep.

It was a good life, marred only by the fact that, once each week just after midnight, Gabriel left the house. At those times, knowing he was going out to feed, Sarah found it impossible to pretend they were just an ordinary couple.

Now was such a time. She watched as he slipped on a black Long Rider coat, then pulled on a pair of black kidskin gloves.

She felt faintly sick to her stomach as she imagined those gloved hands wrapped around some poor unfortunate woman while he drank of her blood.

"Is this something you have to do?" She knew it was, yet the words slipped out before she could stop them. "Couldn't you just rob a blood bank or something?"

"I prefer my nourishment fresh and warm," he replied bluntly.

"I could warm it up in the microwave," she suggested, hoping to erase the hard look in his eyes. "Sort of like a TV dinner."

She glanced away, unable to believe she was making jokes about such a gruesome subject.

"This is what I am, Sarah," Gabriel said quietly. "Can you accept it?"

With a small cry, Sarah threw her arms around his waist and held him close.

"It doesn't matter, really," she said fervently. "But how did you ever get used to it?"

He let out a sigh that seemed to rise from the soles of his feet. "It's a craving, Sarah, an addiction that can't be ignored. I need it to survive. In the beginning, I tried to do without it, but the pain was excruciating, like nothing you can imagine."

"Have you . . . have you killed very many people?"

Gently, he wrapped his arms around her. "I've existed a long time. It's no longer necessary for me to kill to survive, *cara.* I don't need as much blood as I did when first I was made. Those I use feel no pain, nor do they remember anything about what happened."

"You hypnotize them?"

He smiled faintly. "A handy trick, for a vampire."

"There was a story in the newspaper a while back about a woman who claimed to have been attacked by a man just like Dracula . . ."

Gabriel grunted softly. "Someone happened upon us before I could erase the memory from her mind."

He pressed a kiss to the top of Sarah's head, gave

her shoulders a squeeze, and released her. "I won't be gone long."

Sarah nodded, aware of his gaze searching hers, judging her reaction. She should be used to it by now, she thought, so why was it so hard to accept? She'd known what he was in a previous life, had accepted it without hesitation. Why couldn't she do that now? If she was the same woman, why didn't she feel the same? Was it possible that the soul remained the same, but not the mind, or its perception of life?

"I will not let you go again, Sarah." His voice was hoarse, edged with what sounded curiously like regret. "If ever you feel that you can no longer accept me for what I am, if you ever wish to be free of me, then you must destroy me."

"I couldn't!"

"I will not let you go."

His eyes burned into hers with an intensity that she had never seen before. It was a look even more frightening than the blood hunger she had seen blazing in his eyes.

"There are three ways to kill a vampire, Sarah. Drive a stake through his heart. Cut off his head. Expose him to the sun."

She felt the color drain from her face. "No . . ."

"There's a small window in the cellar. If you ever wish to be free of me, you have only to remove the board from the window while I sleep. Nature will take care of the rest."

She pressed her hands over her ears. "Stop it! I don't want to hear any more!"

Reaching into his pocket, Gabriel withdrew a large

brass key and forced it into her hand. "This fits the lock on the cellar door."

"I don't want it!"

"Keep it. The day may come when you'll wish you had it."

"Gabriel, you're scaring me."

"You should be scared," he retorted bitterly. "I am, after all, a monster."

"Dammit, I hate it when you talk like that. You're no more a monster than I am."

"Then why are you afraid?"

She wanted to deny it, but she couldn't. Deep inside where she didn't look too often, she was afraid, not of him, but of what he was.

"What's happened?" she asked. "What's changed? Is it what I said earlier? If it is, I'm sorry. It's just that I hate to think of you doing what you have to do to survive."

"I understand, *cara,*" he said, his voice low and soft. "I understand better than you think."

"I love you." She whispered the words as though they could somehow make everything right again.

"I pray you don't regret it," he murmured, and left the room, the long black coat swirling around his ankles.

She stared after him for a long time, the key clutched in her hand. She had never gone into the cellar; now, as if drawn against her will, she walked through the kitchen, down the short flight of stairs, to the cellar.

The door was locked. Her hand shook as she slid the key into the lock; then she opened the door.

She fumbled along the inside wall until she found a light switch. When she flicked it on, a pale yellow light illuminated the room—a room that was empty save for a sturdy pine box that stood in the corner behind the door.

She glanced at the narrow boarded-up window cut into the wall opposite the casketlike box and shuddered.

It took all her willpower to cross the short distance to the box and look inside. An old-fashioned black cloak made of finely woven wool was spread over a thick black comforter.

Her hand seemed to have a will of its own as it reached into the box and rested on the cloak. She closed her eyes, and a quick image of Gabriel sprang to her mind—an image of Gabriel walking toward her, the long black cloak swirling around him like a dark mist.

A small sob burst from her lips as she whirled around and ran out of the room.

*A cure,* she thought. *There has to be a cure.*

She repeated the words as she ran up the stairs to her bedroom. Repeated them over and over, like a mantra, as she filled the bathtub.

A cure. It was their only hope for any kind of a normal life.

He walked the streets for hours, his shoulders hunched under the long black coat, his thoughts bleak. Somewhere, there had to be an answer, a way that he could share all of Sarah's life. And yet, as much as he longed to be mortal for her sake, he harbored a deep and abiding fear of death, of finally coming face to face with that power that was greater than his own. A fear of judgment. Of eternal damnation. How many centuries would he have to spend in perdition to atone for his sins against humanity?

He was walking up the hill toward the mansion when he felt it—an awareness that he was no longer alone, that another immortal being was nearby.

He paused, his gaze sweeping the darkness, as the sense of another presence grew stronger.

And then they emerged from out of the shadows, two men and a woman. For a time, they stared at him, and then the taller of the two men spoke.

"You sent for me, Giovanni, and I am here."

"But not alone."

"I brought two of my younger fledglings with me."

Gabriel's gaze swept over the other two vampires. The boy was young, no more than twenty, with curly brown hair and limpid brown eyes. He was curious and afraid, and he hovered close to his master, making Gabriel wonder how he'd found the courage to cross the gulf from life to death and back again.

And then he got a good look at the woman, and for a moment he was looking into a face from the past. She had Nina's dark eyes, Nina's long black hair, the same haughty tilt to her chin. She was, he knew, a woman perfectly suited to the life of a vampire, a woman whose heart and soul had rejoiced in darkness even before the Dark Gift had been bequeathed to her.

He sucked in a deep breath, let it out in a fervent sigh of relief as he reminded himself that Nina was dead.

"My house is at the top of the hill," Gabriel said.

Quillan nodded, the gesture telling Gabriel more plainly than words that the vampire already knew where he lived. "Does the woman know what you are?"

"Yes."

A look of surprise flitted across the ancient vampire's face. "And she accepts it?"

"As much as a mortal can."

"Does she know you sent for me?"

"Yes."

Quillan nodded, and Gabriel started walking again, acutely aware of the three who followed him.

Sarah was waiting for him at the front door, a smile of welcome on her lips. A smile that quickly died as three black-clad figures followed Gabriel into the entry hall.

Vampires. She knew immediately what they were. A chill unlike anything she had ever known seemed to enter the house with them.

"Sarah, this is Quillan."

Quillan. The vampire from France. He was tall and lean, almost cadaverous. His complexion was pale; his green eyes burned with an unquenchable fire. His hair was long and straight and brown, touched with streaks of gray.

"*Mademoiselle.*" The vampire bowed over her hand. "May I introduce my protégés, Delano and Sydelle."

Sarah forced a smile as she nodded at each one in turn. The boy smiled uncertainly; the woman's gaze was dark and unfriendly. And hungry.

Delano. A name that meant "of the night." A fitting name for a vampire, Gabriel mused as he led the way into the parlor and invited his guests to sit down.

"In your letter, you asked about the existence of a cure," Quillan said, getting right to the point.

"Yes."

"You are serious about this, Giovanni?"

"Yes."

Quillan glanced at Sarah. "I presume your desire to be transformed into a mortal is because of this woman."

Gabriel nodded. "Can it be done?"

"There is a formula that is rumored to be effective, but I know of no vampire who has survived. Those who have tried it have all suffered long and painful deaths."

"What is it? How does it work?"

"It consists of rare herbs and spices. They must be gathered by the light of a full moon, mixed by a white witch on All Hallow's Eve, and consumed by the vampire at dawn's first light."

Gabriel shuddered. He had felt the sting of the sun once before. Its touch, while brief, had been excruciating. He could scarcely bear to think of the agony those other vampires must have suffered before death claimed them.

"Do you have a list of the necessary ingredients?" he asked.

Quillan nodded. "But I would admonish you to think carefully before you partake of it, Giovanni. The passage from life to death to life is perilous. The journey back to mortality has always been fatal."

"Why would you want to give up the Dark Gift?" Sydelle asked impudently, her black eyes bold with challenge. "Why would you want to spend a few years with this puny mortal, and then die, when all the women of the earth are within your power?"

"Sydelle!" Quillan's voice was filled with quiet authority. "I would remind you that we are guests here. I will not tolerate your insolence."

The woman stared at Gabriel for a moment, her

dark eyes glowing with lust, and then she lowered her gaze.

She wants Gabriel, Sarah thought. Not his blood, but his body . . .

"If you cannot bear to be parted from this mortal, would it not be easier to bring her over?" Quillan asked.

"She doesn't wish it," Gabriel replied.

Surprise flickered in Quillan's eyes. "It isn't necessary that she agree."

Sarah gasped, alarmed by the predatory expression in the vampire's eyes, by the coldness in his voice.

Sydelle leaned forward in her chair. "Tell me, Giovanni," she purred, "have you ever made anyone vampire?"

"No."

"Never?" Quillan's voice betrayed his surprise. "Surely, in four hundred years, you've wondered what it would be like."

"I've wondered." Gabriel took Sarah's hand in his and gave it a reassuring squeeze. "But I would not bring her over against her will."

"That is your choice, of course."

"No," Gabriel replied. "It is her choice."

"I admire your restraint."

"Have you never wanted her blood?" Sydelle asked, genuinely curious now.

"Of course," Gabriel admitted gruffly.

Sydelle looked at Sarah, her expression filled with disdain. "Won't she give it to you?"

Sarah stood up, her hands clenched at her sides, her eyes narrowed as she glared at the other woman. "Get out of my house!"

Sydelle sprang to her feet. "How dare you speak to me in that tone!"

"Get out!"

"Sarah." Gabriel rose to his feet and placed a restraining hand on her arm. "Calm down."

"I will not calm down. And I won't sit here and watch that creature look at you as if you were a plum ripe for the picking!"

"Sarah." His voice was low and filled with warning.

Quillan rose effortlessly to his feet. "We will take our leave, Giovanni," he said. "When next we meet, I think it would be wise for us to meet elsewhere."

Gabriel thought for a moment. "The house at the bottom of the hill is vacant. I'll meet you there tomorrow night."

Quillan nodded. "Midnight?"

"The witching hour," Gabriel mused. "An appropriate time for a meeting such as this."

Quillan sketched a courtly bow in Sarah's direction. "I apologize for Sydelle's rudeness. *Au revoir, mademoiselle*. Giovanni." He sent a sharp look at his two fledglings, then turned and left the room. Delano followed close on his heels.

Sydelle followed more slowly. At the door, she glanced over her shoulder at Gabriel, her gaze blatantly sensual and inviting.

"*Au revoir, chérie,*" she called softly. She glanced briefly, scornfully, at Sarah, then followed Quillan out the door, her hips swaying provocatively.

"The nerve!" Sarah exclaimed. "I'd like to scratch her eyes out!"

"It isn't wise for a mortal to anger a vampire, Sarah," Gabriel said dryly. "Not even a fledgling vampire like Sydelle."

"Maybe you'd like to take her up on her offer!" Sarah snapped. "She's probably waiting for you outside."

*"Cara . . ."*

"She couldn't keep her eyes off you."

"Is that my fault?"

"Yes! If you weren't so darn handsome . . ."

He was laughing at her now, his dark gray eyes merry with amusement. "You're jealous."

"Damn right!"

"Shall I destroy her for you?"

He said it so casually, Sarah was sure he was joking, until she looked at his face, and then she knew he wasn't kidding at all.

"You'd do that?"

Gabriel shrugged. "If you wish."

"No."

"There's no need for you to be jealous, *cara.* My heart belongs to you." His gaze, dark and intense, rested on her face. "Only you. It always has. It always will."

His words, softly and sincerely spoken, made her realize how foolish her anger really was.

With a sigh, she moved into his arms, her head pillowed on his chest. "What are you going to do?"

"About what?"

"The cure?"

"I won't know until I see exactly what it calls for," he answered, but he already knew he would try it, regardless of the danger. They could not go on as they were. If he could not be mortal again, then perhaps it would be best for all concerned if his life came to an end. In time, Sarah would forget him.

She would marry again, have the children he knew she longed for.

"I think maybe you should forget it. I don't want you risking your life for me. And if it doesn't work, you'd be in grave danger."

He nodded, remembering the touch of the sun on his face and hands, the excruciating pain, the fear that he would perish in flames before he could return to the cellar.

"Come," he said, swinging her up into his arms. "There are only a few hours until dawn, and I would spend them with you."

She snuggled against him, her mind in turmoil. She had been so sure that a cure for what he was would solve all their problems. Now it sounded as if the cure was worse than the disease.

And then Gabriel was kissing her, his hands moving over her body, discarding her clothing, caressing her skin with his lips, sweeping her away to a world that was only big enough for two, and there was no more time for thought; there was only the touch of his hands and the rough velvet of his voice as he whispered that he loved her, would love her to the end of his existence . . .

# *Chapter Eight*

She was on edge all that day, unable to concentrate on anything for more than a minute. All she could think of was that Gabriel was meeting Quillan at midnight; that they'd have the formula in their hands. Only two weeks until Halloween, she thought. Only two weeks to make a decision that would have monumental influence on the rest of their lives. Quillan had said the journey back to life had always been fatal. Did she want Gabriel to be mortal again badly enough to risk his life? If the cure didn't work, Gabriel would die a horrible death. Gabriel had said he would not let her go in this life, that he would not stand by and watch her die again, and so there were really only two choices: they must find a cure for what he was, or she would have to become a vampire . . . and she knew that was something she could never do.

Maybe Quillan was right. Maybe Gabriel should

transform her against her will. Maybe she could accept it then, but even as the thought crossed her mind, she knew she would never forgive him, that no matter how difficult the decision might be, it had to be her own.

Never had the hours of the day passed so slowly. She tried to read, tried to watch TV, but she was too restless to sit still, and so she paced the living-room floor, wishing the sun would hurry across the sky, wishing for dusk so she could be with Gabriel. She needed to feel his arms around her, to hear his words of reassurance chasing away her fears.

As the shadows grew long, she went out to stand on the veranda, watching the sun make its downward climb.

It had not yet disappeared when she sensed his presence behind her. With a glad heart, she ran into the house and flung herself in his arms.

"Hold me!" she cried. "Hold me and never let go!"

"Sarah, what is it?"

"I'm afraid."

"Of what?"

"I don't know. Don't go tonight. Forget about the cure. Stay with me."

"*Cara . . .*"

"Please."

"I have to try it, Sarah. If there's any chance at all, I have to try it." He tilted her head up. "It's what you want, isn't it?"

"Not anymore."

"Then it's what I want."

"I don't believe that. You're doing it for me, I know you are."

"I want us to be together, not just at night. I want

to live as a man again, to walk in the sun with you at my side."

"But what if it doesn't work?"

"Then you must go on with your life. Find a man who will love you and give you children."

"No."

"You found me in this life, *cara.* If it's possible, I will find you in death."

His mind was made up, and there was nothing she could say to change it.

He carried her upstairs and made love to her, slowly, deliberately, savoring each sensation, storing them in his mind. If the cure proved ineffective, he would have only these last two weeks to live. To a man who had survived over four and a half centuries, two weeks seemed but a moment.

And now the hours sped swiftly by.

Too soon, it was almost midnight.

Lying in bed, Sarah watched him dress. He left the room for a moment, and when he returned, he was wearing his cloak.

"I won't be long," he promised, bestowing a kiss on her cheek. "Keep the bed warm for me."

She choked back a sob as she watched him leave the room, overcome with a terrible premonition that she would never see him again.

The door opened at his bidding. He stood in the entryway for a moment, his senses probing the darkness of the house.

"In here, Giovanni."

Quillan's voice. Deep. Predatory. Deadly.

Too late, Gabriel realized Quillan had not come alone.

Three vampires materialized out of the shadows; a fourth ghosted up behind him, cutting off his escape. Fledglings all, they circled him like winter-starved wolves, fangs gleaming even in the darkness, eyes aglow.

Fear slithered down Gabriel's spine. "What do you want?"

"We cannot let you rejoin the ranks of humanity," Quillan said flatly. "You know our habits, our weaknesses. We cannot take a chance that you might turn against us."

"Why would I do that? What would I have to gain?"

Quillan shrugged. "Everything. Nothing. As I said, it is a chance we cannot take."

Gabriel glanced over his shoulder. A tall, slender vampire stood behind him, a stake clutched in his gloved hands. "So you're going to destroy me."

Quillan nodded. "A stake through the heart has always been the preferred method," he said.

Gabriel was afraid, and he didn't like it. Afraid for himself. Afraid for Sarah. "What of the woman?"

"She dies, too. Delano and Sydelle are on their way as we speak."

"No!" The denial was ripped from Gabriel's throat.

"We have survived thousands of years only because we have never let mankind know of our existence. They may suspect. They may have seen or heard something for which they have no logical explanation, but they do not want to believe. The woman dies."

"Quillan, please . . ."

"Too late, Giovanni."

They moved toward him, closing the circle. But Gabriel had not survived as long as he had by being foolish. In 464 years, he had trusted no other vampire, and only two mortals.

With a low growl, he sprinted past the two young vampires in front of him, his hand reaching inside his cloak, delving into his pants pocket as he vaulted the stairs to the second-story landing.

Whirling around, he fired the pistol four times in rapid succession. The bullets, made of solid silver, had been loaded into the gun by the man who owned the gun shop. They struck the fledgling vampires with deadly precision, and then Quillan was on him, knocking the pistol from his grasp. Locked together, they tumbled down the stairs. Quillan, heavier, older, was on top when they hit the bottom of the stairs.

His hands closed around Gabriel's throat, his weight pinning Gabriel to the floor as he bent toward him, his fangs bared.

"Do not fight me, Giovanni," Quillan rasped, his hand closing over the stake that had fallen from his fledgling's hand. "You are too late to save the woman, and in a moment, you will join her . . ."

Sarah heard the front door open and breathed a sigh of relief. He was back!

She sat up, combing her fingers through her hair, her heart pounding with happiness. So much for premonitions, she thought.

And then she heard footsteps on the stairs.

Unfamiliar footsteps.

Her gaze darted around the room, seeking a weapon, but found nothing. Muttering a silent prayer, she climbed out of bed and went into the bathroom. Locking the door, she pawed through the drawers, but the most dangerous thing she found was a blow dryer.

Tears of frustration welled in her eyes as she bunched her gown in one hand and climbed out the window. Behind her, she heard someone pounding on the door, and then she heard Sydelle's voice, soft and seductive.

"Let us in, Sarah," the vampire called. "Gabriel is dead, and there's nowhere you can hide."

Dead! No! He couldn't be dead. She slid down the slope of the roof, grabbed hold of a tree branch, and made her way to the ground.

Hide. She had to hide. But where?

She heard a faint crash as the vampires broke down the bathroom door. A moment later, she saw Sydelle's face at the window.

Adrenalin pumping, Sarah ran toward the corral. Never in her life had she vaulted onto a horse's back, but she did so now. Wrapping her hands in the stallion's mane, she drummed her heels into the horse's flanks and Necromancer bolted forward. A sharp kick sent him sailing over the six-foot fence. For a moment, Sarah swayed precariously on the stallion's bare back, and then they were racing toward the back gate.

The horse came to a gravel-scattering halt when they reached the block wall. With fingers that trembled, Sarah opened the gate, then drummed her heels into Necromancer's flanks once again.

She could hear Sydelle calling her name, but she paid no attention. Gabriel, she thought frantically. She had to find Gabriel.

The stallion's iron-shod hooves clattered loudly as he trotted down the middle of the street.

The horse snorted and shied as they reached the bottom of the hill. Sarah screamed as two dark shadows crept up behind her. Delano and Sydelle! How had they gotten there so fast?

With a shriek, Sarah jumped to the ground and sprinted up the walkway to the front door of the vacant house. With a sob, she flung the door open and raced inside.

"Gabriel!"

"Here."

She peered into the darkness, acutely conscious of the two vampires entering the house behind her.

And then she saw Gabriel. He was sitting with his back against the staircase. Moonlight poured through the sliding glass door a few feet away.

"Gabriel?" She ran to his side, Delano and Sydelle forgotten as she saw the dead vampires sprawled on the floor. Nausea rose in her throat when she saw Quillan's body. A wooden stake pierced the vampire's heart. "What happened?"

But Gabriel wasn't looking at her. He was staring at the door.

Afraid of what she'd see, Sarah glanced over her shoulder.

Delano and Sydelle stood silhouetted in the doorway. Even from across the room, Sarah could see the blood hunger burning in their eyes.

"The stake, Sarah," Gabriel said quietly. "Get it."

She looked at him as if he'd lost his mind, her whole being recoiling in horror at the thought of pulling the wood from the vampire's body.

"Do it!" Gabriel hissed, and only then did she notice how pale his face was.

Her gaze swept over him, and she saw the blood,

blood so dark it was almost black, seeping from a hideous wound in his chest.

"Hurry," he said urgently.

She glanced at Delano and Sydelle, saw the rage contorting their faces. Bloodred tears welled in Delano's eyes as he stared at Quillan's body.

Closing her eyes, Sarah wrapped her hands around the wooden stake and jerked it free, and then she scooted back toward Gabriel.

"What now?" she asked, but she didn't need or expect an answer. Everything she needed to know was written on the faces of the two vampires as they slowly stepped into the entry hall and closed the door.

Sarah was shivering now. Cold sweat beaded across her brow and ran in cold rivers down her back. Try as she might, she couldn't draw her eyes from the two vampires. She was going to die, she thought, here, tonight.

There was one brief moment when everything seemed to happen in slow motion.

A soft grunt of pain escaped Gabriel's lips as he stood up.

She saw Delano bare his fangs as he lunged forward, his hands looking like claws as he reached for Gabriel's throat.

And then Sydelle sprang toward her, and time ceased to exist. The vampire's strength was incredible. Sarah gasped as she was driven backward. The breath whooshed from her lungs as she fell against the staircase. Her head struck one of the steps and bright lights flashed before her eyes. She felt Sydelle's hands wrap around her throat, heard a blood curdling growl as the vampire attacked her. Using her teeth and her fingernails, Sydelle savaged Sarah's face and neck.

Fear lent strength to Sarah's limbs and she began to struggle wildly. Lifting her arm, she jabbed the stake she was still holding into the vampire's side.

With a roar, Sydelle plucked the stake from Sarah's hand and flung it aside. And then Sarah felt the woman's fangs at her throat. There was a sharp pain, and then everything went out of focus. The room and its occupants seemed to blur. As if from far away, she heard sounds of a struggle. Gabriel was fighting for his life, she thought numbly. She had to help him. But her arms and legs refused to move, and then everything went black . . .

She was drifting, floating on a sea of darkness, when she heard his voice. He was crying, and the sound of his heartache made her want to cry, too.

*Crying,* she thought, and she knew in that instant that Gabriel was crying for her, because she was dying.

The knowledge didn't frighten her as it should have. She looked around, puzzled by the darkness. Where was the tunnel and the bright light everyone talked about, she wondered.

And then she heard his voice again, sobbing for her to come back, pleading with her not to leave him again. Begging her to forgive him for what he was about to do.

She tried to speak, tried to tell him that everything would be all right, but she no longer had the power to speak.

She heard his voice grow faint as she floated farther and farther away. She tried to call his name, tried to tell him she would find him again no matter how long it took, but it was too late . . . too late . . .

She was on the very brink of oblivion when a sudden warmth filled her. It was thick and hard to swallow, but it drew her back from the edge of the abyss. She felt it course through her body, and then she heard his voice again, urgent, filled with love. And regret.

"Drink, Sarah," he said. "Drink."

Obediently, she opened her mouth, and he pressed his wrist to her lips again.

"Drink," he commanded, and she felt his hand at the back of her neck, holding her in place.

And because she feared the darkness, because she didn't want to leave him again, she did as he asked, her throat convulsing as she swallowed again and again, until, with a groan, Gabriel jerked his arm away.

"Enough, *cara,*" he murmured.

Her eyelids fluttered open and she looked up at him.

"Gabriel, what happened?"

"I'll explain later," he promised, gently brushing a lock of hair from her brow. "Sleep now."

"Don't leave me!" She couldn't bear the thought of being parted from him again. "Please don't leave me!"

He wrapped his arms around her, holding her tight, until she felt her heart beating in time with his.

"I won't leave you, *cara,*" he promised, his voice infinitely sad. "But you must rest now."

She didn't want to sleep. She wanted to know what had happened to Delano and Sydelle, wanted to know why she felt so strange, why the thought of being separated from him for even a moment filled her with such gut-wrenching anxiety, but a lethargy unlike anything she had ever known was creeping over her, dragging her down into oblivion once more.

# *Chapter Nine*

She woke to the sun in her face and a raging thirst. Alarmed, she sat up. "Gabriel?"

There was no answer, and for a moment sheer panic threatened to engulf her. "Gabriel? Gabriel!"

*I'm here.*

Relief flooded through her, sweeter than wine.

"Where are you?"

*Below. Go back to sleep, Sarah.*

"What happened? I feel so strange."

*I'll explain later. Go to sleep now,* he said again, his voice low and soothing. *I'll come to you as soon as I can.*

"No! I need you now. Please."

*Come to me, then.*

Jumping out of bed, she ran through the house, fairly flew down the cellar stairs. She hesitated, repelled by the thought of seeing Gabriel lying in that pine box, but the thought of being separated from him quickly overcame her reluctance.

And then, of its own accord, the cellar door opened.

"Gabriel?"

*I'm here. Lock the door behind you.*

She did as he asked, a cold chill slithering down her spine as she locked herself in the basement. She was reaching for the light switch when she heard his voice in her mind once again.

*Leave it off.*

"Why don't you talk to me?" she asked as she felt her way through the darkness toward his resting place.

*It takes less effort to communicate with you like this.*

She shivered as her hand came in contact with the side of the box. And then he was reaching for her, lifting her over the edge as if she weighed no more than a child, cuddling her against him, and all her fears melted away.

"Gabriel . . ."

*Sleep, Sarah,* he said, his voice heavy as he fought to stay awake. *Sleep . . .*

He drew the edge of his cloak around her, and then he sank back down into darkness, her head pillowed on his chest, his arm around her waist.

She should have been afraid, but she wasn't. She was asleep before she could wonder why.

When next she woke, it was to the sound of Gabriel's voice speaking her name. It was an effort to open her eyes. Feeling strangely disoriented, she blinked up at him and then, realizing where she was, she bolted upright, aghast to find herself sitting in what was, for all intents and purposes, a coffin.

"What am I doing here?" Shivering with revulsion, she started to scramble over the side.

"Relax, *cara*," Gabriel murmured as he gathered her into his arms.

Sarah clung to him, soothed by his presence, by the inimitable strength of the arms that held her.

"Are you all right?" he asked, his voice deep with concern.

She nodded, her gaze never leaving his face.

"You're sure?"

Sarah frowned at him. "Why wouldn't I be all right?"

Wordlessly, Gabriel carried her up the stairs into the kitchen, sat her in one of the antique ladder-back chairs she had bought on one of her shopping sprees.

Going to the refrigerator, he poured her a large glass of orange juice.

Handing her the glass, Gabriel sat down in the chair next to Sarah's, his gaze intent upon her face as she drank the juice.

"What do you remember about last night?" he asked.

"Last night?" Sarah shook her head. "I don't remember any . . ."

Gently, Gabriel pulled his hand from hers. Going to the window, he stared into the lowering darkness. It was going to storm again. He could hear the thunder in the distance, smell the rain. If he let his mind open fully, he could hear the conversation of the people in the next house, smell the exhaust of the cars on the street below.

"Gabriel?"

"You almost died last night," he replied quietly. "I

couldn't let you go. I couldn't. Do you understand?"

"No." She stared at his back, wondering why he sounded so troubled, why he wouldn't look at her.

"Forgive me," he said, his voice raw with self-reproach. "I couldn't hold you in my arms and watch you die again." His hands balled into tight fists. "I gave you my blood, Sarah. That's why you can hear my thoughts inside your head so clearly. It's why you're feeling so strange, why you're afraid to let me out of your sight."

Slowly, he turned around to face her. "You are a part of me now, bonded to me by the blood we share."

*Will you be my slave or my equal?* His words, spoken weeks ago, echoed in her mind.

She remembered the night she had given him her blood. *Am I your slave now?* she had asked, and when he had assured her that she wasn't, she had blithely replied that she wouldn't mind being his slave. Now that it seemed to be a fact, she wondered if that was still true.

"What does it mean, exactly?" she asked. "Being bonded? How long will it last?"

"It will last as long as you live," Gabriel replied. "No matter where you go, or what you do, I'll be able to find you."

"And will I be able to find you?"

"Yes, always," he promised, though he knew that, should he desire, he could shut her out of his mind, but that was something he would never do.

"Can you make me do things I don't want to do?"

He thought of vampires he had known, male and female alike, who had initiated mortals, then used them to do their bidding. In the old days, mortal slaves had often hunted prey for their vampire masters.

"I could," Gabriel admitted, "but I won't."

"Will I always feel so desolate when we're apart?"

"I don't know. I've never initiated anyone before."

"Initiated. Is that what this bonding is called?"

Gabriel nodded as he watched the emotions play across her face: doubt, fear, anxiety, resentment.

Had he done the right thing? Or did she hate him for it? She might have preferred death to being subject to his power, and yet he could not let her die, not when he had the ability to save her.

Sarah released a long, shuddering breath. "Why didn't you just make me what you are?"

"I wanted to, but I found I couldn't make that decision for you, *cara*. I couldn't bring you over against your will."

"I wish you had."

"There's still time. You're young and healthy. Perhaps, in a few years, you'll decide to be as I am. If not, then I will follow you from life into death."

"I've already made my decision," Sarah replied, smiling tremulously up at him. "I think I made it the first time I looked into your eyes."

He knelt before her, his deep gray eyes dark with desire, his hair as black as the night, reminding her of a medieval warrior rendering homage to his lady.

"I'll do whatever you wish, *cara,*" Gabriel said, his voice soft and low. "Only tell me what you want."

*Only tell me what you want*. And she knew, in that moment, that she wanted to be with Gabriel, like Gabriel. She didn't want to live each day knowing they could never truly be one, didn't want to watch the years pass by, knowing that he stood on one side of the vast gulf of mortality that yawned between them, while she stood on the other.

The thought of being what he was, repugnant to her only days before, now seemed far less frightening than the thought of being parted from him again.

"I want to be yours, now and forever," she whispered. "I want to share the night with you, and spend the day resting in your arms."

His gaze moved over her face, his eyes warm with love. A faint smile played over his lips.

"I can arrange that," he murmured, and slanting his mouth over hers, he swept her into his arms and carried her up the stairs to their bedroom.

And there, sheltered in Gabriel's arms, strengthened by a bond of love that would last forever, Sara Jayne found the courage to take the first step in an endless journey of discovery.